KING'S MOUNTAIN

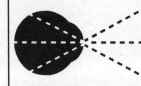

This Large Print Book carries the Seal of Approval of N.A.V.H.

KING'S MOUNTAIN

A BALLAD NOVEL

SHARYN MCCRUMB

• **THORNDIKE PRESS**
A part of Gale, Cengage Learning

GALE
CENGAGE Learning·

Farmington Hills, Mich • San Francisco • New York • Waterville, Maine
Meriden, Conn • Mason, Ohio • Chicago

GALE
CENGAGE Learning

LIBRARY OF CONGRESS CATALOGING-IN-PUBLICATION DATA

McCrumb, Sharyn, 1948–
    King's mountain : a ballad novel / by Sharyn McCrumb. — Large print edition.
        pages ; cm. — (Thorndike Press large print basic)
        ISBN 978-1-4104-6538-2 (hardcover) — ISBN 1-4104-6538-1 (hardcover)
    1. Mountain life—Fiction. 2. United States—History—Revolution, 1775–1783—Fiction. 3. Large type books. I. Title.
    PS3563.C3527K56 2014
    813'.54—dc23   2013038084

Published in 2014 by arrangement with St. Martin's Press, LLC

Printed in the United States of America
1 2 3 4 5 6 7 18 17 16 15 14

*To my fellow descendants of the
Overmountain Men*

CHAPTER ONE
1776

My family might have had a more peaceful
life if we had stayed in the Shenandoah Valley, but *staying put* was not in the blood of
the Seviers. My ancestors had come from
Navarre, that province lodged in the mountains between France and Spain, and, like
most of the mountain people I have met
since, they did not seem to care overmuch
for governments telling them what to do.
Anyhow, my grandfather was a Protestant,
in a time and place where to espouse that
belief was to court death, but instead of opt-
ing for the blessed martyrdom of a public
execution, my practical forebear decided to
suffer the world a while longer and make
his escape from France. When Louis Qua-
torze revoked the Edict of Nantes, which
had protected the Huguenots from persecution for nearly a century, Monsieur Sevier
— or Xavier, as the family name was then
— lit out for the more congenial political

climate of England. I would have done the same myself, I think. I don't say I won't fight for a cause, but I prefer to let the other fellow do the dying.

When Grand-père settled in London, he changed the family name from "Xavier" to the more English-sounding "Sevier," and then he married an Englishwoman to cement his change of nationality. He prospered in his adopted country, but that prosperity did not prevent my father, Valentine Sevier, from setting out for the colonies, to try his own luck at a new beginning.

I was born, then, on September 23, 1745, cradled by the mountains in the Shenandoah. In this colony of Virginia, I was christened "John," all trace of the family's French origins now all but forgotten in the new world, where the telling social distinctions were not country or faith, but skin color: white for station, black for servitude, and red — *oh, red for danger.*

I wondered if the hill country of my boyhood bore any resemblance to distant Navarre, or if the love of mountains in my blood harked back to those far-off Pyrenees, but perhaps the coincidence was only a matter of expedience: mountain land is more easily had than the fertile flat fields along the seaboard, because fewer people want it.

I suppose they think the beauty of the land comes at too dear a price if the fields are steep and stony and the holdings isolated. The mass of humanity seems not to mind living piled in among one another like maggots on a dead crow, but I thought that high hills and elbow room were fine things, and if my people had been cast out of the Pyrenees for their philosophical stubbornness, then we would seek out our mountains elsewhere.

"You have the bloodline of a saint," an old priest told me once.

He was passing through the long valley on his way to Charleston, perhaps to take up a posting at a Catholic parish somewhere to the south. Anyhow, he had stopped for the night in our Shenandoah village where my father kept a store. I passed the time of day with him, for I was always interested in talking to people from "away." Any sort of learning was welcome. He was a little Frenchman, with great liquid eyes and a stillness that made one want to talk to fill up the silence.

I told him my name, and that I shared his French heritage, mentioning that we had once been "Xaviers" of Navarre. To my surprise he knew the name at once, for he nodded sagely and murmured a few words in a foreign tongue — French, or, for all I knew, Latin. Then he said, "St. Francis Xavier, he was. A founder of the Jesuit order and a great missionary in the east." The old man smiled. "Perhaps you will be called to minister to the Indians one day."

I said that I should like to help a good many of them into heaven, at any rate.

If the Frenchman took my meaning, he made no comment. At last he said, "Well, it is a good thing to be of such a lineage. Saint's blood. No doubt you will be blessed in all things. Indeed, you have already the makings of a tall and handsome man. All will go well with you."

If I had ambition in this life, I did not catch it from my father. He farmed and kept a country store, or perhaps it kept him, for as time went on, he was content to idle away his time with the drunkards and the gamblers at Culpeper Court House. He sent me to school at the Staunton Academy, though, perhaps hoping that I would make something of myself and keep him in spirits and card money in his dotage, but I had no inclination for the life of a scholar. I felt no call for medicine or the legal profession, so when my schoolfellows passed on to the college of William and Mary to become pillars of society, I made my way home to the Shenandoah, to become a clerk in the family store — well, somebody had to. There were nine young Seviers, but I was the eldest, and I thought I should see to it that the younger ones were kept fed. Perhaps it is a burden to feel responsible for so many mouths at so young an age, but the gift for leadership that was to show later in life may have sprung from those days when I was the oldest of so many. Perhaps I got in the way of thinking that I was elder brother to the world entire, and that it would always fall to me to keep the rest of humanity safe and fed.

You would think that a man who was content to fritter away his time with dice and whiskey would have been satisfied to have his affairs tended to by a hardworking son who shared neither of those vices, but it seemed that I was the star my father wished upon, for in my sixteenth year when I announced my intentions of settling down, he would have none of it.

"Married?" he thundered at me in a spirituous haze. "Why, you are no more than sixteen, boy! I won't hear of it."

"You have heard of it," I said coldly. "For I just told you. And, as for stopping me, there is precious little chance of that. The other boys are old enough now to take my place as breadwinner. Let Joseph or Robert or Valentine keep the store and tend to the farm. Surely, I have done my share."

"But you are sixteen," my father said again.

I held my peace, for to tell my father that I felt twice that age would be disrespectful, and he was not a bad man — only a weak one. In truth I felt that having the responsibility only for the care of Sarah Hawkins would be a great relief — the day I wed her I would have eight fewer burdens than I'd had before. No one could have been less of a child at sixteen than I.

"Well, boy, you know your own mind," said my father with an ill-concealed sneer. "I only hope you know what a long road you have ahead of you, and if you have chosen badly so soon in life, you will have many years of leisure in which to repent of it."

I replied that I was more concerned that Sarah would have cause to repent her choice of me. I was too much the dutiful son to add that I should take care to see that I did not turn out to be a likeness of my father, but the thought crossed my mind, then and later. There's no telling how far you can go if you are outrunning something.

In 1761, I secured a tract of land and called it Long Meadows, and I set to farming and to siring a brood of young Seviers to help me work the land. Our holdings lay along the westward trail in a wide valley, and thus far at least I imitated my father: I farmed and kept a store of my own, but after more than a dozen years, we were all tired of seeing the world pass us by on that westward wagon road, and we decided to go west ourselves. My brother Valentine had left already, and he was homesteading on the frontier near the Shelbys. I made a couple of journeys out to see him, and to see if this wilderness really was the land of plenty that people said it was. When we finally set our minds to moving, the whole family set out together — my parents, my younger brothers Robert, Joseph, and Abraham — all headed for the backcountry. There were hardships, right enough, Indian attacks and backbreaking toil involved in carving a farmstead out of the endless forest, but game was plentiful, and there were land grants to be had. I never regretted the decision to settle on the frontier. Perhaps I was gambling a safe present for the chance of a prosperous future, but the game was worth the candle.

And the land was worth fighting for.

Perhaps the people along the seaboard were fighting the revolution for philosophical reasons — to escape unjust taxes, to choose their own leaders . . . they had a dozen reasons for wishing to be rid of British dominion. For the most part, those of us in the backcountry had but one reason.

The British wanted to throw us off our land and make us move back east of the mountains. They had made that long-ago treaty with the Indian nation, and they seemed to want to enforce it after all these years. I think they wanted us closer to their town garrisons, so that we could not easily oppose them.

Perhaps that priest from my boyhood meant what he'd said as no more than pleasantry, a social blessing given to a backwoods boy on a summer afternoon, costing him nothing, but I chose to take his words as a prophecy. Many's the time that the memory of those words has emboldened me to courage and to action. *I am blessed,* I tell myself. *I cannot fail.*

And I very seldom do.

Chapter Two

JULY 1776

It was the cows, you see. Bawling. Half a dozen of them out in the fields by the creek, past a grove of sycamores, just beyond sight of the fort. But not beyond sound. No, we could hear them well enough, at first lowing in their discomfort, and then bellowing in outright pain, for the beasts had not been milked in many a day.

Well, the caterwauling will stop when they begin to die, one of the hunters said.

But some of the younger women had begun crying themselves to hear the animals' suffering and to be powerless to help. They were mothers themselves, and perhaps they thought that there was pain enough in being female, without having it made worse by the cruelty of men. *Help them,* the women said. *Else, we will.*

It is a trap, the men told them. *The Indian savages what have laid siege to this fort know that storming the palisades would cost them dear as long as we have powder and shot, but they reckon that if they can trick us into opening the gates, they can rush the fort and kill us all. They have left the cows there to suffer to tempt us into going out. Their cries are meant to test our fortitude. Why, they would torture the beasts with hot knives if they thought it would weaken our resolve.*

All this was unarguable truth. And although that assessment wasn't kind or pleasant, it was indeed sound reasoning from seasoned warriors. *Do not be tricked out of your citadel by an animal.* Why, that advice was as old as Troy.

But when has reason ever triumphed over suffering?

At least we had been warned. We always knew there was danger, of course. On the Carolina frontier, it was never far away. In mid-July, a few days before the siege began, I had been down on Stoney Creek, directing the building of a new log fort that I would command, being the ranking elected officer of our local militia. Then in case of an Indian attack, those who lived on the nearby farms would have a fortified place of refuge. We were still a good ways from finishing construction when someone shouted that a rider was approaching, and

16

we saw the trader Isaac Thomas, bareback on a jugheaded Cherokee horse and gaunt as a scarecrow, calling out to us. The men dropped tools and hastened to meet him, shouting joyfully and pulling Thomas down from the horse, for he had been captured weeks ago, and we never thought to see him again. All summer there had been unrest among the Cherokee, and we had lost several of our number to their raiding parties. Besides Thomas, two other men from these parts had been taken, and — the greatest cause of concern around the settlement — the wife of William Bean was taken as she was riding from their cabin on Boone Creek to Fort Watauga for safety. I hoped for news of all of them, but especially of her, for she left behind a grieving husband and a young child.

I set the mallet down next to the rifle that was never far from my hand, and went out to welcome him. Thomas was dirty and sweat-soaked from his hard ride, but he had no apparent wounds, and I was thankful to see him thus — in one piece with his scalp still attached.

I clapped him on the back, and led him to a fallen log by the river, where I had set a jug of cider and a hunk of bread and cheese for my lunch. "You look like a starving hound, Thomas, but I see that you managed to escape them."

He did not smile. "It was made to look that way, Mr. Sevier. But I had help. *The Ghighau,* Mistress Ward, got some of her clan to spirit us out and give us horses to speed us on our way. She wanted me to carry a message to the settlements up here."

Suddenly I felt cold in the sunshine. "When is it to be then?"

He nodded. "The attack? Very soon. As the tribe's Beloved Woman, Nancy Ward sits on the council, you know, and she may speak when they are making their plans. No doubt she is very wise, but the other council members do not often heed her words. She warns that Old Abram and her kinsman Dragging Canoe are leading war parties. They want us out of here, of course. Thanks to the meddling of the king's army, they are no longer willing to honor the land purchases we made, and, if we won't go back east willingly, they mean to drive us out or kill us where we stand."

I believed him — or rather I believed Nancy Ward, for I had met her, and found her to be both truthful and wise. The honor of being the Cherokee Ghighau is usually given to an old woman, but Nancy Ward had become the Ghighau when she was still

18

a young girl. She had married a young warrior named Kingfisher, and when the warriors went south to fight the Creek nation, she went with him. They said she stayed by his side during the fighting, helping him reload his weapon, and chewing the bullets for his gun. When he fell in battle, the stricken young wife was so overcome with grief and rage that she snatched up her dead husband's weapon, and led the surviving warriors in a charge against the enemy. This brave or foolhardy gesture turned the tide of the battle, and when the war party went home victorious, they declared the widowed girl their "Beloved Woman," *Ghighau,* adviser to the council of chiefs, and so she had been ever since. In later years, when the whites came into Indian territory, Nancy Ward married the trader Bryan Ward, and though their union did not last, she had borne him children, and she knew more of our ways than the rest of her people. They would have done well to listen to her.

Nancy Ward would not have arranged for Isaac Thomas to escape unless she knew the attack to be a certainty.

I nodded. What Thomas said was no more than common currency among our neighbors. The British had given guns to the tribes along the frontier, and encouraged them to attack the frontier forts. For one thing, that would keep our minds off rebellion against the king. "But Nancy Ward saw to it that you escaped. I'll wager she thinks that some of us might survive their attacks, and that if we do, our vengeance against the Cherokee will be terrible. She is wise."

"Yes, sir. And she doesn't trust the British any more than we do. She particularly told me to ask you to spare the Hiwassee towns should the circumstances arise."

In her place, I would have requested the same, but I knew that it might not be within my power to accommodate her. I was a respected landowner, and in the process of building the fort I would command for the settlement here on the Nolichucky, but Colonel Carter and Captain Robertson over at the Watauga fort outranked me in the local militia, and they might have other ideas.

"What of the other prisoners?" I asked Thomas. "Did you see any of them?"

"Yes, sir. Mistress Lydia Bean was a captive in the village where I was kept. Two other white men were tortured to death, and Mrs. Bean was to be next. They tied her to a stake in the center of the huts, and set the tinder alight, but before the fire could take hold, the Ghighau marched out of her hut, walked straight up to the flames, and stomped them out. Then she delivered what sounded like a tongue lashing to those in charge of the burning. I reckon it sickened her to see Cherokee warriors tormenting a defenseless woman who had done them no harm. Then she pointed to the ropes binding Mistress Bean, and some of the men cut her loose. Then the Ghighau herself took Lydia Bean back to her own cabin, and that's the last I saw of her."

"Is she yet alive?"

"From what I could tell, they don't mean to kill her. The Ghighau won't allow it. She has set Mistress Bean to teaching the village womenfolk how to make cheese and butter. I reckon they'll let her go sooner or later if she doesn't cross them. But she wasn't allowed to come with me. I was only set free in order to deliver the message that an attack was coming."

"The Ghighau cannot stop the raids, more's the pity. Though she holds the swan's wing, and she sits with the chief at their council, she has only the power to advise. Still, she must know that, win or lose, this war will be the ruin of her people. There are too many of us out here now. Even if the Cherokee killed us all, more settlers would come. She is right — peace is their only hope of surviving, for we will wipe them out if we have to in order to protect our land. But I can see that it would be difficult for her to convince warriors of that. So they mean to attack despite her counsel to keep peace?"

"They do. I don't know when — perhaps a week or so — but, as sure as I stand before you, it is coming."

I was grateful that we had been warned, but I wished we had more time to finish the work on the new fort.

"Well, our concern now is to warn the others," I told Isaac Thomas. "Water your mount now, while I go and write a note for you to take to the other forts. Carter and Robertson can send word to the neighboring farms, as we will here."

Isaac Thomas looked past me at the framework of the unfinished fort, and I could see that he was thinking that we might as well hide under a blanket for all the protection it would offer. "Will you stay here, sir?"

"Yes, if I can. If we leave it, Old Abram will burn it to the ground, and it would be a pity to see a whole summer's work go to waste."

But we had to abandon it anyway. When I warned those on the nearby farms that a

Cherokee war party was coming, there was great consternation among the neighbors. They had wives and children to think of, and livestock that they would not risk if they could help it. Without delay they packed up what they could carry, herded what cattle they could manage, and fled north to the nearest refuge: James Robertson's post at Fort Watauga. We sorely needed a fort closer to our homes, for if the Cherokee attacked, we risked being cut down on our way to the more distant fort erected by James Robertson's men, on the shoals of the Watauga. That fort was large enough to hold a hundred souls or more — if they could survive to get there. The other workers sent their women and children on ahead to the Watauga fort, accompanied by what men we could spare to protect them on the journey. Soon there were fewer than a dozen of us left to carry on with the construction. I saw that we would never finish it in time, and I could not in good conscience risk the men's lives and families in a vain attempt to continue the work.

I held out as long as I could, but one night over supper when I was holding forth about those men who had left the work to retreat to Fort Watauga, my wife, Sarah, said, "Is it the fort's construction you mind about,

John, or is it the fact that you were to be in command of it?"

I could not answer her.

"I know you want to finish it, but there are lives besides yours at risk here. Your brothers Robert, Joseph, and Valentine, and their families. Our own Joseph, and the little ones. It is too much of a gamble to stake all their lives on the chance that you will finish the fort in time."

She was right, though I did not like to admit it. Finally, though, I faced the fact that a swift completion of the fort was past praying for, called a halt to the construction, and said that we would join the others at the fort on the Watauga.

I had been distracted by the need to get our fort constructed and ready, but as Sarah had reminded me, I had others to think of besides myself — my wife and our eight children, and Richard our youngest, who was still a babe in arms. For their safety, Sarah and I thought we had best gather up our brood, and join my brothers and their families and the remaining neighbors in the flight to Robertson's fort while there was still time.

It would be close quarters, for the fort was not designed to hold so many, but perhaps it was for the best that we should all be gathered there, for then we would have all our militia officers — Captain James Robertson, Colonel John Carter, and myself, a lieutenant — along with seventy-five armed men to defend the settlement, perhaps two hundred souls in all. We would not be comfortable, herded together like penned cattle, livestock and all, but we were used to hardships.

At least we were fortunate that it was high summer, so that there were provisions enough for all of us. The men ventured out to hunt, or to slaughter one of the hogs driven to the fort from the farms. The women prepared trenchers full of stews, cornmeal puddings, and beans, and such dishes as they could concoct from the plants nearby. It might have seemed very jolly to have all our friends and kinsman gathered for a long party, but only the younger children thought it a holiday. Our thoughts lay elsewhere. We kept sentries posted at every moment, watching the forests and the riverbank, waiting for the attack that we knew would come. I think the waiting was harder than the fighting itself when it came.

We had not long to wait, though. Near daybreak on the twentieth of July the Indians launched the first attack. Old Abram's warriors stormed the wooden walls of our little fort, and we managed to drive them back with volleys of musket fire, but our safety was dearly bought, for we lost a good many brave and honest men in that skirmish.

Even the women were drawn into the fighting, fierce as it was. At one point, while we were distracted by the gunfire, several of the Cherokee attempted to build a fire at the base of the log wall. The man who saw it stopped shooting long enough to kneel down on the parapet and shout down a warning to those milling about below. Some of the men began firing down at the Indians with the firebrands at the base of the wall, but they were protected by covering fire from their comrades hidden in the woods close by.

Within the fort, some of the women had been grouped around the big kettle, doing the washing. When they heard the warning shout — attackers trying to burn the fort — one of them responded at once. This was Ann Johnston, the sister of Captain Robertson. Married young and widowed at twenty-one, Mistress Ann had brought her three little daughters to the fort, and she had proved as much of a leader among the ladies as was her brother with the militia.

When the cry of "Fire" went up, Ann Johnston snatched up a wooden pail and dipped it into the boiling wash water. She carried the bucket to the side of the fort where the men were shooting at the marauders, and called to the women nearest her to help her scale the wall to the parapet. Once she gained her footing on the walkway near the top of the wall, she pushed her way past the marksmen, hoisted the bucket to the top of the palisades, and poured boiling water on the warriors below. By then the women had filled another bucket, and passed it up to her, so that she could do it again.

The scalded Indians soon abandoned their efforts and ran for the woods, but not before the Widow Johnston herself was wounded in the hail of arrows and shot flying past her. She did her part, though, in saving the fort, and she set an example for courage that helped all of us face the prospect of the long siege to come.

After that, all was quiet for hours, though we kept a full strength of sentries up on the parapet, watching in every direction, and the women kept that kettle boiling until nightfall.

The Indians did not come back, though. The next day dawned and the one after that, without a sign that there was anything out in the woods except wild turkeys and squirrels.

"They mean to starve us out," James Robertson told me as we took our turn on guard duty one evening. "They have all the forest to hunt in, and the whole of the river for water, while we sit here elbow to elbow within these walls. Our provisions won't last forever, and they know it."

I was watching the dark forest, but there was no movement there, no sign that we were not alone. "What choice have we? We can't go out and attack them in force. They would slip away before we got a hundred paces from the gates, only to come back in their own time. We must wait for them to attack again."

Robertson watched a bat soar up out of the forest in search of moths in the twilight. "I hope their patience is wearing thin. Mine certainly is."

July turned to August, and we sweltered inside the fort, waiting for an attack that did not come. It had been nearly a fortnight since we had seen any sign of Old Abram's men. Some of our people began to say that the Cherokee had given up and gone back to their villages. This was more wishful thinking than good sense, but we were all mortally tired of whiling away the summer days cooped up in a wooden pen.

The young people minded the most, I think. I mentioned this to my Sarah, and she smiled. "I expect the children do mind being cooped up," she said, "but except for the pall of danger, I reckon it hardly matters to the women. We are doing what we always do — cooking, washing, scrubbing floors, and tending to babies. One place is much the same as another for that."

No one liked the waiting, the short rations, or the close quarters, but mostly the women bore it with Christian fortitude until the cows started to bawl. We had kept the cows within the fort as long as we could, but when the fodder gave out, we had no choice but to turn them out to pasture and to hope that the Indians would not steal or slaughter them. So far they had grazed unharmed, but two days had passed, and the unmilked cows were bawling in distress.

"We can't let the poor things die," said one of the young mothers. "It isn't their fault we're in a war. Besides, our little ones need the milk."

The older women, whose children had shed their milk teeth and could subsist on the fare of the adults, hugged their young'uns close against them, and declared themselves persuaded by the arguments of the old Indian fighters. Since they had no urgent need for the milk, they were more concerned that it was not safe to venture outside the fort. They said that they could bear the sacrifice of the cows for the safety of the community. But, after another day, those among the women with babes in arms or just-weaned lap babies grew more insistent. They knew that we would have need of the cows' milk sooner rather than later, for the younger children could not eat the rough rations that the rest of us were making do with. The fact that two of my own children swelled that number made me mindful of the urgency of the situation.

Siding with the young mothers were a few tenderhearted girls of sixteen or thereabouts, those who likely tended those very cows and knew each one by name, and would not be swayed by arguments of prudence. They clamored to be let out to tend to their animals.

Perhaps the young never really believe that they can die.

I believed it, both for them and for myself, for I was a man of thirty by then, married these thirteen years and father of eight, and in a sense a father to all those within the fort, for I was one of those in command of

Fort Watauga. Two hundred lives depended on our ability to lead.

The young girls brought their argument to me. Colonel Carter and James Robertson were busy with the men, planning for the rationing of the provisions and ammunition, in case the siege should drag on for even more weeks. They sent me to reason with the women. I tried to persuade Robertson to talk to them in my stead, but he laughed and said, "A handsome fellow like you holds much more sway with the ladies, Sevier. Put your charm to good use." Robertson's sister Keziah was married to my own younger brother Robert, which made us kinsmen of a sort, or at least uncles to the same little boy, but he insisted that he had no patience for the wailing of women over a bunch of cattle, and he all but ordered me to do what I could to pacify them.

Thus I was doubly besieged — Indians without, and weeping maidens within. Four flowers of the frontier encircled me, their lips set with determination and their moist eyes flashing with indignation at the suffering of the animals.

"We don't even know that Old Abram and his men are still out there!" declared the doughty blonde whose hair fluffed around her ruddy face like a dandelion.

I looked into her gooseberry eyes and sighed. The poor girl was no beauty. I wondered if she thought that a show of bravery would add luster to her charms. Well, I did not think so. Courage from a stout woman is the sign of the shrew, the termagant, endearing her to no one. The willowy Sherrill girl was the oldest of the four women, past twenty-one and still unwed, though I would warrant it was not for lack of beauty. She had the look of a storybook heroine — too small and too pretty even to have to smile. And there they were, the two of them, and two more unmarried girls besides, asking my leave to die — a futile gesture for the stout girl and a waste of the beauty of Catherine Sherrill. Perhaps the others were followers, ready to fall in with any enterprise proposed by their companions. Or perhaps boredom at the tedium of our confinement had made them foolhardy. The boys their age — like my own firstborn Joseph — had been allowed to serve alongside their elders as guards and musket men, and so they felt like men, but the girls had done nothing except help with the chores and tend to the babies, and they were restless. In some measure, we all were. It is difficult to live day after day with the threat of an impending storm that never breaks.

"We want to go," the stout one said again. She gave me a mulish look that told me my arguments would fall on deaf ears.

The others were nodding in stony agreement. "We have heard no shots, seen no movement all day," said one.

"Surely it is safe, Mr. Sevier."

"I cannot open the gates," I said again, for to contest the point with reasoned arguments would be futile. They had an answer for everything. These fair flowers had thorns aplenty between them.

"Well," said dark-eyed Catherine Sherrill with a trace of a smile. "If you will not let us bring the cows *in,* you will have to let us *out.*"

I stared at her, but she did not back down. "Let you leave the fort without protection?"

She nodded, and the others murmured assent. "We need the milk for the youngest children," she said quietly. "We haven't enough food as it is. Let the four of us slip out through the gates. With buckets. Let us milk the cows, at least, even if we must leave them there in the field. If we see any sign of trouble, we can drop the pails and run back to the fort. We are the fastest runners in the settlement."

I doubted that, and I directed my gaze to their trailing skirts to make my point, but they all nodded in agreement that this preposterous statement was so.

"Not faster than the flight of an arrow," I muttered, but they paid no heed. The bawling of the distant cattle drowned out my objections, and I could not deny the truth of their argument: food was indeed scarce, and we did not know how long it would have to last. But the danger was a consideration as well. Already, we had lost two of our number to a quest for supplies.

It was only a week or so before the cows began their pained exhortations, when we'd sent out two of our own. It had been quiet for an entire day, so James Cooper and a brave young boy called Samuel Moore had ventured out of the fort and down to the river in search of wood for roofing a hut being constructed within the fort.

The Cherokee must have been watching them from the moment they slipped out of the gate, but they let them get all the way to the river's edge before they made themselves known. The ambush, when it came, happened close enough to the fort that we could hear the two men's screams, but too far away for us to provide any covering fire for them. It was too late by then, anyhow.

When their cries for help reached us, I rushed to the gate to assemble some of the militia and attempt a rescue, but Captain Robertson blocked the way, and ordered us to stay within.

"But they'll be killed!"

He nodded. "That may be. But you know full well that the Indians sometimes play tricks upon an unwary enemy. The attackers themselves will scream and call for help as if they were the captives, and foolhardy defenders will rush to the aid of these imaginary victims, only to be slaughtered themselves. We will not chance it. Your life is worth more than the risk."

I was all but certain that Cooper and the boy were in mortal danger, but I could not disobey the orders of a superior officer, though sometimes I wish I had, for many is the night since then that the screams of those men have troubled my sleep.

We watched as James Cooper tried to swim across the river to the comparative safety of the wood beyond, but before he reached the opposite shore, the Cherokee warriors brought him down with arrows and shot. Then they hauled his bleeding body out upon the riverbank, within sight of the fort, finished the job of killing him with their knives, and then took his scalp for a trophy.

As for the boy who had gone with him — poor little Sam Moore — we heard that he had been burned at the stake. There was little to choose between the two fates — being killed outright or being taken prisoner.

At the time, the four women knew of Cooper's fate, and they could guess at the probable end of young Sam Moore. How could they suggest that I let them leave the fort?

The cries of the cattle echoed around me. *Oh, yes.*

"The Indians are gone," one of them said. "Else they'd have killed the cattle already."

"Unless they left them alive to torment you," I replied.

Catherine Sherrill gave me a steely look. "We cannot let the beasts suffer, sir. Give us the pails and let us take our chances. In this war, sir, are we not all soldiers?"

I could not dispute that. If the fort were overrun, all our lives would be forfeit. Perhaps, though, the young women could slip more quietly in and out than armed men would be able to do. I hoped that to be the case, but whether true or not, the fact was that we could spare the girls more than we could the men, for if there were too few men left to defend the fort, then all within would die.

"Very well," I said. "You four may go at your own risk, but if you hear anything — the slightest sound in the underbrush — you are to drop those pails, and run straight for the fort without a thought for your companions. If you stop for one another, you may all perish. So you will run straight back as if you were alone. If you hear *anything*. Even a bird call. It might be a signal. Do you promise me that?"

Solemnly they nodded. They'd have promised me golden goose eggs to get my leave for their reckless errand.

If they heard anything. Did they think me foolish or had they, too, forgotten that no one could hear a twig break when a field full of cows is bellowing in agony. And if they were indeed ambushed at the meadow, would they in their terror remember what they had been told? I knew what a risk they were taking, and I hoped that their bravery was illuminated with the knowledge of the danger they faced, for if they were merely softhearted simpletons, then, in letting them go, I would be consigning more helpless creatures to suffering.

They were right, though. We needed the milk, and more than that, we could ill afford for the cows to die. The risk must be taken. The men were needed to man the guns, and the older women had children to tend. If anyone could be spared, it was indeed these unmarried girls. I felt heartless even as I thought it, but life on the frontier is a lesson in hard truths.

It had been quiet for days. I decided that we could wait no longer, or the cows *would* die, Indians or no. With many misgivings, which I forebore to speak of, I escorted the four maidens and their pails out of the log building and saw them safely to the great wooden gate. "Godspeed," I said, but, intent upon their mission, they hurried away with their oaken buckets without a backward glance. I watched them go, admiring their courage, for even though they were soldiers as much as any of us, they had willingly set out on a mission from which I doubted they would return.

I wished that there were a clear view of the meadow, instead of the curtain of trees into which they vanished only a few yards from the fort.

The young man who stood guard next to the gate touched my arm as I turned away. "Do you think the Indians have gone, sir?"

I shrugged. "I wouldn't have."

PATRICK FERGUSON
PITFOUR, SCOTLAND
1758

"There are better tombstones in Strachur."

I was startled, that's all. Anybody would be, hearing a voice like that, as if out of nowhere in a gloomy kirkyard. I was glad to be alone — glad that I had managed to stand my ground, and that my sister Betty had wandered off into the sanctuary of the kirk, for she would have laughed and pointed to see me tremble so as if I were a quaking bairn.

But I wasn't afraid, not of old graves on a gray afternoon. Of course I wasn't. We Fergusons are an educated family, not a tribe of superstitious bumpkins. And isn't my uncle a famous general over the water in Canada? If I am to follow in his path, I must not be skittish over a sudden rush of movement or noise — for what else are battles but that?

It was just that I hadn't seen anyone else about among the tombstones, that's all.

■ ■ ■ ■

High summer it was, and we had journeyed up from Edinburgh to our country house at Pitfour, in Buchan, just inland from Peterhead. The place had belonged to my Grandfather Ferguson, who had been Sheriff-Depute of Aberdeen, though I never knew him, for he died a decade before I came into the world. Upon his death, Pitfour was inherited by my father. One day it will go to Jamie, I suppose, along with any titles that happen to be going, for he is the eldest, and was born with his nose in the trough right enough. He will follow our father into the law, I have no doubt, and while I do not envy him that sedentary life, I would wish that mine were not so uncertain. The family is trying to decide what to do with me. Perhaps my solemnity comes from the uncertainty of my future, for I knew my childhood to be nearly over, exchanged for I knew not what.

I was called Patrick after my other grandfather Lord Elibank, but that is all I am likely to get, for a second son is only a spare, not an heir, and unless Jamie breaks his thick neck, I will have to shift for myself in this life. I tell Jamie that it's a blessing to have the freedom of the world from which to choose one's path, but he only smiles as if he knows that choosing is the greatest burden of all.

I had just turned fourteen in June, and the shape of my life had begun to occupy my thoughts for I was no longer a child, and the future seemed to be coming upon me in a great rush — unlike Jamie's fate, which would sit square in the road years ahead of him like a great braw hound, only waiting for him to reach it.

"At least no one has to die to give me a foothold," I told him.

My brother did not trouble to reply because as soon as I said it, I knew it to be a lie. Uncle James Murray, who assumed command in Canada after General Wolfe died at Quebec, had surely reached his new eminence through someone else's demise, and it was he who proposed that I should follow him into the army. Uncle James had seen me playing with my wee tin soldiers a year or two ago, and he told my mother that they ought to think of buying me a commission in a good regiment. The idea pleased me, not least because I was a frail child, the very antipode of a great warrior. All the more reason to prove myself.

When I was twelve, and Uncle Jamie was

lieutenant colonel of the 15th Foot, he prevailed upon my father to buy me a commission in the regiment so that he might shepherd me into his profession. It came to naught, though, for I was such a wee, frail lad at twelve that the regiment, looking ahead to war in Canada, had no choice but to throw me back, and to refund to my father the purchase price of my ensigncy, for I'd have been no use to them on a battlefield.

For now, there was little to do besides my lessons and to go for country walks with my sisters. I fancied myself protecting them on our rambles, though I was no bigger or stronger than they.

"Pattie, how shilpit you look," said Betty, peering into my face. "Are you taken ill?"

I shook my head. "Mortal thoughts, Betty," I said, trying to make light of it. "Consider our surroundings."

My sister Betty and I had gone walking in the kirkyard, threading our way among the tombstones, stopping now and again to examine the mossy carving or to read a weathered inscription.

"You're not afraid of a graveyard, are you?" The voice was all tender concern, but Betty's gray eyes mocked me from beneath her prim blue bonnet.

"I am not. But I'm not a child to go larking about among the dead, either. Show a bit of respect, Betty."

She tossed her head. "Perhaps Father should train you up for a parson instead of a soldier," she said. "I wish I had come with Jean instead of ye, dour old man of fourteen!"

Jean is our youngest sister, and normally Betty thinks herself too grand and grown to consort with a bairn like Jean. She only wished for her now to taunt me, but my black mood and a dearth of other society in the neighborhood had combined to make the pair of them allies if not friends in the few days we had been in Pitfour, so that any excursion planned for an afternoon would necessarily have included wee Jean as well, but today she was taken ill with a summer cold, and Mother deemed it best not to let her go out walking in the damp mist of a drizzly day. Jean must stay at home with George, the youngest, who was thought too delicate to be abroad in foul weather, whether he had a cough or no. Thus my sister was left with only old sobersides — me — for company.

Betty soon tired of walking in the gloomy shade of the kirkyard. "Would you like to

43

see the inside of the church, Patrick? It isn't grand at all compared to the kirk in Edinburgh, but there's a pretty colored window. I like to see the sun making rainbows through the glass. I thought I might try to sketch them. Will you come?"

I shook my head. On such a gray day as this, I thought little of her chances of seeing rainbows in sun shafts. "Go along, Betty," I said. "I am happy out here, parsing the words on these headstones."

She looked doubtful. "All right, but if it begins to rain, you must promise me that you will come inside. You mustn't take a chill."

I assured her that, as I had no wish to catch my death in a kirkyard, I would come in the moment a drop of rain touched my cheek. With that she was satisfied, and she left me at last in peace. I strolled among the rows of headstones, more preoccupied with my own thoughts than with concern for the dear departed. Once I thought I saw a stoat slink down past a stone mausoleum in the distance. Hunting church mice, I thought, or perhaps young rabbits too fresh from the nest to know the dangers. Bit early for a stoat to be out hunting, though, surely, even if the day was dreary.

■ ■ ■ ■

I had wandered alone for a wee while after Betty departed, reading the epitaphs, and wondering what my own might say in the fullness of time. The place made thoughts of death inevitable, even for a merry lass like my sister, much more so for her dour younger brother.

A soft voice startled me out of my reverie.

"There are better tombstones in Strachur."

I spun round, alarm giving way to annoyance at being thus rudely accosted. "Who the de'il?"

In the shadow of the great tree stood a lass who looked no older than I. Great green eyes peered out at me from a whey face beneath a gray hooded cloak, the color of the rain clouds. Beneath the cloak she wore a dark homespun dress, and I glimpsed wisps of damp red hair curling at her temples. She had knelt down before a headstone, and was tracing its lettering with one bony finger.

The wind bit into me, and I shivered as I peered over her shoulder, attempting to make out the faint inscription, half worn away by weathering. The only word on the stone that yet remained discernible was

"Ferguson."

"That is my name," I said aloud.

The pale girl nodded. "Aye. 'Tis. There be Fergusons buried at Strachur as well."

"Are you connected to the family?" I asked her.

Solemnly she nodded again. She did not look up at me when she said it, for she was intent upon her tracery of the lettering.

I thought, though, by the clarty look of her homespun clothing and her rough speech that she was not of the gentry. A servant girl perhaps, or a nursemaid, brought hence with some family, working on a neighboring farm. "I am Patrick Ferguson of Pitfour," I said, drawing myself up to not much height. "My father is a lawyer in Edinburgh."

I suppose I expected her to be covered with confusion upon hearing whom she had disturbed with her ill-mannered prating, but she only shrugged, as if she had known that already and it did not trouble her overmuch. She seemed intent upon studying the stones. I wondered if she could read them or if her scrutiny was only for show.

"And who are you?"

"Nobody," she said. I heard no bitterness in her voice. So simply was it said that it nettled me, as if to mock my own pride in

46

my rank and lineage.

"I intend to be somebody one day," I said. "Do you live near here?"

Solemnly she nodded. "Quite near indeed."

I waited, but she did not say to which family she belonged. Perhaps she was ashamed to have me know, but she seemed to know a fair bit about my own people.

"And, pray, what is so special about the headstones at Strachur?" I asked her, annoyed by her complacence and by the thought that our Pitfour kirk should be outshone by some distant village in Argyll.

If she heard petulance in my tone, she did not heed it. "Some of the stanes there ha' faces upon them."

"*Faces?*"

"Aye. Graven atop the stane will be a face with wings on ither side of it."

"Angels, do you mean?"

"Not angels at all. 'Tis the *brideag* on those stanes."

I did not understand the word and shook my head impatiently.

She raised her eyebrows and looked at me as if to question my ignorance. "Do you not know it then? And you a Ferguson?"

"I am from Edinburgh. We set no store by rustic superstitions. Anyway, I do not speak the Gaelic, which I presume that word to be." In my tone I gave her to know how foolish and unfashionable I thought both her language and her quaint notions.

"It is an old word," she said. "There are other names for it."

"Well," I said. "We have fine kirkyards in Edinburgh, too. Have you ever seen the monuments at Greyfriars?"

She shook her head. "I have not. But there will be Fergusons there, too, perhaps," she said.

"Yes, I expect I shall be buried there one day," I said, trying to make a jest of it.

She turned and looked at me with great green eyes, and suddenly I was put in mind of an owl's gaze. *"No, ye will not."*

The shrill scream of a small creature rent the air, and I flinched, startled by the sound, but the girl reacted not at all to the sounds of the death agony. She could not have been calmer if she had been expecting it. I supposed that the creeping stoat I had seen a while before had found its prey — a young rabbit, judging by the sound of it.

"A merciful death," she murmured. "Scarcely any pain. Soon over."

"I wouldn't want it," I said.

She turned her green owl eyes on me then. "Would you not?" she said, as if she really wanted to know.

"Signifying nothing," I said. "A death which means something would be worth the price of pain, I think. Of course, I'm meant to be a soldier."

She nodded. "And would you die to save an empire, then?" she asked me.

I thought she might be making sport of me, but she regarded me with a grave expression as if she really wanted to know.

"To save an empire would be worth my life," I allowed grandly. Easy enough to speak of such things in peaceful churchyards when you are yet a schoolboy, I suppose, but I meant it.

"So you would rather have a protracted death in service of a cause than a meaningless, but merciful, release?"

"I am a Ferguson of Pitfour," I said. "I have my honor to consider. I don't suppose you could understand such a thing."

Her eyes widened for an instant, and I thought she might reproach me for my hasty words, but then she simply shrugged, and said, "It shall be as you wish then, Ferguson of Pitfour."

Before I could ask her what on earth she meant by that, it began to rain in earnest, and Betty appeared at the church door, shouting for me to make a dash for shelter before I caught my death in the downpour. I pulled my coat up to cover my head, and hied myself off toward the sanctuary. When I turned to look for the owl-eyed girl in the gray cloak, she had gone.

CHAPTER THREE
AUGUST 1780

When Isaac Shelby came to find me in August of 1780, it put me in mind of the time four years past, at Fort Watauga, when I had allowed four young girls, armed only with wooden buckets, to venture outside the wooden walls. Shelby's news made me recall the one thing I had learned from the incident of the suffering cows: that it is better to attack than to be besieged. Shelby had come to tell me that an even greater war might at last be coming into our territory.

"We cannot wait for them to attack us here, Sevier. We must go out and meet them." When he told me that, I found myself thinking of young girls going forth into the fields armed only with wooden buckets.

Our strategy had changed, and so had the enemy.

■ ■ ■ ■

Isaac Shelby and I were old friends, and, more than that, comrades in arms, for we had fought together in many a battle on the frontier. The country had been at war now for four years; and we had done our share of fighting, though not with George Washington's Continental Army, whose battles were taking place elsewhere. We had little enough time to think of the northern campaign, and day to day we had little evidence of our own eyes that anything was amiss beyond our valleys.

The larger war was not here. The Continental Army was fighting it in the northern colonies — Pennsylvania, New York — and they left us to fend for ourselves. We were *beyond the pale,* that ancient term for those who lived removed from civilization. When bands of Indians attacked our farms and killed our neighbors, no standing army marched to our rescue. So we built our own forts and served in a citizens' militia, and we protected our own.

The truth was that those in power didn't want us out there on the frontier in the first place. We would have been easier to manage if we'd all stayed hemmed in on the coast, within half a day's ride of one of their cities, where their troops were quartered and their rules enforced with the rope and the lash. The British had signed a treaty back when they were fighting the French, who were in league with the Indians. To end that war, the British agreed that no whites would settle the mountain lands — the Treaty of Paris, that was, and nobody asked us settlers what we thought about it — but they could no more stem the tide of folk heading westward than they could dam up the ocean.

When they finally realized that the frontier was going to be pushed west whether they liked it or not, they started to parlay with the Indians to reach yet another agreement, which would be a fine alternative to fighting, if the savages could be trusted to keep their word. A dozen years back at Fort Stanwix, the government made a treaty with the Iroquois that was supposed to give them the rights to the lands south of the Ohio River. But the Iroquois nation does not speak for all the Indians, and the Shawnee who hunted there would not abide by it — I reckon nobody asked their opinion, either.

We suffered for that.

Battles were waged and, thankfully, won by us — but not without a heavy toll. Our eventual peace treaty bought us only a little time. The revolution itself commenced up in the Massachusetts colony some six months later, but it did not touch us that soon. Between the Indians and the vicissitudes of farming, we on the frontier had little time to spare for thoughts of war with our British overlords. By 1780, though, we had been bloodied in the fighting, and we did know that the war would reach us soon enough. The Continental Army's struggle looked grim, and the outcome was by no means assured to be a happy one. Shelby was just on thirty, but with his hawk-billed nose and his ramrod carriage, he seemed a stern man even in idle times. He had arrived at my farm that afternoon with his grim tidings, only to find that he was intruding upon a joyous celebration already in progress. In truth, though, I don't think his somber nature stood out against our revelry any more than it might have on any other day. It was late summer, a time of harvest and plenty, and my second wife and I were newly married, so we were hosting a barbecue for all our neighbors. A pig was roasting on the spit, and the long tables had been dragged out onto the lawn and laden with bowls of food.

Shelby, weary from forty miles of hard

riding over from his family's holdings at Shelby's Fort, rounded the bend to see a horde of people making merry under the trees, eating and laughing, while others danced and clapped in time to the music of fiddlers. I was getting ready for the horse race, for I had a fine young stud that I wanted to try against my neighbors' stock, but when I saw Shelby riding up — the grim-faced bearer of bad tidings — I handed over the reins to my oldest boy, Joseph, and bade him take my place in the race. One of the younger boys took Shelby's horse to be cooled down and watered, while Shelby himself downed a cup of water, and then I led the colonel into the house, away from the revelers.

The cows' bellowing echoed through the woods as the four young women had set out in a line from the fort on that still evening. They walked slowly, single-file, and not talking amongst themselves. Even if they believed that the danger was past, they would be cautious and quiet anyhow. They had been raised on the frontier, and such wariness was in their blood.

In the fort all was quiet as well. The sentries gazed over the palisades, alert for signs of trouble, and the rest of us were listening, praying that until those girls came back we would hear nothing.

The crack of distant gunfire sent me running to the parapet. I had been right. Of course I was. The Indians had not left — why should they? We were trapped in the fort, existing on a meager food supply while they had our farms, the great forest, and the rivers to sustain them. What had they to do but wait it out, and the longer they waited, the greater their triumph, for in our privation, we would grow weaker by the day.

I only hoped that I might have the satisfaction of hearing the stammered apologies from those foolhardy lasses when they came crashing through the bracken back to the safety of the fort. *Drop the buckets and run,* I thought. Surely they would not be foolish enough to do otherwise.

Run.

I could only hope that they were closer to the fort than the renegades, and that they could run fast enough to save their lives. I hauled myself up on the parapet, gun in hand, while my eyes scanned the distance, looking for some sign of those girls, or, failing that, for some enemy to aim at.

If we could set up a covering fire, it might slow down the attackers enough to enable the girls to gain the fort.

Captain Robertson and those of us up on the parapet waited for what felt like an eternity, but it was only the space of time that you could hold your breath. One girl ran headlong up the path toward the great wooden gate, but she was cut down in a hail of gunfire and arrows. As I had suspected, the Cherokee had not gone away, after all. In the night they had crept close to the fort and hidden themselves in the woods, re-appearing only when the girls tried to return to the fort. I recognized the bleeding body below as the stout girl with gooseberry eyes. Who'd have thought she could have run so fast? It was her misfortune that her speed and her bravery had not been enough, and I was sorry to see her courage repaid with tragedy.

Where were the others?

For another moment I glanced at the crumpled form of the fallen girl near the walls of the fort and then I turned my gaze back to the path searching for the remainder of the party. Only one appeared.

Catherine Sherrill.

There she was, running for all she was worth. On the parapet I called out to Captain Robertson, "The Sherrill lass," I said, pointing, but I saw that he had already caught sight of her. "The gate. Can't we chance it?"

He shook his head. "If they open it for her, the Indians can get in as well. They are practically upon us. Even if we could kill them, they could cut down as many of us before they were all dispatched."

I could not dispute the truth of what he said, but it was a bitter choice: save the brave young woman or safeguard all those within it?

I leaned over the poles of the stockade. The wall was perhaps fourteen feet high, and too steep to climb — it had to be, to keep us safe from attacks. Around me, the men were firing blindly into the woods, trying to guess the location of the attackers from the smoke and the direction of the arrows' flight. But the trees shielded the attackers, making it difficult to bring one of them down, but we hoped to distract them so that they could not take a proper aim at the running girl.

By now Catherine had reached the gate, and found that it was closed. Her shoulders sagged, and I swear I could see the reality register in her fear-stricken eyes. My heart sank for her, and my own despair grew. I caught my breath, willing her not to give up. She hesitated for no more than an intake of breath, and then she sped away, around the perimeter of the fort, staying close to the wall, and calling out for help when she had the wind to manage it. I watched arrows fly past her, and bury their points into the wall of the fort. Bullets struck the logs and made little clouds of wood dust where they hit. Silently, I cursed the British army that had given those guns to the Indians. At any moment one of their bullets would find its target and strike her down, making us all unwilling witnesses to her fate.

I could not bear the cruelty of it, and perhaps it was my dread of watching her die that gave me the idea. Some of the men had rushed out of the blockhouse and were standing in the open space below. I called down for them to climb up on the parapet. We had but moments to effect a desperate plan.

As they ascended the ladder, I set aside my hat, my powder horn, my weapons — anything that would weigh me down. Then I turned to them: "Lift me up over the wall, boys. And two of you hold on to my feet. Mind you get a good grip, though."

They might have tried to reason with me if there had been time, but I outranked them, and, even though we were not a formal army here on the frontier, an officer's orders were beyond question. Or perhaps in those few moments they realized that what I proposed to do was the sum total of that young woman's chance to live.

The fact that I am tall and lean gave me an advantage in the prospect, for my reach would be long, and I hoped my shape would make me less of a target for the Cherokee marksmen lurking in the nearby woods. I scarcely had time to take a deep breath before the men hoisted me up and dangled me down over the pointed logs atop the fort. I felt myself falling and then just as abruptly I pulled up short, as the lads who had hold of my legs tightened their grip and held me fast.

I hung there headfirst, like a ham from a smokehouse rafter, with my arms outstretched but still able to reach no closer than seven feet off the ground. I spared a thought for my leggings, hoping that the deer hide would be equal to the strain of the grip of those who were keeping me aloft. If any shot or arrows were aimed at me, I would be powerless to avoid them. But, one way or another, a minute would see me to the end of it.

When Catherine Sherrill rounded the corner of the stockade wall, I called out to her above the shouts and the crack of gunfire, "Jump, Kate!"

She heard me and glanced up. Without breaking stride, she sprang into the air, reaching up as far as she could, but as I strained to reach her out-stretched arm, she fell back again, a hand's breadth shy of the distance she needed to catch hold of my hand. "Circle around!" I screamed down to her. She stumbled for just an instant, and then ran on, just as a Cherokee arrow hit the wall close behind her. Apparently, so intent were they upon dispatching her that they did not spare a volley up at me. Or if they did, their aim was faulty, for I stayed unharmed.

We had perhaps a minute, if she and I succeeded in staying alive that long, before she would appear again. I needed to stretch lower to the ground to be within her reach, yet still have the force to hoist her up with me over the wall, for I did not mean to land outside the fort myself and keep her company in dying.

I called up to the men who had hold of my legs, "A little lower, boys! Now swing me side to side! Like a pendulum!"

This was our last chance, and then we would have done all we could. Now her life depended upon Providence, and on her own strength and will. Once again she rounded the corner of the fort, seeming to run at me in a blur as I dangled there swinging back and forth, a hanged man in reverse, with the blood coursing to my head. I stretched out my hands as far as they would go, and upon the low arc of my passage above her, she hurled herself upward with a great leap, and managed to grasp my wrist. I wrapped my fingers around her own slender wrists, and let the swinging motion carry us upward and toward the men at the top of the parapet leaning over to grab us.

It seemed to me that a dozen hands grabbed us both. With a collective heave, they hauled us up and over the log spikes atop the wall, where Catherine and I tumbled down together in a heap on the parapet.

It was only then that Mistress Sherrill began to weep.

The full, coordinated attack from the nearby Cherokees came later that day, and we managed to beat them back. We lost a good many brave souls in the fighting, but we had killed enough of Old Abram's war party for him to call off the siege. We watched the few surviving warriors fade back into the forest. We waited a while to make sure, and then sent out scouts. They were gone.

The gates of Fort Watauga swung open,

and, family by family, we all filed out, cradling our wounded, and keeping our children as close as we could, still watching for shadows in the dark woods. The battle was over . . . but not the war.

Three years after that day, Sarah, my loyal wife of nearly twenty years, died after a lingering illness, following the birth of our tenth child.

The following summer I married Catherine Sherrill.

It was the celebration of that occasion that Isaac Shelby had happened upon when he rode up to Plum Grove that afternoon with his news of yet another enemy sent to try us.

We lingered outside long enough to collect tankards of applejack, and then I led Shelby inside the house, and settled him in our little parlor. We talked for a bit of inconsequential matters — the harvest, the children — while he finished his drink and cooled down from the long ride.

"You know Sam Phillips, I think? A kinsman of mine."

I nodded. "I have heard talk of him recently. Was he not captured by the Tories down in South Carolina?"

"He was. We had all feared the worst for

him, for you know how brutal they are with their prisoners. They are neck and neck with the Indians for savagery. But Sam arrived at our place on the Holston a day ago, not much the worse for wear for his ten-day journey, and bearing a message."

"They let him go?" I had not thought to hear that, for those loyal to the king are overly fond of using the rope on those that they deem traitors.

"They did — but only because they wanted him to bring that message to us. And I came to you, because we must decide how best to answer it."

I stared. "A message — from whom, exactly?"

"Ferguson."

We knew of him. Maj. Patrick Ferguson was a Scotsman, regular British army, and recently he had been sent down from the war in the northern colonies, charged with the task of persuading more southern citizens to side with the Crown. His methods tended more toward ruthless coercion than sweet persuasion.

For much of the summer, Isaac Shelby had been away to the south of here, leading a company of militia and joining other Whig commanders in the fighting against the British and their homegrown Tory soldiers. The

British would bring the war up into North Carolina, and so they had asked for troops to defend the border. My brother Valentine was one of our Backcountry soldiers who went south like Shelby to fight.

I had elected to stay at home with my own troops, in case the Indians should stage another attack. We had not forgotten the bitter siege of Fort Watauga four years before, and many of us believed that the British were trying to forge a treaty with the Cherokee; distraction here would keep the Backcountry militias from helping those opposing their armies farther east.

While my troops stayed north, waiting on word from the Backcountry soldiers, news reached us that Ferguson himself had led a troop of Tories out of South Carolina, on raids near Gilbert Town and farther north to steal cattle and supplies for his regiment, and to harry the landowners who favored independence. At the time, I'd thought ruefully that if Ferguson tried to apply that tactic to the likes of us here on the frontier, the major's efforts would have the opposite effect.

I looked wonderingly at Colonel Shelby. "Ferguson has sent us a message?"

"Yes. He demands that the 'officers west of the mountains' cease their opposition to the king's forces. And he says that if we do not comply, he will bring his army here and lay waste to our lands."

I raised an eyebrow. "Does he now? I wonder what he thinks of his chances."

Shelby permitted himself a tight smile. "From what transpired this summer, I think Ferguson might have a time of it up here."

"You led the Tories into a trap, and managed to dispatch two hundred of them. And what were your losses?" I knew the answer, roughly, but I was underscoring my point, that we would not be easy pickings for Ferguson's Tory soldiers. Back in the early summer, when Colonel McDowell of Quaker Meadows had asked for help from the militia commanders over the mountains, Shelby and James Robertson joined their forces to those of McDowell, and routed the Tories at Thicketty Fort and later at Musgrove Mill.

"Including wounded? Eleven men." Shelby drained the last of his applejack. "I'm happy to fight the Tories again if they haven't yet learned their lesson about our backcountry fighters, but I'd rather keep the war well away from our territory, for even if they lose, they are like locusts for taking crops and livestock to feed their troops. We should have ended it after Musgrove Mill, when we had them on the run. Robertson and I thought we ought to march straight down into South Carolina, to their main camp at Ninety Six and finish the job, but we were held back."

I had heard this already from my brother Valentine, who agreed with Colonel Shelby. Their troops were only thirty miles from Ninety Six, mounted and ready to advance, but before they could get under way, they were stopped by a courier from Charles McDowell. He was delivering a dispatch that McDowell had received hours earlier from General Caswell. The letter advised them that Gen. Horatio Gates had been soundly defeated at Camden. South Carolina was now controlled by the Loyalist forces under Lord Cornwallis. This was deemed to be such a blow to the Revolution that our commander could not risk the loss of any more troops.

"I heard of it from my brother," I said. "That letter from Caswell, informing you of Gates's defeat. Infernally bad timing, wasn't it?"

"We had to pass Ferguson's encampment on our way north, and they gave chase. We hastened with such speed that we dispensed with encampments altogether. We drank from streams as we crossed them, and ate what he found in the fields we traversed. Finally, we reached McDowell at Gilbert Town, not long after our pursuers called a halt to their chase and faded back to the south. And so we came home."

"But this threat from Ferguson is your pretext for another chance."

"Well, it's only the gravy, Sevier, not the meat. Before we even got back from the Musgrove Mill expedition, Robertson and I talked about it, and we decided that it would be a good idea to raise as large a force as we could muster, and send them all back to engage the enemy in one fell swoop. And this time I don't mean to let any timid commanders hold us back."

"But you are proposing to head back there and join forces with McDowell again?"

He scowled. "That cannot be helped. We need his support, but not his leadership. He is an old sheep and I mean to lose him in a mighty flock.

"Look here, Sevier, just think. You with the Fort Lee contingent, and Robertson with his Watauga boys. William Campbell can bring Virginia troops, and I have my command. Benjamin Cleveland down on the Yadkin. If we put all the militias together, more will join us — some South Carolinians perhaps, and some units from even farther east than the Yadkin. Why, we could put together a force of more than a thousand men."

"I suppose we could. And how many have agreed to join you thus far?"

Shelby hesitated for a moment and in the silence, the shouts and laughter from the lawn filled the little parlor. I looked out at the golden afternoon. There under the trees, the younger children were chasing one of the puppies, and from a bench in the shade of a towering poplar, the older ladies were keeping an eye on the courting couples. It was odd to think of my bride Catherine as one of the settlement's matrons now, though she was all of twenty-six by now, and the new stepmother of a sixteen-year-old lad, my Joseph, as well as the nine younger Seviers.

I knew that Shelby was asking me to leave all this — leave my bride of three weeks — to march off to war a hundred miles and more from home. The war had been going on for four years now. Why must it come after me now?

"Who else has agreed to this, Colonel Shelby?"

He stared out the window for a few more moments, and then he met my gaze without a qualm. His purpose, after all, was to see that all of us on the frontier were safe, and so my wife and children were the very reason to go. "I came to ask you first," he said. "But I don't think we have much of a choice. We can't sit back and let the government in the north fight this war against the Tories when it's all happening on our lands — and they don't know how to fight the battles. It's not just McDowell anymore. Now it's the likes of Gates, too. We're the frontiersmen, Sevier. We're the ones who know how to fight; and I'd prefer to do so before the battles creep into our own backyards."

"Tell me about Gates, then."

"You know that Congress appointed him the commander for the southern department of the war, as they call it."

"Yes, Horatio Gates. English by birth. They say he is the son of a duke."

"And also the son of that duke's housekeeper. He is a mule of a man, trying mightily to be a thoroughbred, and thoroughly irritating everyone who crosses his path with his airs and graces. Leaving aside all the tittle-tattle about his behavior in the northern colonies, he comes south, and decides to attack Camden, despite objections from the local commanders that their troops are not ready to do battle. Then he, knowing nothing of the terrain himself since he just arrived, insists on marching the army by the 'direct route' to Camden, through swamp and pine barrens, instead of taking the road that would have taken them through farmlands, where friendly Whigs would have fed the troops along the way. So he arrived with tired and ailing soldiers, and ordered a night march on the town. Cornwallis, who was headquartered there in the home of some poor Whig, ordered a march that same night, knowing full well that Gates's army was coming. The Tory spies are quite efficient, I fear."

"My brother Valentine has said that the battle was a rout, but he gave me little of the particulars."

Shelby waved a hand dismissively. "Oh, they were outnumbered, sick from trying to eat green corn, and footsore from the long march. It is not the battle that I wished to speak of. It is the aftermath. They say that Gates left the battlefield at a gallop. Major Davie was on his way to the battle with a small group of reinforcements, when — ten miles from Camden — he encountered a rider in full flight, heading north. Davie says that Gates ordered him to turn back, to which the major replied that his men were ready to fight against Tarleton, despite his reputation as a butcher. General Gates looked back as if he expected to see all the devils of hell in pursuit of him, and then he spurred his horse and sped on northward."

"Gates abandoned the army?"

Shelby shrugged. "What was left of it. We had nearly four thousand men on the field at Camden, and General Cornwallis claimed that his men had killed a quarter of that number and wounded another quarter. Meanwhile, as these men lay maimed or dying at Camden, their illustrious commander rode more than a hundred and eighty miles in just three days, and fetched up in Hillsborough."

There were so many thoughts crowding my brain that I seized upon one at random and said it aloud. "General Gates . . . He is not a young man, is he?"

"He is past fifty. You may consider that ride an admirable feat for a man of his age, but as behavior for a general it is monstrous."

"And is he still in Hillsborough?"

"The last word that I had said he was there with the few hundred survivors of his folly at Camden, trying to reassemble an army. If you are thinking of appealing to Gates for help —"

"Not after what you've said," I assured

him. "It sounds as if we are on our own. But we cannot do it alone, you know, Shelby. Not just with your militia and mine. We haven't enough men."

"No, but people look up to you, Colonel Sevier. If I can tell people that you are with us, then the rest will come. You can raise at least a hundred men or so, can't you?"

"Yes, but you know it will take more than numbers. If you propose to march a few hundred men down to Ninety Six, or wherever the fight will be, then you'll need powder and shot, rations, supplies . . . It takes a deal of money to grease the wheels of a war wagon."

"Yes, it does indeed, but no one will give us the money until we have the army. We'll cross that bridge farther along. What I need to know right now is — will you come?"

I considered it. "So Ferguson threatens to bring the war to us."

"Yes. That's the nub of it. I do not think any of us has a choice of whether or not to fight. You can only decide whether you want to do it in the low country or" — he pointed to the sunlit lawn beyond the window — "there."

"Where are the armies now? Do you know?"

"Lord Cornwallis and Banastre Tarleton

are thought to be in Charlotte, but Major Ferguson was headed for Gilbert Town, and we deem it likely that he is still there in the foothills burning and thieving his way to converting the people to his side. I don't want him here."

"No. It was good of him to warn us, though. I wonder why he did."

"It's peculiar, isn't it? I can only assume that he meant to frighten us into submission."

We looked at each other and laughed. "He doesn't know us very well, does he?"

Virginia Sal

I joined up with him that summer, a week or so after Ramsour's Mill. Some of the folk hereabouts would take umbrage at my doing that, for they were saying that the British were only trying to keep us from being free, but I never had any time for wrangling about politics. I reckon I will still have to chop wood and boil water no matter who is in charge of the country. I listened to all the arguing, though — you could hardly help it unless you was to sit off by yourself the livelong day, which I had neither the means nor the leisure to do. I kept my opinions to myself, but hearing both sides of the wrangle day in and day out, I saw the most sense in those that held with keeping our ties with England. Maybe it's all right for those folk in the big cities by the ocean to harp on being independent, but here we are in the hill country, a few far-flung farms and patchwork fields hewed out of a tangle of forest that goes on forever. Who is to save us if the Indians make another war? Or if the Spanish should decide to come north? If that was to happen, I reckon most folk around here would go down on their knees and beg the British to stay.

Anyhow, I did like the look of that fellow I saw commanding the Loyalist troops in these parts.

I caught a glimpse of him from afar as his regiment went marching down the road one day. Some of the men had on the scarlet coats of the regular army, and they made a fine show on their horses, with their swords and their brass fittings glinting in the sunshine. Most of the soldiers, though, were just South Carolina farm boys, not real soldiers at all, and they just looked dusty and hot, and ordinary, trudging down the road in the wake of the gentry. The commander caught my eye at once. I took him for a general, with his fine white horse and his faraway look, as if he was so important and noble that it was beneath him to notice anything so common as a muddy trace cutting through the hills of Carolina, and a bunch of gawking rustics, peering at him from over their fences.

Folk who had seen him up close were full of tales about the commander's fancy way of talking, and the prissy way he had of insisting on proper meals and clean clothes, even when he was soldiering and camped out in the back of beyond. He was quality. You could tell. But when I went along to the army camp that summer morning, I hadn't any notion of meeting up with him at all. He was just a sight to behold, riding by on a white horse, and I had no more thought of getting closer to him that you'd have about keeping company with a waterfall or a snow white deer — he was just a marvel to say you had seen one time, that's all.

His manservant, Powell, found me in the camp, a few days after that set-to they had at Cowpens. Their side had won that battle, and so I came along out of curiosity, but mainly to see if there were pickings to be had, for I have to make my own way in the world. There are some I know who would have run away from an army, and if I had been a man, I reckon I might have done that, but, on my own like I was and sick to death of being the hired girl on an upland farm, I thought I would go and see what the war was like, afore things around here went back to being dull again. I was young and pretty enough to be sure of my welcome among soldiers. And I reckoned I was safer with an army than I would have been as a lone, lorn woman on some farmstead when they came through, a-foraging. You fare better if they can count you as one of their own, and if you are not afraid of them, for one on one they are mostly just farm boys, same as all the ones you've seen a-plowing and hoeing corn. Besides, from what I had seen these past months of Loyalists and Rebels raiding farms, stealing livestock provisions, and hanging them that disagreed with them, I judged that it might well be safer to be with an army than staying at home and trying to ignore one.

So I set out that morning before sunup, looking for the war.

It didn't take much to find them, neither. The Indians may slip in and out of the woods without ever you knowing they were there until too late, but the king's army rampages around like so many rutting bulls, making all the noise and commotion they please and proud of the display of it. So I had to ask the way a time or two, along with a dipper full of water, for it was a day of breathless heat, but finally I found them along about mid-morning, and I strolled into the camp, smiling and nodding how-do as if I had been sent an invitation.

I attracted attention enough. Some of the

Loyalists were older men, and mindful of families left back at home, and bone weary besides from all the marching, but there were enough young bucks in the ranks to create quite a stir at the sight of me. I smiled broader and edged away from a grasping few, looking for somebody worth my time.

A likely-looking bunch of the younger soldiers had gathered around me, and they were making free with their flasks and their rations, when a fussy little terrier of a man — name of Elias Powell, I was to find out — spied me talking amongst them, and he swooped in like a duck after a june bug, cut me out of the pack, and hustled me away, with his hand gripped tight around my elbow so's I couldn't run.

"What did you want to do that for?" I asked, trying to shake him off. "I wasn't doing nothing, but only just passing the time of day with those boys back there."

He tightened his grip on my arm and shook it a little to show he meant it. "How do we know you aren't a spy for the Whigs then?"

I blinked at that, for it wasn't what I was expecting to hear. This Elias Powell wasn't much older than me, maybe twenty-five, I judged, though not at all as handsome as them he had dragged me away from. He looked like a chinless rabbit, and he sounded like a local farmer, but even so I thought that he had taken me away from the militia men either because he disapproved of stray women in camp, or else because he had designs upon me his own self, though now I could see that his thoughts lay elsewhere entirely.

"A spy?" I couldn't help it: I laughed in his face. "Where's the money in that? I came here hoping to earn my keep."

His eyes narrowed, and he nearly let go of my arm. "As a camp follower?" *He'll wash his hands in the nearest creek when he leaves off shouting at me,* I thought. "More fool you, girl!"

"Why? They might be a fearsome sight as an army, all coming at you at once with guns a-blazing, but take them one at a time and they ain't nothing but Carolina country boys. Though they do give themselves airs about fighting for the king, as if he'd know anything about it or care if he did know. Much good may it do them."

"You have the sound of a Whig to me, making sport of the king. I do believe you are a spy. We hang spies when we catch them, same as the other side does."

I shrugged. "Why would I bother to spy upon you? Nothing will change for the likes of me, ever who wins, so why should I help either side in this? I came here for my keep, that's all."

He kept peering at me as if he expected some words of truth to break out in letters upon my forehead, but I returned his gaze stare for stare, never showing a flicker of fear, and presently he stopped looking so fierce and said, "What is your name?"

I give as good as I get, and for all his high and mighty ways, this little man did not frighten me. He was in a military encampment, right enough, but he hadn't the look of a soldier, and I had seen enough of them to know. "Come to that, what's yours?"

He drew himself up to his full height, which wasn't much. "Powell. Elias Powell, Esquire, and 'sir' to you. Now, then, I asked you your name, girl."

When I hesitated, he tightened his grip on my arm again, and I knew that by midday I would have his finger marks in purple on the skin of my forearm. Finally I muttered, "I am called Sal." I didn't want to tell him much about who I was, for I had no wish to be sent back to the place I'd left, where they would never miss me anyhow. This Elias Powell didn't look like the sort of nosy parker who could be bothered to do such a thing, but I trust nobody, especially in these times, when neighbors are at one another's throats over some fal-lal of ideas about liberty and such, as if such notions would buy you a pot of beer or a crust of bread. I couldn't see the sense of it.

"And you live around here?"

"I come from Virgininy," I told him. Well, one time I had come from there, and I saw no reason to tell him more. It was true enough.

He grunted, as though he begrudged the fact that my answer had pleased him. "Well, then I shall call you Virginia Sal. You've come a long way, but I am not yet twenty miles from home, myself. But, like you, I wanted a taste of army life. I'll wager there's little else of common ground between us, though. Why are you hanging about this camp like a stray dog?"

"Because I am one, I reckon." I picked a dry leaf out of the tangles of my hair, and that set me to wishing that I had given myself a wash in the creek this morning afore I come into camp, cold as the creek water was. There was no use being sorry about my dirt-streaked, ragged dress, though, for I had no other. "I got no family, so I thought I'd come find the soldiers, and mayhap hire on as a cook or a laundress. Whatever the army needs. Armies always have money."

He shook his head. "Maybe they do, but earning it a penny at a time from the likes of yonder hounds would be hard labor indeed." He held me at arm's length and looked me over. He muttered to himself, thinking aloud, and heedless of whether I heard him or not. "A right ragamuffin, I'll be bound. And it wants to be a laundress, if you please. The first thing in need of a wash are those hands and face. Young and fit, though. No sign of the pox. Good teeth. Curly red hair. He's partial to gingers, though the Lord knows why. I don't fancy 'em myself."

I stiffened when I heard him say this. "*He?* Who are you speaking of that is partial to red hair?"

"The commander. He's a bit of a ginger himself, so perhaps that accounts for it. He's a proper Englishman. Well, Scotch, then. He is particular about that, as if one place there over the water is any different from another. At any rate, the commander is a gentleman, son of a lord or some such title, and they have a fine country estate somewhere that he talks about when the mood takes him. So it stands to reason that he won't stand for the ordinary privations of soldiering, even out here in the wild-wood."

I resolved then and there to get a closer look at this high and mighty fellow. "And what are the needs of a gentleman general?"

"He is not a general, but only a major, though I'll warrant that is a high enough perch in the king's regular army. They buy their way into the officers' ranks, the British do, so you'll hardly find any commoners among them."

"If they are as rich as that, you'd think they would have better things to do than come out here to the wilderness to fight."

"They are younger sons, mostly, so the money settled to buy them an army com-mission is their inheritance and their one chance to make good — unless of course the eldest brother dies, and then perhaps they'd go home and get on with the busi-ness of managing the family estate." Elias Powell scowled. "As to the commander's personal requirements, that need not con-cern the likes of you, unless he accepts you into his service, and then I reckon you'll be apprised of them soon enough, and roundly punished if you should forget them."

"What service would his lordship be need-ing then?"

Powell took a breath, as if he were about

to trot out a lecture on how to address my betters, but he must have thought better of it, for he only shrugged and said, "He takes special food, and he's particular about the cooking of it, so there's a cook in camp just to look after him, apart from them that does for the rest of the men. He has a washer-woman already — leastways we call her that — and I am his body servant, seeing to his clothes, and cleaning his boots, unpacking his cases, and the like."

I stared at him, trying in my mind's eye to picture this runty fellow nipping about the commander's tent, setting up a silver teapot upon an officer's trunk and spooning cane sugar into a china cup. I almost laughed. "You do for him? You? I thought he'd have a black slave, same as most of the quality folks from around here."

Elias Powell shook his head. "We're all blackamoors to him, girl."

I always got the feeling that he talked to me the same way another person might talk to their favorite hound, more to hear the sound of their own voice than to be understood or answered back by the listener. Maybe it was on account of my mare's nest of red hair, which folk have said gave me the look of the Irish over the water. 'Course the commander, he was a Scotchman, but I don't suppose there's much to choose between them, for judging by the ones I have seen, they both have voices like music and pale skin that reddens and burns in the sun.

Elias Powell sat me down on a rock that first day, while he went to see if it was convenient for the commander to look me over. It wasn't above a quarter of an hour before he came back and motioned for me to follow him to a tent pitched in a clearing a little away from the rest of the camp. I had smoothed down my hair as much as I could, and brushed the mud from my skirts. Now I resolved to stand up straight and meet his gaze to show I wasn't to be bullied or cowed by a man, no matter what his station.

As I stooped to go through the tent flap, Elias Powell gripped my elbow again, and in a harsh whisper he said, "You mind your manners here, girl! He'll have you flogged if you sass him, but, worse than that, you will make him think ill of my judgment, so have a care."

I nodded to show I understood, and then I wrenched free of his grasp and followed him in.

The officer didn't take any notice of us at first, so we stood there at the entrance waiting to be spoken to. He was sitting on a little stool scratching away with a quill and ink on a bit of paper set atop a polished wooden box. I could not decide if he was trying to put me in awe of him by taking no notice of me standing there, or if he was so lost in thought in his letter-writing that he had not seen us come in. I didn't mind, though, for it gave me a chance to look him over, same as he'd be expecting to do to me. He wasn't young by my lights — he'd see forty afore I ever saw twenty-five, but he held his years better than poor men do, and he was still a fine figure of a man — clean and carefully dressed, as if he were a-settin' in a fine parlor instead of in a tent on a piney ridge. He was light-haired and angular, and I wondered from the strained look on his bony countenance if he had been ill or wounded. As soon as I had that thought, the officer shifted a bit on his stool, and I saw that his right arm was bent up close to his chest and that even when he moved, it did not. That surprised me, for I could not see how a man with only one good arm could command an army. I would have expected him to be sent home to his rich family, or perhaps to some sort of job back home that could be done with papers at a desk, for surely he could not ride and fight, maimed as he was. I didn't feel sorry for him — he looked so grand and stern that pity would be an impertinence. Besides, wounds are the wages of war.

Elias Powell shuffled his feet and made a little noise in his throat, so perhaps he had decided that the commander had not seen us enter.

He did glance up then, only for a moment, and then he bent over his paper again and scratched another line or two, and then signed his name grandly with a flourish before he laid aside the quill and turned to look at us. "Well, Powell, what is it?"

The little manservant was as meek with his master as he had been high and mighty with me, and I saw that he was one of those weak terrier fellows who tailor their tempers to the measure of those about them. I had no intention of bowing and scraping to the man, not even if he had been the king's son instead of a Scotchman, so I kept my eyes steady on him, for I didn't see there was much that he could do to me however I behaved.

Powell shifted from one foot to the other, still keeping his gaze directed at the dirt floor. "Begging your pardon, sir. This here young woman has presented herself here at camp, asking to be taken on in some capacity, and I thought I'd bring her along to you, to see if she would suit."

Without a word the officer looked over at me, and found me staring back at him, bold as brass. I doubt if he'd have stood it from a man, but he didn't seem to mind it from me. He took care not to show even a flicker of a smile.

"So, you are a servant of the king, are you, girl?"

"Only if he pays me wages," I said. "Same as anybody."

Powell edged me aside. "She's only a simple girl, sir, and the rights of this conflict are beyond her ken. But she might suit as a maid of all work."

The officer was still looking at me, and he said to me — not to Elias Powell — "Well, what use are you? We have no cows to milk and no floors to scrub."

If he meant to frighten me, he had made a poor job of it. All that time he had kept us waiting while he wrote had given me time to think up my piece, for I knew he'd be asking me something of the sort, and I had my answer ready. "You've clothes, haven't you? I don't reckon you wash them yourself when they get dirty."

"We engaged a washerwoman already."

"Mending, then. I am a dab hand with a

needle, sir. And I can be useful tending the sick. I done that before."

"Still, I suppose there is enough work at camp for you to do, helping the cook as well as the laundress. And if you can be of any assistance to Dr. Johnson, there is some value in that."

"I can do all of that well enough." I would have told him I could break horses and mend cannons if it would have made him take me on. But I judged that a womanly silence would do more for my cause than any further arguments about my skills.

He thought the matter over for what seemed like a good long while to me, holding my breath, but at last he said, "Well, young woman, if you are in my service, I should expect you to comport yourself properly. No goings-on with the soldiers, no drunkenness, or slatternly habits. Do you understand?"

I nodded, and forced myself not to grin.

"See that you do, because if you do not abide by my rules, you will be dismissed at once."

"As long as I have my keep, I'll do what you say," I told him, and that was true enough. I might miss taking a drink now and again, but I don't reckon anybody would make free with a smelly bunch of soldiers if they had any other choice.

He looked back at his manservant. "All right, Powell, I suppose her keep will cost us little enough. She may stay if she behaves herself."

"I'll see to it, sir," said Powell, shooing me out of the tent ahead of him.

So that's how I came to be on the king's side in this war. Maybe if I had chanced upon an encampment of the other side that day, I might have cast my lot with the Americans, for I never yet had a conviction — political, religious, or heartfelt — that could not be scotched by an empty belly or the need for a dry place to sleep.

Elias Powell took charge of me for the rest of the afternoon, rabbiting on about camp rules, and washing, and a long recital of the commander's wants and wishes. "And mind you keep yourself clean in body, girl," he added, "In case he adds you to his list of wants."

I shrugged. "That will cost him extra."

He took me to the cook's tent, and saw that I was given a bit of boiled beef and corn, soldiers' rations, for my midday meal, washed down with a pot of ale. I wondered whose cows had been taken to feed the army, but even if they had come from the farm of someone I knew, I would have eaten it just the same, for my going hungry would not change anything for them that had lost their livestock.

Finally, when I had finished my food and Powell had run out of commandments, he took me along to one of the tents used by the commander's servants, where I would be staying, alongside the other maidservant. "Go on inside," he said, "and tell her you're here on my say-so. Reckon she can tell you whatever else you need to know," and I decided that he had thought of somebody else that he needed to order around, and on account of that, he was willing to let me go for a while.

I went into the tent, but nobody was there. Just a woven basket of soiled clothes, some bedding, and a tin plate next to a wooden pail of water. The sparseness of the tent was more what I had expected for an army on the move, instead of the rug and trunk and silver and I don't-know-what-all that the commander needed to keep body and soul together in the wildwood.

"You looking for something?"

It was a woman's voice, low and quiet, but colder than snowmelt, and for a heartbeat I felt my body tense to run at the sound of it, but then I shook off that foolish notion, and turned to face her. "You'd be the other maidservant? That Elias Powell said to tell you I am hired on to help you serve the commander."

She stood staring at me without a word of welcome. It was hard to put an age to her, though of course she must have been about the same as me, for her thick ginger hair was unsilvered, and her face was smooth as a child's. I decided that it was her eyes that belied her youthfulness. They were as green as persimmons, big and dark-lashed, set above sharp cheekbones in a face as pale as moonlight. But those eyes were as cold as her voice, as if she could cut right through you with the harshness of her gaze. For all her beauty, hers was not a face that I cared to look at overlong, and I could feel her still looking at me even after I turned away.

I tried again. "I hope I'll be some help to you, looking after the officer."

Her smile was mostly a sneer, but she seemed to make up her mind to tolerate me, for she said, "What do I call you?"

"Name's Sal. Elias Powell called me Virginia Sal, on account of I told him I come from there."

She shrugged. "He had another reason, too. I am called Virginia Paul."

I wondered if she was saying *Paul,* like the apostle in the Bible, or *Poll,* which is a nickname among some folk for "Mary." The first was no name for a woman, though, and the second, being the name of the mother of Our Lord, did not suit her at all, so I reckoned "Paul" was her last name. I didn't like to ask, though, for I didn't think she'd take kindly to my notions about her name, so all I said was, "Are you from up in Virginny, too?"

"No."

I listened to see if I could tell where she came from by the sound of her voice, but she hadn't said enough for me to be able to tell. She didn't sound much like the Englishmen I'd heard talking, nor the fellows from the northern colonies, but she didn't talk like someone from these parts, either. A time or two I thought her words sounded like the commander's way of speaking, with odd, rolling *r's* and sounds that came from the back of his throat and seemed to struggle to come out of his mouth at all. I wondered if she and the commander came from the same place. I made up my mind to ask her about it, if she ever thawed out enough to be civil to me.

After another minute or two of silence, she said, "Well, you came to work, and there's washing to be done. Pick up that basket. I'll show you where the creek is."

I followed her out of the tent, carrying the basket of soiled linen shirts, and I tried to keep up with her, though the washing was heavy, and I had to watch my step on the uneven ground. Finally, though, I managed to call out to her to slow her pace, and, with a scornful glance in my direction, she did so, leaning up against a tall pine and watching me stumble down the slope to reach her. I managed not to spill any clothes out of the basket, though I had caught my leg on a branch of briars, and the cuts stung as they seeped blood about my ankle.

I spied the creek at the bottom of the hill, a shallow little stream that was as much rocks as water, though that wasn't a bad thing if you were aiming to wash clothes in it, for you needed to beat the garments against the stones to get the dirt out. I set the basket down alongside the creek, and took a shirt out of the pile and held it under the water until my hands tingled.

Virginia Paul came up beside me, and picked through the pile until she found a cloth with red stains on it. I knew it for blood, so I said, "Did he cut himself shaving?"

She gave me another scornful glance. "He doesn't shave himself," she said, pushing the towel down into the clear stream between the rocks, and rubbing at the stain until the cloth turned loose of the blood. "We do the washing for the regiment's doctor as well. This is his."

"Have you been with the commander long?" I asked her, thinking that this was as good a time as any to get acquainted.

"A few weeks," she said, without looking up from her scrubbing.

"So you haven't know him for very long, either."

She smiled at that. "I've known Patrick Ferguson a deal longer than he thinks I have."

I wondered what she meant by that, but when I asked, she only shook her head and went right on beating cloth against the creck rock.

I settled into the routine of the regiment soon enough, and I got better acquainted with the others, though the men didn't take much notice of a servant girl, but Virginia Paul kept to herself, as much of a stranger to me as she had been on the first day. But our work was mostly the same, and so we spent time together, and, though I never found out much about her own life, she seemed to know a lot about the commander.

"He's the son of a lord," she told me once, when I wondered aloud about him. "Back in Scotland. He talks about it sometimes of a night. His father is an earl, the chief of the Fergusons of Pitfour, though he is a lawyer as well."

"Are you kin to them?" I asked, for she seemed to know so much about the family.

"The Fergusons of Pitfour are my clan, though I am no blood of his." She nodded in the direction of the commander's tent. "Just as well, since we share a bed now and again."

Well, I knew that, though I never thought to hear her say it out loud. I couldn't see that there was any love lost between them on either side. It was just something they did to pass the time, perhaps, or to snatch a bit of comfort out of the hardships of army life. Virginia Paul was pretty enough to look at, but it was a cold beauty, like a winter tree silvered in ice.

I thought it best for the time being to keep away from the question of her and the commander, so to get on safer ground, I said, "Fergusons of Pitfour? What's Pitfour? A castle?"

She shook her head. "Just a big old barn of a house. The laird and his family live in the capital city, but they have the country place farther north, and he misses it sometimes, though I think it's because he was a boy there. He left home a long time ago and he will never go back."

She said that as if it were a known truth, but I didn't see how she could know such a thing, so I said, "Mayhap he will, though. When his father dies, he could go home and take over the family farm."

Virginia Paul laughed at my ignorance. "Not he! Patrick Ferguson is nothing but a younger son, good for nothing unless the eldest dies. They sent him off to the army while he was still a beardless boy, and he has been there ever since. His mother's brother is an important general, and they had hopes that he would smooth the path for young Patrick in the king's army. And, by the by, that *farm* you speak of is the size of this county."

"Did he tell you all this?"

She shrugged. "Never mind. I know."

I thought she must have come from his part of the world, and I wondered if being in the same clan was like being a cousin.

"I am no blood of his," she said, as if she had heard me thinking, and that made me shiver, for I could be careful of what I said around her, but I didn't see how I could hobble my thoughts.

CHAPTER FOUR
EARLY SEPTEMBER 1780

Isaac Shelby stayed the night at Plum Grove, and after a brief respite to partake of the barbecued steer and exchange pleasantries with the guests, he and I talked until the evening fire burned low. Maj. Patrick Ferguson had invited us into the war, and we aimed to oblige him.

We talked over the logistics of getting a thousand armed men over the mountains and into the territory held by the enemy, with sufficient resources to fight once we got there. A decade or so of living in the back-country served us well in this respect, for we had both taken part in campaigns against the Indians. That experience had schooled us for the coming fight.

We knew how to move an army through the wilderness, how to make camp without being ambushed, how to keep troops armed and fed, and how to draw up a plan of battle. The expedition to Point Pleasant with

Lord Dunmore was the pattern upon which we would base our campaign. The one thing we lacked now that had been supplied for us in Lord Dunmore's War was the money it took to finance a military campaign. The colony of Virginia, backed by the resources of the Crown, could afford to engage in any wars it took a notion to fight, but we were backcountry farmers, and our worth, such as it was, lay in land and livestock. We could defend a fort with a hundred souls under our protection for a week or two, for we were equal to that task in supplies and in the courage of necessity, but now we were proposing to fight the king's army, a long way from home. They did not lack for funds or supplies, or for professional soldiers to lead them.

"Nobody will want to be paid for going with us," I pointed out to Shelby, seizing on the one favorable aspect of the whole daunting prospect.

"Good," said Shelby with a wry smile, "because I had not calculated on paying them. That is the least of our worries, though. It will take us ten days or more to get to that part of the country where Ferguson is reported to be, and if among us, we militia commanders can get a thousand men to make up an army, we'll have to supply them with powder and shot. And feed them and their mounts the whole way there and back."

I could not deny the truth of what he said, but I had no wish to give up the fight for want of a few paltry supplies. "I suppose if the need were great enough, we could get Whig sympathizers along the way to feed us. We are making sacrifices for this cause, and so should all those who side with us. Many of them are rich enough, and it's harvest time, after all. They can spare it. Or else we could take what we need from the farms of the Tories. They're even richer."

"No," said Shelby. He yawned and stretched, and began to pace back and forth before the hearth, fighting the weariness that had overtaken him. "I thought about that on the long ride over here. I journeyed past fields full of fat cows, and cornfields that stretched for miles along the river, and I thought, 'There's enough bounty here to feed an army.' But as soon as I thought it, I put myself in the place of those landowners, and I realized that if any army came like a plague of locusts and stripped my land and took my stock, I would hate them until my dying day, cause or no cause."

"But such sacrifices have to be made in time of war. Look at what we've gone through here in the Indian wars."

"Perhaps, but all the same, I think that refusing to demand provisions from the populace would be our great strength. Major Ferguson is doing that, you know."

"It hardly surprises me. It is usual for armies to live off the land."

"Yes, but it does not endear them to the citizens in their path. After Ferguson went up to Gilbert Town, he ranged west, trying to frighten people into his fold, and offering them his *protection* if they will remain loyal to the Crown. Those who choose not to side with him are relieved of their goods, and in particular their livestock." He laughed. "Ferguson was so intent upon rounding up beeves that you'd think the beasts could pay taxes."

"Well, he has an army to feed, and I'm sure that his master, Lord Cornwallis, would never countenance paying money to mere subjects to supply the needs of the king's troops."

"No, it never occurred to them to buy the cattle. McDowell and I discussed it after Musgrove Mill, before I set out for home. We thought we might make some political capital out of saving beeves instead of requisitioning them. So we went along to some of the landowners along the Yadkin, those who had the most to lose, and we offered them our protection. If they would pledge to support the Whigs, we said, we would keep their livestock safe from Ferguson by driving their cattle back into the hills for them. And others, who refused to side with us, saw the sense of our tactics, and drove their own herds into the deep mountain coves where the Tories would never find them."

"That was all to the good, whether the landowners pledged to you or not. At any rate, hiding the cattle in the hills kept the enemy short of provisions."

"Yes." Shelby laughed. "I later heard from McDowell that we had help from unexpected quarters in this endeavor. When Ferguson reached the area around Quaker Meadows, he found so few beeves for the taking that he consulted John Carson, whom he took for a Loyalist, and Carson told him where he could find some cattle."

"Was he telling the truth?"

"That's a question for lawyers, I suppose. Did Ferguson's men come back with cattle? Indeed, they did, proving that in that respect Carson had told the truth."

I puzzled over this for a moment, and then I had it. I could hardly speak for laughing. "John Carson told them where to find *Tory* cattle, didn't he?"

Shelby nodded. "So he did. You can imagine the wrath of those landowners who were loyal to the king, upon finding that the very army they supported had robbed them of their livestock. After that, I think they'd have favored the devil himself if he happened to oppose the Crown. So, you see, Ferguson's cattle raids are helping our cause, converting more people than a hundred speeches about liberty could ever sway. There are plenty of people sitting on the fence right now, trying to make up their minds whether to support the Whigs or stay loyal to the Crown. All we need to do is to refrain from preying upon these farmers, and they will count us on the side of the angels."

"It's an expensive virtue, though. We cannot fight the British with starving unarmed men, so we must pay our way. I think I see a way to do that, Shelby."

"Do you? How?"

"Oh, we'll borrow it from the king."

VIRGINIA SAL

I never did mention any of the things she told me to Major Ferguson himself, for I wouldn't like him to know that we were whispering about him behind his back, being servants of his, like we were, but as I got used to being around him, I listened carefully whenever he talked, to see if I could piece together some of what he told me with what Virginia Paul had said. He didn't seem to take much notice of me at first. I had mending to do, and Elias Powell secured permission for me to sit in the commander's tent of an evening, so that I could work in the lamplight. I suppose that being from a noble family like he was back in Scotland, he was accustomed to having servants underfoot, and he paid them no more mind than I would the kitchen cat. So I kept quiet and listened while I sewed.

Often of an evening the commander would have Capt. Andrew DePeyster come and pass the time with him, and sometimes the camp doctor, name of Uzal Johnson, would stop in, for he was an educated man and fitting company for the son of a lord. They weren't neither of them thirty yet, and both of them came from the northern colonies. Dr. Johnson had a fine education, and he had left a medical practice in New Jersey to be an army doctor for the Loyalists, and Captain DePeyster was a fine-featured gentleman from New York, who had been soldiering since the start of the rebellion. I reckon he and the doctor were good friends because they were much the same age, and they came from the same part of the world.

Even though they were well-spoken and educated gentlemen, the both of them generally had a pleasant word for me. Virginia Paul told me once that true aristocrats are mostly civil to everybody; it's only them that have just climbed up out of the muck themselves that are rude to their underlings. It made sense to me that the major would choose to spend his evenings in the company of these learned and kindly fellows. Perhaps they reminded him of the evenings with the gentry in Edinburgh — at least, if he closed his eyes to the shabby surroundings of his army tent and ignored the boiled and burnt food that sometimes passed for his dinner.

Once he got to know me, Dr. Johnson even asked if I would mind helping him with the sick and the wounded soldiers if he ever had need of any help, and I said I would. I reckon he could have just made Major Ferguson order me to assist him, but instead he asked me politely himself in that clipped and formal way of his, and I set a store by him for that bit of kindness.

Many nights I got to sit in a corner of the tent and listen to the gentlemen's conversation. And sometimes, after the fires burned low, Major Ferguson spent the rest of the night with me, but we never did talk much then. I didn't take it too personally. It was just that he had been alone so much of his life, and being in the middle of a war, he could never count on having much of a future in which to remedy that. So little by little, we got acquainted, there being nothing else to do after sundown between set-to's with the enemy.

Sometimes, when the mood took him of an evening, especially if it was raining and cool and he had no other company, the major would sit in the opening of his tent, staring out into the darkness, and he'd talk a bit about his home and the times he had growing up in Scotland. I never asked him any questions when he talked of home, even when I didn't understand what he meant with a strange word or a peculiar turn of phrase, for to interrupt the flow of his words would have broken the spell. He would have thought me impertinent, besides, to speak without being spoken to, for whatever else we were to one another, every now and again, he was above all my master and the commander here. Even when I shared his bed, I never called him by his given name, which was Patrick, or Pattie, as his family called him when he was a lad, but he would never stand for being addressed as such by anyone on this side of the ocean. I never heard Virginia Paul call him that to his face, either, though she said it often enough behind his back. A word from him and they'd flog you until the skin of your back was in ribbons. Anyhow, at such times it was plain that, though he spoke aloud, he was not talking to me, but only airing his thoughts for his own comfort. He could have been talking to a hunting dog for all the answering he expected.

Odd that he never talked about military matters. He seldom spoke of his postings in the islands or up in New York, except in passing. He had lived through a fair few battles and such, but they were not uppermost in his mind on the evenings when he went to woolgathering. No, mostly he harked back to his boyhood, and his home in Scotland, though he hadn't been much more than a boy when he left there, Still, I suppose we all see our youth as an Eden of perfect days, and we think that if only we could go back there we would be content. But it was more than that with him. At first I thought it was because his father was a lord, and that he missed the mansion and all the trappings of being an aristocrat, but though he made it clear that we have nothing here to compare to the fine estates in Britain, he did have his nobility here, for being a commander in the king's army gave him position and servants, and the best of what there was to be had. Anyhow, leaving home at fifteen like he had, I reckon he had long got out of the habit of rich food and the finery of the gentry. I came to think that he dwelt so longingly on thoughts of his home and family because he sensed that he would never see them again.

What I learned of his history in the army I found out piecemeal, some from Dr. Johnson, but mostly from the lips of Virginia Paul, while we were doing our chores. Sometimes in the late afternoons, if all was peaceful thereabouts, she and I would get out of earshot of the camp, and, since there wasn't much else to talk about, leastways nothing that seemed to interest her, I'd get her to talking about the commander. I wondered if he had told her all she knew about him when he took her to his bed, but he never spoke of his military past with me in similar circumstances, so I did wonder. Virginia Paul never did seem to mind him being with me, and he never let on to me that they were close, so I couldn't make sense of it. She knew about him, though. Sometimes she talked like she had been there her own self, she knew so many of the particulars.

I knew how he had begun his military life as a young cornet on the continent, and now he was here in the Carolina backcountry, commanding Loyalist troops, but I wondered what had come in between.

On another long afternoon in the wagon, journeying from one back-country nowhere to another, I reminded her of where she had left off before. ". . . So after young Ferguson recovered from the sickness he caught in the Prussian war, he went back to the regiment, but they had forgotten all about that foolhardy stunt of his with the dropped pistols?"

She nodded. "That war on the continent was over, and everything having to do with it was old news. All he could do was start over, and hope to get noticed again. He spent a few months in England, assigned to put down local riots of colliers — them that mines coal, ye ken — and then he was garrisoned here and there about the country, though of course he longed to do real soldiering again. He tried to get posted to the command of his mother's brother in Canada, but that came to naught, for his father fell ill, and he felt he must stay close by the family. By then he was twenty and not much further along than he had been when he began."

I sighed. "It must be hard to do everything you can to make your way in the world and still have all the luck run against you."

"Like a salmon swimming upstream, fighting the current," she said, with one of her rare smiles, but I did not know of such things, for here in the Carolina hill country we have trout and bream, and mostly they drift along in the streams living peaceful lives in the backwater. For the hundredth time I wondered where she was from. You couldn't really tell by how folks talked, because some of them whose parents were foreign, or them that had come over the

111

water as children, still had the cast of a foreign tongue in their speech. But Virginia Paul knew more about what went on over there than anybody not born and bred over there ought to know. I asked her more than once, but not a word would she say about it. I kept her talking, though, in hopes that she would let something slip one day, and I could put the pieces together.

I opened my mouth to say, *"Did you come from where his family lives?"* but I knew it was no use asking her for the twentieth time, for she never would answer, so instead I said, "Well, at least he had recovered his health —"

"Not entirely. He tired easily, and limped a bit, and he was given to fevers. But worse than that for him was that time was passing. All the young officers who had begun when he did now outranked him, and he knew that he had to do something to begin moving forward again."

"He needed another war, did he not?"

"Well, he needed more of one than he was likely to find with the Greys, chasing smugglers on the coast of Sussex. So he did what many an ambitious officer had done before him — he sold his commission in the Scots Greys, and purchased a new one in a regiment being sent abroad."

"Back to the continent?"

"No. Not to that continent or this. He transferred to the 70th, to serve under a cousin of his, Lieutenant Colonel Johnstone. It was his best chance for advancement, and his new commission was a captaincy, but when he told the news, he got more condolences than congratulations."

"Why?"

"Because the 70th was posted to the West Indies, where most of the battles are fought against pestilence. Why, a man could die just trying to get there."

I waited a moment, and then asked lightly, looking anywhere but at her. "The Indies? Have you been there?"

She was silent so long that I turned to look at her, but her gaze was as empty as a stone. "Those islands be a long way from the solitary firs of Pitfour, in every way at all," she said at last. "Hot and strange, those islands, with fauna and flowers that seem to come from another world. You'd think he would have hated it there, wouldn't you? So wild and strange to a Scots lad that it would take a sea of rum just to keep him afloat for duty. But he gloried in the place."

Well, he might have told her that, I supposed. "What's it like then, those islands? Do you know? And what captivated him?"

"Well, he was but twenty-four then. Perhaps new places and things are more enchanting before people get set in their ways. He called it an everlasting summer. It was rich in game — wild hogs and doves and pheasants — and the waters around the island teemed with fish, which were anybody's for the taking. Not like Scotland, where the very streams belong to one laird or another, and you must pay for the right of fishing them. And the fertile soil of those tropical islands must have seemed a miracle to one accustomed to the cold, thin earth of the Highlands, where little grew of its own accord save thistles and heather." She laughed and shook her head. "On Tobago, he actually made his soldiers plant gardens, so that they might grow their own vegetables. Would you credit it? And proud as a peacock he was for having thought of it."

I blinked, trying to imagine the proud and stern commander turned farmer. "Do they promote officers for such as that?"

"You know they don't. But 'twas a way to pass the time until real duties called."

"If the islands were such a paradise as that, what would they be needing soldiers there for?"

"Well, it wasn't a paradise for everyone. There were slave revolts. 'Twas a hard life

114

for them that toiled in the cane fields. They died young. Disease and hard labor in the hot sun carried them off. But Captain Pattie, as he was then, dealt with it all, and stopped the revolts. He'd have got his precious promotion out of that, I don't doubt."

"Did he not then?"

She smiled. "He did not. For just as he was beginning to glimmer like a hero again, he took sick. Malaria — easy enough to get in the tropics, especially for one who was in delicate health to begin with. They shipped him home to Scotland yet again, and he spent months in his mother's care, fighting to regain his health. When he was well again, the islands were forgotten, for the war had begun here. So here he came, hoping that the third time would be the charm."

I shivered. "Do you think it will be?"

"No."

Chapter Five

The next morning Shelby and I mounted our horses and took the trace along the river to the home of the Irishman, John Adair. The day was fine with a blazing blue sky, and the road, which lay between the green wall of mountains and the winding Nolichucky River, made for a pleasant morning's ride, or it would have if we had been able to leave our troubles at home, but we scarcely noticed the late summer glories of woods and fields, for our thoughts were already fixed on the coming battle.

John Adair knew both of us well, for he had been elected to office last year when the North Carolina Assembly passed an act to create a new county here on the frontier, calving the lands around the Holston settlement away from Washington County. Thus, Sullivan County was formed, and, along with a sheriff, a clerk, and other functionaries, Isaac Shelby was appointed colonel of the new county's militia. John Adair was the entry taker, the man who kept the county treasury, mostly from land sales, which were to be sent back to the state's government in New Bern. We were counting on Shelby's rank as militia commander to carry the day.

We found John Adair at home on that bright September morning. Someone in his household had spotted us from afar over the fields, and had no doubt run to tell Adair that two gentlemen on horseback were headed to his door. By the time we reached his yard he was waiting for us, and trying to smile a welcome, though his eyes showed his unease. He knew that this was no social call, and during the moments while he waited for us to dismount he must have run through all the dire possibilities that could have prompted our visit. On the frontier, unexpected callers often heralded bad tidings: an Indian attack in the offing, a small-pox outbreak, or perhaps the death of a neighbor.

One of the Adair boys took our horses to be walked about the yard until they cooled down, and we followed John Adair into his little frame house. I'd as lief stayed outside in the sunshine, but our mission was a delicate one, and the gravity of the occasion behooved us to speak in a formal setting.

117

He offered us cold water from the spring-house, which we took to put him at his ease, and when this little chore of hospitality had been effected, Adair sat down on a little pine stool facing us and waited to hear what we had come about.

Isaac Shelby held out the letter that his kinsman Sam Phillips had delivered. "The British army, in the person of one Major Ferguson, is threatening to call on us here in the backcountry."

Adair opened his mouth and closed it again. He hunched over the creased and rumpled bit of paper, his lips moving soundlessly as he read the lines. He read it twice over, to be sure of its message, and then he looked up at us, ashen to the roots of his red hair. "We're to be attacked? By the army? Is it not enough that we've got the heathen savages biding their time in the wildwood, waiting to hack us to pieces? Have the soldiers nought better to do than to come and pester us?"

Shelby smiled. "I think they mean to pester everybody before they're done, but just now, they seem to have taken offense that we have been sending our militias down to help the men of the Yadkin and the Catawba in this summer's skirmishes southeast of here."

"They mean to frighten us into staying home," I said. "Then they hope to defeat the Whigs down there, before they come up and settle scores with us."

Adair stared at us, taking it all in, and liking none of it. "Can you not stop them then?"

"We think that the only way to stop them from invading here is to stop them altogether."

Isaac Shelby took up the thread. "We mean to put together all the men we can muster, and head over the mountains to fight them there."

Adair nodded. "Yes, yes. I see. Better to fight them there than here. And are you recruiting men to go along with you? I'll go."

Shelby and I glanced at each other, and then he said, "You'd be welcome, Adair, but we have not yet got to the point of calling up troops."

"We need money."

Adair blinked at me when I said this. He was still so discomfited by our visit and our disquieting news that his wits wanted catching up to the thread of the conversation. "Money? Ah, well . . . I haven't much put by, gentlemen. Just a bit for salt and lead, and the like, same as most folks hereabouts.

But if you're having a whip-round about the settlement, I suppose I could —" He looked wildly about, as if he were about to start from his seat and retrieve his cash box from within a blanket chest.

I willed myself to keep solemn, and Shelby favored him with a reassuring smile. "We are grateful for your trust, Mr. Adair, but hear us out. It isn't your coins we came for. It will take a good deal more than any of us has to outfit the militia for the journey south. We've horses and men to feed, and powder and shot to procure. War is not cheap in any way, shape, or form."

I said gently, "We have come for the money from the land sales. About twelve thousand pounds, I make it. You haven't been able to send it back to the capital because of the troubles. We are asking for the loan of it."

The poor man looked from one to the other of us as if we had demanded his firstborn in a stew pot. "But . . . it isn't mine to give. It belongs to the government. I've no authority . . ."

We waited while he worked it out for himself.

"But . . ." He took a deep breath and met our gaze, calmer now. "It is true that I have no authority to give that money to anyone, but if the enemy overruns the country, then our liberty will be gone. And if that happens, the money might as well go, too. If you mean to use the funds to fight in our defense, then you had better take it. I can think of no one I would trust more to have it."

"We will give you our personal guarantees for the sum," I told him, and Shelby murmured in agreement. "Give us a bit of paper and we will write our pledges for the loan of it."

"While you go and get the money," Shelby added.

Before the sun was much higher in the sky, Shelby and I were out in the yard again, preparing to mount our horses, with heavy saddlebags of government money to take with us.

John Adair shook our hands and wished us Godspeed. "When will the gathering be for the long march?" he asked.

Shelby and I had talked about the mustering site this morning on the long ride to John Adair's place. "We'll assemble the various militia units in each settlement," I told him, "but we mean to join them all together for the march over the mountains on the twenty-fifth of this month at Fort Watauga. Sycamore Shoals."

"I'll be there, gentlemen. Put me down on your roll. And my son as well." He nodded toward the slender youth holding our horses.

"So we will," said Shelby. "And you'd oblige us if you would pass the word along to any of your neighbors who would be willing to go."

We turned our horses back to the road and rode off in silence for a bit, savoring the crisp air and the first tints of autumn in the trees along the distant ridges. A flock of wild turkeys skittered across in front of us, and dived into the underbrush a moment later.

"Well, Colonel," I said. "The first and most difficult of our tasks has been accomplished now. We have the funds to field an army."

He nodded. "But we have precious little time to make ready, and much left to do. And we have pledged our personal fortunes to the government for the loan of that money."

"I wouldn't worry about that, if I were you, Shelby. If we lose this war, I doubt if either of us will live to pay it back."

CHAPTER SIX
EARLY SEPTEMBER 1780

That evening after a weary Colonel Shelby had retired to the best bed, kept for guests in the parlor, I withdrew to my own room, and told my bride Catherine about the message Shelby had brought, and of our plans to take the war to Ferguson instead of waiting for him to bring it here. The first of many sacrifices we would make would be our honeymoon, for I must spend the coming weeks gathering supplies for the mission and, with her mending and needlework, Catherine and my brothers' wives would help the men of the family prepare for that journey. As I enumerated all the tasks that I must accomplish between now and the gathering of the militias at Sycamore Shoals, Catherine looked up from her sewing, and gave me an impish smile.

"Well, Mr. Sevier, outfitting an army sounds mighty like planning a wedding, what with all the people you must invite, new clothing to be sewn, and then procuring enough food to feed a multitude." She laughed. "And will you be needing a parson as well?"

I knew that she was only teasing, but she had hit upon a telling point. I was not a conspicuously pious man, but asking the Lord to bless our venture seemed a prudent thing to do, and as it would cost us nothing, I resolved to see to it. I answered Catherine's jest in all sincerity. "A parson? Why, yes, now as you mention it, my dear, I believe we will be more in need of a minister than any betrothed couple. I hope the Reverend Mr. Doak will see fit to pray over us at the mustering and wish us Godspeed on our journey. I must remember to pay a call on him and ask him, but first I have more pressing matters to see to, chief among them: the one thing we did not require at our wedding."

Catherine's eyes sparkled with firelight. "Oh, yes?"

I smiled. "Why, gunpowder, my dear. When Mr. Wilson read us the vows, I was your willing captive, and so there was no need of it, but for the coming ceremony with Major Ferguson we will need all of it that we can carry."

■ ■ ■ ■

The next morning Colonel Shelby headed home to Sapling Grove, intent upon enlisting the support of Col. William Campbell and the Virginia militia. My task was to meet with another of our proposed allies, Colonel McDowell. He had known of the proposed march even before I did, for Shelby had laid out the plans for confronting Ferguson while they were encamped near Gilbert Town, hiding out after the battle at Musgrove Mill a few weeks back, and trying to get home before Ferguson caught up with them. McDowell, Elijah Clarke of Georgia, and some of the other Whig officers had agreed with Shelby that the best solution would be to hit Ferguson with a combined force of as many militia units as we could gather — North Carolina, South Carolina, Georgia, and Virginia. If Cornwallis wanted to take the war to the south, we would oblige him.

The summer's fighting had cost McDowell and his people dearly. He and some of his men had been driven from their homes in Burke County, and they had taken refuge here in the backcountry where Buffalo Creek runs into the Watauga. These folk, some of them owners of fine plantations back home, were living in makeshift huts. For food and supplies, they depended on the charity of the people in the settlement. It was high summer, though, and the woods along Buffalo Creek were full of game: men whose shooting skills had been honed in battle were in no danger of going hungry as long as they had powder and shot.

Some of them brought their families with them, and they took what livestock they could to keep it from falling into Tory hands. Those who remained behind were ordered to take the Tory oath of loyalty. The reasoning was that by seeming to changes sides, those men would have the freedom to look after the property and kinfolk left behind by those who were forced to flee.

The refugees from Burke County wanted the fighting finished once and for all so that they could go home.

I rode out to McDowell's encampment that morning, not to persuade them to join us — for they would be the first in line to go in pursuit of Ferguson, needing no invitation from me — but to gather information. They had fought Ferguson throughout the summer, and the territory to which we were headed was home to them. I needed to know everything they could tell me about what to expect once we crossed over the mountains.

I knew that Shelby had deliberately left this task to me. He was still resentful of Col. Charles McDowell for insisting on a withdrawal after Musgrove Mill, instead of advancing farther into Tory territory in South Carolina. He would be seeing McDowell soon enough when we began the march over the mountains, and then he must swallow his ire and behave like a good compatriot, but for now he preferred to negotiate for the cooperation of Colonel Campbell of the Virginia militia, letting me meet with the Burke County commander. I was content with that, for, although my brother Valentine had fought at Musgrove Mill, I had remained to keep watch over the settlement during the summer months, but I heard much of what transpired in messages from him.

When I told my brother that Shelby was leaving me to talk to McDowell, Valentine had been quick to point out that Shelby was not the only one of our officers with hard feelings toward McDowell. Capt. Andrew Hampton had even more reason to shun him.

He had come by to pay his respects to Shelby as he was preparing to depart for

Sapling Grove, and after we had wished him Godspeed and watched him canter off down the river road, Valentine followed me back inside, and we shooed everyone out of the parlor, and set to talking about Shelby's plan.

"It's a bold plan, Jack," my brother said, "but if we manage to put together a force of a thousand men, I believe it can be done. One question, though — who's to be in charge? Did you and Shelby talk about that?"

I shook my head. "We never got down to details. I was too worried about getting the money to buy supplies for the men, and making sure that nothing is forgotten. Shelby is going to ask Colonel Campbell of Virginia to bring his troops to join us. He asked me to talk to McDowell. He didn't seem to want to, himself."

Valentine nodded. "There were hard feelings when McDowell refused to countenance an advance into South Carolina after we won at Musgrove Mill. That's why I asked you who was going to lead the army. Charles McDowell is the highest ranking officer among you, you know."

"I hadn't thought about it."

"You should, though, Jack. There's some

128

who won't follow him. I don't know that I would."

"There's still hard feelings about the Hampton boy, isn't there?"

"Lord, yes, Jack. Colonel Hampton will never get over it. Can you wonder at it? Suppose it had been your Joseph?"

I knew about this. Col. Andrew Hampton was an able officer in the militia. He had settled east of Gilbert Town, but his military service in the Whig cause had taken him far afield at times. At the beginning of the war, he had fought in the eastern part of Carolina, at the Battle of Moore's Creek against the Scottish Tories, and lately he had been among those who tried to prevent the fall of Charleston, and thereafter he had fought at Thicketty Fort with McDowell and the others. He had a son, Noah, still in his teens, who was in the militia commanded by Col. Charles McDowell. Back in early July, a militia colonel from Georgia, one Elijah Clarke, had crossed into South Carolina intending to do battle against what Tories they could find, but when scouts informed them of the size of the enemy force in the area, Clarke's men decided that it was too dangerous to pursue the campaign, and they elected to withdraw. One of their party, Col. John Jones declared that he would stay and he would lead any who cared to go with him back into North Carolina to join forces with the militia there.

Jones and thirty-five volunteers made their way north, passing themselves off as loyal supporters of the Crown, and thus received help along the way from local Loyalists who offered to guide the party on their way north. Less than fifty miles from the North Carolina border, one of these guides happened to mention that there had been a battle the night before, and that the Loyalists were defeated by a Whig force.

Colonel Jones, who was perhaps more clever than prudent, saw this news as an opportunity for mischief. He professed great sympathy for the defeated soldiers, and he asked the guide to conduct them to the Loyalist camp, so that he might join his forces to theirs in preparation for a new and more successful engagement. The trusting guide agreed to this plan, and hours later, at nearly midnight, he delivered Jones and his men to the Loyalist encampment. At once Jones ordered his men to attack the sleeping enemy. In a quick skirmish, only one of the Tories died, and the rest surrendered and asked for quarter, so Jones paroled them, confiscated what supplies he wanted, and forced the hapless guide to lead them onward to Earle's Ford on the North Pacolet River, where they would join forces with the Burke County militia of Col. Charles McDowell the next day.

There were Tory troops nearby, occupying a captured fort, originally built by the local population as a refuge against Indian attacks, much like our own Fort Watauga. The fort's commander didn't know that McDowell's militia was in the area, but he had already been given an earful about the deceitful Colonel Jones and his attack on the sleeping Loyalists. He dispatched a troop of dragoons and some regular soldiers to go after Jones.

The dragoons and infantry sent out by the fort commander arrived at the campsite on the North Pacolet in the dead of night, just as Jones had done the evening before. Intent upon repaying the raiders in kind, the Tories crossed the river, and launched their attack upon the sleeping encampment before the Burke militia's sentinel could sound the alarm.

Because the Georgia troops were the ones encamped closest to the river, Colonel Jones died early in the fighting, hacked to bits by the sabers of the dragoons. As the attackers fought their way forward toward McDowell's Burke County militia, the newly awakened soldiers, alerted by the sounds of the skirmish, grabbed their weapons on the run, and rallied to halt the charge, forming a line behind a nearby fence. Within moments they had organized themselves and were preparing to advance. By then the attackers from Fort Prince must have realized that the army they had encountered was larger than the one they had expected to find, because instead of a quick raid against thirty men or so, they found that the encampment stretched on and on, and that hundreds of soldiers were making ready to fight back.

Taking stock of the situation, their commander ordered them to fall back across the river, thus they exited the fray after suffering only a few casualties. This sudden encounter with many more of the enemy than expected was more of a battle than they had bargained for, and, having dispatched Jones, the object of the raid, they were ready to call it even, and head back to Fort Prince.

In the brief skirmish before they withdrew, they had managed to kill eight men and to wound another two dozen or so, but the one casualty for which that night would be remembered was young Noah Hampton, the son of the famed Burke County officer.

The boy had been asleep in his bedding

on the ground, when he was awakened in the darkness with the point of a bayonet prodding his throat. Angry voices demanded his name.

"Hampton," he murmured.

That name was well known to the area Loyalists, through the exploits his father, Col. Andrew Hampton, and others of the Hampton clan, who had done much to earn the hatred of their enemies, even as far back as the Moore's Creek battle, in which North Carolina's Highland Scots settlers were defeated, attempting to support the very king that they themselves had rebelled against thirty years earlier at Culloden Moor.

They say that young Noah Hampton had time to beg for his life before the dragoons pushed the bayonet point into his throat, but I hope it is not so. I hope he died as bravely as the rest of the Hamptons lived. I do know that his death was a loss deeply felt by his comrades, and tantamount to a wound to his grieving father.

Col. Andrew Hampton vowed to make the Tories pay for this outrage — most of those present did the same — but the bereaved parent did not reserve his anger for the attacking Loyalists, for, in war such acts constitute a soldier's duty, however much we may deplore them.

Now we come to it.

Andrew Hampton also blamed Charles McDowell for the death of his son, for letting it happen.

Why was McDowell so negligent about taking the most ordinary precautions during a bivouac? Why were there so few guards for a force of three hundred men, and none of them posted far enough from camp to sound an alarm in time for it to do any good?

Colonel Hampton confided to some of his fellow militia officers that he did not feel that McDowell could be trusted to command. According to Shelby, many Whigs believed that McDowell's overcautious actions in the aftermath of the Musgrove Mill battle corroborated that judgment of his unfitness to lead. Others said that he drank too much, clouding his judgment at crucial times.

But, putting all that to one side, I had to consider the fact that Charles McDowell had a few hundred troops at his command, and we sorely needed them. Shelby had confided all this to me during his recent visit to Plum Grove, although I had already heard a good bit of it from my brother, and we all agreed that, like him or not, we had to have the support of his militia in the coming venture.

Now, I had stayed home all summer, guarding the settlement against possible attacks from the Cherokee to the south, so I was not present for the fighting on the Pacolet or at Musgrove Mill. Any reservations I had about McDowell's ability were relayed to me at second hand, so it was decided that I should talk to him. I kept it uppermost in my mind that McDowell was on our side, capable or not. He might prove to be an encumbrance, but he was not the enemy.

People say that I have charm, perhaps from my French heritage. I can get along with almost anybody, unlike these brooding Scots and Irishmen, who store their grudges in the cellar with the winter apples. If ever I do harbor any ill will toward a fellow man, I hope I am careful not to show it, for to let an enemy see your feelings is to disarm yourself. Enemies are a luxury, and I try to choose them sparingly, because between the Indians and the British I generally have all I can handle.

Perhaps, for all his resentment of McDowell, Col. Andrew Hampton felt the same, for when Ferguson raided his home territory around Gilbert Town, Hampton, too, had gathered some of his followers and come over the mountain to take refuge along the

Watauga. So he and McDowell were neighbors, maintaining an awkward truce perhaps, but, because there was still a war to be fought, they would be forced to coexist in peace for yet a while longer. We knew that we all must put aside our differences and work together for the common cause as best we could.

So I rode off to the Burke encampment that morning, as bright and welcoming as the September sunshine, bearing what I hoped would be good news for the colonel: another chance to engage the enemy. I had been a visitor there before, of course. McDowell was a man of substance, and we had all gone to pay our respects at one time or another in the past few weeks as a matter of courtesy as well as prudence. I had sent supplies from Plum Grove to help them settle in to a bearable exile.

I found McDowell in camp, alone, eating his midday meal of stew and beans off a dented tin plate. Charles McDowell had been a lifelong bachelor, and perhaps solitude and the enforced idleness of temporary exile from his plantation weighed upon him, for he seemed even more somber than usual. Still, he managed a taut smile as he padded forward to meet me, and to bid me welcome with starched courtesy, proffering a dipper gourd of water, which was most welcome after my journey on that hot morning. Then he hovered close to my horse's withers, making inconsequential pleasantries while I watered the animal at the creek, unsaddled it, and saw to its tethering in a patch of grass.

When I had completed these small tasks, Colonel McDowell led me to a fallen log in the shade of a sycamore tree, and we sat down there together, a stone's throw from Buffalo Creek. Other militiamen in the camp had seen me when I arrived, and some of them waved as I rode past. I decided that after I'd had my talk with Charles McDowell, I would seek out Andrew Hampton and perhaps David Vance, another able officer from Burke County, to apprise them of what had transpired. Some of the exiled militiamen gathered to watch me pass, but none of them approached when I sat down to confer with Colonel McDowell.

They knew at once — as did he — that I had not made the long ride merely to pass the time of day with him. Colonel McDowell might have had idle days to fill, but I — with a farm to run, ten children and a new wife to see to, and the ever-present threat of Indian attacks to occupy my thoughts — had no time at all for aimless social calls. I hope I was cordial and unhurried that morning, but I was not without purpose.

All pretense of bonhomie aside, McDowell fixed me with a grave stare, and murmured, "Is there news?"

I nodded. "Yes, sir. I have lately had a visit from Isaac Shelby. He came bearing a letter that was just delivered by a kinsman of his, a prisoner freed by the enemy for the express purpose of carrying this missive to Shelby. It was from Maj. Patrick Ferguson. He orders us to keep out of the war."

"Ferguson?" McDowell's answering smile had not an ounce of mirth in it. "Orders us? That man would take a battling stick to a beehive, wouldn't he?"

"I think it amounts to that. We aim to sting him, anyhow."

Idly, he picked up a stone and tossed it in a lazy arc toward the creek. "You'd better make that sting a deadly one, then, for Ferguson is already a menace in the territory south of here. If you stir him up and then leave him at large, you will only make a misery for those of us whose holdings are there."

"Oh, we mean to end it, Colonel McDowell. I promise you that. We were fed to the teeth with Ferguson already, for all his cattle raids, and for turning his horses loose to

138

forage in Whig cornfields, but now with that letter of his, he has made it personal. We mean to stop him, but the task will take all of us working together to accomplish. I know that you and your men can be counted on to join us."

"You have settled on a course of action, then?"

"We have, sir. We are mustering at Fort Watauga on the twenty-fifth of this month, and then marching over the mountains to hunt down Ferguson. I can vouch for Shelby's men and mine."

McDowell digested this information for a moment, and then he growled, "And what about Campbell and his Virginia militia?"

"Yes. That is — I hope so. Colonel Shelby has gone home to write to him, setting out the reasons for him to cast his lot with us. Surely he'll see the sense of the plan and join us."

"Sevier, Shelby, McDowell, Campbell." He ticked off the names on his fingers. "I make it fewer than a thousand men. What about Benjamin Cleveland of the Yadkin, then, and the other militias farther to the east around the Moravian settlements, and what about the South Carolinians? Are they with us?"

"Yes, of course, sir. All the Carolina commanders we can persuade to fall in with us. We hope to have all of them."

McDowell grunted, which meant that he could find no fault with my answer. "I don't doubt you will need them all. The twenty-fifth of September, eh? We can all meet up at Quaker Meadows and unite our forces there with those of Cleveland and Winston and the rest."

I hesitated. Meeting at McDowell's plantation would further solidify his position as commander, but I did not object. *He sounds as if he is taking charge already,* I thought, but I resolved to overlook his preemptory attitude, and to respond with a civil answer, for his was indeed a reasonable suggestion. By the time we reached that point in the journey, we would be in need of more provisions, and it made sense to head for a place where we could be sure of getting them.

"Well, I hope you may persuade the other militias to join you in this venture. I don't doubt you will need them all. Perhaps my influence can be useful in asking them to join."

"I came here to enlist your support," I told him. "Well, more than that, for I know that you need no urging to lead your troops for the fight. But what we also need is information. Once we get over the mountains, we will be heading into your territory, and you know it better than any of us. The rivers. The fords. The location of the homes of Whig sympathizers. And where the enemy strongholds lie."

McDowell raised his eyebrows. "But I will be with you, Sevier. I can show all of that to the rest of you when the time comes."

I was on shaky ground here, and so I chose my words carefully and bound them up in a smile. "Of course you will be with us, Colonel, but we must be prepared for every contingency. Our forces could become separated. People could be lost to ambush or illness. It's best that we not keep the keys to our survival locked in the head of just one man. The risk is too great."

He saw the sense of that, and indeed it was true enough, as far as it went. I would not want such details to be the sole property of any one member of the party, for that would put us one bullet away from disorder and defeat.

After a long appraising look at me — for, after all, who completely trusts anybody these days? — McDowell nodded. "Very well, then. Have you a bit of paper with you? Well, we can find some in my cabin, I expect. I will draw up maps and make lists. You will want to commit all of it to memory and destroy the notes, of course, but at least you will have a few weeks to learn the information as best you can. I hope you will not have to rely upon your memory for these matters, though. I mean to be with you and Shelby, every mile of the way."

I smiled, which seemed safer than saying anything.

As if reading my thoughts, McDowell said, "I am the senior commander, you know. I have been a colonel longer than any of you, and so, when we do unite our forces, by rights I should be the one in charge of this campaign."

I did know it. Shelby and I had talked about it at length, looking for some way around that disagreeable fact. The solution we finally agreed upon was not ideal, but it was better than the alternate, which was to give the reins over to McDowell and let him have sole command. I willed myself to keep smiling. As gently as I could, I said, "We think it best if we rotate the command every couple of days, instead of having just one leader. We are not a regular army, you know. Our soldiers are volunteers, and they follow us at their own pleasure. We think it more likely that the militias will come willingly if each one's own trusted leader is in charge of the campaign at least part of the time."

His eyes widened and his lip curled in scorn. *"Come willingly,* Sevier? These men in the militias are soldiers. They have taken an oath. They ought to do as they are told — obey orders from superior officers and trust their betters to decide on the strategy of the campaign. Choice does not come into it."

I sighed. "Well, Colonel, you will find men in this war who obey orders and trust their betters, without any thought at all to their own rights or liberty. But those men are mostly fighting on Ferguson's side, not ours. We do things differently on this side of the mountain."

Virginia Sal

It was September now and we had been on the move, heading up into the hill country, looking for converts to the cause and for livestock to feed the army. It was still warm, even at night, and sometimes we'd come upon apple trees bearing their fruit, so our sojourn in the foothills suited me all right, but I did notice that some of the trees on the high hills were already beginning to turn red and gold, which made me wonder what the army would do when winter came. I hoped we'd stop camping in the woods, and go somewhere like Charlotte Town until spring came. The general's headquarters were there, and I reckoned that the major could take over any house he wanted there.

I asked Virginia Paul about it, but she only shook her head and said that I needn't worry about the winter, that I should not pass a day of it cold or hungry. I suppose she was just trying to ease my mind so I wouldn't pester her with my worries, but she sounded as if she knew it for a fact, so I tried to believe her and to put the matter out of my mind.

There were other things to worry about soon enough. But for a while it seemed like summer and good fortune would go on forever.

Dr. Johnson stopped by the tent one afternoon while I was sitting on a blanket in the tent opening, mending one of the major's shirts. The doctor rubbed his hands together, looking big with news. "We shall eat well tonight, my girl!" he said. Uzal Johnson thought a fair bit about food, even though we generally had enough. I thought that tending to sick people made him more determined than most people to take enjoyment where he found it. Or maybe he was used to more and better meals than I was.

"Did somebody shoot a wild turkey?" I said, for we were not in farm country now. Instead of broad fields of corn and tidy gardens of beans and carrots at the big farms in the river valleys, there was now about us only woods and fields of wild grass, that even the major's fine white horse seemed loath to eat. The major had ridden off earlier in the day with a dozen soldiers, but he seldom bothered to tell us what he was about, and, being just his servant girl, I would hardly have asked him for an accounting. As often as not, I didn't care where he went, anyhow. It was just a bunch of men riding out, armed to the teeth, talking or fighting, and feeling mighty important about whatever it was they were doing. It was all one to me. Sometimes Virginia Paul would know the particulars, but she didn't seem to care any more than I did.

"Well, someone may shoot a turkey, now you come to mention it, Sal, for I think I caught sight of one in the weeds last evening, but what I am talking about is beef!" He hit his fist against his palm, and grinned. "At least I do hope so. Major Ferguson has gone to parlay with a landowner who has persuaded himself to stay loyal to the king. It seems this gentleman farmer knows where McDowell's militia hid their beeves before they fled over the mountains. The cattle are pastured in coves up the mountain near here, and the major has taken some men to go after them."

None of that had anything in particular to do with me, except that if we did manage to round up some cattle, I'd eat better, same as the major, because he was good about seeing that his people were fed. More cattle to feed the men was good news, but even without them I had few complaints about the victuals we were given on the march, for we always passed by a goodly number of Loyalist farmers along the way, and the major prevailed upon them to feed his men. He also prevailed upon the rebel farmers to provision his army, but he did not ask them politely. He took what he wanted. Since it amounted to losing their crops and livestock either way, I thought that perhaps some of the Loyalist farmers were simply making a virtue of necessity, to keep us from burning their farms as well as taking their goods. Maybe when the other army passed by, they'd switch sides again. Anyhow, we never went hungry. I supposed that Major Ferguson was making a point of finding the Burke militia's beeves simply to deprive them of the use of them, but I'd be happy to help him eat the meat.

"I hope he finds those cattle, and that doing so will raise his spirits," said Dr. Johnson. "The major has been unsettled of late, though he insists that he is not sick, and since I can find nothing wrong with him, I suppose I must believe him." He stepped past me, and sat down on the major's trunk, watching my needlework. "Does Major Ferguson seem ill to you, Sal?"

"Well, no sicker than usual, I reckon," I

said, for I remembered what Virginia Paul had told me about his bouts with fever in Europe and again a few years later in the islands. I wondered if that ailment might come back one day, for the Carolinas can be fever country in hot weather, but the major had passed the whole summer without a sign of it, though he did seem restless and foul-tempered sometimes, and his sleep was troubled. I hadn't been with him that long, though, so for all I knew that was how he always was. Dr. Johnson knew him better, so I took his word that something was amiss, though it seemed to me that the major might have a good many reasons to feel poorly.

"Can't you fix his arm?" I asked him. "He can't straighten it out, but holds it up against his chest all the time. I reckon that affliction would get anybody down, much less a soldier, who is supposed to be able-bodied. Does it pain him?"

The doctor considered it. "I shouldn't think so. It has healed. And for that reason, I can do nothing for him. The wound was treated, and the joint has fused in place. That cannot be changed."

"It's a good thing he is left-handed, so that he can still write and eat."

Uzal Johnson shook his head. "The major

was born right-handed. He has taught himself to use his other hand so as not to be completely incapacitated by his injury. It's wonderful what he managed in so short a time. He is trying hard to retain his commission. I gather that the army is his home now. It is his inheritance, anyhow, and all the fortune he is ever likely to get."

"About his wounded arm — I never heard what happened to him." I wondered if Virginia Paul knew, but I reckoned she did, because she seemed to know everything. She had not got around to telling me yet, though.

The doctor watched me wielding the needle. "Have you asked him?"

"I have not. He'd take that as an impertinence, and I wouldn't like to ask, anyhow. He hates being a cripple. You can tell."

"Well, he's not accustomed to it yet. It happened less than two years ago. Bad luck for a career soldier, even more than for most men. It's all on account of that infernal gun of his, though I think he blames everything but that."

"Tell me, please. Did you attend him when he got hurt?"

"I did not. But I know the particulars. We have dined together often enough, and exchanged the tales of our troubles."

I looked up from my needlework. "Well, you look fit enough, doctor."

He smiled. "I am sound in body, but this war has cost me dearly, too. Eight years ago I graduated from King's College in New York, and set out to practice medicine back home in New Jersey. I had four prosperous years until the rebellion began brewing, and then the Whigs commissioned me for a surgeon. Presently, I left them, for I decided that my allegiance lay with the king, and besides the Whigs were losing."

I nodded. "It seemed that way to me, too."

"I cast my lot with the New Jersey Volunteers. The rebels confiscated my medicines and such of my property as they could get their hands on, which did nothing to endear me to their cause. So, now, four years later, here I am in this temperate jungle, where the air in summer feels like cotton wool when you try to breathe it. It has been a long war."

We fell silent for a bit, while I plied my needle, and the doctor took out his little book and began to write in it, as he often does of an evening by lamplight. Finally, though, my curiosity got the better of me, and I said, "But you know how the major came to be crippled?"

"Oh, yes. He was badly wounded up in

Pennsylvania, at Brandywine. That's the short of it, but if you want to hear all that led up to it, I know a good bit of that, too."

I squinted up at the sun, which was still above the treetops. The major wouldn't be back for a couple of hours yet, and I could make the mending last as long as the tale. "Tell me then, if you please, an' the soldiers can spare you a while longer."

Dr. Johnson nodded. "They seem well enough. Well, where to begin? Back when I was learning to name the bones at medical college, the good major was stationed in the Caribbean, keeping the peace for the English planters. He managed to get through those skirmishes unscathed, but he fell ill with malaria, which is not at all uncommon for soldiers who are sent hither and yon across the empire. Banastre Tarleton has it, too, you know. It can go away for months at a time, but then it comes roaring back, and lays the sufferer low for weeks."

I nodded. "I knew about that. I don't reckon you doctors can cure the malaria fever, either."

The doctor shrugged. "There's precious little we can cure. Sometimes I think we simply amuse the patient until he gets well on his own — though wounds are different, of course. We can patch those up, after a

151

fashion. But rest and a better climate can sometimes help those suffering from fever. Anyhow, Ferguson was not in my care in those days, so I cannot say what ailed him. When he fell ill, they sent him back to Scotland to recuperate. And as he recovered his strength, he began to devote his time to developing a new-fangled weapon that he hoped would replace the army's Brown Bess."

"Is that what the soldiers here are carrying?" I didn't know much about guns, except to get out of the way of them.

Dr. Johnson shook his head. "No. His invention did not replace the Brown Bess. But the major will tell anyone who will listen that it should have. His new weapon had a far greater range and accuracy — or so he says. I have never seen one myself, I am no expert on weapons, though I fear I am becoming well versed in treating their consequences."

I scooted over a bit, so that the light shining through the tree branches would fall on the seam I was working on. "How was the major's new gun different from the old ones?"

"I couldn't tell you in terms of the mechanics of it. If you ever have trouble sleeping, ask the major for the particulars, and he will talk about it until cock crow. It was a breech-loader, I do know that, while the army's Brown Bess loads at the muzzle."

"Which one is better?"

"Well, heaven only knows. The major says that his weapon would be easier for soldiers to reload while lying down or when hidden in underbrush. I suppose that would be an advantage."

"Did he ever make one to try it out?"

"Indeed, he paid for a gunsmith to make several of them, and he tested them himself. Why, he even went to Windsor Castle and demonstrated the thing for the king. Can you imagine? Had it been me, I doubt if I could have held the rifle steady."

I shrugged, as if I didn't care a bit about seeing any old king, but I ached to ask the major a thousand questions about his visit there. What did the king look like? What furniture was there in the castle? Did they give you anything to eat — and did they serve it to you on plates of gold? It wasn't any use, though. Men never talk about things like that, and like as not they don't even notice. But it felt like I had a little hot coal in the pit of my stomach just to think that I was acquainted with somebody who had met the king.

Well, it was no use even to dream about

such as that, so I pretended to take this news in stride. "The major is the son of some kind of nobleman, ain't he? Maybe he feels a little closer to the king's level than the rest of us on account of that. And maybe he didn't hold the rifle steady, either. From what you say, the king wasn't impressed enough to buy any."

"The major would have it that King George was impressed indeed, but His Majesty may not know any more about guns than we do. Anyhow, ultimately it isn't the king's decision. The army has a Board of Ordnance to choose their weaponry."

"A what?"

"A committee of high-ranking officials who are empowered to make decisions of that sort."

"People who do know about guns, then?"

"One would hope for that to be the case," said the doctor with a weary sigh, "but my experience with armies tells me that they are simply aristocratic and well-connected people, the sort who feel that any decision is right because *they* have made it, whether they know anything about the matter or not. And such people are not fond of change."

I nodded. "They might be afraid that one of the changes might be *them.*"

He laughed. "There's no cure for that,

either. But the major jumped all the hurdles for them. And in the end they decided that Ferguson's marvelous rifle-gun was too expensive to make, unreliable in conditions of rain and mud, and too difficult for the ordinary soldiers to use. Who knows? Perhaps they were right, but he swears his breech-loader was the better weapon. Nevertheless, when he was deemed fit to return to duty, they gave him his own special company of soldiers, equipped with the new weapon, and they shipped them off to America to join the war."

I looked up at the sun again. The major could come back at any moment now, and the chance might not come again to find out about his wound. "Tell me the part where he got hurt, Doctor."

"It was at a place called Brandywine, where they fought against the Continental Army. Major Ferguson was looking forward to the battle, because he had his own troops, all equipped with the rifle he invented. In the course of the battle, he was shot in the arm, shattering the elbow. He says that the surgeons wanted to amputate, but he refused. He spent a year in the city of New York, recovering. He saved his arm, but it healed frozen in place as you see. With great determination and more than a little courage, he learned to write and to eat with his left hand, and he was determined to continue his military career, but his superiors sent him south, perhaps because they don't think there's much of a war here. No one wanted a crippled officer in his command. So here he is."

Outside the tent someone laughed. I froze for a couple of heartbeats, and when I turned I saw Virginia Paul shadowed in the opening. "That's about half the story," she said. "But you don't have time for the rest. The major is on his way here, and he's asking for you, Doctor."

Uzal Johnson scrambled to his feet. "What? Is he injured?"

She shook her head. "No. But he needs a doctor all the same. Not that you'll be any use. But you'd better go and meet him." As the doctor started to leave the tent, Virginia Paul called after him, "Oh, and, sir, if you need any help, please send for me, and not Sal here."

He looked as if he wanted to answer, but then we heard voices in the distance, and he simply nodded and hurried away.

When he was gone, I turned in fury to Virginia Paul, "What did you tell him that for? I'm supposed to be the one helping the doctor, and you know it!"

She turned to me with the saddest look I'd ever seen in her cold green eyes. "Fool girl! I'm doing you a kindness. You'd be wise to take it."

In the end they did not call for either one of us, and the major and the men who were with him rode away again without even stopping to rest their mounts. I had waited a few minutes after the doctor left, and then I got out of the tent, and tried to see what was going on, but I didn't see anything until they took to the road again. As soon as I saw them ride away, I went running in search of the doctor to see what the matter was, because he had not been with them when they rode out again. If there had been an ambush or if a battle was in the offing, the soldiers would be scurrying around like ants near a campfire, but everything seemed as quiet as it had before.

The sun was low in the sky now, setting the clouds alight, and I found Uzal Johnson down at the creek at the edge of the camp, washing his hands and arms over and over in the cold stream. Virginia Paul was nowhere in sight.

"They have set off again, Doctor," I told him. "Did they not need you after all?"

He sighed. "The major wanted only my

opinion as the regiment's physician. And he knew that if he was right in what he suspected, then all my skill would be useless."

"What's the matter with him, then?"

"With Major Ferguson? Nothing, thank heaven. It is poor Ensign Evans who is afflicted."

I shut my eyes for a moment, trying to place Ensign Evans among the scores of young officers here in the regiment. I thought he might be the jug-eared boy from an upper South Carolina farm who hunted rabbits everywhere we camped to supplement the army rations. He looked to be about the same age as me, so I couldn't imagine what would be ailing him, if he hadn't been wounded in an ambush.

"Evans? What's the matter with him?"

"He was taken feverish this afternoon, and when I saw him, he was beginning to redden with a rash. 'Tis the smallpox, poor devil. I've seen it enough to have no doubt of that."

I shivered, remembering Virginia Paul's parting words to me, *"I'm doing you a kindness."* So she had been, for anyone would want to keep well away from a body afflicted with smallpox.

"Couldn't you do anything for him, sir? He's young and strong. He could fight it.

I've heard tell of people who lived through a bout of smallpox. Of course, they were pockmarked and fearful ugly ever after, but anyhow they did live."

Dr. Johnson shook his head. "We were all heartily sorry for poor Ensign Evans, but the prospect of his recovery cannot be an issue in Major Ferguson's decision. He has a thousand men under his command, and he cannot risk losing them to pestilence for the sake of one man. The major consulted me only so that I could confirm that Evans was indeed stricken with the pox. When I agreed that this was so, he had no choice about what to do." Dr. Johnson plunged his arms up to the elbows in the creek, and began to scrub again.

I knew he was trying to wash away any contagion he might have got, and I was so affrighted by the thought of that, that I squatted down beside him and commenced to washing my hands as well.

"Was Ensign Evans with them when they rode away just now?"

"Oh, yes." He paused for a long time, staring up at the trees, but as last he said, "Evans will not be with them when they return."

I let the words sink in, trying to work out what he wasn't saying. "Are they going to

159

kill him?" I whispered.

The doctor turned to stare at me, and I thought he might have laughed at my foolishness if the situation weren't so sad. "No, Sal," he said. "Though it might be kinder if they did. One of the other officers mentioned that he had seen an abandoned cabin a few miles back along the trace, and they decided to take him there and leave him."

"What do you mean, leave him?"

"They will put Ensign Evans in the cabin with a few days' rations, which I doubt he will need, and he will die in God's good time. A few days at most."

My throat felt too small to get the words out. "But, Doctor, I told you: people with the pox get well sometimes."

"I know they do. And let us hope that poor Evans is one of them. I would pray for such an outcome, but as a medical man I would not wager a penny on it. Once his supplies run out, he will have no water, no one to look after him, and he will be too weak to build a fire or to fend for himself. It might be more merciful to pray that for him the end comes quickly."

I opened my mouth to ask whether the doctor could leave someone to tend to Ensign Evans, but my mind knew better before I even uttered the words. No one would be fool enough to stay in close quarters with a man dying of smallpox, for they would most likely follow him sweating and raving to the grave before the month was out. Oh, a wife or a mother might be fond enough to risk it, but the fellow was all but a stranger to us. No one would risk their own life on the off-chance of saving his. Would I offer to take on such a task? I knew I would not, and, if I really plumbed my heart, I reckon I was as glad as anybody here that the man with the deadly pestilence was being taken out of our midst, so that I could not catch it from him. Even if I took the pox and lived, my life as a likely looking wench would be over, and I'd surely die young from toil in the fields, for I'd be good for nothing else.

I'd be haunted in my sleep, though, for many a night to come, thinking about that poor dying man shut up alone in a dark little cabin, with maybe a few days' rations and a jug of stale water, knowing what was to come, and having to face it friendless and alone. I wondered if they would leave him his weapon, for he might choose a quicker death than the one the pox would give him — but, no, I reckoned they wouldn't. Guns are more valuable than young soldiers. They can always get themselves another farm boy to shoot it.

"I wonder how he came to get the pox?"

Dr. Johnson shook his head. "Nobody knows the answer to that, girl. Perhaps it floats about in the air. Some get it and others don't. The will of Providence, I suppose. Anyhow, I shall have to inspect all the men before we break camp tomorrow, and every day thereafter for a week, to make sure that no one else has been stricken with it."

I could not sleep that night for thinking about that poor boy left to die in a solitary cabin with only his sword and a sackful of victuals to comfort him, but when I said as much to Virginia Paul, she only shrugged and said, "There's worse things than dying."

CHAPTER SEVEN
SEPTEMBER 1780

A day or so thereafter I set out to secure the most crucial item in our campaign against Ferguson: the powder to blow him to hell.

We were fortunate here in the Watauga region: we had a powder mill. The making of black powder is arduous and dangerous work, not a job I would wish for, but in these perilous times I could think of no greater blessing than to have such an operation within a day's ride. Like John Adair, who kept the settlement's treasury and had lent us the money for the campaign, the proprietor of the powder mill was an Irishman, one John Patton, who had come over from Ulster as a lad, and settled first in the Pennsylvania colony. Patton's great good fortune here lay in his choice of a wife, for he had married another Pennsylvania settler, an Englishwoman named Mary Mc-Keehan, whose father owned a mill, and had passed on to his daughter the trade of powder-making. Thus provided with a better livelihood than most of the neighboring farmers, John and Mary Patton had set up a powder mill of their own in the village of Carlisle, where they prospered and began their family. They might have stayed there forever, but for the fact that the war in the colonies arrived in Pennsylvania some years before we felt the blast of it here in the Carolina backcountry.

I'd had occasion to hear their history from the Pattons themselves, for like most of the other men in the Watauga settlement, I called on them regularly to purchase black powder, mostly for hunting, but sometimes in preparation for another attack on our lives. No one ever grudged them a penny of what they earned selling black powder. Our lives depended on their skill at their trade.

Often I passed the time of day with Mistress Mary Patton when I came to buy a new supply from them, for it was she who had the tending of the saltpeter kettles, supervising the workers, while her husband, John, managed the crops in their fields. She always seemed glad of the company, for the necessary stench of her powder-making would discourage many casual visitors. I suppose she had grown used to the foul smell herself over the years, but, between the smoke-filled air and the reek of dung, few people cared to linger long in her society.

Because of the prospect of war, the Pattons had received little enough from the sale of their mill in Carlisle, for, distaste and danger aside, not many folk were anxious to take on such an enterprise with the threat of a British occupation looming. Nevertheless, the Pattons were determined to go, and so they accepted a meager offer, cut their losses, and headed down the great wagon road with their daughters to start anew. Another of our neighbors, Andrew Taylor, himself a transplanted Pennsylvanian, had urged the couple to come westward on the Wilderness Road to the Watauga settlements. Taylor had eased the way for them by helping them to construct a new mill on the small stream situated next to Taylor's own holdings. Because of the mill, that stream soon became known as Powder Branch. I expect that Taylor meant his generosity to be Christian charity to the Pattons, for he had known them during his time in the militia back in Pennsylvania. But his benevolent gesture was an even greater kindness to the rest of us here in the backcountry, for the establishment of the powder mill meant that we were not dependent upon shipments from away to keep us supplied with the ammunition we needed to hunt and to defend ourselves.

When the Pattons arrived here in the Watauga settlement and made ready to set up their operation, in addition to a grateful and welcoming community, they found another bit of good fortune awaiting them here, for they soon discovered an abundant source of saltpeter less disagreeable than the usual ways of obtaining it. The big powder mills back east import the saltpeter they need to manufacture black powder, but a man-and-wife mill operating on the frontier has not the luxury of obtaining that crucial ingredient ready-made. Obtaining and preparing the saltpeter was the most unpleasant part of the process, and I've often wondered that anyone would willingly embark upon the operation of such an enterprise, necessary though it was for the survival of all of us.

Saltpeter is distilled from the excrement of livestock in the barns and pastures, and if that supply should not prove sufficient to the task, even the night soil of human beings would be put to use. The thought of having to deal with such a foul substance gives me pause, but the Pattons must have been used to it, I suppose, and indeed life on the frontier was not easy for any of us. Someone had to do it, and it had the virtue of being a profitable enterprise and a product for which there would always be a market.

At least, here in the Carolina mountains, the Pattons were spared the indignity of having to collect their raw material from the waste matter of people and livestock, for at the base of the nearby mountains that towered over Powder Branch, there were caves. Countless generations of wild beasts and roosting bats had used those caves as a refuge, and over the years these feral inhabitants had carpeted the cave floor with their foul droppings. The Pattons were able to collect this rich source of nitrate from the caves, not a pleasant task, perhaps, but certainly better than the alternatives.

There was no mistaking the location of the powder mill. As my horse followed the trace along Buffalo Creek, I could see plumes of gray smoke unfurling in the distance, making a haze over the forest in an otherwise cloudless sunny day. Not long after I saw the smoke, my senses were assaulted by the reek of boiling excrement in the open kettles. The powder-making operation was going full force that morning.

I tied my horse to a sapling at the edge of the open field where the powder-making operation took place. He would have been reluctant to carry me farther in any case, for he had no love of the smell of the place, either, but even worse were the half-dozen sod-covered pyramids of burning timber set a few yards apart across the field. The flames were kept contained within the earthen covering — unless something went wrong — but plumes of smoke arose from the vent hole at the top of each stack, and a horse does not need to see fire to know it is there. My mount rolled his eyes and edged backward as far as the rein would permit him. I patted his neck and spoke a few calming words to soothe him, and then I headed for the wooden hut near the creek, where Mary Patton sat, keeping watch over the timber pyres from the open doorway. If ever the flames broke through the earthen covering, she or one of the workers would have to rush to the pyre and repair the damage.

As I crossed the field, giving the pyres a wide berth, she caught sight of me and waved a greeting, but she did not get up. Mary Patton was a slender, sturdy woman nearing her thirtieth year, ruddy of face, and weather-beaten, for she worked with fire and noxious materials, and she spent most of her days out in the elements. Her brown hair was tied up in a kerchief to keep it out of harm's way while she worked, and sweat beaded in the furrows on her wide forehead. When I got close enough to bid her good day, I saw that she cradled an infant to her breast, swaddled in a cotton shawl.

"A fine-looking child," I said, though I could see little but the tip of its nose. "My congratulations to you."

She shrugged. " 'Tis another lass, this one, and we've three of them already." She nodded in the direction of the creek where three little girls, the eldest no more than seven, were playing at the water's edge. "If they don't bring husbands into the business, I suppose they'll learn the craft from me, as I did from me own father."

"You don't allow them near the fires yet, surely?"

"No. That will keep until they are older."

I looked out across the field to the little stream, to watch the three copper-haired Patton daughters, too absorbed in their game to notice their elders. I had expected to see them laughing and splashing one another, as my own young ones did at play, but the Patton daughters were as solemn as owls. Each of them was holding a corner of a large white cloth, stained with red streaks, and they were dipping it into the creek and pulling it out again. After a moment, the oldest girl turned back to look for her mother. Finally catching sight of me watching them, she pointed her finger at me and uttered a low moan. Her sisters, stair steps to her in age, let the wet cloth fall upon the rocks, and joined the eldest in pointing and moaning in my direction. Their utter solemnity rendered the scene chilling, rather than charming.

My smile faded and I took an involuntary step backward. "What on earth are they doing?" I asked their mother, endeavoring to banish the thought of madness from my mind.

Mary Patton sighed and shook her head. "Oh, it's all a nonsense, but it's their favorite pastime nowadays. I beg your pardon if they startled you, but it's only part of that silly game. They call it being *washers at the ford*. Their father has filled their heads with wild tales from the old country. He gathers them around the hearth of an evening, and spins tales of fairy folk, and magic swords, and all manner of fanciful moonshine. So now the girls play at being the creatures in those old stories of his."

"But what is a washer at the ford?"

"Well, John would have it that there are female spirits called *bean-sidhes,* who appear to those who are about to die. He says that if you come upon a strange woman washing bloody clothes in a forest stream, then you have met the bean-sidhe and shortly thereafter you are bound to die. You'd think the girls would take fright at hearing such a tale as that, especially the little one, but, no, they are all three enchanted. Instead of fearing such a creature, Margaret and her sisters are playing at being the fairy women themselves. They've taken to washing that old sheet in the stream, and you arrived at just the right time to be their victim today. It's only nonsense. Pay it no mind at all." She began to fuss with the baby's shawls, and the older girls turned back to their washing.

I managed a weak smile. "Children are savage little creatures, aren't they? In happier times, I think I would be charmed by such a singular pastime, and your little woodland fairies are lovely creatures. But the mission that brings me to see you today is so fraught with danger that I am wary of any omen at all that might cast a shadow on its success. Still, these fairy washers are only little girls, and not magic beings, but I would wish that those lasses had pointed

171

their bony little fingers at Major Ferguson instead of at me."

At the sound of that name, Mistress Patton stopped arranging the baby's shawls, and grew very still. "So that's the way of it?" she said softly.

I sat down on the grass close to Mistress Patton's wooden stool. "Yes," I said. "That's the way of it. Ferguson is somewhere north of Gilbert Town, last we knew, and he has had a message delivered to Colonel Shelby, threatening to invade our settlement unless we keep out of the war."

Mary Patton was looking past me, keeping a watchful eye on her timber pyres, but her very stillness told me that she was listening intently. When she was satisfied that nothing was amiss with any of her charcoal fires, she turned her attention back to me. "Well, I don't suppose that you gentlemen do intend to keep out of the war, since you have come to pay a visit to me."

"True enough. We have talked it over at length, Colonel Shelby and I, but I don't think either of us ever had a moment's hesitation in charting our course of action. We agree that if we allowed ourselves to be cowed by Ferguson's threats, sooner or later he would find an excuse to bring his troops here to the settlements, anyway, if only to steal our livestock to feed his army."

Mary Patton's expression did not change. "So you mean to get into the fighting. We've heard tell that Charles Town in South Carolina fell back in the spring."

"Yes, but we've had battles with the Tories since then, and acquitted ourselves well. We don't mean to fight the lot of them — just the forces commanded by Ferguson. We fancy our chances, providing we can take him by surprise without his getting reinforcement from Tarleton." I doubt if I would have spoken with such frankness or in such detail with any other woman of my acquaintance, but the nature of Mary Patton's work gave her more familiarity with military matters than most members of her sex. It was the fruits of her labor that would enable us to go to war in the first place, and if we lost, the consequences to her family would be dire. She deserved to know.

She was nodding. "Take the Tories by surprise and hope they don't outnumber you, yes. And also providing that you have enough supplies and ammunition to hold your own against the king's army for however long you need to."

"Yes, and it is on that account that I came to consult you, Mistress Patton. How is your stock of black powder these days?"

She looked appraisingly at me. "Depends on what you reckon you'll need. How many men are you taking over the mountain?"

"All of us together? Upwards of a thousand. My men, and Shelby's and those of Colonel McDowell. We can persuade William Campbell over in Virginia to come, I hope. Other militias east of the mountains will join us as we go, but they'll have their own supplies. But, say, a thousand men."

She blinked. "So many? Perhaps I'd better be making powder for the rest of us first, then. After you've gone, will there be any able-bodied men left behind to protect us from the Indians?"

"Yes. We planned for that. James Robertson and his militia will keep the settlements safe while we're gone. But I do not expect there to be any Indian raids this soon. The Cherokee are well aware of our war with the British. If I were Dragging Canoe, I would wait to attack until the invaders reached the settlements here. That distraction would increase his chances of making a successful strike. Anyhow, Robertson should not have to hold the territory for long. Our journey will be brief — one way or another."

I glanced back at the three little girls, but they were taking no further notice of us. Now they were kneeling on the rocks at the water's edge, sailing leaf boats along in the swirling current.

Remembering the words of Shakespeare, I mused aloud, *"There is a tide in the affairs of men, which, taken at the flood leads on to fortune . . ."*

Mary Patton paid no mind to my wool-gathering. "When are you planning to set out then, Colonel Sevier?"

"We are mustering not far from here — at Robertson's fort, at Sycamore Shoals — on the twenty-fifth of this month. You have until then to make the powder we need."

"I will need until then," she said, glancing back at her workers, tending the charcoal pyres. "Unless weather or mishap hinders me, I reckon I can deliver five hundred pounds of powder by the twenty-fifth, but . . ." She hesitated.

I suspect there is Scots blood somewhere in the lineage of Mary Patton, and the French and the Scots have always under-stood each other. "Never fear, madam. We can pay you for your work. John Adair has advanced us funds from the settlement's treasury, and we have no greater need for that money than to purchase black powder for our weapons. The success of the venture depends upon it. Name your price, but remember that it is for a good cause."

Mary Patton smiled. "Well, that's all right then, Colonel. You shall have your powder on the mustering day, as ordered."

Virginia Sal

There is a time in late September when the leaves are still green, and the days are still warm, but somehow you know that it is all about to end, as if summer was holding its breath, and when it let it out again, it would be autumn.

I felt that way about the golden days we had spent racketing around the hills of Carolina, feasting on stolen cattle and swilling the apple wine of the Whig landowners. I didn't feel too sorry for the Whigs, though, because I knew they'd do the same thing to their Loyalist neighbors when they could, and I didn't feel guilty because it wasn't me that did the stealing. It would have happened just the same, whether I'd been there or not. But I kept on having this feeling that the glorious excursion was coming to an end.

I said as much to Virginia Paul, when we were rattling around in one of the supply wagons, on the way to somewhere else, which is what we usually did in the daylight hours, while the regiment went looking for rebels to fight. It wasn't any use to try to do the sewing in the wagon, for the rocky road jostled us so that we could not hold our needles steady enough to make a proper seam.

When I ventured to say that it felt like things were coming to an end, Virginia Paul stopped combing her hair, and gave me a less disdainful smile than usual. "What makes you say that, Sal?"

It was a feeling, but I couldn't put it into words. I shrugged. "It just seems like things are changing. There wasn't much fighting all summer, and most of the time I felt like we were on an excursion instead of fighting a war."

The scornful look returned. "I suppose it was an excursion for you, Sal. Seeing new country and eating your fill every night. Nobody asked you to fight. You didn't so much as steal a chicken. There has been precious little fighting, at least in your purview, and not many losses. You have yet to see death at close hand, and feel the pain of it."

That stung me, coming from her, for she couldn't be much older than I was. She was being awful high and mighty for somebody who hadn't seen much more of the war than I had. "I suppose you'd be an expert on dying," I said. "I expect you know all about it."

Virginia Paul took no offense at my mockery. With a solemn expression, she tilted her head to one side while she considered the matter. "Yes," she said at last. "I have seen a fair number of deaths, and I reckon I know the way of it better than you do, Sal. But I never could feel it the way you can. You'll know more of the sorrow of death than I ever will."

I knew there was no use asking her what troubles she had lived through, for she never would answer any questions about herself. Sometimes she spoke as if she were an old woman who had seen many years of toil and sorrow. But since she was so young, I thought that she must have meant that somewhere she had seen too many horrors to be moved by anything more.

Suddenly she looked up and became still, as if she were listening to something outside, but all I heard was the rumbling of the wagon, and the *clop clop* of the officers' horses in front of us. After a moment she sighed. "Well, we shall soon know the truth of it, Sal. Let us see how you feel then."

She would say nothing more on the subject, and at last she curled up in the blankets at the back of the wagon and went to sleep, but I sat still for a long time, expecting at any moment to hear the crack of gunfire that would signal an ambush. All was quiet, though, and I decided she'd only been trying to frighten me with her talk of death.

That evening we fetched up somewhere near Gilbert Town, for the regiment had been circling that town for weeks, like a moth to a candle flame. We might go a ways north or west of it, but sooner or later we ended up back again, ready to set off in a different direction in a day or so.

Virginia Paul and I jumped down out of the baggage wagon and went looking for the creek, for we were sweat-soaked and dusty from the day's sojourn on the road. When we had finished what the major would call our "ablutions" and were heading back toward camp, we heard a piteous wailing, followed by shouts of alarm.

An ambush, I thought, but Virginia Paul kept on calmly walking toward the camp, as if the noises had been no more than birdsong.

I took hold of her arm. "What is it?"

She turned to me and smiled. "Go along

180

and find out, Sal. They'll have need of one of us, and this time it should be you."

I hitched up my skirt and ran toward the shouting. When I neared the circle of baggage wagons, I found a cluster of soldiers gathered around something that I could not see. Before I could make my way into the crowd to see what had happened, I saw Uzal Johnson with his black satchel, hurrying along in the wake of one of the farm boys. The crowd parted to let him through, and I followed him into the gap.

I saw the blood in the dirt before I could take in anything else. Sprawled on the ground lay a rawboned boy, one of the local recruits, holding his leg, from which the blood gushed like a stream of snowmelt. I turned to the man beside me. "What happened to him?"

Without taking his eyes off the injured recruit, the soldier said, "That there's Malcolm Hardie, from over in South Carolina. They say he tripped on something — a rock — like as not, and it pitched him under the baggage wagon, just as the rest of us were rolling it in place in the circle of wagons. One of the wagon wheels ran over his leg. Crushed it, I reckon."

"Come here, girl!" Uzal Johnson was kneeling next to the wailing boy, probing the wound with his fingers, when he looked up and caught sight of me. I had helped the doctor now and again with the washing and dressing of wounds, so I reckoned he had need of me now.

Pushing my way through the onlookers, I squatted down next to Uzal Johnson. "They say he fell under the wheel of a baggage wagon," I said. "Did he break his leg?"

The doctor nodded. "That's not the worst of it." He grabbed my hand and set it down on top of the fountain of blood spurting out from a tear in the soldier's britches. "Keep your hand there, Sal," he said. "Push hard, while I think what can be done."

"Won't you set the bone?" I asked. "I can find you a likely stick to make a splint with."

Uzal Johnson sighed. "It won't come to that, Sal. Look closely where the wound is."

I tried to peer down through the stream of blood, and then I saw what the doctor meant for me to see. A jagged piece of bone stuck out from beneath the skin near the wound.

"Keep pushing down, Sal." When he saw that I had managed to staunch the flow, the doctor gestured to one of the officers. "Get all these men away, sir. I don't want them here."

The officer nodded and began to herd the

crowd away from the fallen soldier, shouting orders for them to gather firewood and such.

Malcolm Hardie had stopped wailing now. His eyes were open, and he kept taking in great gulps of air, while he tried to lie still.

"What has happened," said the doctor, speaking to both of us, "is that the wagon wheel snapped that leg bone in two, and when it broke, the splintered bone poked its way up through the skin, tearing the femoral artery; hence all the bleeding."

I nodded, fighting the urge to pull my hand away from the pooling blood. "How long do I have to hold the wound like this, Doctor?"

Uzal Johnson wiped his eyes with the sleeve of his coat. "Why, for the rest of his life, Sal."

"But . . . but . . . can't you sew up the cut and stop the bleeding?"

He shook his head. "He would bleed to death before I could get in a single stitch. His life is draining away now, and all that is keeping him alive is the pressure of your hand upon the wound. When you take it away, this man will die."

I pushed harder, and tried not to look into the face of the wounded man, but at last I did, and I saw that he was staring at me, calm now. "It don't hurt too awful much," he said. "It'll be quick, won't it, sir?"

Dr. Johnson nodded. "Quicker than you can say the Lord's Prayer, soldier. But you have a little time yet to prepare yourself. Sal here can hold that wound shut yet a while, can't you, Sal?"

I nodded, feeling tears sting my eyes, and then I looked away so that he might not see me cry. Away at the edge of the field I saw Virginia Paul, looking above her into the branches of an oak tree, and paying us no mind at all. She was singing.

Chapter Eight
LATE SEPTEMBER 1780

The remainder of September went by in a storm of activity and preparation, as the men of the militia and our womenfolk made ready for our expedition. True to her word, my Catherine set out to sew clothing for me and my eldest boy, Joseph, who would accompany me.

Joseph and I were cleaning our weapons, and talking about the coming journey, when from her sewing table, Catherine called out to me, "Mr. Sevier, here is another of your sons who wants to go with you!"

I set down my rifle, and glanced at Joseph. "Wait here, boy."

I found Catherine seated among her sewing things, and, beside her, red-faced and sullen, stood my second boy, James, sixteen years old, and chafing at the bit to be a man. Catherine tried not to smile. "He has been bending my ear half the morning with all the reasons that we should let him go. You'd better hear him out."

James blushed at this, but he lifted his chin and met my gaze with a steady stare. "I want to come with you. I'm as good a shot as Joseph is, and I'm as old as you were when you married Mama and set off on your own, so don't tell me I'm too young to go, because I'm not."

I sighed. "This will not be an easy journey, James, nor a safe one."

"I know that. But if Joseph can do it, so can I."

"The Tories would as soon hang prisoners as look at them. I hear tell that sometimes even the Whigs make a mistake and hang someone on their own side without taking the time to establish his bona fides."

He grinned. "They'll have to catch me first."

I wavered. He would have to learn to fight sooner or later. Life on the frontier was an endless war with nature or hostile tribes, so the boy might as well fight Tories as Indians. At least they didn't scalp their victims. Besides, it wasn't as if I would have my hands full with him. He was a steady lad, who gave little trouble. Besides, Joseph could look after him, and my own brothers Robert and Valentine would be with us. But there was one last objection to his going.

"We have but two horses, James. And it is a hundred miles or more over the mountain to where we must go."

He beamed with joy when I said this, for like all children he recognized a parent's feeble objection over a minor matter as a sign that grudging permission was soon forthcoming. "Oh, a horse! Why, that's nothing, Daddy. Somebody will give me a horse. I'll ask Uncle Robert. His boys are way too young to go. He'll gimme his other saddle horse, for certain."

I thought it likely that he would, too. I had talked to him about it a day or so before, and told him what the plans were.

"I'll come with you," my brother Robert had said.

I hesitated. "We need to leave some men here to guard the settlement, you know. Some of your wife's people are staying. James Robertson would be glad of your company, if you wanted to stay."

My younger brother shrugged. "I'm going. You're going. I reckon Valentine is going. What about Joseph?"

I nodded. "Yes. Both of them — our brother Joseph, and his namesake, my son. The boy is eighteen now. I said he could come."

"Well, I may be your youngest brother,

187

but try to remember that I am an old man of thirty. If you're letting your eighteen-year-old boy ride with you, don't even think of telling me to stay home with the women and the babies. I'm going."

We were sitting outside Robert's house on a bench under a big shade tree with the mountains rising up before us like a blue curtain, so misty that it was hard to tell where the hills stopped and the clouds began. I had wanted a word with him in private. After I said my greetings to Robert's wife, Keziah, and to little Charlie, and duly admired their red-faced newborn, named Valentine after our father, I had beckoned my brother outside with a solemn expression that told him my visit was more than a social call.

I sighed. "I knew you'd be hell-bent to come, but that new son of yours is just on two months old, isn't he? And little Charlie is not but two. Shouldn't you think about staying with Keziah?"

He laughed. "Aren't you one to talk, Jack? With a brood of ten of your own, and a new-made bride who joined the family less than a month ago. If anybody in this family is tied down with apron strings and wrapped in baby bunting, I reckon it's you."

"Well, I'm a colonel, Bob. Nobody can

make me stay home. And you're a Sevier, so I don't suppose anybody can tell you *anything.*"

Then we laughed and clapped one another on the shoulder, and began to talk about the plans for the march.

Now here was my second son, James, sporting the same obstinate expression Bob had worn, still standing there defiantly next to Catherine's sewing table, looking up at me awaiting an answer. I sighed. Perhaps if his mother were still alive, she'd have had objected to my letting him go to war so young, but we had buried her early in the year, and perhaps the boy's childhood had died with her. Catherine, only a few years his senior and his stepmother only a scant few weeks, would have no such qualms about letting him go. He must have seemed quite grown-up enough to her. Or perhaps she simply trusted me to make the decision regarding my own son.

Looking at young James's anxious smile, I was struck again by how much he reminded me of my own youngest brother. Neither of them was going to be left behind when the older ones were allowed to go. Robert would see James's feelings as a mirror of his own. James would get his horse.

■ ■ ■ ■

While I was arranging for the purchase of black powder from the Pattons' mill, ordering ground corn from the mill of Baptist McNabb, and meeting with William Cobb over at Rocky Mount to obtain other supplies from his store, Colonel Shelby was attending to the diplomatic side of the enterprise, for he had to enlist the support of William Campbell and his Virginia militia to join us.

He was a well-connected man, Col. William Campbell, as well as a man of substance. A man of my own age, but with more formal education and the airs and graces of eastern Virginia's aristocracy, Campbell had married a sister of Virginia's former governor Patrick Henry, and the Campbells lived on a fine plantation called Aspenvale, near the Holston. Although he had aspirations to the gentry, Campbell was as seasoned in war as the rest of us. He had done his military service in the first Virginia Regiment under the command of Patrick Henry, and then under the able Col. William Christian. Since Campbell's return to his home on western Virginia's frontier, he had been hunting down Tory bandits and conspirators in the area. He had hanged a few of them, and so enraged the rest that they nailed signs to the gates of Aspenvale, marking him for death. There had been at least one attempt on his life by his enemies, but it did not succeed, and he carried on, unfazed by the threats of retribution.

Rather than ride another forty miles to call on Colonel Campbell, Shelby wrote Campbell a hasty letter explaining the situation and the plan for the march south, and he dispatched his brother Moses Shelby to deliver it and await an answer.

But the answer was no.

"There is more urgent business than chasing after Ferguson," Campbell told Moses Shelby, as he penned a reply. "I am lately come back from fighting down in the Yadkin Valley, and I have heard all the talk about Lord Cornwallis's intention to invade Virginia. What's more, I believe it. I think Cornwallis will avail himself of the Great Wagon road, and push north with his forces, crossing into Virginia a hundred miles east of here. I cannot leave the Commonwealth undefended to go looking for trouble in South Carolina. I plan to march my men eastward to wait for the invasion forces in a mountain pass on the Virginia border with Carolina."

He said as much in the message he sent back to Isaac Shelby, but that could not be the end of the matter, for so great was our need for support from Campbell's militia that Shelby could not take no for an answer. Shelby and I had reckoned on being able to round up two hundred and fifty men apiece, give or take, and we calculated that the Virginia militia would double that number. Without them we would be hard pressed to hold our own against the enemy's troops. We hoped to have other forces join us as we pushed on toward Gilbert Town, but we could not be sure of their number. Campbell had to be persuaded to join forces with us.

Colonel Shelby wrote again. He read Campbell's refusal carefully, taking note of his objections to the plan, and then he penned a second missive, and this time he wrote at greater length, taking pains to explain the plan more thoroughly and to address Campbell's objections.

Suppose it were true, as Campbell contended, that Cornwallis intended to invade Virginia, just as Ferguson had threatened to attack the backcountry settlements? Would it not be better to prevent such an invasion at the outset, rather than to stand by idly waiting for it to happen?

We thought so, Shelby wrote, and that is

why we were prepared to seek out Ferguson before he could make good on his threat. In this new letter Shelby argued that if Campbell joined his forces to ours, and if we succeeded in defeating Cornwallis's men, then such a victory would surely delay any planned invasion of Virginia. Perhaps it would eliminate it altogether.

Campbell thought about it. It must have occurred to him that if he stuck to his original plan, he would face the enemy with only half the forces he'd have if he united his troops with ours. And the prospect of fighting the battles on some territory other than your own was always pleasing.

In short order, Shelby had a new reply. This time William Campbell agreed to join forces with us, and he outlined his plans in some detail. He would, he said, gather his men together on the twenty-second of September in the village we knew as Wolf Hills, though it had taken the name of Abingdon two years earlier. There was a meadow there, just west of Black's Fort, alongside Wolf Creek, a clear stream for drinking water, and enough space for an encampment of two hundred men or more. They would gather there.

The following day, the twenty-third, William Campbell himself would proceed to

Shelby's house, Sapling Grove. On the twenty-fourth, his men, taking a more direct route westward on the old Watauga Road, would catch up with the two commanders en route to the mustering grounds at Sycamore Shoals.

Shelby sent this information and other details of his own preparations to me in a long message, saying that he would see me at the mustering grounds in a week's time. I was glad that my own tasks — arranging for supplies of food and for lead from the local mines to be made into bullets, and making sure that the two hundred and two score men under my command had the clothing and weapons they needed — had kept me so occupied that I had little time for worrying about what might go wrong with the expedition or whether we would prevail once we found Ferguson. I tried to spend as much time as I could manage with Catherine and the children, all the while attempting to banish the thought that I might never see them again. Catherine did her best to maintain her smiling good humor, but at times, when she thought I was not looking, a faraway look would come into her eyes, and she would dab a tear away from her cheek with the corner of her apron.

The smallest children were too young to

understand the gravity of the situation, and my two oldest boys, Joseph and James, were aflame with anticipation for the great adventure to come. John, the third of my sons, was in a bate because he was forbidden to go along with his older brothers, so that he scarcely spoke a civil word to anyone in those weeks. It was only the middle children — Valentine, Richard, Betsey, and Dolly — who grieved to think of my leaving, for they were still mourning the loss of their mother earlier in the year. I was glad that I could entrust my brood to someone as tender-hearted and brave as Catherine; it was a blessing to know that I could be single-minded in the mission at hand, without having to worry about how my family fared at home.

The great day came at last, both too quickly for all the needed preparations and fare-wells, and too slowly to allay the lingering doubts that plague a man in the darkest hours of the night, but as the men began to gather there in the great field near the river, I forgot everything in the rising tide of excitement that at last the waiting was over.

We had arisen well before first light to make our way to the muster grounds. Catherine and John rode along with us, on the old plow horses that would stay behind on the farm, as would they, but we had said our farewells to all the younger children the night before, and they were left at home in the care of a servant. The boys and I had packed all we could the night before, and we set out that morning in the darkness on the road to Fort Watauga. Joseph and James were in high spirits, laughing and teasing each other, and boasting to their sullen brother John about all the brave deeds they intended to accomplish on the campaign while he was mired at home with the babies. Catherine and I rode side by side mostly in silence, but from time to time hazarding some chance remark on any subject at all except the fact that we were parting.

By the time the rising sun began to tint the clouds with pink and turn the wooded hills to gray, we were nearing the muster ground, and the trace was no longer a lonely road through the forest, but a bustling pike, crowded with militiamen and their families, all headed to the same place. They called out to one another, and some of the women joined their voices together in a hymn, and the quavering notes I heard in the tune made me think that they were singing in order to keep from weeping.

I left my boys to tend to the horses, while

Catherine and I walked across the field, stopping here and there to greet our neighbors and to wish them well. Valentine and Robert had come with their wives, and Catherine left my side long enough to visit for a few minutes with them. I heard Catherine ask after Keziah's new baby, and then in one breath the three Sevier wives were promising to help one another while we menfolk were away. I was watching for the Pattons' wagon to arrive bearing the black powder we had ordered, and keeping a mental tally of which of my men were accounted for.

There was little distinction between officers and men, and unless you were acquainted with them, you might have difficulty telling which was which, for all the militiamen wore our customary long hunting shirts over leather breeches. Their belts bristled with long knives and short-handled axes, and each man had his rifle close to hand. Presently I caught sight of Colonel Shelby across the field, and I hurried forward to pay my respects.

Isaac Shelby, when he saw me, clasped my hand, and said with a wry smile, "Why, Sevier, I could almost believe I am back at the same celebration that I interrupted when I first came to bring you the news."

I looked out across the sunlit field where hundreds of people were gathered, and I saw what he meant, for this looked more like a festival than the beginning of a military campaign. Young children with their dogs were laughing and shouting as they chased one another across the grass. The mothers, and wives, and sweethearts had all come to say good-bye to their men, and many of them had brought food, so that the family could share one last meal together before they were parted.

"Yes, Colonel Shelby, it is very like my barbecue a few weeks back. And, just as last time, we will be obliged to leave the celebration prematurely. Did Colonel Campbell accompany you?"

"He did. I think he is seeing to his own troops, if they have arrived yet. Campbell's men came by the old Watauga Road, you know. He reckons there will be about two hundred of them. And my brothers Evan and Moses have come as well. Shall we go and find them?"

I glanced at Catherine, but she seemed happily in conversation with my brothers' wives, so I followed Shelby toward the far end of the field, where William Campbell stood in the company of the Shelby brothers. Colonel Campbell was a tall, robust man of my own age. His ginger hair and blue eyes were a testimony to his Scots blood, and the dour disposition of his forebears was reflected in his own stern and unyielding countenance.

"Campbell will be a great asset to our mission. He is the scourge of the Loyalists along the Holston," said Shelby. "Have you heard about his encounter with Francis Hopkins?"

"No, though that name strikes a chord. Was there not a robber of that name in these parts? A Tory sympathizer?"

"That is the man. He was a constant troublemaker in the area, a thief and a ne'er-do-well, and finally when he was caught counterfeiting money, the authorities clapped him in the local jail, but one night his villainous friends broke in and helped him to escape. What must the blackguard do next but present himself at a British fort, with the intention of doing further mischief to his Virginia neighbors. The fort's commander, happy to help cause trouble among the Whigs, gave Hopkins credentials and a letter to take to the Cherokee, offering support for a murderous attack on the settlements."

"I would have put him down like a dog," I said, for I had seen too many of my neighbors and comrades tortured and killed in

Indian attacks to feel any spark of mercy for a man who would bring about such an infamous deed.

Shelby nodded. "We are of one mind about that. The wonder is that after all his treachery, Francis Hopkins should dare to venture again into the Holston settlement, but one Sunday afternoon, that is exactly what he did. Campbell and his good lady were heading home after Sabbath services at the church at Ebbing Springs in the company of some of their neighbors, when suddenly a rider crossed their path, and, upon seeing them, immediately turned and spurred his horse away into the nearby woods. When Campbell registered astonishment at the stranger's peculiar behavior, his companions told him the identity of the fleeing rider."

"Francis Hopkins?"

Shelby nodded. "The very same."

"Campbell and the other men immediately rode off in pursuit of the fugitive, leaving Mrs. Campbell and the other ladies in the party to await their return. They chased Hopkins, who tried to elude them by fording the river. Campbell — you know what a burly fellow he is — plunged into the water after the villain, and they fought hand to hand there in midstream, until Campbell wrested the knife away from Hopkins and hauled him back to shore to the waiting justice of Campbell and his men. A quarter of an hour or so passed, and presently Squire Campbell returned to his wife, who wanted to know what had transpired. He said, *'Why, Betty, we hanged him,'* and without further comment on the incident, he proceeded to escort his good lady home."

I smiled politely. "The sister of former governor Henry must find things a bit more rowdy here on the frontier than she was accustomed to in genteel Williamsburg."

"She comes of bold stock, though, despite their gentility. I'll warrant she is equal to the challenge. And the incident pales beside what your lady wife has lived through these past years."

"Ah, you've heard of that incident on this very ground, during Old Abram's attack, when poor Catherine ran for her life, and had to be hauled over the wall of the fort with the Indians in pursuit."

"Why, that story will outlive all of us, Colonel Sevier." Shelby patted my shoulder. "Are your men in readiness for our departure?"

"I think they are saying their good-byes."

We joined Shelby's brother and Colonel Campbell, and shook hands all around.

"We have among the three of us about seven hundred men," said Campbell, "and another hundred or more of McDowell's have already arrived here to join us, but I hope to see that number doubled once we get across the mountains and into the Yadkin territory. Ben Cleveland will join us, come hell or high water."

"They know we are coming," said Shelby. "Let us just get safely and quickly over the mountains, and then we shall all join together, and as far as Ferguson is concerned it will be 'come hell,' indeed."

One of my men came up just then. "Sirs, the Reverend Mr. Doak is about ready to commence the preaching, if you'd care to lead the way. He's yonder under the sycamores."

Campbell looked surprised. "A clergyman? Come to wish us well? We are fortunate then. Back in east Virginia, the usual breed of minister uses his office to urge his flock to stay loyal to the king. They declare that rebelling against the king and his appointed officials here is not only treason, but a sin against Almighty God, by whose divine right the sovereign rules. They have frightened a good many pious men into submission through fear of the Hereafter."

"Reverend Doak is not that sort of parson," I told him. "He seems to believe that rendering unto Caesar and rendering unto God are not one and the same."

"Or else he is persuaded that the Whig cause is a just one," said Shelby. "At any rate, he is a learned young man, and the Watauga settlement is blessed to have him. He has studied at the College of New Jersey and also at another institution in Virginia. I hope that God spares him for many years to be a spiritual leader."

Campbell nodded. "Indeed, but why is such a scholar here in the wilderness?"

"His sister Elizabeth has settled here with her husband," I said. "So presently Mr. Doak came along here and bought land of his own to be near them. But he did not leave civilization behind altogether, for he brought his personal library of classical literature all the way down the Wilderness Road on packhorses. Preachers are scarce in these parts, so the reverend preaches at a number of settlement meeting houses, each in turn. We could not wish for a better man to deliver our valediction."

We joined the throng of people making their way across the open field to a stand of sycamore trees. Samuel Doak, a youthful, but solemn figure in black, stood in the shade of the trees, perfectly composed as he waited for his flock to gather round. The laughing and chatter had ceased. Even the children were quiet as they approached the sycamore. I would not have thought that a thousand people all gathered in one place could make so little noise. For a moment all I heard was the gurgle of the river tumbling over the rocks of the shoals, and the call of a bird from the nearby woods. Then the Reverend Mr. Doak raised his hands in supplication to the heavens and commenced a discourse with the Almighty.

Many of those present bowed their heads in prayer as they listened to his oration, but as he spoke, I took a last look at my family, for none of us could know if we would be coming back or not. I hope that the men found comfort in Sam Doak's conviction that the Lord would be with us and that He approved of our cause.

As he prayed, he allowed as how the journey on which we were embarking would be one filled with hardship and danger, but he assured us that we would not travel alone, for God would be with us, guiding us every step of the way. He went on for a bit about the righteousness of our fight for independence, and he urged us to go forth and help those people east of the mountains who were oppressed by the Tory armies. He reminded the men that they were no strangers to battle, for they had been tested and tried by the attacks of the savages upon our settlements, and they had survived those battles and emerged victorious, as, with the Lord's help, we would do again this time.

Then he asked God to protect us and give us the strength and the courage to face the enemy. Then he likened our mission to the Biblical tale of the Children of Israel at war with the Midianites, and he spent a good many minutes on the scriptural details of that ancient conflict, in case the particulars of it had slipped the Lord's mind.

I hope my soldiers took that comparison to heart, for if they could believe that they were God's chosen army, it would give them the strength and courage we were praying for.

After close on to an hour of preaching and prayer, for we had no time for more, Sam Doak ended his exhortation with a battle cry straight out of the book of Judges. Citing the Bible verse from his prodigious memory, he echoed the words of Gideon: "When I blow with a trumpet, I and all that are with me, then blow ye the trumpets also on every side of all the camp and say, *The sword of the Lord and of Gideon!*"

Twice more he called out those words, and, as he began a third time, his mighty voice was drowned out by a thousand men taking up that battle cry, and shouting it until the valley rang with the echoes.

Then it was over.

The cheers faded back into silence, and the solemnity of the occasion quenched our high spirits. The militiamen and their families turned away, retreating into their own private rituals of parting. Some of the women and children were weeping and clinging to their departing menfolk, but Catherine and I said our farewells to one another with somber restraint, for I was mindful of the example that I had to set for my men: courage and duty before all other considerations.

"Just keep things steady here for a couple of weeks, Kate," I said. "And at the first sign of trouble, you take the children and set out for the fort. Promise me that."

"Of course, I will."

"Good. The family is in good hands then. I'll be back before the leaves are gone. Depend upon it."

She nodded, with a tremulous smile. "Set your mind at ease about us. Just keep yourself from harm."

Reverend Doak was moving among the

crowd, clasping hands, patting shoulders, and offering comfort and encouragement to those who needed it.

"Your faith will be your armor," he said more than once, to those men who seemed reluctant to set out.

We made the last preparations, saddling our mounts, and packing the provisions and gear. Some of the men had not been able to secure a horse for the journey, and they were prepared to walk along in the wake of the riders, keeping up as best they could. Others made ready to drive the cattle along behind us on the march.

Before the sun was much higher in the sky, the men had assembled into the separate militias, and when the command was given, we mounted our horses and rode slowly away from the meadow, following Gap Creek upstream, back toward Roan Mountain, that strange bare-topped mountain on whose summit no trees would grow. The Cherokee told tales of a monstrous wasp, which had lived upon that mountain, so big that it had carried off human beings to feed upon.

As we ambled along at the snail's pace required to move a thousand men and a herd of cattle along a narrow trace, I reflected on that old legend, trying to remember if some bygone Indian warrior had killed the monster, or if it had simply gone away.

My two boys were a ways behind me when we set out, in company with some of the younger riders who were friends of theirs, and so for a while I had only the company of my own thoughts as I rode along, but presently my brother Robert trotted up alongside me, slowing his horse back to an ambling gait that made it as easy for us to converse as if we were sitting on a porch. The path along the creek was dappled with sunlight, shining through the leaves on the trees of the bordering woods. Those leaves would be red and gold by the time we made our way back this far on the return journey, but for now summer still held sway here in the valley, and there was no sign that it was coming to an end.

Robert grinned up at me. "Well, we've gone and done it, Jack. The die is cast. I hope you and Shelby know what you're doing, because I don't reckon you could stop this thing now even if you wanted to. There's more soldiers here than John ever saw."

I nodded, knowing which John my brother meant: the prophet who penned the Book of Revelations. "I wish I had more soldiers than *Caesar* ever saw."

Robert squinted up through the overhanging branches at the sun, now high in the sky. "We have a long way to go, Jack. And at this pace, it's going to take an almighty long time to get there. Why, Ferguson might die of old age and save us all the trouble of killing him."

I scowled at my younger brother's levity, but, though I would not admit it, I took his jest to heart. It wasn't the boredom of the tedious journey that concerned me — enduring hardship was our duty. I was worried, because I knew that the more slowly we proceeded, the more danger there was of our route becoming known to the enemy, and, because of that, we could be attacked somewhere along the way. Also, a slow journey was a longer one, which would mean that we would use up more food as the days passed, perhaps leaving us less than we would need when it was vital to maintain our strength for battle.

After Bob dropped back in the ranks to talk to other riders, I turned these thoughts over in my mind for a while. Presently, I rode a bit ahead so that I could have a word with Colonel Shelby.

"We must find a way to go faster," I told

him, after we had exchanged the usual pleasantries.

Shelby turned partway around in his
saddle, and surveyed the long line of soldiers
stretching out behind us until they were
obscured by the trees at the bend in the
road. Behind them was the herd of cattle,
not within sight of us, but occasionally we
could hear their bawling echoing through
the narrow valley.

Shelby shook his head. "There are nigh
on to a thousand men in this caravan, all
trying to make their way down a narrow
mountain trail. I don't think you can expect
them to proceed at a gallop."

"No, but there ought to be a way to go at
more than a crawl." I told him my concerns
about an ambush and about depleting our
supplies on a protracted journey.

Shelby listened carefully to all my explana-
tions, then he smiled. "Let's think on it as
we go, Colonel Sevier. We'll see how far we
get by nightfall. Then, if you are still of the
same mind, we can take the matter up
among ourselves."

The sun, now low in the sky, was obscured
by shoals of gray clouds that had begun to
roll in from the southwest, following behind
us as surely as the bawling cattle. By the

time the rain began to fall, we had reached the Doe River, with the great wall of mountains rising up in front of us. It was too close to nightfall now to attempt to cross over them, and we called a halt to the procession. My great concern was neither the fatigue of the men, nor the encroaching dark: it was the danger that the rain might ruin the powder. On the steep side of the trail, a rock overhang created a natural shelter from the elements, and as soon as I saw it, I directed the men to stow the powder there. The nights were still warm enough, and we could sleep in the sodden field beside the river and be none the worse for it, but in a week's time our lives would depend upon the efficacy of Mary Patton's powder, and I meant to look after it in the meantime.

We had no tents or official military issue for our expedition. All we had was what had been brought from home. We made camp in the field beside the river, wrapped in blankets to protect us from the chill and the damp, and, after we had fed and watered the horses, we ate what rations we had brought with us: jerky and cracked corn, mostly.

John Miller, a young man from a nearby farmstead came out to see what all the commotion was, and the soldiers dismounted and crowded around him, eager to tell him where they were going and why.

John Miller nodded as they spoke, but he was looking at their horses, lifting one mount's forefoot after another, and shaking his head. "You've got a mighty long ride ahead of you, boys, and the trail gets rocky from here on over the mountain. It'll wear those horses' hoofs down to a nub if you don't get 'em shod."

Seeing their worried faces, he added, "I'm by way of being a blacksmith. If you'd care to come back to my place, I reckon I could do the job for you this evening."

The officer in charge granted permission for them to do this, and half a dozen men walked their horses down the path to Miller's farm.

I suppose I was as weary as anybody, but before I crawled into my bedroll, I wanted to talk to the other militia commanders about how we might go faster for the rest of the journey. I collected Shelby and McDowell, and we hunted up Colonel Campbell, who was sheltering under a tree with a group of his Virginia officers before a sputtering campfire.

The four of us squatted there next to the

fire and talked in low voices about the march.

"Colonel Sevier thinks we are not moving fast enough," Shelby said.

"I was thinking that as well," said Campbell. "Word is already spreading among the little settlements we pass by. I would not want the news to reach the Tories too far in advance of our own arrival."

"What can we do about it, though?" said McDowell. "Nobody is slacking or lagging behind. And that is a herd of cattle yonder, not blood horses. You cannot make them gallop down the trace."

I had spent most of the afternoon mulling over that very point, and Shelby was right: the cattle were the problem. That set me to thinking back to the siege of Fort Watauga in the summer of '76, where those infernal cows bawling to be milked almost cost the life of my Catherine. I began to see them as an omen, and wondered if the bane of my existence would not be the usual black cat crossing the path of some unlucky soul, but a great oafish cow, always in my way.

Campbell must have been thinking the same thing about what a millstone they were around the neck of the militia. "Let's get rid of the cows, then," he said. "They cannot go any faster, and we cannot confine ourselves to the pace they set, and so we must part company."

I nodded. "They were an encumbrance today, on relatively level terrain. Tomorrow when we begin the steep climb to Carver's Gap, they will become an obstacle. Perhaps that herd could make the treacherous ascent, but not with any speed."

"But we need the cows," said McDowell. "We can't feed an advancing army on parched corn and then expect them to walk a few hundred miles and fight a battle. We'd be defeating ourselves."

We were silent for a few minutes, turning over the problem in our minds. Finally, Colonel Shelby said, "No. I cannot see any way around it. We have to slaughter the cattle."

"All of them?" McDowell frowned as a raindrop fell from a leaf and coursed down his cheek. "How would we ever carry all that meat? How would having to transport the carcasses of five hundred rotting cows help us any?"

"Then let's not kill them all," I said. "Choose a few of the men to drive some of the cattle right back to the settlement. By now a few of them may be willing to volunteer to turn back. Then we can butcher the rest of the beeves and cook the meat to take with us. If that enables us to move faster, we may get most of the way to our destination before it becomes inedible."

No one said anything for a few moments, until Colonel Shelby broke the silence with a quiet, "Are we all agreed then, gentlemen?"

We all nodded our assent.

McDowell said, "I suppose it must be done, but I hope that in slaughtering our food supply, we are not doing the enemy's work for him."

Shelby shrugged. "The faster we move, the less time we'll have to be hungry."

Chapter Nine
SEPTEMBER 26, 1780

The day dawned clear, and at first light each of us told our troops what the order of the day would be: dividing the herd; slaughtering the cattle we would keep; and boiling the meat. Only a few of the men would be occupied in performing those tasks. The rest would be set to practice military drill, a step toward learning how to function as a united fighting force. Colonel Campbell was the most experienced among us in such formal military matters, and we deferred to his judgment about what would best serve the needs of our army. We were anticipating a battle upon a flat field, and we needed to be more prepared for such an engagement than Buford's troops had been.

After the herd was divided, and more than half of the cows sent lurching and bawling away back up the trace toward home, we turned to the task at hand. The troops spent the whole of that morning beside the river, dispatching the cattle, and preparing the meat. Although butchering the herd had been my idea, a way to speed up the march, this very action had cost us half a day in which we made no progress. I hoped that the sacrifice was worth the time it cost, and that the outcome would justify the decision.

Perhaps I should have thought of sending a message back to Catherine with the men who were driving the cattle home to the Watauga settlement, but there was much to be done in camp that morning, and by the time I could spare a thought for home and family, the riders had disappeared back up the trace in the wake of the stumbling cattle. There was little I could have told her, anyhow. We had scarcely begun.

Finally, a little past midday, the meat was cooked and stowed away for transport, and we gave orders for the men to mount up and head out. They would not be on horseback much of the way, however, for we were following an old buffalo trail called Bright's Trace that would take us through the woods and then up into Carver's Gap, through which we would ascend the steep slopes, ridge by ridge, until we had crossed over the crest of the mountains. For much of the climb, we would have to lead our mounts and go single file along the path.

As we followed the Bright's Trace higher and higher into the mountains, we left summer behind in the valley below, where the wildwood was still cloaked with green leaves, and the warm sun gilded the fields. We took our leave of that summer country as we climbed into the very clouds that had showered rain on us the night before. Now the air burned cold as we breathed it into our lungs, and the sun was obscured in a wet mist. We threaded our way upward through sparse pines and past boulders lodged on the slopes from spring rock falls.

We halted our march again a few hours later in the gap that led across the mountain. A few miles away, though we could not see it from the gap, stood the high knob of Roan Mountain, whose summit is a great treeless meadow, and once the abode of that great monster wasp of Cherokee lore. I put no stock in fanciful tales of monsters, and of course we saw no sign of such a creature hovering over the mountain when we finally reached that high gap, but we marveled all the same, for having left the late-summer fields of the valley below, we found ourselves ankle-deep in an early snow.

The air was clear now, and looking out from the height of the gap, we could see the Yellow Mountains spread out before us, ridge after ridge of red and gold, resplendent against the cope of heaven. Somewhere to the west of us was home, the settlement we had left behind a day ago. How strange to see that green valley nestled in the curve of the river, and yet not be able to go back there. I was almost glad when the gray clouds folded back over us, blocking the scene from my view.

"Perhaps this is what it would be like to be dead," I mused aloud, thinking of the vista below us. "You can look down from heaven and see the place you came from, but you cannot return."

We called a halt to the march so that men and horses could rest, and we broke out our midday rations to fortify us for the rest of the day's journey. But first the other colonels called for more drilling by the soldiers, and so they trampled down the snow marching and doing close order drill, practicing so that the officers' commands would become second nature to the regulars.

Again we took roll to make sure that no one had become lost or left behind along the way, but this time something was amiss.

As an officer from each militia took a tally of the men, all was well, until Major Tipton took the head count of those under my command. When he had finished the roll, he blinked and straightaway took it again, and finally, when he was sure, he reported to me.

"Two men are missing, sir." The young officer looked as if he could not believe it himself.

"Are you sure? Oh, yes, of course you are, or you wouldn't be telling me, would you? Well, then, which two, Major Tipton?" It crossed my mind that they might have become separated from the group, or met with an accident somewhere along the trace. I even hoped that that might be the case, because the alternative would be somber news indeed.

"Well, young Sam Chambers is nowhere to be found."

I relaxed a little. Sam Chambers wasn't much more than a boy, and not an overly bright one at that. "Perhaps his nerve failed him," I said. "Or else he got homesick for his family and hightailed it back there before we got any farther from home."

Tipton did not return my smile. He stood there watching me, and his expression told me there was worse to come.

"Who else, Major?"

"James Crawford."

There it was. Now that was a serious matter indeed. I knew the man Crawford of old, and he was no wavering youth. I had served with him in the Indian wars, and I knew him to be a wily fellow and an able soldier. He had neither lost his way nor his nerve. If he had deserted our forces, it must be because his conscience had put him on the side of the king, or else his soldier's instincts told him that our ragtag army was likely to be on the losing side when the final reckoning came. He was looking out for himself, which is counted as a virtue on the frontier, and is only an inconvenience when there is a higher cause to be served. Perhaps Crawford had not been outspoken in his support of our cause, but he is an able fellow, and we were sorely in need of soldiers, so when he joined our ranks, we did not question his loyalty.

"He might have gone home," said Jonathan Tipton, and I knew he meant that remark more as consolation than as a serious suggestion. The major did not believe it, and, though I wished I could, neither did I. I liked Crawford. He had served well in earlier battles against the Cherokee, and I wished that he had been able to see his way clear to support us in this campaign.

"We will have to tell the others, Tipton. I am afraid that the man means mischief. He might sell our plans to the Tories for who-knows-what reward."

Tipton grunted. "I hope the blackguard gets more than a jug of whiskey for selling us to the enemy."

"Thirty pieces of silver, then?" My smile faded even as I uttered the impious jest, for it was a grave matter. "Even if he has simply gone in search of a Tory militia to join up with them, I think he will certainly cost us the element of surprise."

"Will you send some trackers after him?"

I shook my head. "There's no telling when he left, or which way he plans to travel, and we cannot afford to waste any men on a fruitless effort to overtake him. Though I'll wager he is headed for Gilbert Town, since Major Ferguson is reputed to be there. I'd better tell the others."

While the men practiced their military maneuvers, I again took counsel with my fellow commanders, telling them of the defection of two of my men, and confessing my fear that they would betray us to Ferguson.

Red-faced with anger, Campbell said, "Well, that's torn it! Now we know that we would be marching straight into a trap. I suppose we will have to turn back."

Shelby was silent for a moment. He thinks things through before he makes a decision, but once he does, he will stay the course. "We have slaughtered the settlement's cows, and spent their tax money on supplies and black powder. If we abandon the mission now, all that will be for naught."

I had hoped one of the others would take that line, for I did not want to quit. I said, "Shelby is talking sense here. The enemy will know we're coming sooner or later, anyhow. And that's all Crawford knows, really, isn't it? That we're taking a raft of troops into their territory, intending to fight. But Crawford doesn't know which way we're going, or what our tactics might be, so I doubt that his information will be any great help to Ferguson."

Campbell considered it. He was by no means pacified, but he was a seasoned soldier, and he saw the sense in our arguments.

"We may never get another chance with a force of this size," said McDowell. "We need to put an end to Ferguson's raids, sooner rather than later. My people want to go home."

Campbell sighed. "Well, if the three of you are set on it, I suppose I must see it through as well. All right, then, let's do what we can to limit the damage. We can divide our forces, alter the route a bit, and make as much haste as we can. That way at least we may avoid an ambush somewhere upon the trail."

I clapped him on the shoulder. "Good man! We will do all those things. When we make camp tonight, let's go over the routes, and decide how to divide up our forces before we proceed."

Campbell nodded. "And when we catch that traitorous man of yours, let's hang him."

At the end of the drilling that afternoon, we ordered the men to fire a volley with their rifles, as if to inform heaven itself of our resolve. But even the thunder of a thousand weapons fired in unison was swallowed up by that great wall of mountains that enveloped us. My first thought was how insignificant we were, dwarfed by that vast wilderness, but I consoled myself with the thought that if we were so small, it would be all the harder for the enemy to find us until we were ready to meet them in battle. *The sword of the Lord and of Gideon.* His army was a small one, too, as I recall.

"We must divide our forces now," said Campbell, when we met again later that afternoon. "If we do that, the Tories cannot ensnare all of us at once."

"Agreed," said Shelby. "And by splitting up, we will occasion different rumors about our passage, if anyone along the way is inclined to betray us to the enemy."

"Perhaps we should first send a scouting party ahead, to tell us if we are walking into a trap."

Charles McDowell gestured with the hand that held his flask. "I'll go. My men have just lately come over the mountain, and we know the way back. Let me take some of my men and go on ahead."

We looked at one another, but no one voiced any objection to McDowell's offer. He did know the trails, and he had resources where we were going. It made sense to let him go on ahead. "It would help to know where Ferguson is," I said.

"So it would," Shelby agreed. "It would shorten our journey and make our provisions last longer if we knew exactly where to find him."

Campbell nodded. "But you'll meet up with us soon and tell us what you find, will you not, Colonel McDowell?"

"I will," said McDowell. "The rest of you can stay together a day or so longer. No one will find you in these mountains. Keep heading southeast. We'll find you in a few days once you've come down into the valley of the Catawba." He stood up, brushing wet leaves from his breeches, and squinted at the westering sun. "There's still a good hour of daylight left. No time like the present, I suppose. I'll collect a few of my best men and be off. Safe travels, gentlemen."

A bit later we watched him mount up and ride off at the head of his small band of Burke County soldiers. He followed a straight path along the creek that would lead him down into the valley of the Roan, and then onward to the foothills of the mountains.

Soon the trees and the slope of the trail obscured them from view, and the three of us turned away. "We won't get much farther today," I said, for the sun was low in the sky and we would not be moving at the pace of McDowell with his smaller force. "Still, I've no wish to make camp here, so let's get as far as we can toward lower ground, else we get caught in a fresh snowfall up here in the clouds."

Shelby and Campbell nodded in agreement, and we gave the word to our officers to make the men ready to move on. We would follow a more arduous path across the mountain than the one McDowell had taken, proceeding in the shadow of the high mountains so that a false twilight seemed to overtake us even before the sun had set. We pressed on, following an east-leading path, and we managed to travel perhaps two miles farther along before the dark came in earnest, leaving us still high in the Yellow Mountains, shivering from the bitter chill of the autumn night. We camped beside a spring, wrapped in blankets that afforded us little relief from the cold winds that whistled through the hollow. Those who had brought extra clothing put it on now, and some of the others complained about the wintry air, perhaps regretting that they had exchanged their homes in the Watauga Valley, still wreathed in the warmth of summer, for a cold dark mountain pass in the wildwood.

It was an easier trek than we'd had in the morning, though, for we had crested the mountain and were now making our way downhill. We'd never have made two miles that evening if we hadn't been on the downward slope.

That night I sat at the campfire with my boys Joseph and James, sharing our rations of cracked corn and fresh-killed beef, and talking over the day's events. We were wrapped up in our coarse woolen blankets, but the cold mountain air still found its way into our bones, and we huddled close to the fire to ward off the chill.

"Well, James," I said to the younger boy, "you were adamant to come with us. What do you think of soldiering now?"

He grinned up at me in the firelight, and wiped his mouth against his sleeve. "It's fine, Daddy. I reckon I can march as well as any of the other fellows now, with all the drilling practice we had today. But I'll be glad when we can quit walking and go to fighting."

"You'll walk three miles for every minute of a battle, boy," I told him. "Soldiering is as much walking and waiting and sleeping rough as it is adventure and excitement. Best make up your mind to accept that now."

"It's worth it, though," said Joseph. "If we whip those Tories, we'll have a tale to tell for the whole rest of our lives. We can say we were there. We fought in the glorious Revolution. Maybe adventures sound better when you're telling them than they feel when you're a-living them."

"Oh, I'm sure that's the truth," I said. "For when you tell this tale to your children in years to come, you'll leave out all the tedium of the marching and you'll forget the times that the bad food put knots in your belly or the blisters pained on your heels. You'll only talk about the glory of the battle. They say that women forget the pain of childbirth and remember only the joy of the babe that comes of it. Maybe men are like that about war."

The morning dawned clear and bright, and we made ready to continue our journey in good spirits, for we knew that the hardest part of the march was behind us. From here on, we would be heading down the mountains, covering more miles every day as we made our way into the broad river valleys to the east. The nights would be warmer, and the food more plentiful, as we came into farming country at harvest time. Now we had only to find Ferguson before he could get reinforcements from General Lord Cornwallis, and all would be well.

We followed a bold stream that tumbled down the mountain, and by mid-morning we had descended from the heights of the Roan to summer country once again, where the sun burned away the last of the chill from our night on the mountain. When the slope of the mountain gave way to a valley, the creek flowed into the Toe River, which was our guide for the remainder of the day's travel. The banks cut by the river were often steep and warranted the utmost caution as we traversed them, but the path was a royal road compared to the hard climbing of the previous days, and by pushing forward to the limits of the men's endurance, we were able to put twenty miles behind us before the coming of night.

We halted for the evening at the mouth of Grassy Creek at Cathee's Plantation, not many miles from the gap that would take us on the final descent into the rolling valleys. If nothing went wrong, we should reach the McDowell plantation at Quaker Meadows in two days.

"We must divide our forces soon," Shelby said.

While the men were making camp, and building the evening's campfires, Campbell, Shelby, and I walked around the encampment, making sure that all was going smoothly, and taking the opportunity to confer once more on the situation at hand. It had been a peaceful journey so far. We had seen no hostile Indians, experienced no ambushes, and lost no men to the rigors of the march. I hoped that our luck would hold, but I knew that we could not count on it. We must do all we could to protect ourselves from misfortune, and, now that we had reached the eastern edge of the mountains, we could no longer consider ourselves safe from ambush. Ferguson could be a day's ride away — and we didn't know where.

"I think we must do it first thing tomorrow," said Campbell, "before we get too far into the valley. I hope that McDowell will send word to warn us if the enemy is in our path."

We all nodded in agreement. "At the gap, then," said Shelby.

After tonight's encampment, we would push forward to the Gillespie Gap, and then, perhaps by midday, go separate ways.

I think Campbell was haunted by the thought that his militia would be annihilated, and leave Virginia at the mercy of the advancing army of Cornwallis. I did not share his sense of dread, partly because I did not think we would be roundly defeated, but also perhaps because with the war going on northeast of here, I did not think the Tories would go so far out of their way to attack the Watauga settlements in force, and if they finally sent over a splinter of an army, I reckoned we could take 'em.

I expect Shelby felt the same about the safety of his territory, or else, like me, he liked our chances of surviving the battle and getting home in one piece. But, worried or not, we saw the sense in the suggestion to split up. It was only for a day or two at most, and then our combined forces would be bigger than ever. By now the Yadkin militia of Ben Cleveland and Winston's forces from the Moravian settlements would have mustered somewhere northeast of here and they, too, would be heading for Quaker Meadows. I wondered if James Crawford had managed to find Ferguson yet, and whether Ferguson had any thoughts of coming after us before we reached McDowell's plantation.

James wolfed down his rations, and wandered off to find some of the young men his age, but my eldest boy stared into the campfire with a scowl that said more than he could have shouted. I wondered if the cracked corn was making knots in his belly, or if he was sore from the climb, but since he was half my age, and I was hale and hearty, I thought something else was amiss.

"Something bothering you, boy?" I said.

Joseph shrugged. "Just I didn't sign on to be no nursemaid, is all."

"Looking out for James, you mean?"

"He's like a new-weaned pup, running all over the place, getting in everybody's way, and never shutting up. I feel like I'm running cattle all by myself, riding herd on him. Why didn't you leave him home with the rest of the young'uns?"

Now it was my turn to stare into the

firelight. "He needs to grow up, Joe. Your mother is gone, and Mrs. Sevier has all she can do to look after the little ones. It's time for James to start becoming a man, and the only way he can do that is if we let him act like one. Sure, he will put a foot wrong at the outset, maybe more times than we'd care to count, but he's got the chance to watch the rest of us, and see how men behave. I don't know of any other way for him to learn."

"All right," said Joseph, still not happy about it.

"And you need to learn something, too, son. I see you becoming a leader, and that means being able to control all manner of men that come under your command — the weak, the lazy, the timid, and the reckless. And you need to be able to look after a man who needs help, even if it means putting your life at risk. There's a lot of trust in soldiering. Your life depends on them and theirs on you. Do you understand?"

He nodded unhappily.

"Good. Then the sooner you can settle your brother down and make a useful soldier out of him, the closer you are to having troops of your own to oversee. And someday the skills you learn from looking after James may be worth something to you." I handed Joseph my flask of spirits, and nodded for him to take a swig. "This journey is a test for both you boys. You see that, don't you?"

The boy nodded, and looked away. "Reckon so," he said in a voice gruff from the raw spirits, or perhaps from tears. "But I swear, Daddy, James would try the patience of St. Peter."

I laughed. "If I remember my Bible, son, St. Peter wasn't known for patience any more than you are. Didn't he cut off the ear of a Roman soldier in Gethsemane? Well, do your best, anyhow. We have a long way to go, and it's too late for any of us to turn back now."

The night was so chilly and the cold ground so uncomfortable that I scarcely minded when the dark blanket of stars above my head gave way to the first gray streaks of dawn. I had no wish to linger there in an effort to sleep. The sooner we got down the mountain, the sooner we could settle our score with the enemy and go home. Then, in a warm feather bed with my dearest Kate, I would sleep.

We made a hasty breakfast of some of our rations, packed up our gear, and, still together as an army, we headed up the valley of Grassy Creek to the Gillespie Gap. The trek up the valley to the gap was a good ten miles, mostly uphill, and I threaded my way carefully along the trail, for I knew my horse was tired after the past few days' arduous journey across the Yellow Mountains, and I did not want his strength to give out when we were half a day's ride from the gentle grasslands of the broad Catawba Valley.

When we reached the gap, we paused there in the September sunshine looking at the ripple of mountains stretching away into a blue haze of clouds on the horizon, so that at times it was hard to tell where the ridges stopped and the mist began. I was looking at the mountain as I had looked at clouds when I was a boy, turning their shapes into familiar images in my mind — the face of an old man, or the round hump of a buffalo's back — when the procession of riders parted, and William Campbell guided his horse up beside mine. He did not spare a glance for the sprawl of hills around us, and, though he looked a bit worn down from the hard ride, I could see that he only had thoughts for the mission at hand.

"It is time to part ways," he said. "Have you a preference for a trail?"

"Why don't you head down through Turkey Cove?" I said. "If you can make it as far as Colonel Wofford's fort tonight, you should be able to reach McDowell's sometime the day after. Shelby and I will go down Catawba Creek."

Campbell nodded. "So you and Shelby's militias will be going along one side of Bald Mountain, and my men will be going down the other."

"Yes. We won't be many miles apart, but with a mountain between us, no army will catch us both at once. We'll reunite again before Quaker Meadows, if nothing goes amiss. Cleveland will be following the Yadkin River, and I'd expect him to camp near Fort Crider tomorrow night and meet us at McDowell's on Saturday as well, don't you think?"

"I hope so," said Campbell. "I am looking forward to a decent meal at the house of Colonel McDowell, and a proper night's sleep before we get underway again."

They headed off then, and before long the hills and the forest enfolded them, and we went eastward down the mountain by the trail along the North Cove of Catawba Creek, within earshot at first, but gradually the paths diverged to skirt around the mountain, and they were gone. If an enemy force should beset us now, they would be unaware of it. We were on our own.

The wilderness is wide, though, and for an enemy to find us on the march would be like finding a gob of spit in the rapids of a roaring creek — not likely. Anyhow, we met no hostile forces on our way.

We made camp that night in the woods alongside the Catawba, near the mouth of a stream called Honeycutt's Creek by those who live nearby. The men were still building the campfires and breaking out their evening rations, when Joseph emerged from the trees with an armful of wood, and called out, "Colonel McDowell's on his way, looking to find you, sir!"

I stood up, and set down my tin plate on my bedding. "Well, then, reckon I'll make it easy for him," I said. "Bid your brother to go and fetch Colonel Shelby and bring him here to the fire. He'll be wanting to see McDowell as well."

I started walking off in the direction that Joseph had come from, looking for McDowell. Farther along the path of the creek, I spied him, still astride his horse, with a couple of his men behind him. I waved him over toward our campfire, and he turned to the others and told them to go and make camp among the rest. Then McDowell dismounted and led his horse over to where Robert and Joseph were tending the fire.

"Have a seat, Colonel McDowell," I said. "My boy James has gone to fetch Shelby, and you can have a bite of supper while we wait on them to get back, so you won't have to tell your tale but once."

We gave him a hunk of beef and settled him near the fire, talking of inconsequential matters to pass the time. He told us that there had been a killing frost the other night down near Gilbert Town. Then the colonel turned to Joseph and asked how he liked soldiering.

Joseph shrugged and looked down at his food. "All right, I guess, sir. Ain't done much of it yet. Just riding trail, mostly."

McDowell smiled. "Your father and I could tell you from experience that being a soldier mostly is a matter of riding and waiting, with only a little dollop of fighting every now and again. It's just that when soldiers grow old and get to telling tales about their wars, they mostly forget all the tedium and they talk about the exciting bits. It gives folks the wrong idea, I expect, but men have been making a glory of war for two thousand years, and every generation of boys has to learn different for themselves."

"Shouldn't be much longer now, though,"

I said. "Another day will see us into the Catawba Valley, and then we'll stop traveling and go to stalking our quarry."

McDowell nodded. "I believe I can tell you where to find him."

It was full dark by then, but I could tell James by the shape of him, a shadow in the dark between the circle of campfires. Behind him was the taller, heavier silhouette of Colonel Shelby. Joseph and I stood silently, waiting for them to join us, a courtesy we thought proper for his rank, but McDowell stayed where he was by the campfire, and bolted down the last bits of his meal. Shelby took no notice of this, but shook hands all round, and took his place next to Joseph while we waited for a report on the whereabouts of Ferguson.

Finally, when he had taken a pull from his flask, and settled himself a bit closer to the fire, Charles McDowell looked around at our expectant faces, and nodded that he was ready to begin.

"Well then," he said. "Here's your report on the enemy's movements. I said I'd find him, and by god I did."

Shelby leaned forward, his face aglow with firelight. "Well done, sir! You saw him then?"

McDowell shook his head. "Not to say *saw* him, exactly, but I have had reliable reports."

Shelby and I glanced at one another, and I was glad that the darkness obscured our expressions. "Oh, have you?" said Shelby, his voice carefully neutral.

"Yes. There was quite a lot to manage, so I thought I wouldn't waste my time riding all over creation, looking for Ferguson. Instead I sent out some men to make inquiries."

"Where were you, Colonel?" I said.

"Well, I went along home to Quaker Meadows, to dispatch a message to Benjamin Cleveland and his men, telling them to hurry along to my plantation as quick as they could, for we all aimed to meet there on Saturday. Got ambushed for his trouble, too, poor old Blair. Some blasted Tory was lying in wait along the road, and he put a load of shot in Blair as he passed by. Didn't kill him, though. He'll be all right, presently." He took another pull from his flask, and smiled, pleased that he was able to impart such happy news.

I felt my muscles tighten, but I resolved to ignore the slurring of McDowell's words, and to put my questions to him as civilly as I could, but my patience was wearing thin. "I'm sorry to hear that your man was injured, Colonel, and I hope that in due time we can make the enemy pay for their treachery, but right now we are so anxious for you to tell us what you know of Ferguson's whereabouts that we can hardly think of anything else."

I glanced over at Shelby, and he nodded in agreement.

McDowell took another pull on his flask. "Long ride today, gentlemen. The fact is, I sent out my men to collect information, and I kept myself at Quaker Meadows to be sure that I received their reports."

The unspoken thought hovered above us that Colonel McDowell had not only received reports while staying comfortably at home, but also: clean clothes, hot dinners, a feather bed to sleep on at night; a new supply of spirits for his flask, and a fresh horse to make the return journey to our position. No wonder he had volunteered so readily to scout ahead for us, though I think we differed on the meaning of the term.

Shelby took a deep breath, and said quietly, "And did your informants provide you with anything useful?"

"He's somewhere near Gilbert Town. Has been for some time now. We can go after him there or take him when he is headed back to join Tarleton and Cornwallis in Charlotte Town. I have even better news than that, though, gentlemen. Not only is

Cleveland making his way down from the Yadkin to meet us, but he is bringing forces under Major Winston from the Moravian settlements. And my riders to the south brought back the news that we will soon be joined by militias from our South Carolina neighbors. Militias under colonels Edward Lacey and James Williams are making their way toward us, and by the time we confront Ferguson, we should have twice as many men as we had reckoned on at the outset."

"That is good news, sir," said Shelby in the same calm voice as before.

McDowell chuckled in the darkness. "Yes, when the battle comes, I shall indeed have a mighty force at my command."

No one made any reply to this sally of Colonel McDowell's, and for what seemed a long time, it was so quiet that we could hear the crackle of the fire, and the distant notes of a sad song carried on the wind.

Chapter Ten
SEPTEMBER 30, 1780

With the dawning of Saturday morning, both the hardest and the easiest part of our journey had ended. The steepest terrain lay behind us, and all that remained was a quick scramble down the last hills and into the Catawba Valley, but when we left the high country behind us, we also relinquished the safety of the mountains. Even an army of a thousand men would be hard to find in the coves and woods we had come from, but once we reached the plain, with its sprawl of farms and villages, everyone in our path would know of our progress, and soon enough the news would reach the ears of the enemy. Well, let them seek us out, though. Let them find us. We had come to fight, after all.

We broke camp early Saturday morning, but before we resumed our march, Shelby, McDowell, and I gathered beneath a spreading beech tree, and we decided to carve our names on its trunk.

"This is an historic occasion," McDowell declared, scoring a long *M* into the bark. "Here we are commanding an army to oust the king's forces from our lands. Let us record the moment for posterity."

As he went on carving his name, Shelby and I, drawing our own blades, glanced at one another. "I hope we are not tempting fate here," said Shelby.

I hoped not, too, but I said, "I hear that fortune favors the brave, so let us say that this is a show of courage, proof that we are fixed in our resolve."

"And good luck to us all," said Shelby, cutting the *I* of his first name into the beech tree. "May we all live to pass this way again."

After that impromptu ceremony, commemorating our passage toward the battle to come, we climbed one last mountain before heading down Paddy Creek, whose waters would lead us downstream to the Catawba River. We had not gone far along the creek path before we saw movement in the bordering woods, and then mounted figures emerged from the trees. For a flash of a moment, my gut felt as if it were full of cold creek water, but then the riders hailed us. It was William Campbell's Virginia militia, coming to reunite with us after going their separate way down the mountain. They looked none the worse for wear; perhaps their night had been as peaceful as ours.

I trotted across the clearing to meet them, and presently Colonel Campbell himself, catching sight of me, rode up to the fore, and we let our horses amble along the verge of the creek for a bit so that we could confer.

"Quiet night?" I asked. "You seem as hale and hearty as when last we met."

William Campbell nodded. "It was not entirely without incident, but we did make our way down the trail unchallenged. I do not believe that the enemy force is in these parts."

"No. McDowell turned up again last night. His scouts report that Ferguson is still in the vicinity of Gilbert Town, well southwest of here."

"Good." Campbell smiled. "As anxious as I am to settle accounts with Ferguson, I am happy to have a few more days to join with the other militias, and to rest a bit at McDowell's plantation before we seek him out. Did McDowell have a skirmish with him?"

I took a deep breath before I answered, willing myself to keep my answer light and neutral. "If the British officer happened to drop by Quaker Meadows for a spirited game of cards, Colonel McDowell did not mention it." I savored Campbell's look of amazement for a moment, before I went on. "Our comrade spent his scouting days comfortably at home, while he sent others out to do the reconnoitering for him. They assured him that the Loyalists were still in the territory around Gilbert Town, well away from here."

Campbell was quiet for a moment. "I see," he said at last. "Well, leaving that aside for the nonce, I had better tell you about what little transpired last night with our militia. On our way down to Turkey Cove, some of my men stopped at the cabin of a man named Gillespie, and they questioned him about the particulars of Ferguson's movements."

"What did he tell you?'

"Nothing. My men say that Gillespie knew nothing, and that he cared not at all about the war in general. Living as he does in the wildwood, with few possessions and no society, I suppose it is all the same to him who rules the country. He means to wait out the war on his little patch of land, without getting involved any more than he can help. Well, if the Loyalists should happen that way, I expect that they will find him as unhelpful as we did. We stopped at the new farm of William Wofford as well. Have you heard of him?"

I nodded. "He is lately relocated from South Carolina, for the Loyalists destroyed his foundry there."

"On the Pacolet, yes. Now he has built a gristmill on his new holdings, and he is resolved to regain his prosperity in his new situation. Wofford wished us well on our journey, but he had no information about our quarry, either, barring the fact that they had not been in the area for some time. I don't doubt that he is glad of that."

"McDowell did offer one bit of cheering news," I said. "He reports that the militias of Benjamin Cleveland and Joseph Winston are on their way south to join us at Quaker Meadows."

"That is heartening news. And the South Carolinians? Are they on the way as well?"

"He assures us they are."

Campbell smiled. "Well, then, let us just reach McDowell Brothers' plantation, and join all our forces together, and then Ferguson can come as he pleases. We are as ready as we'll ever be."

We must have traveled nearly twenty-three

miles that day, and Campbell's Virginians nearer to thirty, but the land was gentle here past the mountains, mere rolling hills, instead of the precipitous peaks over which we had toiled to get here. And with our descent into the green valley, summer had returned to grace our progress. After the cutting winds and the snow we had trampled underfoot on Bright's Trace, now we rode once more past green woodlands in full leaf, cloaked in bright sunshine. Heaven was smiling down on us, and I took it as an omen.

The sun was low in the sky by the time we reached Quaker Meadows. Those broad fertile fields were a welcome sight, and, though we would still be sleeping rough on the ground, the air was mild and promised a good night's rest.

Maj. Joseph McDowell, the colonel's younger brother, rode out to meet us, and welcomed us to Quaker Meadows. He was a young man, only twenty-four, but he was a brave and steady soldier, as kindly to his friends as he was formidable to his foes. I found him a more congenial soul than his brother.

"Camp where you will," McDowell told us, indicating the green pastures enclosed by board fences. "Your men will be exhausted from the day's journey, so don't bother about trying to scour for firewood among the trees. Use the fences to build your cooking fires."

"That's uncommonly kind of you, Major," said Campbell. "Are you sure?" Shelby and I murmured similar sentiments.

Joseph McDowell smiled. "Quaker Meadows' workers can always build more fencing. And if your troops leave here well rested, they are more likely to win the battle. That in turn lessens the chance that Ferguson and his men will burn this whole place to the ground one day. I call it a bargain, gentlemen."

The men were weary after five days of hard traveling over rough terrain, and we decided that it would be fitting to celebrate our success in reaching this point without incident. We were greeted by some of the Burke County men who had stayed behind when Colonel McDowell and some of his militia left in the summer to camp on the Watauga. Anticipating our arrival, they had rounded up some of the cattle that had been hidden in the upcountry coves to protect them from Ferguson. They slaughtered the beeves, and even now they were being parceled out to the many cooking fires in the meadows. No one would go hungry tonight. I had not yet eaten, but I checked on my boys, Joseph and James, and found them settled in by a campfire with Valentine and Robert, and with my sons' uncle John Crockett, the husband of their late mother's sister. I hoped to get back to them later, and bade them save me some of the meat.

One thing still troubled us, though. Before the major turned to go, Shelby called out, "What of the other militias? We had farther to come than they did."

Major McDowell smiled again. "They'll be here by nightfall, gentlemen. We sent word for them to hasten along, and we received a response this afternoon by rider. Colonel Cleveland and the Wilkes County militia and Major Winston with the Surry County men are traveling along the road that runs south along the Yadkin River. They mustered on Wednesday, and camped last night at Fort Defiance, the home of William Lenoir, who rides with them today. If there have been adventures along the way, I doubt not you'll hear it from them when they arrive."

His words were borne out before the sun had set, when a great cry went up through the pastures, and the men at their cooking fires stood up and waved their hats. I turned and saw a procession of riders making their way up the path toward the main house. I hurried that way myself, so that we all could meet with Cleveland and Winston, once they had got their troops settled in, but as I neared the McDowell house, I saw that there were further complications to their arrival.

Close to the front of the procession was an open wagon, surrounded by grim-faced riders as if they formed an honor guard. I mounted to the porch and looked down into the wagon. A burly young man lay there on a bed of straw with a blood-soaked bandage bound around his thigh. He was pale and grimacing with pain, but he did not cry out.

Ben Cleveland, colonel of the Wilkes militia, rode at the head of the formation. I recognized him at once, for tales of him were passed throughout the Whig militias as if they were tuneless ballads. He was a giant of a man, both tall and great in girth, but no less vigorous for his size. He seemed to belie the tradition of fat men being jolly and mild in nature, for many of the tales about Ben Cleveland centered on the hangings of the Tories that he pursued so relentlessly in the Yadkin Valley.

Joseph McDowell hurried forward to greet Cleveland, and seeing that Shelby, Campbell, and I had reached the porch, he made hasty introductions, but Cleveland barely spared a glance for us, so intent was he upon seeing to the wounded man.

"A casualty already?" murmured Colonel Campbell, nodding toward the wagon.

Benjamin Cleveland, swinging down from his horse, called out. "My brother. He has been shot by those murderous villains. I hope we kill them all."

From what I had heard of Colonel Cleveland, for his fame preceded him, he had made a good start on that task already.

"Bring him inside," said Joseph McDowell, throwing open the door.

We all moved to help, but Cleveland waved us away, and we saw that the men who had accompanied the wagon were more than equal to the task of removing the injured man and conveying him into the house.

"Perhaps we'd better wait out here," I said to Campbell and Shelby. "Let them see to the wounded first."

Shelby nodded toward a spreading oak tree within sight of the house. "We can wait there, and talk a bit. From there we can see them when they come out again."

We threaded our way through the clumps of militiamen resting upon the ground, heading for the great oak, which as yet had no one making camp beneath it.

"Good man, Cleveland," said William Campbell. "I rode with him in the summer, chasing Tories. He came from Virginia originally, you know. Married Mary Graves, whose sister Susannah is the new wife of Gen. Joseph Martin. The Martins live next to Leatherwood, the plantation of my brother-in-law. Great friends of ours."

Neither Shelby nor I said *"Patrick Henry,"* when Campbell casually mentioned his brother-in-law, but I'll warrant we were both thinking it. Fortunately before I could remark that we had no need of a pedigree, as we weren't thinking of using Colonel Cleveland for breeding purposes, Shelby said, "I believe Martin is our best hope for the safety of our families back over the mountain. He has connections with the Cherokee nation, and he is using his influence to keep them from attacking our settlements while we are away."

I held my peace again, but I, too, was well acquainted with the Cherokee, and, though nothing would be said of it here among gentlemen, I also knew that one of Martin's principal connections with the Cherokee was his marriage to Betsy Ward, the daughter of the tribe's Wise Woman, Nancy Ward.

Since this Indian marriage was concurrent with his present union with Susannah Graves, I doubted if either Campbell or Cleveland would thank me for mentioning it. I suppose that this alliance with Betsy Ward increased Martin's influence with the tribe, and enabled him to make pacts with them for the benefit of our settlements, but, though I saw the sense of it, I would not do such a thing myself. I had too clear a memory of the attacks on our homes . . . of seeing poor James Cooper scalped and murdered while we watched helplessly from the fort. And most of all I remembered my new bride — as she is now — running for her life around the wooden walls of Fort Watauga, saved from the same fate only because I was able to grab her hands and lift her up out of harm's way. No, I would not be bringing any Indians into the family fold. Not I.

"Something of a changeling, Martin is," Campbell was saying. "His father was the son of a wealthy merchant in Bristol. He was sent to the colonies to pursue business interests, but when he told his father that he proposed to marry a Virginia woman, the outraged patriarch disinherited him. He may not have been good enough for the aristocracy of England, but in Virginia he counted the Jeffersons and James Madison as his neighbors, and no doubt Captain Martin envisaged a gentleman's life for his son and namesake."

I was still watching the house, but no one had as yet emerged. "Perhaps rebelling against a father's expectations runs in the family."

Campbell smiled. "So it must. Young Joseph was indifferent to schooling, left an apprenticeship, and ran off to the backcountry. He became quite the explorer. He loves to tell the tale of how Daniel Boone, some ten years back, was leading a party of settlers into the Powell Valley, only to find Joseph Martin and his men already there, constructing a fort. I'd love to have seen the look on Boone's face. Anyhow, Martin knows the backcountry as well as anyone. If anyone can keep the peace with the Cherokees, it is he."

"He is well acquainted with the Indians, certainly," I said mildly.

"I hope for all our sakes that he succeeds," said Shelby. "Have you any such stories to tell us about Colonel Cleveland before he joins us?"

Campbell nodded. "I recall a tale or two from his wild days, before he settled down with Miss Mary. He is a steadfast fellow now, but some of Cleveland's exploits before the war are the sort of yarns best suited to fireside tale-telling, shared over brandy."

"Well, we will have to make do with just the firewood," I said, tapping the broad trunk of the oak tree, "though I daresay I could fetch you a dram of corn whiskey if you should require it, Colonel."

He waved away the offer. "The stories themselves are brandy. He is the scourge of the Tories in the Yadkin Valley, you know. They call his militia 'Cleveland's Devils,' but in his salad days, he was a bit of a devil himself, much more suited for hunting and trapping — and drinking — than farming. But — now this was a dozen years ago, before he moved over the border into North Carolina — Ben Cleveland had a little farm on the Pigg River. He and Joseph Martin were ever the best of friends, and so the pair of them decided to plant a crop of wheat on the farm, but they were not temperamentally suited to agricultural endeavors."

"Never cared for it overmuch myself," said Shelby.

Campbell smiled. "No, it is hot, hard work. Especially when a man is young, the fine summer days tend to get away from him. The wheat crop made it to harvest time, suffering somewhat from the indifference of its tenders and perhaps more from want of the fence that Cleveland had neglected to put up around the field to keep the animals out. But still there was a wheat crop to be gathered in, and Cleveland and Martin duly invited all the neighboring farm families over for the harvesting and the celebrations that went with it."

"That's the best part of farming," I said. "When you gather the community together for a big barbecue, with all the fiddling and the dancing and the passing of the jug. That's a fine thing, after all the work of harvesting."

"Yes," said Campbell with a wry smile. "*After.* Unfortunately, in those days Cleveland and Martin were impetuous young men, and they gave the party before they held the harvesting. What with all the drinking and the dancing and the celebrating, nobody ever did get around to bringing in the sheaves. So Cleveland went back to exploring and land-speculating. Of course, the war has matured him, as it must do for many a man."

I thought that some of Ben Cleveland's ordeals in the wilderness over the mountain might have had a good deal to do with turning him into a leader, and perhaps into the pitiless foe that he had become. Everyone who has ever spent any time on the frontier has lived through something that haunts him. I should know. I'll warrant that Cleveland could tell many a harrowing tale that would put the harvest story in the shade. Anyhow, that hapless young farmer of twelve years ago was gone now, and in his place was a man who was keeping score against the world. For every wrong the Tories did in his bailiwick, Cleveland struck back. He would hang them all if he could.

I looked again toward the house. Time was short, and the others would be joining us soon. "Setting aside all these fine pleasantries, sirs, there is something else we need to settle, though for my sense of honor I could wish we were standing on someone else's land while we talk about it."

Shelby caught my meaning at once. "Charles McDowell."

"Yes. He is taking it for granted that he will be in command."

Campbell shifted uneasily, glancing back toward the door. "Well, he is the senior officer."

We were all silent for a moment, contemplating that unpleasant fact.

At last Campbell said, "Is there any way around it, gentlemen?"

Shelby sighed. "McDowell is a staunch patriot. An honest man. A steadfast soldier, but . . ."

"He won't do," I said. "He is too old and slow. He drinks too much, and he is indecisive when he ought to be bold. This foray is our last, best chance to end this, and we cannot risk it in the hands of the man who turned back after Musgrove Mill, and who did not post pickets at Earles Ford on the Pacolet."

"We've been alternating command thus far," said Shelby. "Perhaps . . ."

"Yes, and I suppose we could simply hope that when we find Ferguson and begin the battle, it will not be on McDowell's day."

"Well, no, of course we must —"

Campbell put a restraining hand on Shelby's shoulder. "We must talk about this later. They are just coming out now." He left us under the tree, and walked a little way out into the meadow, waving to the McDowells and Cleveland, motioning for them to join us.

With a last glance back at the closed door, Ben Cleveland stumped down the steps and ambled toward us, with both the McDowell brothers and another officer following in his wake. The men who had carried the injured fellow into the house hurried back to join their comrades in the pasture. The smell of cooked meat filled the air, and here and there we could hear the strains of a merry tune. The set-to with the Tories was yet to come, but the men obviously felt that they had won the battle with the mountains. After the snows of the Roan, it was pleasant for them to rest in a summery meadow, however briefly.

Cleveland was red-faced and huffing when he reached us, and though he shook hands all around, it was plain that his thoughts were still elsewhere. "Do you know Major Winston here? Surry militia. Good man. I had the honor of fighting at his side in Alamance, and again when we went after a hornet's nest of Tories on the New River."

We hastily greeted Joseph Winston, a somber-looking fellow near my own age, but it was impossible to divert one's attention for long from Cleveland in his agitated state. Still, the big man made an effort to be congenial. "Congratulations are in order for the major, gentlemen. May I tell them your news, sir?"

Joseph Winston finally managed a smile and a brief nod. "Just as you like, Colonel."

"Mistress Winston has just recently given birth to three fine sons, and all are thriving. Is it not a marvel, gentlemen? The major here will be going home to a ready-made family. And I hope they may all live a long time in perfect happiness."

We made suitable noises of congratulations, but Cleveland was still distressed, and finally he burst out, "They shot my brother. The Tory vermin." Now he was pacing back and forth under the tree, flushed again with anger.

"Robert?" said Campbell, who had also ridden with Cleveland heretofore.

"No. Robert is well. That was him riding alongside the wagon, and he's out in the field somewhere, making camp. It's our younger brother Larkin. They shot him."

"This is grave news," said Campbell. "When did this happen?"

"Just a few hours ago, as we were making our way here. I reckon some of the local Tories had heard of our progress, and they were determined to make mischief. They hate me, y'know. I think they may have mistook my brother for me. We look rather alike, especially at a distance." He patted his ample girth, but there was no humor in the gesture. "Anyhow, we had left Lenoir's house — Fort Defiance, it's called — and we were perhaps ten miles from Crider's fort on our way here. We were crossing the river at Lovelady Ford. There are heights on both sides of the Catawba there, and the blackguards were hidden up there in the rocks, waiting to ambush us. I'd like to know who told them of our movements."

His voice left us in no doubt about what would befall the traitor if Cleveland should discover his identity.

"So there was Larkin, fording the stream, and they got him in the thigh, shattered the bone. Once he fell, some of my men went up the rocks after the shooters, but they were too quick for us. Got clean away. We shall hang them someday, if I have my way. Anyhow, Larkin could not ride, so our brother Robert and one of the men set off in a canoe with him, and the rest of us continued the march here by road. They met us near here. Larkin only came in the wagon up from the river. Just as well. He was in pain enough without rattling eight miles along the rutted road."

"He is upstairs with my mother now," said Joseph McDowell. "And he will have every care that Quaker Meadows can offer while we are gone. It is a serious wound, but he is young and strong, and I think he will overcome it."

"We Clevelands are big enough targets, I grant you, but we are hard to kill. And if it is not his time, he will not be called from this life. Gentlemen, I believe that."

"So do I," said Joseph McDowell. "One of the South Carolina soldiers told me a tale about their colonel Edward Lacey. 'Tis said that when he was a boy, a gypsy fortune-teller told him that he need have no fear of battles, for he was fated to die by drowning. She has proved right so far for he has come through many a skirmish unscathed. You heard about the taking of the blasphemous Tory Huck back in June? He was in that company."

"I'll bet he takes care when he is fording rivers," I said. But I, too, had nearly drowned in my boyhood. I was rescued from the stream by two young girls, who managed to pull me out. They say that those who escape such perils are born to be hanged; I hoped that would not prove true in my case.

There was a sudden silence, for all of us were mindful that time was short and the day of reckoning was near. All the commanders were now assembled under the great oak: Campbell, Shelby, Cleveland, the McDowell brothers, Joseph Winston, and myself. The troops from the south would rendezvous with us elsewhere, but when we broke camp in the morning and set out on the last leg of the journey, we must be ready to face the enemy at any given hour. We talked for a while about what we knew — that Ferguson was in the vicinity of Gilbert Town, and that before we encountered him, we expected to meet up with additional forces from South Carolina and Georgia. And we knew that before we set out to do battle we must choose a commander, because an army must have a fixed chain of command, and not simply someone who is in charge for the day. We resolved little except that we would set out toward Gilbert Town in the morning, still passing the mantle of command back and forth among ourselves.

"What we need is a spy," said Campbell. "Someone who can venture out ahead of the army, and bring us back information on the whereabouts of Ferguson. Someone who doesn't look like a militiaman."

Charles McDowell nodded. "That would be a great help, certainly. I've heard Major Hampton speak of such a fellow. Tomorrow, let us take up the matter with him."

We spoke a while longer about matters connected to supplies and such, and then we all shook hands and wished one another well, before retiring to our respective encampments for an evening's rest. If anyone went to the house to share a fine dinner at table with the McDowells, I did not take note of it, though it was only to be expected that Ben Cleveland would go back to see to his wounded brother.

CHAPTER ELEVEN
OCTOBER 1, 1780

The next day, the Lord's Day, and the first of October, dawned clear and fine. The roads would be dry and flatter than the terrain we had crossed to get here, and the men were rested and eager to get on with the mission. We would make better progress from now on than we had thus far. Gilbert Town lay nearly thirty miles southwest of our present position at Quaker Meadows, and it would take us several days to reach it — if, indeed, we got there at all without encountering Ferguson's troops somewhere in between.

The South Mountains lay along our route, just when many of us thought we had done with steep terrain, but there were valleys and passes cut by the streams and rivers traversing it, and we reckoned that we could thread our way through those passages without having to make another arduous ascent.

We headed for those rugged hills, hoping to pass them by nightfall, but our luck with the weather ran out long before dark, when it began to rain hard. I was riding with my sons at that point, and Joseph wiped the rain from his face with a fearsome scowl. James seemed not to mind the downpour, though. Young as he was, and having had to wheedle his way into the expedition in the first place, I think he would have happily forded streams of molasses in his joy at being allowed to accompany us.

To lighten our spirits, I summoned up a bit of scripture from memory: *"For He maketh His sun to rise upon the evil and on the good, and sendeth rain on the just and on the unjust."*

"Amen," said James, grinning.

"I sure do hope that Ferguson and his Tories are getting as wet as we are," grumbled Joseph.

"We should be thankful for the good weather the Lord has already given us to get us over the mountains. A little delay now isn't much to complain about. We have come far enough for one day, I think. Let's look for a sheltered campsite."

The commanders conferred — hastily — for none of us was eager to be drenched in the saddle in order to carry on a prolonged debate. We agreed to call a halt to the march, and the men set about making camp in a gap, near the headwaters of two creeks.

We had no tents and no other protection from the cold rain except for our sodden blankets and whatever shelter was afforded us by rock overhangs and the canopy of trees around us. I was sure that Major Ferguson, wherever he was, would be much better accommodated for the evening, for he had tents, baggage wagons, and servants to dance attendance upon him. We were not even an army, strictly speaking, and we had to make do with what we had, which was precious little. This would not be so pleasant an evening as the one before, but at least it lessened the chances of an ambush. Nobody would be out in this weather unless he had to.

We made camp that evening near the creek, and when we had eaten the evening meal and settled in with what shelter we could manage from the drizzle, Colonel Cleveland appeared, and seeing that my boys and I had not yet bedded down, he eased himself down onto a blanket-covered saddle.

"Too early to sleep," he said, "especially in this blasted weather. Thought I'd come and pass the time."

We spent a while in desultory conversation about family and past skirmishes with the enemy, and I could tell by his rapt expression that my younger boy James was fascinated by Cleveland. He had a slight defect in his speech, which probably had kept him out of political life, but his charm was manifest, and this would stand him in good stead as a leader. Finally James got up the courage to ask the colonel a question.

"They say you've hanged men, sir? Have you really?"

Cleveland nodded, recognizing a boy's natural thirst for adventure. "That I have," he said. "A good many, in fact. It's a consequence of war, you know."

James shivered. "I don't reckon I could, sir."

"Well, that's on account of your impulse to kindness. Does you credit, son, but it won't do in wartime. I recall back in Wilkes, when we were hanging that Tory traitor, William Riddle, a crowd gathered to watch the proceedings. Among their number were two young boys, who had thought that the spectacle might afford them a fine day's adventure. They soon decided otherwise, though, for it was a sorry sight, and with tears in their eyes, those boys tugged at my coattails, a-begging me to spare the wretch's life. The fellow had been injured when he resisted capture, and he cut a pitiful figure, standing there with the rope around his neck, sobbing for his life. The tenderhearted lads thought that the prisoner's distress ought to move me to mercy, but I had seen so many hangings by then that I was unmoved by the sorry spectacle. I scarcely remember when the ritual of hanging aroused any feeling at all within my breast, except the desire to have it over with. Death comes to us all sooner or later, and I judge that there are many worse ways to set out for the Hereafter than dangling at the end of a clean rope."

James nodded. "The Indians burn their captives. I reckon that is worse."

"A terrible death," said Cleveland, nodding sagely. "Every now and again you hear of a poor woman who has caught alight when the hem of her gown trailed through hot cinders from the fireplace, so that her dress goes up in flames and she with it. Burning is a terrible lingering death, accompanied by unbearable pain, and I would not wish such a fate upon any sinner in this world. They burned people to death in our mother country in the not-too-distant past, but here in the New World, civilized men do not. They call me cruel for I do not stay my hand at the hanging of a scoundrel, but if his death is warranted, then it must be done, and I can think of few ways as kind as the rope."

James considered it. "You could shoot them."

Cleveland nodded. "Yes, I suppose you could shoot your prisoner, but most of these wicked wretches would be a waste of good powder and shot, and, besides, there's the chance of missing a vital organ, and thus prolonging the process, which is cruel to the condemned and distressing to the bystanders. But stand a man up under a sturdy oak with a noose around his neck, and you have him a scant ten minutes away from eternity, with next to no chance that the execution will fail. Not if you know what you're doing, and we have had enough practice by now to be experts in every particular."

Joseph had settled into his blanket to go to sleep, or pretended to, and, although I was listening, I thought I'd stay out of the conversation, so that James could have his own talk with the famous Ben Cleveland.

"Did you ever show mercy to any of them?" the boy asked, and I could see that he was struggling with the thought of this jolly stout fellow acting the part of a pitiless executioner.

Cleveland smiled. "Show mercy? Why, I may have done a time or two. I remember once, we hanged a fellow for horse-thievery, while his partner in crime looked on in great distress. When it came to be the second man's turn for the rope, I told him that I would spare his life if he would cut off his own ears then and there, and leave the area straightaway and never return."

After a shocked silence, James managed to say, "And did he?"

"He did. Hacked off his own ears with my hunting knife, and took off down the road with the blood running down his neck. So you see, I can be a kindly, forgiving fellow if I don't keep reminding myself of the urgency of the cause we're fighting for. If we want this Revolution to succeed, we must be willing to set an example by dispatching those who oppose us, serve as a warning for the rest. It is a matter of resolve of purpose — our foes must die so that our cause may live. I reckon I come by it honestly, this practical way of looking at matters, for I am descended from a man who ordered more executions than I can even count in support of his revolution: Oliver Cromwell, who saw the king himself into the Hereafter, and I only wish I could do the same."

My boy's eyes widened, for of course he recognized the name. "You're descended from the Lord Protector, sir? Are you really?"

He nodded. "My family — the Clevelands, that is — does not bear the Cromwell surname, for the tale of my ancestral origins is a romantic one, and I take pride in it." Here he glanced over at me, and said with a rueful grin, "You know, Colonel Sevier, my dear wife, Mary, winces when I speak of my ancestry at social gatherings. She looks no further than the coffers of her wealthy planter father for proof of her own aristocracy. It is not seemly of me, she says, to boast of my forebears when they were born outside of wedlock, but, when one of them ruled a country and his good lady was herself a duchess of the realm, then I say there's plenty to be proud of without worrying overmuch about the legalities of the matter. Besides, I think that Mary is secretly proud of my noble ancestors' forebears."

"I had not heard of your family history," I said.

"It's in a book. My family origins are recorded in a great slab of a book that a traveling peddler fished out of his pack and sold to me, when he learned that my name was Cleveland. *The Life and Entertaining Adventures of Mr. Cleveland, Natural Son of Oliver Cromwell,* the tome is called, and it is a daisy of a tale, though it bids fair to run as long as the Bible. The book says that the mistress of King Charles was cast off by him, and that she then took up with his supplanter, Oliver Cromwell, the Lord Protector of England. He threw her over as well, I regret to say, and he tried to have her killed to boot, but not before she gave birth to this son, Cromwell's own. Well, it must be true, mustn't it? To be written down in a book like it was."

James gasped. "And you are descended from the duchess's baby?"

"Well, she was the Duchess of Cleveland, so there you are. My ancestor. Bound to be. At any rate the tale in that book suited me down to the ground. I tell you, boy, I couldn't be happier if they were to tell me that I was descended from the Archangel Gabriel. Oliver Cromwell overthrew the king of England, don't you see? Defeated his armies, signed his death warrant, saw him beheaded, and then took his place as ruler of the country. Now that's a sign if I ever saw one. Here we are in the colony of North Carolina at war with the troops of the king, and here am I, Ben Cleveland, fitted by blood and destiny to follow in the footsteps of my illustrious ancestor."

With the barest squeak in his voice, James managed to say, "You wouldn't hang the king, would you, Colonel Cleveland?"

The big man smiled and shook his head. "Well, perhaps not, son, but I don't propose to let him hang *me,* either."

Virginia Sal

"If this is war, I believe I could get used to it," I said, downing the last of my wine.

In the major's tent, we had dined upon confiscated beef and roast corn, and I was thinking that this life was a deal better than the one I had left behind. For a servant girl, the work had been hard and the victuals meager. Here, instead of scrubbing and mopping, and helping cook, and doing everybody's bidding the livelong day, I had only to do a bit of washing, and sewing, which is no more than a fine lady does, for many's the night back at the plantation, I had caught a glimpse of the mistress, sitting in her chair up close to the fireplace, plying her needle on silks and linens that gleamed in the firelight.

Of course, now I was a mistress, too, but of quite another kind than the planter's lady.

I don't say that I loved the major, for I knew myself to be no more to him than his white horse or his china plates — something useful for serving his needs, but otherwise of no account, and easy to replace. Still he didn't stink, like the cowherds do, nor hit me when he drank, and he was kind to me, when he thought of it. I didn't mind him, and sometimes I got to thinking I was fond of him, for I knew I'd never have a man like him again, and I resolved to make the most of my days as almost-a-lady. That would end when this war was over, I reckoned, for then he would be posted somewhere else for some other war, but, in spite of all the killing and the laying waste of people's farms, I wished this war would go on and on.

The major was in a jaunty mood tonight. The men had raided a Whig plantation that afternoon, and, while he said he cared nothing for the spoils of war, he pronounced himself cheered by the thought of having deprived an enemy of his goods.

"I have something for you, Sal," he told me, when his officers had left us alone in the tent. "One of the men took it from the daughter of the house this afternoon, for he said she was too plain and stout to wear such a thing. He gave it to me, and I suppose it will do for you, my girl, for you are neither stout nor plain."

He reached into his pocket and drew out

a string of green glass beads that glistened in the lamplight like the jewels of a queen.

I reckon I liked him better then.

He fastened the string around my neck, and held up a silver dish so that I could admire my reflection. I squealed with delight at the sight of myself in such finery, for I had never had such a thing before. Then I threw my arms around his neck and declared him the most gallant soldier in all the world.

A while later, after I had given him his reward for the gift, and we lay there in the lamplight, spent but not ready for sleep, I said, "This war suits me down to the ground. I reckon you're accustomed to such a life, though, ain't you?"

I heard him sigh. "The army has been my home for a long time."

"Your family sent you away then?"

"Oh, I wanted to go," he said with a hint of laughter in his voice. "A commission in a fine regiment and a war to boot — what more could a boy wish for?"

I couldn't imagine, and I said so.

"Well, for a better war, of course. Back then, the only fighting to be had was the Prussians fighting the French and the Austrians, but that is hardly the stuff of Shakespearean heroics."

"Which side did you favor?"

"Between the Prussians and the French? I don't know that I cared, but Britain had sided with Prussia and so we were in it. Anyhow, I deemed that conflict better than no war at all, and considerably better than doing lessons at the Royal Military Academy in Woolwich, which is where I had spent the last two years, waiting for a chance to live through a battle instead of writing essays about them."

"You went to war as a boy?" I suppose some of the farm boys we had in the regiment here were still waiting for their voices to change, but at least they weren't officers. I wondered what a grown foot soldier would think of being ordered about by a stripling boy.

He laughed and stroked my hair, which was the same color as his. "Didn't I hear that question often enough when I first went off to the army, and always from the lasses. *'Will you go to war then, Pattie?'* Even my sister Betty put that question to me one evening at Pitfour. I was already used to being asked that, for I had heard it often enough on my visits home, usually in the sorrowful tones of my mother or from various young ladies of my acquaintance. *'Will you go to war then?'* they would ask, their voices hushed, as if the wake for me had already begun."

He mocked the accents of the worried young ladies, to show his disdain for that foolish question.

"And what did you tell them?"

"Why, I gave them all the same somber answer, to the effect that I was only a low-ranking officer, and that wiser heads than mine would make those decisions, but I hoped that God would give me the fortitude to do my duty, come what may, though of course I would not wish the scourge of war upon the innocent, and so on — what gentle ladies wish to hear, it seems. It satisfied my inquirers at any rate, for they would pat my arm and inform me with great solemnity that I would be remembered in their prayers. It was all I could do to keep from laughing at their theatrics. I thought I should be lucky to see anything besides a regiment of books, and a volley of examination questions. Still, an officer must be gallant as well as brave, so I told them all what they wished to hear.

"But by God, I hoped there'll be war! I had need of one."

"So you weren't afraid to go to war then, even as a boy?"

"My family had chosen the army as my

career, and war is the army's stock in trade. When I was but twelve, my uncle advised my father to purchase an ensigncy for me, and so he did, but when Uncle's regiment the 15th Foot was posted to Canada with a war in the offing there, they thought better of having a lad of twelve in command of anybody, and so they gave my father back the money he had paid out for my commission, and my military career languished until I should be old enough and sturdy enough to be of some use to the army.

I thought the officers were wise not to let a boy of twelve have command over anything, just because his parents could afford to buy him a commission, but I told him what he wished to hear as well. "I'm sure you would have made a fine officer, even then, Major."

"Well, I never got the chance to prove it. My father sent me off to a college to learn soldiering, and by the time I was fourteen I was ready. Nothing quickens a military career like a war, for it gives a soldier a chance to show his mettle and then creates a few openings within the ranks for advancement. I was ready."

"I cannot see you as a soldier," I said, nudging him in the side, for I could feel his ribs poking up under his pale skin. "Back then you must have been so slight that you barely cast a shadow."

He shrugged. "Less of me to make a target then."

"But a battle! You might have died."

"I was quite accustomed to hearing about battles. There were battles in Scotland the year I was born. Charles Edward Stuart, son of the old Pretender — and not even the eldest son, at that — had raised an army to fight for his father's claim to the throne."

"What throne? Scotland?"

"Ah, no, Sal. They keep the king in London nowadays."

"Did the fellow" — I had forgotten his name, but even I had heard of London — "attack London, then?"

"Not quite, but he got within striking distance of it, before the British army pushed him back across the Scots border. Then there came a battle that even I would not have wished to be in — a travesty of fighting on Culloden Moor against the army of the Duke of Cumberland." Playfully, he put his finger on the tip of my nose. "And before you ask, Sal, the Duke of Cumberland was a son of the king."

"Which king?"

"Why, the same one that we have now. His Majesty, King George."

"Oh. That king. Strange to think he has been king since before you were born." Then I remembered what Dr. Johnson had told me, and I made bold to ask him about it, to see if it was true. "Did you really meet the king at his castle?"

"I was asked to demonstrate my breech-loader for his majesty, so, yes, I went to Windsor and shot at targets to show him how well my invention worked."

"Did you shake his hand and sit supper with him?"

He laughed out loud at my foolishness. "My father is a lawyer, not a prince. In fact, after the Jacobite defeat at Culloden, he defended some of Prince Charles's supporters in the trials."

"Trials? Then I reckon Prince Charles lost."

"That he did. My father managed to save his noble Jacobite clients from the rope, though, and when they visited our home in Edinburgh, my brother and I heard their stories. How the prince's men had been marched all night so that they came to the battle exhausted, and how the quartermaster had left the food behind in Inverness and brought the wrong size shot for the cannon. Swords against muskets. What followed was a slaughter, and when it was over, the men of the Duke of Cumberland had paced the field, prodding the bodies of the Jacobites for signs of life and bayoneting any who moved or groaned."

"Just like Major Tarleton then?" We had all heard about the Waxhaws, and I was sorry for the poor rebels who died like that, but it did not make me want to cast my lot with them. "Were you sorry your Scotch friends lost their battle?"

He shook his head. "I suppose we were sorry to hear of such horrors being inflicted upon our fellow Scots, but as good Protestants, we were not sorry the Catholic Highlanders lost, nor were we much surprised. Anyone who would face muskets and bayonets with great unwieldy swords and useless cannons is ultimately past saving, I'd have thought. It cheered me to think that I had joined the side that had fought with the muskets and bayonets."

"You could still get killed, for in this war the other side has guns, same as you do."

"Just remember which army I've joined. Surely we are a match for any fighting force on earth."

"Even good armies lose soldiers."

"But I am an officer, Sal." Then his voice took on an odd note, and he said, "Of course, so was General Wolfe."

Well, I didn't know who that was, but he had got out of the mood of talking now, and he turned to me again, kissing me on the neck, and unfastening the glass beads. "We wouldn't want to break your necklace with our sporting, Sal. You may have it back — after."

Chapter Twelve
OCTOBER 2, 1780

We had hoped that the storm would pass during the night, but when the light thickened at daybreak there was only an unbroken sea of clouds in a clabbered sky, and the rain was still falling like pellets of lead from a shot tower. My brother Robert, who had bedded down near us the night before, crawled out of his damp bedroll and peered up at the sky. "Well, the storm didn't pass. Do you think we'll move out in this weather, anyhow, Jack?"

I shook my head. "I doubt it, but I won't know for sure until I talk to the others. My head must be waterlogged — I can't even remember offhand whose day it is to be in command. You keep an eye on things here while I hunt them up."

As I went in search of the other commanders, one of my men called out, "I hope you officers ain't aiming to make us drill in this foul weather, Colonel! 'Cause I reckon we wouldn't!"

I gave him a brief stare until he turned his gaze away from mine, and then I quickened my pace. The problem with this army is that it wasn't any such thing. These men had taken no oath to the nation, received no training, and no pay. They had simply come on this mission because they were asked to by leaders that they trusted, and although most of us were trying our best to act like military men, the fact is that we weren't. We were old Indian fighters, and our trust and obedience was based on our personal knowledge of those who fought alongside us. That acquaintance would be lacking for us in this expedition when we'd have to fight in the company of strangers. The longer this expedition lasted, and the more unpleasant conditions became, the more likely we were to have problems among the ranks. The men were tired, cold, and sore from their journey over the mountains, and the more time they had to think about going up against a trained enemy force, the more fractious some of them would become. It worried me.

I said as much to the others when we stood together in a thicket of trees, which was as much shelter from the downpour as we could find. "I hope we find Ferguson soon," I told them, "before this whole army falls apart around us. Our several militias are like squares of a quilt, but held together only with basting stitches. The fabric will not hold for long, and it will not take much pressure to pull it apart."

"Agreed," said Campbell, "but I see no sign yet that this storm is breaking up. If we tried to march the men out of here today, we might lose more in illness than we gain in discipline. We cannot fight with sick soldiers."

"More than that," said Shelby. "The mud will slow us down. The streams might be too swollen to ford, and, above, all, we cannot risk the gunpowder. If the powder is ruined, it destroys our mission. I think we had better wait another day before we set off again."

"Ferguson will keep," said Andrew Hampton. "I doubt that he will change his position in such weather, either."

I saw the force of their arguments, and, though it did not suit me to sit about idly while our enemy was still abroad in the land, waiting was the reasonable course. So we sat out Monday, doing what chores we could despite the rain, and when Tuesday, October 3, proved no better, we remained in camp for another frustrating day, while Ferguson ranged about heaven-knows-where, and we crept one day closer to winter, when such foul weather would be a commonplace.

We kept a close eye on our men that day, to ensure that they did not while away this dreary day interval of inactivity with excessive drinking or fighting. Boredom was an enemy in itself.

That evening, as the rain continued to fall in leaden sheets, we made the best of our rations for a soggy repast, and then set off from our respective encampments to confer at the headquarters of Charles McDowell. Finding that I had arrived somewhat in advance of the others, I resolved to spend the time until they arrived in making pleasant conversation with Colonel McDowell.

His men had managed to rig a makeshift canvas cover under a spreading oak tree. Its abundant foliage helped to divert the rain, and the colonel himself looked relatively dry, seated in the opening of the tent before a sputtering fire. I bade him good evening and sat down beside him on a pile of clothing and blankets.

"I hope your family is faring well back home," he said. "You've had no word, I suppose?"

I shook my head. "I tell myself that I'd have heard if anything were amiss. Robertson would get word to us."

"I envy you your fine family," he said. "I have heard, of course, of your recent marriage, and I offer you my heartiest congratulations. Even my envy at such domestic happiness, for I have never married, you know. And the tale of your daring rescue of your good lady at the Watauga siege of '76 is a wonder to hear. She is a brave woman, your bride."

"Yes, she is," I said, smiling at the memory of her, as I wiped a droplet of windblown rain off my cheek.

"I know of another such woman," said McDowell. "They are as rare as double rainbows, but what a treasure it is to find one."

I looked around. The others had not yet arrived, and McDowell's men were busy with their rations. We could not make plans without the presence of my fellow commanders, so I decided to humor him in his choice of subject, sentimental as it was. "And have you found a rainbow of a woman, Colonel?"

He smiled. "I have, indeed. She is a kinswoman of mine, Mistress Grace Greenlee Bowman, whose mother is a McDowell. But she is in deep mourning still over her husband, who was one of our officers. He fell at Ramsour's Mill, back in June. When word was sent to her that he was mortally wounded, Grace saddled a horse, put their infant child on the saddle in front of her, and rode the forty miles to the battlefield — heedless of her own safety, heedless of the enemy soldiers who might still have been in the vicinity. She stayed there on the field and tended Captain Bowman until he departed this life. A handsome woman, as brave as any soldier I have."

"Well, she has the McDowell mettle in her bloodline," I said. It had begun to rain in earnest now, and the campfire sputtered out into smoldering ashes. I thought it might be some time before the others joined us.

The colonel smiled. "Yes, that mettle is evident in her mother as well. Once Mary McDowell was offered a horse by her neighbors if she would retrieve their daughter from the Indians — which she did. She was so clever and able that some of the people thereabouts said she was a witch." Charles McDowell chuckled. "As for young Grace, that fighting spirit was evident in her from an early age. Back in Virginia, where they had settled then, her father was anxious for her to make an advantageous marriage, so that the family could advance socially. He fixed it up for her to marry a wealthy planter, an elderly man. She said not a word when they told her she had to go through with it, and hauled her into the church for the wedding ceremony."

"To marry this Captain Bowman?"

"No, indeed. A much older gentleman. When the parson got to the part about 'Do you take this man for your lawfully wedded husband?' — quite clearly and firmly, in front of the entire congregation, my cousin Grace said that she did not. They asked her more than once, but she was quite obstinate. She would say nothing except 'No,' and at last they gave up, and she was not required to wed the elderly planter. Instead, she made a match of it with young John Bowman, and they came to Carolina along with her brother James and his wife to start a new life in the Yadkin Valley."

"And Bowman was killed at Ramsour's Mill, you say? How sad that their happiness was so brief."

"Indeed. Her life has not been easy, but she has lost none of her courage. I had word of her recently, for all our family and some of Bowman's comrades are looking out for her whenever possible. I would have been at her service myself, except that I had to flee over the mountains into your territory."

"Is she faring well?"

"She is in as much peril as any of us in these difficult times, but the last news I had of her indicates that she is equal to the challenge. While I was away over the mountain, the Tories quite overran this part of Carolina. One day, Cousin Grace heard a commotion in the yard, and found a troop of soldiers there, one of them leading her horse out of the barn. Upon seeing her, the Tory said, 'Madam, the king hath need of your horse.' Her response was to go back inside the house, and to return with her husband's gun, which she aimed at the man holding the reins of her mare. The soldier took a long look at the stalwart lady leveling the gun barrel at his head, and he said, 'Madam, the king hath no further need of your horse.' They put the animal back in its stall, and rode away, leaving her in peace. For now."

I smiled politely at this story, but then I said, "Your cousin Mistress Bowman must be quite young and pretty."

"Indeed, she is. But what makes you say that?"

"Because a woman who was not young and pretty would not have gotten away with such behavior. A stout matron who behaved thusly would have been lucky to lose only her horse. Are you thinking of rescuing this brave lady from her widow's weeds, Colonel

McDowell?"

He sighed. "By heaven, I would, if I thought she'd have me. But I keep thinking of the way she spurned the advances of that wealthy old planter. And I fear I am something of a wealthy old planter myself."

I smiled, choosing to ignore the fact that I was only two years shy of his age myself. "Do not lose hope, McDowell. You are not so old as all that. I fancy the lady will have you." I forebore to mention the reasons for my believing that, for they were not nearly as romantic as the old fellow's ardor. I was thinking that Mistress Bowman was no longer the headstrong young girl she had been when she refused the old planter in Virginia. The war had made pragmatists of us all. Now, the lady was perhaps a decade older, and with at least one child to consider, and I thought, the offer of wealth and security might be more appealing than they were when she was a maiden. McDowell could offer her a prosperous home, a safe haven for her baby, and the comfort of a family already known to her. One did not have to believe in the true love of storybooks to think that McDowell might get his happy ending. Still, I wished him well.

Someone hailed us just then, and we looked through the curtain of rain to see the other commanders approaching. I saw that Andrew Hampton had joined Cleveland, Shelby, and Winston, and I knew that the very presence of that grieving father would serve as a tacit rejection of Charles McDowell as commander.

It was time for us to decide who would lead our makeshift army into battle, but, as ready as I was to settle the matter, the others shied away from it. At first they found other things to talk about — pressing matters, all of them — but, excepting Colonel Hampton, at the back of their eyes I could see the hesitation. The decision, when it came, would hurt the pride of Charles McDowell, and, much as we all knew that he was not suited to command our forces, we all respected the fellow, and we would have spared his feelings if we could.

It was McDowell himself who ended the desultory conversations and called the council to order, for he was still the senior officer in charge. "I have been thinking this through, gentlemen," he said. "It is our duty to inform General Gates of our plans. He is the supreme commander in the south, and he may wish to send more troops to join us. Anyhow, he needs to be told."

Shelby glanced at me, and I knew that a good many harsh thoughts were going through his mind — thoughts of Gates's shameful behavior after the battle at Camden, when he deserted his army, and rode at breakneck speed for the safety of Hillsborough. None of us would set much store by Gates's opinions or his offers to help, but McDowell was right: military protocol required us to apprise him of our plans.

"I agree," said Campbell. "We are a union of militias from several states — and more on the way, if the South Carolina troops join us. Strictly speaking, none of us has the authority to command the forces from states other than our own. There should be someone with the authority to command, and General Gates has the power to confer that authority. We must consult him."

"Gates is in Hillsborough," said Shelby. "If we sit around cooling our heels and awaiting the general's pleasure, it could get us all killed."

Andrew Hampton gave a quick nod of agreement to this, and I knew he was thinking of earlier battles and opportunities lost.

"That's true enough," growled Cleveland. "Our greatest advantage is speed and surprise. We must corner Ferguson before he can get reinforcements from Cornwallis. We must proceed."

Joseph Winston spoke up then. "But how

can we proceed without an appointed commander?"

"Just as we have been," I said. "We will all meet every evening to discuss the day's events and to decide how to proceed, and we will continue with an officer of the day, to be given command by our general consent."

Shelby scowled at me. I knew he wanted more decisive measures. "Do you know where we are, Colonel Sevier? Perhaps sixteen miles away from Gilbert Town. We could encounter Ferguson's men at any hour, or at any given place within the next mile. We don't know. Discipline is already becoming a problem. Our supplies are limited. We cannot hang about waiting for word from the general, but neither can we weaken our forces by changing leaders every day. We need to choose one."

"But Gates must be consulted," said McDowell.

It occurred to me then that, as useless as Gates was, he might do us a service, after all.

"Why, you must go and report to him, Colonel McDowell," I said. "You are senior among us, and it is fitting that you should be the one to confer with him and to explain our position."

Shelby took my meaning at once, and warmly supported my suggestion.

McDowell hesitated. "But my men . . . the Burke County militia."

"Surely your brother Joseph can take your place until you return," said Cleveland. "As young as he is, he is an able fellow."

Several of the others murmured their assent. Despite his youth, Joseph McDowell was a good soldier, and he was well liked by those who had served with him.

Charles McDowell was silent for a moment, thinking it over. "Yes," he said at last. "As senior officer here, it is my duty to go. I will leave at once. Joseph is indeed a capable leader, and in my absence the men will follow him. Let me have a word with him, and then I'll be off."

"Not just yet," said Cleveland. "Perhaps we should compose a joint letter to General Gates, explaining our position and our requirements. You can, of course, elaborate on the particulars when you see him, Colonel McDowell, but the letter will let him know that we are all acting in unison in this matter. Whether Gates assists us or not, we will have discharged our duty regarding the chain of command."

All of us agreed that this was a good idea, and we spent the better part of an hour deciding on the wording and the form of the missive, while Joseph Winston made notes of the phrases, so that when we were satisfied with it, he could make a fair copy for us to sign. After much discussion, we arrived at a draft that satisfied all of us. Joseph Winston read it aloud one last time for final comments.

Sir,

We have collected at this place about fifteen hundred good men, drawn from Washington, Surry, Wilkes, Burke of North Carolina, and Washington County, Virginia, and expect to be joined in a few days by Colonel Williams of South Carolina with about a thousand more. As we have at this place called out Militia without any order from the executives of our different States, and with a view of expelling out of this part of the country the enemy, we think such a body of men worthy of your attention and would request you to send a General Officer immediately to take the command of such troops as may embody in this quarter. Our troops being Militia, and but little acquainted with discipline, we would wish him to be a gentleman of address, and be able to keep a proper discipline without disgusting the soldiery. Every assistance in our power shall be given the Officer you may think proper to take command of us. It is the wish of such of us as are acquainted with General Davidson and Colonel Morgan (if in service) that one of these Gentlemen may be appointed to this command.

We are in great need of ammunition, and hope you will endeavor to have us properly furnished.

Colonel McDowell will wait on you with this, who can inform you of the present situation of the enemy, and such other particulars respecting our troops as you may think necessary.

Your most obedient and very able servants,

Benj. Cleveland
Isaac Shelby
John Sevier
Andrew Hampton
Wm. Campbell
Jo. Winston

We nodded to one another when Winston had finished reading it. It was a good letter: very forthright.

"That's very well said," I remarked to Shelby.

He nodded and murmured, "Yes. Very . . . plausible."

I took his meaning at once. On the face of it, the letter seemed quite logical and modest, humbly asking the general to send us a commanding officer. I hoped that neither McDowell nor Gates would trouble themselves to read it more carefully. Both Morgan and Davidson were fine soldiers, and most capable of leading an army, but it wasn't going to happen.

Before taking up arms here in North Carolina, William Davidson had fought the war in the north: he saw action at Germantown and Saratoga; he froze at Valley Forge, and of late he had been second in command to General Rutherford here in Carolina. But Davidson had been gravely wounded back in July at Colson's Mill, and he had been out of action ever since. He would not be taking command of anything for a good while to come.

And we had said in the letter that we wanted a "gentleman of address." Daniel Morgan, stalwart old warrior that he was, was not quite that. He came of humble Welsh stock from Pennsylvania, or perhaps New Jersey, and he had very little in the way of education, though there were few men more skilled in gambling and toping. Back in the war against the French, Morgan had served as a mule skinner with the forces of General Braddock, and he managed to survive a punishment of 499 lashes for the insubordination of striking an officer. The hatred for the British army kindled upon that occasion turned Morgan into the most ardent of patriots. I knew him in Lord Dunmore's War, and deemed him an excellent soldier, but he was not a man of tact or social graces. Despite all his service, he was passed over for promotion in favor of men who had less combat experience but more powerful friends. Morgan might have risen to the rank of brigadier if he had courted the favor of Congress, or troubled to cultivate friendships with his superiors, but he could not or would not do so. That was a great pity, for he would have made a better job of Commander of the Southern Department than the craven Horatio Gates. We all wished they had given the supreme command to Morgan instead. And rumor had it that Morgan himself, infuriated by being passed over while others were honored, had resigned his commission and gone home to his farm. Gates could hardly appoint a commander who had withdrawn from service.

All that was perhaps beside the point, though. Morgan was not *here.* That's what mattered. And General Gates was two hundred miles away in Hillsborough, while we were less than twenty miles from Gilbert Town, where Ferguson was reported to be.

By the time Charles McDowell rode from here to Hillsborough, conferred with Gates, and rode the two hundred miles back to wherever we would be by then, with or without an accompanying commander, our campaign would be over. One way or another, it would be all over.

So the contents of that letter to Gates, although entirely courteous and well reasoned, in actuality signified nothing. We had requested two men who could not possibly accept the commission, and in sending the letter we had rid ourselves of a third nominally qualified leader in the person of Charles McDowell. We meant to go on as we were, no matter what we had said or wrote to the contrary.

One by one we signed our names to the document. Then Charles McDowell stretched out his hand, and, with a deferential nod, Joseph Winston handed him the letter.

"I'd best be off soon," McDowell said.

"It's a long way to Hillsborough. I make it nigh on two hundred miles." He looked around for confirmation, and Cleveland and Winston, who knew that part of North Carolina, nodded in agreement.

"Yes, I thought so. Two hundred miles. I'm glad my horse has had a bit of a rest." He reached for his saddlebag, and slid the letter inside it, wrapping leather breeches around it to protect the ink from the rain. Then he stood up, and pushed his way out of the makeshift shelter. The rain had slacked off again, and the rest of us followed him outside, and away from the dripping branches of the tree, but we did not disperse. We wished him Godspeed, and watched him stride away, calling out for his horse to be saddled and for someone to find his brother so that he could transfer the command of his troops.

"Well, that was easy enough," Shelby said to me, in a quiet aside not meant to be overheard, and then he turned back to the others, and in a louder voice he announced to the company, "Now, gentlemen, let us choose a real commander."

William Campbell blinked at the abruptness of this sally. "Without McDowell?"

Shelby nodded. "Oh, yes. He is well away, and we won't be waiting for word from him.

There's not a moment to spare, and we must have a real leader before we proceed. Mind you, Charles McDowell is a fine, loyal fellow, and a good soldier, but he won't do for command overall. I fear he is too . . . well, too *old* . . . to be entrusted with that responsibility."

At this last utterance, the others stared at Shelby in amazement. Charles McDowell was thirty-seven years old, only two years past my own age. That made McDowell five years younger than Benjamin Cleveland, who was forty-two, and, even with his enormous girth, no one would dare suggest that the relentless Colonel Cleveland was unfit for command. I knew what Shelby meant, though, even if he forebore to say it. McDowell was not a satisfactory choice for commander, and age was as good an excuse as any, for the truth was considerably more awkward.

McDowell had a sense of caution bordering on timidity, and the poor management of his campaigns made him seem like a pettifogging old woman. I knew, too, that Andrew Hampton would never forgive Charles McDowell for the incident on the Pacolet, when he had neglected to post pickets, and Hampton's son had died that night in the attack. Although he had said very little during our discussion of the matter, he and his men might well have refused to proceed under the general command of Charles McDowell. No one disputed Shelby's objection to McDowell. He was right in the spirit of his objection, if not accurate in his complaint of the colonel's age as the excuse for it.

There was a moment of silence, while we all considered this proposition. Then Benjamin Cleveland looked around the circle, weighing his choices: Shelby, Winston, Campbell, Hampton, and myself. Even though he would now assume command of the Burke militia, Joseph McDowell would not be considered for the job of chief commander. Joseph McDowell was a fine fellow, and as a leader he was a great improvement over his brother, but he was a mere twenty-four years of age. In his case, age most certainly was the deciding factor to disqualify him.

"It had better be you, Campbell," Cleveland said at last.

William Campbell looked startled, as well he might. Many of the rest of us were old comrades in battle, with closer ties to one another than to him. "What? Me?" he said. "But why? Surely, it is Colonel Shelby who should be chosen to lead us. Please take my name out of contention, gentlemen. I have no claim to such a primacy above the rest of you."

Shelby shook his head. "No, no, sir. Colonel Cleveland is right. You are the best and most logical choice, Campbell, though your modesty does you credit. Perhaps any one of us would do as well as you in the overall command, but there are other considerations beyond that. First of all, I contend that we must not hurt Charles McDowell's feelings any more than we have to. Agreed?"

We all nodded. There was no malice in our wish to replace Charles McDowell as leader, only our grave concern for the success of the enterprise. The presence of Joseph McDowell among the commanders would also make it imperative that we act with the utmost tact in making our decision.

"Right," said Shelby. "We are agreed on that point. Well, then, that being the case, I believe I am the last person you should consider. I am the youngest of all of you, and I have served under McDowell. If you should promote me over McDowell, I fear he would take offense."

"I believe you are the least objectionable choice, Campbell," said Ben Cleveland.

"The rest of us are all from Carolina, and to elevate one of us in McDowell's absence would be . . . unwise. But you are a Virginian. Your appointment would be less of a direct challenge to his authority. And I daresay none of us would object to your election." He looked around at the rest of us. "Gentlemen?"

We all nodded. The force of Shelby's logic had won us over. Campbell was indeed the sensible choice, and it was a choice that we could all live with. Fair enough.

We put the matter to an informal vote — a show of hands — but that was merely for form's sake. The Virginian commander William Campbell would lead our combined forces from now until the battle with Ferguson was over. And if anyone remembered how hard Shelby had to beg in order to persuade Campbell to join our enterprise in the first place, no one remarked on it.

CHAPTER THIRTEEN
OCTOBER 4, 1780

We passed a quiet night, with only the rain to break the silence of the woods, and much to our relief the day dawned clear and fine. We began to break up camp, making ready to go on with the march, when word went around the camp that Old Roundabout wanted to address the men before we got under way. I wondered what Cleveland wanted to tell them. Leaving James and Joseph to pack up our gear, I went along to find the other commanders. The men from each of the militias were beginning to congregate around a clearing, and a little apart from the crowd I saw Cleveland conferring with Shelby, with the other officers grouped nearby.

When they caught sight of me, they waved me over.

"I mean to talk to the troops," said Cleveland, after we had dispensed with the initial formalities. "They have got a bit wild with all this idleness, and too much time to think before a battle can wear away a man's resolve. We need to ginger them up, and I'm the man to do it. Speech-making doesn't come naturally to me, on account of this infernal halt in my way of talking, but, being descended from Oliver Cromwell and all, I reckon I can summon up the spirit to rally them to the cause."

I said that a speech to the men was a fine idea, and that I looked forward to hearing it myself.

Even without a platform or a pulpit, Benjamin Cleveland was an imposing man — tall and corpulent, with a girth that was already more fat than muscle, but despite the jesting nicknames like "Old Roundabout," the men knew that he was no buffoon. There were a goodly number of Tories hanging lifeless from trees attesting to the fact that Ben Cleveland was a deadly serious man. They would follow his every word, and, even if he stumbled over a few of them, no one would mock him for it.

A hush fell over the assembly, and the men stood in a semicircle waiting to hear what Colonel Cleveland would say. He was still for a moment, letting his gaze go from one upturned face to the next, and then with a deep breath he began.

"Well, my brave fellows, I have come to give you the news. The enemy is at hand, and we must up and have at them. Now is the time for every man here to do a priceless service for his country — one that will cause your children to rejoice in the fact that their fathers aided in the conquest of the hated Ferguson. When the time comes, rest assured that I shall be with you. But if any of you have misgivings about sharing in the battle and the glory to come, why you may now have the opportunity to withdraw from this company. You may leave if you choose to, and we shall permit you a few moments to think the matter over."

He fell silent then, but his eyes never wavered from the company, and not a man among them moved.

In the stillness, Maj. Joseph McDowell called out, "Those of you thinking of backing out, what kind of story will you tell your families when you get back home?"

More silence, except that William Campbell standing beside me murmured, "Shakespeare's Henry the Fifth, is it not? *Gentlemen in England now abed shall hold their manhood cheap while any speaks who fought with us . . .*"

The moments allotted for a decision had now elapsed, and it was Shelby who urged the men to take a stand. He called out, "Right. Those who want no part of this campaign will upon my mark retreat three paces to the rear of the company."

After another pause, Cleveland himself barked out the order, and we waited. Some of the soldiers looked around at one another and smiled, but to a man they stood their ground. When they all realized that no one had chosen to desert the cause, a great cheer went up from the ranks, and the officers exchanged sheepish grins that were equal parts pride and relief.

Now that we knew we had faithful soldiers, with no cowards or traitors among them, Shelby offered a few words of counsel regarding the battle to come. "We don't know when we may encounter the enemy, but it will be soon, and when we do, you need not wait for a word of command to proceed. Every one of you will be his own commander. If we are fortunate enough to be able to fight them in the woods, then we must give them Indian play: hide behind the trees, and do not let them get a clear shot at you. But if the enemy yields to us, then you must be alert and wait for an officer's orders."

He spoke a bit longer, more of the same, gingering up the men so that they would be spoiling for a fight by the time we found Ferguson. Then to celebrate our unity of purpose, Major McDowell produced a barrel of spirits that he must have brought by wagon from his home near Quaker Meadows. One of the men doled out a cupful to each of the soldiers, and there was much banter and boasting as they partook of it. Then each man was told to pack two days' rations in his kit, for we would be on the move again directly.

When we judged that the morale of the company was running high and strong, Campbell gave the order for the militias to make ready to break camp. The horsemen mounted, and the foot soldiers fell in behind them, laden with weapons and blankets.

My oldest boy threaded his way around the other riders, and Major Tipton edged away so that he could come up beside me. "Do you think we'll find Ferguson today, sir?"

"I hope so, Joseph. We are all fed and rested, and as fit as we're going to be. Where is your brother?"

"Oh, I got tired to playing nursemaid to that young'un, so I fobbed him off on Uncle Robert. They're riding together awhile to give me a rest."

"All right, but James is your responsibility.

I expect you to look out for him. I can't command this militia and ride herd on you boys at the same time."

Joseph hung his head, and it struck me that he was in many ways still a boy. True, I had been married and a father when I was his age, but he was still living at home, so perhaps he'd had less of an opportunity to mature. I wished he could take his time in coming to manhood, but war has a way of making boys grow up whether they mean to or not.

We snaked our way along the banks of Cane Creek, heading in the direction of Gilbert Town. We figured we would reach the town by nightfall. The tension in the air put me in mind of a summer thunderstorm, but it wasn't the weather causing that feeling: it was us. There was no singing or shouts of laughter, no raucous calling from one group to the next, as there had been now and again in the early days of our march. Now we were in enemy territory, and the next bend in the trail could bring us face-to-face with Ferguson's army. The men were not afraid of what was to come, but they were solemn, for death is a serious business, whether you are giving it or receiving it.

Suddenly there was a commotion far

ahead of us at the front of the procession. We were riding a good ways behind the leaders, which was Joseph McDowell's Burke militia, and so we could only tell that something had made them stop. No shots had been fired, though. I told Valentine to take command for a bit, and I worked my way up through the line until I reached the front.

As I headed for McDowell, I heard the Burke men calling out to one another that up ahead a lone rider had emerged from the woods. I heard no shots, though, and no sounds of combat.

A minute later I could see that McDowell, Campbell, and Andrew Hampton were in conversation with a young man who bore a passing resemblance to Major Hampton. I trotted forward to join the parlay.

I soon learned that the young man was Jonathan Hampton, brother of poor Noah, the boy who had been slaughtered on the Pacolet when Tory raiders ambushed McDowell's militia. We were nearing the area where Andrew Hampton's landholdings lay, as well as the area where Ferguson was reputed to be.

"He's gone," Jonathan Hampton said again for my benefit. "He left Gilbert Town a few days back, and the word is that he

315

went a-hunting Elijah Clarke."

"I doubt he'll find him," said Major McDowell. "But I hope he crosses our path before he crosses Clarke's."

Jonathan Hampton scowled. "There's something you ought to see." He reached into the pocket of his coat and drew out a folded piece of paper. "Ferguson has posted copies of this here broadsheet at general stores and on signposts far and wide." He handed the paper to Isaac Shelby, who had just appeared, saying "Your name's on it, too, Colonel Shelby."

We all dismounted so that we could examine this broadsheet together. The proclamation, dated three days earlier — October first — gave the author's location as "Denard's Ford, Broad River, Tryon County," which I knew to be a few miles southeast of Gilbert Town. It was addressed to "The Inhabitants of North Carolina."

Shelby read it aloud.

Gentlemen:
  Unless you wish to be eat up by an inundation of barbarians, who have begun by murdering an unarmed son before his father, and afterward lopped off his arms, and who by their shocking cruelties and irregularities, give the best

316

proof of their cowardice and want of discipline, I say if you wish to be pinioned, robbed, and murdered, and see your wives and daughters, in four days, abused by the dregs of mankind — in short, if you wish or deserve to live or bear the name of men, grasp your arms in a moment and run to camp.

The Backwater Men have crossed the mountains; McDowell, Hampton, Shelby, and Cleveland are at their head, so that you know what you have to depend upon. If you choose to be pissed upon forever and ever by a set of mongrels, say so at once, and let your women turn their backs upon you, and look out for real men to protect them.

Pat. Ferguson, Major 71st Regiment

Slowly, Shelby lowered the paper. "Well, he knows we're coming."

"That's about all he knows," said Major McDowell. "*Backwater Men?* Why, Hampton and Cleveland and I are a good forty miles east of you, Colonel Shelby. Does that English fool think that the Catawba and the Yadkin rivers are on the other side of the mountains?"

"At least you rated a mention," I said, trying not to grin. "Poor Campbell and I were

317

cruelly snubbed, and we *are* Backwater Men."

"And what is this business about a son being murdered before his father?" said Hampton. "Arms lopped off?"

"Fanciful, ain't he?" Shelby was laughing. "I think he must have made up that part. But what I want to know is: just who is he hoping to convert to his cause? The men or the ladies?"

Cleveland was not amused. "*Pissed upon forever.* I shan't forget that turn of phrase. I think we owe him something for that. We should read this notice to the troops when we make camp this evening. Major Ferguson's words are likely to inspire them a good deal more than mine did this morning."

"So Ferguson is no longer in Gilbert Town. What should we do now?" asked Joseph McDowell.

Campbell considered it. "Let's go on as we planned. From there we can deliberate on what next to do. But we had better see about getting a spy to scout out the whereabouts of the enemy."

Andrew Hampton spoke up. "I know a fellow from these parts who could manage it. Name of Enoch Gilmer. He is one of William Chronicle's men. We can talk to him when we meet up with them."

We headed out again, with Jonathan Hampton riding alongside his father, for he intended to stay with us and see the mission through, and when we reached Gilbert Town late in the afternoon, we learned that Ferguson had indeed left the area, for we camped that night on the very ground that he had vacated only days before.

The next morning, we were waiting for reports on the whereabouts of Ferguson, and hoping that the South Carolina militias would find us, when a lone rider came galloping up the road. Seeing as how he was alone, we took him for an ally, for no Tory would be foolish enough to ride into our encampment on his own. I was sitting with the other commanders, finishing up our morning's rations, when the rider approached. He was a red-faced man of about forty, with a prominent nose that deprived him of any vestige of good looks, and his thickset body rivaled Colonel Cleveland's for girth. He had evidently asked where to find the commanding officers, for he made straight for us, with an upraised hand, conveying that he came in peace.

While the rider was still out of earshot, dismounting, and handing his horse's reins to a nearby soldier, I murmured to McDowell, "Who is he?"

It was Isaac Shelby who answered, addressing all of us in tones of quiet vehemence. "That, gentlemen, is James Williams. I know quite a bit about him — none of it good, I'm sorry to say."

He had no time to explain further, for the fellow was striding toward us, smiling as if he had not a care in the world, but I noticed that he was glancing from one of us to another, evidently trying to decide who was the overall commander.

Scarcely pausing to draw breath, the stout fellow gave a slight bow to each of us, and repeated our names as we gave them. "And who is in charge here?" he inquired pleasantly.

"I am," said William Campbell, and no one elaborated on his answer, though we were all wondering about the purpose of this visit. Surely General Gates had not sent this officer to take command? We had certainly requested such action from him, but we did not mean it, and we had counted on his not receiving our message for another week.

"Ah, excellent news, Colonel Campbell," said Williams, beaming. "Your name precedes you. I know that Governor Jefferson will be pleased to hear that the kinsman of his predecessor is upholding the honor of Virginia. Commend me to him in your dispatch, if you will."

William Campbell was no doubt used to such sallies from ambitious strangers, for he ignored the remark, merely asking, "You have not yet identified yourself, sir."

The smile never wavered. "My apologies. I am acquainted with some of you, so I fancied you knew. I am Brigadier General James Williams, recently appointed to that rank by Governor Rutledge," he declared. He paused for a moment, perhaps expecting us to show deference to this exalted rank, but all he got for his trouble was hard stares from all of us.

When he said that he was a general, I saw Major McDowell give a little start as if he had been bee-stung, but he said nothing. Williams had pulled a crumpled bit of paper out of his pocket — the official documentation of his appointment to general by the governor of South Carolina — and he waited while we passed it from hand to hand. The document was genuine; obviously the man was who he said he was.

"Delighted to find all you gentlemen well and none the worse for your journey," he said, as he stuffed the paper back into his pocket. "The excellent General Gates will be gratified to know that I have found you. I sent him a dispatch just three days ago, apprising him of my position, and telling him that my four hundred and fifty horsemen expected to form a junction with you in a day or so. Well met, gentlemen!"

No one spoke for a moment, but Isaac Shelby made a great show of looking around and peering over our visitor's shoulder, as if hoping to espy these 450 men, who were nowhere in evidence. I endeavored not to smile.

"Four hundred and fifty more soldiers would be a welcome addition to our enterprise, sir," said Colonel Campbell. "But you seem to have misplaced them."

Williams's smile suggested that he was delighted with Campbell's powers of observation. "Indeed, they are not here," he said cheerfully. "I wished to ascertain your position, and since you took a bit of finding, I thought it best to make the search alone. I have just left the encampment of colonels Lacey, Hill, Graham, and Hambright. Together we have more than a thousand men. We plan to join our forces to yours farther along, before you catch up with Ferguson."

"Why have you come, sir? Have you news for us?"

"I do indeed. We have received reports

from local spies about Ferguson's movements. He was here only a day ago, you
know."

"Yes, but do you know where he is now?"
asked Campbell, voicing the question for all
of us.

Williams nodded. "An old man came to
our camp yesterday with information on
Major Ferguson's movements. He is in my
home territory. You know it, I'm sure.
Ninety Six, just down in South Carolina,
perhaps a few days' miles from here. You
should proceed there at once."

Ninety Six . . . That area was deep in South
Carolina, and suddenly the information that
Ferguson was there made terrible sense.
Waxhaws had been the scene of a great
Loyalist victory — and a terrible massacre.
Earlier this year, in May, Bloody Ban Tarleton and his dragoons had slaughtered
Colonel Buford's men, and when the defeated army asked for quarter — that the
survivors be spared — none was given. The
dragoons butchered the wounded on the
field, and Buford himself barely escaped
with his life. The memory of that battle
spurred many a man to walk another mile
and to fight another day, in hopes of aveng-
ing that dishonorable deed.

Ferguson would be glad to face us on that

flat, open field where his side had triumphed so handily in the earlier engagement. If he had somehow managed to get Tarleton to ride out from Charlotte Town as reinforcement, the outlook for us would indeed be bleak: a ragtag group of farmers with weapons off the mantelpiece and five hundred pounds of powder against regular British army dragoons.

We all realized the implications of this news. It was Cleveland who growled, "Ninety Six, is it? Is Bloody Ban with him?"

"No," said Williams. "At least not yet. We've seen no sign of him. If you hurry, you can catch Ferguson on his own."

When Williams paused for breath, we peppered him with questions, but he hadn't much more in the way of useful information. He did say that Ferguson had not received reinforcements from Charlotte Town, so it would only be his regiment that we must contend with, and not the dragoons of Bloody Ban Tarleton. That was welcome news.

Campbell invited Williams to partake of some food, though we had next to nothing to give him, and perhaps he divined that this was the case for he declined the offer, saying that he must go back and join the other militias, as he had left his own soldiers with them, and that he would see us again at the rendezvous at Lawson Fork. We tried to question him further, but Williams scarcely lingered long enough for a cup of water before he called for his horse to be saddled and brought to him, saying that it was urgent that he return to the South Carolina forces.

We watched Williams ride away in startled silence, and I glanced at Shelby to see if he was going to say anything about the visitor, but no one spoke for a bit, and then William Campbell ended the matter: "Well, gentlemen, you heard the general. The enemy is within striking distance. Let us proceed to Ninety Six without delay."

CHAPTER FOURTEEN
OCTOBER 5, 1780

After General James Williams rode away, we broke camp and gave the order to resume the march onward into South Carolina. Ninety Six was some eighty miles away, halfway between here and Georgia, and even if our forces had all been mounted troops, we could not have hoped to reach it in a day, nor would we wish to, for if a great battle lay at the end of our journey, we would not want to arrive there footsore and weary. As it was, with worn-out foot soldiers as well as horsemen, it would take us at least two days to reach Ninety Six. Still, if that's where Ferguson was camped, we had no choice but to go. We were concerned, though, worried that we were overtaxing the endurance of our men and horses, and, for myself and Shelby, also worried that in traveling so far from our territory beyond the mountains, we were leaving our homes and families open to an attack by Dragging

Canoe. Ninety Six was a good deal farther than we had counted on going, but having come so far already, we could not waste the effort and supplies by giving up now.

We made it only part of the way by nightfall, and, still on the North Carolina side of the state line, we camped along the Green River, planning to continue the long journey southward at first light. I hoped that food would be more plentiful farther along, for I dreaded the thought of going into battle with weak and hungry soldiers.

There was little laughter or conversation in camp tonight. I passed group after group of gaunt, blank faces — weary men with next to nothing to eat, staring into campfires, too tired to speak. The roasted meat that the McDowells had given us at Quaker Meadows was now a distant memory, and we had subsisted for days on whatever provisions we could find. A thousand men swarming across a valley like locusts left little for anyone to eat, especially when they traveled in the wake of an enemy army who had passed that way only days before. Our men ate turnips when they could find them, and many had to make do with parched corn, washed down with a few drops of honey. Soon they would become weak from the constant traveling and the lack of nourishment, and I dreaded to think how they would fare in battle in such a worn-out condition. The horses, too, were showing signs of failing. Two weeks of ill use and indifferent fodder had rendered some of them unfit to continue. The commanders would have some hard decisions to make when we met to plan the next moves.

Despite the fact that Colonel Campbell was now the nominal commander, we all continued to come together as soon as we had finished our evening rations, so that we could talk about the situation, and reach a consensus about what to do next. We were not an official army. Not a one of us could be compelled to do anything. We led our militias because the men trusted us. I hoped that trust was not misplaced. If we failed them it would be from misfortune, and not for want of effort or ability.

I threaded my way through the clumps of men huddled around campfires, spread out across the open ground like a field of stars.

As I passed through the Burke militia's campsites, I caught up with a wiry rustic-looking fellow who was wandering across the field, carrying a battered hat full of apples. He grinned at me, and held out the hat to offer me one.

"Thank you, no," I said. "But I am looking for Campbell. Can you tell me where to find him?"

The fellow gave me a beaming gap-toothed smile. "Why, you must have had a drop too much to drink, your lordship. There ain't no camels at all in these parts. Just horses and beeves. And an ox every now and again."

"Campbell," I said, a bit louder. "With the Virginia militia."

The fellow put his forefinger up to his temple, deep in cogitation. Then he shook his head sadly. "I never heard tell of no Virginia militia, sir. Now there's a Virginia McMillan over to Sherrill's Ford, and she's as purty as a speckled hen. 'Cept for her squint, of course. But she don't have no camel that I ever heard about. . . . Is you certain sure you don't want an apple, your worship?"

The poor man was a simpleton, probably brought along to camp by some of his relatives in the militia, I thought. I must find out whose company he is attached to, and make sure he is kept well in the rear of any encounter with the enemy. But right now, he was hindering my progress.

Swallowing my impatience, I pushed my way past him, determined to find Campbell's campsite for myself, but as I hurried along, he trailed after me, calling out jaunty comments that he apparently intended to be helpful. He was still dogging my steps when I reached the spot where the commanders had gathered for the evening conferral.

When McDowell looked up and caught sight of me, he smiled. "Welcome, Colonel Sevier. We were just talking of the need for a spy to help us locate Major Ferguson. One of our area officers, William Chronicle, recommended a local fellow. He says this man is able to get information out of Tory households without anyone ever being the wiser. We are just waiting to speak to him now."

A strong steady voice spoke up behind me. "Yes, sirs, I am here. Enoch Gilmer, at your service, Colonels."

I turned to find myself looking into the face of the simpleton with the hatful of apples. The look of vacant amiability was gone now, though, and I saw before me a calm and resolute young soldier, whose bearing spoke of intelligence and purpose. A hint of humor was alight in his brown eyes. He turned and gave me a cordial nod. "Care for an apple, Colonel Sevier?"

■ ■ ■ ■

Gilmer's cleverness in deceiving me gave my fellow commanders a much-needed moment of levity, and I did not begrudge them the chance to laugh at my expense, though I think that Colonel Cleveland is entirely too fond of such idle jests. A few nights ago, when he appeared at Campbell's tent for our nightly meeting, Campbell himself was waiting at the entrance to greet us, and Cleveland pretended to mistake the colonel himself for his half-caste servant, John Broddy. He clapped William Campbell on the back, and said, "Hello there, Jack! I know you are taking good care of your master's fine black horse. See you do as good a job of taking care of my own mount, for Roebuck is my pride and joy." Both Campbell and his manservant are tall and lean, but no one could mistake one for the other, not even in the deepest twilight. Cleveland was simply playing the fool, the jolly fat man people expect, but his size and girth ought to make people think not of a clown, but of a bear: Ben Cleveland can be just as quick and deadly when he is roused.

When we were all assembled in Campbell's tent, with Enoch Gilmer taking a place beside Andrew Hampton, Campbell summed up the situation for all present. "As you gentlemen know as well as I, we will be on the march to Ninety Six at first light. Williams has told us that Ferguson is encamped there, and so another two days should see us to the end of our quest, but before we meet him on the field of battle, we need more information. We need to know how many men Ferguson has, and whether he has had reinforcements from Cornwallis in Charlotte Town. Do you know this country, Gilmer?"

"No, sir, but I know country people well enough. And I'll get them to tell me more than they know — you see if I don't."

"I hope you will," said Campbell. "We need as much information as we can gather. Set out tomorrow and visit some farms along the way. See what you can glean from the inhabitants, but don't stray too far from us."

Gilmer nodded. "You won't see me, but I'll be around, sirs, and mostly out ahead of you, since one man can travel faster than an army. I'll be playing the rustic simpleton that deceived Colonel Sevier this evening." He gave me a rueful smile. "Begging your pardon, Colonel."

I smiled back. "I am honored to have been

shown a sample of your work."

"In keeping with my pose as a simpleton, I have thought of a signal that I could use to let you know when all is well up ahead. There is a jaunty song, well known and liked these days among the country folk for its many comical verses and lively tune. 'Barnie O'Linn,' it's called. Do you know it?"

Cleveland was already humming it, and McDowell's grin showed that he, too, was familiar with the song. Gilmer sang a verse of the song, in the clownish voice of his simpleton guise, so that the rest of us would recognize it when we heard it again.

"It's settled then," said William Campbell. "Good luck tomorrow, Mr. Gilmer. I hope you bring us a wealth of news."

Gilmer bade us good night, and exited the tent, leaving us to our evening conference. Once he had gone, we talked about the day's march, and commiserated with one another over the scarcity of the rations.

"We need to increase the sentries," said Andrew Hampton. "We don't know how close we are to the enemy, and they are notorious for night raids. We should post twice as many as usual, and change them every few hours, to make sure they stay alert."

He was right, and everyone nodded in

agreement. I thought, though, that he was thinking of his son Noah, murdered on the Pacolet for want of a few vigilant pickets standing guard. We were careful not to look at Joseph McDowell when we agreed, for no one wanted to make him feel that we were reproaching him for his brother's errors.

"Well reminded," said Campbell. "Thank you, Colonel Hampton. We will arrange for the posting of extra sentries at once. Have any of you other suggestions to make?"

"The hardships of this journey are taking their toll," I said. "The foot soldiers are tired, and some of the horses are nearly spent. I think we shall have to cull the ranks before we make the last push toward Ferguson."

"Surely we need all the men we've got for the battle," said Joseph Winston.

"No," said Shelby. "Exhausted men are no use to us." He looked around at the rest of the commanders for confirmation, and there was a murmured chorus of agreement.

"Colonel Shelby is right," said Campbell. "Now that we are within striking distance of Ferguson, speed is more important than numbers."

"Striking distance?" said Winston. "Ninety Six is a good two days' journey from here.

We could delay such a move until we are closer, if we must do it at all."

"No," said Shelby. "There have already been rumblings among some of the men. They are afraid that we are straying too far from the settlements over the mountain. Ferguson and the Tories are not our only enemies, you know. We also have to worry about Indian raids, and they may take advantage of our absence to attack. The men want to be only a few days away from home, in case the Indians do raid the settlements."

"Yes," I said. "If we cull the troops now, that will leave half our forces closer to home, and they can leave for the mountain settlements if we get word of an attack. I think we should divide the men now, before we head farther south."

"But suppose they're needed when we encounter Ferguson?" said Joseph Winston. He came from the Moravian communities more than two hundred miles west of the state capital, but still nearly a hundred miles shy of the mountains, so he had no worries about renegade Indians despoiling his home while he was gone.

"We have faced this sort of decision already," I told Winston. "On our way here, we slaughtered some of the cattle we had brought with us, and we sent some of the remaining beasts back home. Much as we needed the meat they would have provided, we could not confine ourselves to the leisurely pace they required, so we had to sacrifice them. It's the same now. We ought to choose the fittest soldiers and the freshest horses, and leave the rest in camp."

"This plan seems sensible to me," said Campbell, looking around at those present. "Does anyone object?"

No one did.

"Very well, then. We shall carry out the plan directly. Each commander should select the men from his own forces," Campbell said. "If we proceed with seven hundred or so of our most able men, we can increase our speed without sacrificing much of our strength."

"When shall we do this?" asked McDowell.

Campbell sighed, for we were all as tired and hungry as our men, but I knew the answer already. "Why, we must do it now, Major," he said. "This very night. Much as we would all like to rest and sleep before tomorrow's travels, we must do this now. We can leave some of our supplies here at Green River, with the men left behind to guard it. They can rest, and make themselves ready for the journey home — or perhaps for another run at Ferguson, if we should fail in our first attempt."

Ben Cleveland stood up, stifling a yawn. "Well, it's going to be a damned long night," he said.

We had come many miles that day in the heat of the Carolina plains, and we were too tired to linger for long after we reached our decision. I made my way back to my own camp, wanting nothing so much as to bed down near the fire with the rest of the Seviers, waiting for sunup, but instead I sent for Major Tipton, my brother Valentine, and the other officers, and told them the commanders' decision.

"Assemble the men," I said. "The commanders have agreed to select only the fittest men and the freshest horses to go forward from here. We need to inspect them all to see who would best be left here in camp. If any of them are sick or if any volunteer to stay behind, or have foot injuries or the like, then eliminate them first. And assign another officer to inspect the horse as well. No excess supplies — only what the men can carry, and rations only for a day or two. From here on out, we will be traveling light — and fast."

"I'll make a start on it now," said Tipton, hurrying away.

"How many men do you aim to take with you?" asked my brother Robert.

I considered it. "Perhaps a hundred, if we have that many soldiers fit enough to go forward."

"You're taking James, then?"

I hesitated, for in the rush of all the other concerns, the thought of leaving him behind had not occurred to me. "He is a bit young, I know, but he might be safer where we can keep an eye on him. He's been all right thus far, hasn't he? Not given you or Valentine any trouble?"

Robert smiled. "Well, not as much as Joseph would have you believe. I just wondered whether he might be safer left in camp."

I sighed. "If I could be sure of that, Bob, I reckon I could leave him with a glad heart, but it seems to me that he might be in just as much peril if we left him here, especially with all the commanders gone. Ferguson isn't the only enemy in these parts, you know. Some local band of Tories could swoop in after we've gone, and slaughter all those left behind."

"I don't believe they will, though, Jack. There'll still be an awful lot of soldiers left to put up a fight."

"I suppose you're right, but he's such a little rooster that I reckon we'd never hear the end of it if we left him behind. If his older brother is allowed to go, he'll insist on coming, too."

"Reckon he will." Robert laughed. "We'll have to take turns looking out for him then. We mustn't let his first adventure be his last."

"Look after the family, Bob, because I have my hands full with the rest of the militia from here on out. And get some sleep tonight if you can."

The other officers had hurried away to assemble the militia, and to get out the supplies so that we could decide what we could take with us. I spent a long chilly night making the final decisions about who should go, and what supplies we should take with us. Finally, with only a couple of hours left before first light, I finished my appointed tasks, and, exhausted into a stupor, I crawled under my blanket to get whatever rest I could in the little time before it was time to move out. When I closed my eyes, though, I could still see lines of men and horses shuffling past me, and I drifted off to sleep counting them as they went by.

■ ■ ■ ■

Despite the chill of the night air and the rumbling of my stomach, I fell into a sound sleep, but I did not linger long in that blessed oblivion, for an hour or so before daybreak one of the sentries shook me awake. Keeping his voice low, so as not to alarm the rest of the men, he said, "Colonel Sevier, you're needed at the camp of Colonel Campbell to meet with the other commanders."

I sat up at once, wide awake and cold with dread. "What has happened?" I whispered, straining to listen for sounds that something was amiss. "Are we under attack?"

"No, sir. Not yet, leastways. But the sentries have detained a rider. They're questioning him at Colonel Campbell's headquarters. Follow me, sir."

I woke Robert to let him know where I was going because I thought someone in our camp besides the sentries ought to be awake in case anything was wrong, and I didn't want the boys to worry if they woke to find me gone. Then with my blanket still about my shoulders, I hurried after the sentry, knowing that further questions would be useless, for he had probably told me all he knew.

They had built up the fire outside Campbell's tent, so that it was bright enough to illuminate the faces of the men gathered around it, and two stout logs were set on either side of the blaze, so that everyone could be seated while we conferred. The expressions of those already there ranged from bewilderment to anger, and all of them were looking in the direction of the one unfamiliar face. The stranger's expression was clear enough: he was sputtering with rage.

I could see that a blindfold was hanging loose about his neck, and, though his hands were not tied, a guard stood a few feet away from him, holding his rifle in the crook of his arm, and never taking his eyes off the prisoner.

"I am not a Tory spy!" the man was saying, probably not for the first time that night.

Ben Cleveland leaned in and fixed him with a menacing stare. "Why should we believe that? I hang Tories, you know."

"Well, you won't hang me. When I was a boy, an old gypsy woman told me that my death would come by drowning, so I've nothing to fear from you — or Ferguson, for that matter. Now stop blustering, and listen to what I am telling you."

"He says he is Colonel Edward Lacey of the South Carolina militia," said Campbell, for the benefit of those of us who had missed the conversation that transpired when the sentries first brought their prisoner to headquarters. "One of the officers of Colonel Sumter."

Cleveland scowled. "What does he mean sneaking up to camp in the dead of night then, all by himself?"

"I had a guide," Lacey said, nodding toward another man under guard. "I nearly shot him, too, for more than once I thought he had deliberately led me astray on the journey here. We had some difficulty in finding you, and that delayed us. But I rode thirty miles to find you — to warn you, blast it! And this is the thanks I get."

"Warn us of what?" said Campbell. "Are the Tories attacking?"

"Well, I haven't seen any. I come from a group of South Carolina militias who came out to join forces with you."

"Where are they, then?"

"Where I left them. Maybe twenty miles south. What I came to tell you is that you have been deceived, and that you are embarking on a wild goose chase in search of

Ferguson, for he isn't where you think he is!"

No one spoke for a moment, and I think we all wondered whether this fellow was a spy who had come to mislead us.

"We've already been told of the enemy's whereabouts," said Campbell. "General James Williams, also of the South Carolina militia, and with papers from the governor to prove it, sought us out at a godly hour yesterday morning. He informed us that Ferguson is camped in South Carolina at Ninety Six. We head there at first light."

The prisoner smiled. "Oh, yes. His precious Ninety Six. Was it only Major Ferguson he claimed to be there? Not Julius Caesar or Robert the Bruce?"

"What do you mean?" said Shelby.

The prisoner shook himself free of the guard, and sat down on the log next to Colonel Campbell. "Let me tell you about James Williams, gentlemen. The man is an utter scoundrel."

Ben Cleveland burst out, "What? Are you saying he is a Tory, then?"

"Oh, no. I'm not sure Williams takes any side except his own. But before I tell you exactly why he is sending you to Ninety Six, I should tell you a bit about his past. You have time before sunup to hear that tale."

"Go ahead then," said Campbell wearily. We all knew that it was too late now to try to get back to sleep, and one way or another we needed to know what this man had to tell us. If he was a spy attempting to deceive us, we would hang him at daybreak before we continued the march.

"Earlier this summer, I was under the command of Colonel Thomas Sumter, who was gathering his forces to combat Ferguson's invasion of the area. James Williams showed up at his camp, with no troops of his own, saying that he wished to do his part to resist the Loyalists, and so Sumter gave him the post of *commissionary*, which put him in charge of two dozen men and four wagons of supplies. Williams served ably enough in this capacity, but in mid-August, after the Battle of Hanging Rock, Sumter discovered that Williams had decamped without a word to anyone. A few men had left with him, and they had taken some of our militia's horses, supplies, and provisions. Stolen them, to be blunt."

"Why didn't you hang him?" asked Cleveland.

"What did he do with the supplies?" I put in before Lacey could answer, for I had heard nothing of this incident.

"I did not wait to find out. The instant we

realized what had happened, with Colonel Sumter's permission, I went after Williams myself," said Lacey. "I took a few men with me, and we trailed them to the banks of the Catawba, but Williams's forces outnumbered mine, so I decided against trying to take the militia's property back by force. Instead, I dismounted and asked Williams to take a walk with me, out of sight of his encampment. I was calm and civil, leading him to expect just a friendly discussion with a fellow officer. I steered him away from the others, out of earshot, talking of inconsequential matters. Then when I got the scoundrel off in the woods by himself, I drew my pistol and held it against his heart, and I told him that if he cried out or made a single move to summon help, I would shoot him where he stood. With that I proceeded to tell the thieving blackguard what I thought of his base and dishonorable conduct, and I demanded that he return the property he had stolen, and rejoin Sumter's forces at once."

"What did he say to that?" asked Campbell.

"Oh, he said he had hoped to use the supplies to defend his own territory, and he tried to pass it off as a misunderstanding. He said at once that he would return the stolen supplies, and that he would go back to Colonel Sumter with as many men as he could persuade to accompany him. But then he was looking down the barrel of my weapon, so what else could he say? I did not trust the man an inch, so I made him swear an oath to that effect, and then I released him."

"Did he keep his word and go back?" asked Campbell.

"No."

"James Williams joined us at Smith's Ford," said Joseph McDowell. "My brother's command. Williams said that he was anxious to return to Ninety Six, for he lives there, and that area has been much beleaguered by marauding Tories. He seemed to feel that he was doing a greater service to his neighbors by returning to fight for them than he would by staying with Sumter. My brother was heading to that destination also, but Colonel Sumter was not. Williams may have appropriated supplies from Sumter, but that public property and the troops who went with James Williams still contributed to our cause. There can be no doubt of that. They were put to the use for which they were intended — to combat the Loyalists."

Lacey scowled, and looked as if he were ready to make a biting rejoinder, but then

Isaac Shelby said, "James Williams and I fought together at Musgrove Mill. He acquitted himself well enough then. It was he who took the prisoners on to headquarters in Hillsborough."

"Yes, and he inveigled Governor Rutledge into making him a general on the strength of it, didn't he? I don't doubt he took credit for the entire battle. And do you know what he did next? He came sauntering into our camp, waving his new commission and informing Sumter that he now outranked him, and on the strength of that he would be taking command. Sumter and his officers refused to allow this, and Sumter rode off to consult with the governor himself about the matter."

"Leaving Williams in charge?" asked Joseph McDowell.

"Oh, no. He'd have found himself in an empty camp if he had tried that. Instead, he hunted up the governor of North Carolina, waved his magic commission under his nose, and got permission to raise one hundred mounted troops of his own from North Carolina. He was heading back to his home territory of Ninety Six when he encountered us. Colonel Hill and I are in charge, Sumter being still away conferring with Governor Rutledge. The governor promoted Thomas Sumter to brigadier general, but we didn't know it then. Williams, who had the papers at hand to prove his exalted rank, at once informed us that he was taking command on the strength of his being a general. We threw him out on his ear, and finally he agreed to join forces with us, but in command only of his own troops, not of the whole militia. We thought we had found a way to manage him, but then a courier arrived with the news that you Backwater Men were massing near McDowell's plantation, planning to hunt down Ferguson. That must have set him thinking."

"How did Williams find us?"

"Oh, the same way I did," said Lacey. "Colonel Charles McDowell stopped by our camp on Wednesday, on his way to Hillsborough. He told us that you were headed to Gilbert Town. It was easy enough to find you. People tend to notice when armies pass by."

While Lacey was regaling us with all this information, we were stealing glances at one another, wondering if this could possibly be true. Obviously either Lacey or Williams was a madman or perhaps a scoundrel, but we had to guess which one to trust. Finally, in carefully noncommittal tones, William

Campbell said, "And what about Williams's information regarding the whereabouts of Ferguson?"

Lacey smiled. "Oh, we know where Ferguson is headed — and it isn't to Ninety Six. Do you know why Williams told you to go there? Because that is his own home territory, and he means to defend it against his Tory neighbors, even if it costs us the war!"

"He assured us that we would find Ferguson there," said Cleveland.

"Well, you won't!" Lacey heaved a weary sigh, probably wondering how we could be so dense. "James Williams told you that lie simply to lure you to Ninety Six. Because some of his Tory neighbors are wealthy planters, and with your army to reinforce him, he hopes to help himself to everything they have. He said as much when he returned to our camp last evening. And I thought I'd better come to warn you."

"So he doesn't know where Ferguson is, then?" I asked Lacey. The squabbles of South Carolina's officers interested me a good deal less than the object of our quest.

"Oh, we know, all right. We had information about the movements of the 71st yesterday morning. An ancient gentleman from these parts, known to some of my men as a reliable patriot, tottered into our camp

349

yesterday, fresh from a visit to Major Patrick Ferguson himself. The old fellow had passed himself off as a staunch Loyalist, and on the strength of that, he got an audience with the major. Ferguson told him that he had sent word to General Cornwallis in Charlotte Town, asking that Bloody Ban Tarleton and his dragoons be sent out to serve as reinforcements for him. In the meantime, Ferguson said that he was heading back toward Charlotte Town, in hopes of meeting Tarleton on his way out, and he declared that he intended to find himself a likely looking hill and take possession of it, in case the battle should come to him." Lacey finished this recital with a decisive nod, and then he looked around the circle of faces before him, to gauge the effect of this news on his audience.

He saw our anger at having been deceived by that scoundrel Williams, and then expressions of resolve that, having at last been given the information that would put the enemy within our grasp, we must complete the mission with courage and dispatch. Above all, though, Lacey saw proof that his journey to warn us had not been in vain. After the ignominy of being hauled blindfolded into Campbell's tent, and subjected to a rude interrogation by suspicious strangers, at last we had come to believe him. He was forthright, knowledgeable, and he spoke with the authority of one accustomed to command. His explanation of James Williams's behavior made terrible sense.

Finally, Campbell spoke for all of us, echoing our thoughts. "But you are sure, Colonel Lacey — completely sure — that Ferguson is headed back toward Charlotte Town?"

Lacey nodded. "I know he is. Already he is southeast of where you are now, and you have a day or two at most to overtake him before he receives reinforcements from Cornwallis. There is no time to lose."

Joseph McDowell took out the crudely drawn map that had guided us on the latter part of our journey through the Catawba Valley and southward. "We must choose a place where your militias can meet up with us, surely by the end of the march tomorrow evening. The sooner we join forces, the better. Colonel Lacey, have you a suitable place in mind?"

"I do, sir," said Lacey, bending over the map. "There is a place that folk call the Cowpens, a large meadow with a number of pens for holding the cattle of the landowner, who is a Tory, by the way. If you want to help yourselves to some of the livestock while you are there, you should have no compunction about depriving the man of his cows. He has it coming."

"Beeves for the taking. Well, that's welcome news," said Cleveland, patting his ample belly. "I've been on field rations for so long now that my stomach thinks my throat's been cut. Can we make it there in a day?"

"Yes. It's just over the border into South Carolina, and then a few miles due east. I'll ride back to my encampment, and Colonel Hill and I will get our troops on the move by midday. We should reach the Cowpens by early evening. Once we are together, we can proceed east until we overtake Ferguson."

Stifling a yawn, Colonel Lacey stood up and stretched. "I thank you for your hospitality, gentlemen," he said, removing the blindfold from around his neck and handing it back to Campbell with a flourish. "I will head back now. I should reach our encampment by midmorning, and we will set out for the Cowpens at once. I know that my fellow commander Colonel Hill will be glad to see me. I borrowed his horse to make this journey."

Virginia Sal

We were up around Gilbert Town when he got word from some of the spies that there was an army of Backwater Men coming out of the hills, a-hunting us. I was there in his tent when the word came, but of course I had to look busy with the mending and act like I didn't hear nothing. I stole a glance at the major when no one was looking, and he seemed more surprised than scared. He curled his lip, and jerked his head up, like a horse on a tight rein, and he said, "Are they coming, by God? After I warned them to stay out of this?"

The rough-looking fellow who brought the news just nodded, and said, "You riled them up with that letter you wrote to Colonel Shelby."

The major smiled then, but it was a cold smile, without a spark of pleasure in it that I could see. "I am glad to hear it. I can make good use of this little invasion of theirs." He looked over at DePeyster, who had sat supper with him, while they talked about plans for the coming days. "Let us draw up a proclamation, DePeyster. If the frontier rabble is headed this way, we ought to warn the Carolina gentlefolk of their impending arrival. Write as I dictate."

He rattled off a string of words about how the lowland gentry ought to band together to fight off the frontier savages from over the mountains. He and Captain DePeyster laughed right smart when he said that the rabble would "piss upon them forever" if the plantation folk didn't stop them. I didn't laugh, though, especially when the major said he wanted fair copies made of the notice to be posted at stores and inns around the settlements. I thought those Backwater Men were likely to get hold of one of those notices, and it wouldn't sweeten their tempers any to read what he said about them. If they were already headed this way with blood in their eyes, I didn't see any point in stirring them up any more. I said as much to the major, after Captain DePeyster left and Elias Powell had scuttled away for the night.

"I know some of those mountain folk," I told him. "They're not long on forgiveness."

But he had been drinking with the captain,

and now he was too far into his cups to feel fear or prudence. He only laughed and said, "Let them come. If they want a fight, they shall have one. Here and now is as good a time as any."

"Reckon there'll be a battle?" I said, for I didn't much like the sound of being caught up in that.

"Oh, don't *fasht* yourself," he said, and I knew that to be one of his words from over the water that he used when the whiskey or some ghost of a memory took him back. He meant I wasn't to worry overmuch. "Tomorrow we shall begin to head back east again toward Charlotte Town. We ought to be able to get word to Lord Cornwallis before the Backwater Men can find us. So let them chase us. They will find themselves caught between Tarleton's dragoons and my good marksmen."

I shivered. "You've seen a deal of battles, haven't you?"

He smiled again. "A fair few. Not as many as you might suppose, given my score of years in the king's service."

"You were wounded, though," I said, touching the sleeve of his pinioned arm. "How?"

"That was some of your rebels' doing, my girl. A proper battle up in Pennsylvania, that was, not these little hole and corner skirmishes they have 'round here." He reached for me, and I knew he would rather use me to forget than to dwell on past sorrows, but battles were uppermost in my mind then, and I wanted to know, so, trusting the drink to keep him tame, I asked again.

He sighed, and I suppose he could easily have brushed it aside, but just then the dead white face of Virginia Paul appeared in the opening of the tent, and she said, "Yes, tell us about Brandywine."

She scooted inside, and curled up next to me, giving him a challenging stare, as if she dared him to summon up the memory. I don't suppose the son of a lord was afreerd of a servant girl, but the look he gave her is the one horses get before they bolt from a sudden fright.

He stared into the little candle flame then, and I don't think many heartbeats passed before the drink and the silence made him forget we were there. He spoke slowly at first, unfolding the memory, and I knew better than to make a sound, for that would have broken the spell.

"That was the last time they used my weapon," he said, as if that mattered more than his arm. "My beautiful breech-loader that could shoot farther and truer than any they had ever seen. They balked at the cost, of course — as if it wouldn't be worth more than those ancient Brown Besses they insisted on keeping! Tradition can be a prison as well as a fortress.

"But at least they gave me a thousand of my rifles, and the troops to use them. I thought I could show them. Why, I might have won this war for them, if I were not hamstrung by honor.

"There I was, the day before the battle was to begin, and I had gone off alone into the woods to practice my aim. I had not begun shooting yet, I recall, for that would have warned anyone else away. But I stood there, holding my namesake rifle, and suddenly, perhaps fifty yards away, the branches parted and a Continental officer rode into the clearing. He was as clear as a paper target in the dark blue of his uniform, astride a strapping gray that shone in the pale sunshine. And I remember thinking, *Now here is a proper target!* and I raised the weapon to the ready and drew a bead on the man. I could have felled him like a stag in the space of a heartbeat.

"But he looked back at me. Now I think if he had shown fear, or turned to flee, or reached for a weapon of his own, I would have taken the shot with the next breath I drew. But he only looked at me. And rebel that he was, there was bearing in his stance — so does a lord look at a chimney sweep. His lip curled, and in my head I heard all the words implicit in that stare. That the battle would not begin for yet another day . . . that I was a craven assassin to be thus concealed in the wood, instead of taking the field with honor like a gentleman . . . that he had no fear of the likes of me. . . . We held that stare between us for a long moment, and then he simply turned and rode away, showing his back to me, daring me to be such a coward as to shoot him thus. And I lowered my weapon and let him pass, thinking we would meet upon the field tomorrow.

"I never saw him, though, when there was a chance to remedy my clemency. I fell before the battle ended, with a musket ball shattering my elbow, and so I only glimpsed the man on the gray from far afield, as I lay there bleeding. It was the rebels' commander. Washington. And I might have ended their hopes for sovereignty there and then, if I had taken the shot. That was the last time I ever saw my rifles. I heard they were stored in a warehouse. God knows what became of them. Sometimes I think I am cursed."

I heard the bitterness in his voice. He looked down at his useless right arm, as if he wished it gone entirely.

"They wanted to cut it off, but I forbade it. What use is a one-armed soldier? So they sent me back to New York to recuperate, and they did what they could for the wound, which was mainly to bind it in place so that it stuck fast in this bent position. Well, I kept the limb."

As always, his arm was bent at the elbow and drawn up against his breast, quite useless. Had it been me, I would have left the army, I think, but Patrick Ferguson was not one to be dictated to, even by fate.

"I stayed there a year, and I taught myself to write and to wield a sword left-handed, and to use that remaining good arm for everything. I told them I was fit to command in the field again, but nobody wanted me in the northern command, so I was banished south to this godforsaken place to recruit Loyalists for the cause, while Banastre Tarleton piles up the military honors with his dragoons. I will show them, though; by God, I will. I will defeat these Backwater Men, and prove that there's more to commanding a regiment than having two good arms. God will give me a sign, so that I will know that victory is nigh."

He was mumbling by now, and his Scots burr thickened. He downed the last dram of his whiskey, and his eyes fluttered shut.

Virginia Paul touched my arm, and inclined her head toward the opening of the tent. I followed her out into the cold night air, and we slipped away, leaving the major to his dreams of past and future glory.

CHAPTER FIFTEEN
OCTOBER 6, 1780

By the time Edward Lacey had said his farewells and ridden away, the sky had lightened to that purple hue that signals the coming of daybreak. The night air was still cold, and I thought lorgingly of my feather bed back in my house over the mountain, and of Catherine, burrowed down under a pile of quilts, waiting for me to come home. No one would be getting any more sleep tonight. It was time to assemble the men chosen to go forward, and to make our way south to the rich Tory's cow pens. We reckoned we had twenty miles or so to go before we reached it, but we would travel faster now without so many foot soldiers to slow us down. We reckoned to be there before nightfall.

By the time Campbell, Cleveland, Winston, McDowell, Shelby, and I had finished culling the weak and weary from the ranks of our militias, we had about seven hundred men to make the last leg of our long journey. I was torn between wanting it all to be over and hoping for one more day so that we could all get some rest before we had to fight.

We were just finishing our morning rations, and getting ready to douse the campfires when the sentries called out that there were riders coming into camp. *Ferguson has brought the fight to us,* I thought, and the same idea must have pervaded the camp, for every man I saw was reaching for his rifle, and getting ready to make a stand against the enemy. No shots were fired, though, for before we could take any action, the message was relayed from sentries to officers across the field: *The riders were our allies, come to join us in our pursuit of Ferguson.*

While Major Tipton and my brother Valentine were keeping the men in order, I hurried away to join the other commanders and see if the newcomers had brought news as well as reinforcements. I found Joseph McDowell on his way to Campbell's encampment. "Who are these new arrivals?" I asked him. "Have you heard?"

"One of the sentries said he thought it might be Clarke."

We soon learned that it wasn't Clarke

himself, but some thirty of his men who had come to join us led by Colonel Graham, along with another two dozen troops under the command of Major William Chronicle, another Catawba Valley patriot.

"Well, that will swell the ranks," said Shelby, who had ridden up to see what was going on. "I feel better about leaving some of my ailing men now that we have fresh troops to replace them."

"Let your sick ones give their powder and their horses, if they have them, to the able-bodied men that are going with you," I said. "We need supplies and mounts as much as we need soldiers."

The march was delayed long enough for us to confer with Major Chronicle, and to let him know that we were meeting Hill and Lacey at the Cowpens this evening. Chronicle agreed to this plan, and ordered his men to join the rest of the militias. At last we were ready to resume the journey. The men who were well enough to fight, but who had no horses, were left behind under the command of a Wilkes County officer, Maj. Joseph Herndon. He was to bring these foot soldiers along in our wake, making as good a progress as they could.

The scouts rode out ahead of us to make sure that we didn't stumble into an ambush, and I saw Enoch Gilmer setting out on foot, with his hat pulled down over his ears, and a rolling gait that made him look like the rustic simpleton he was pretending to be. I hoped his disguise would serve him well, and would bring us news of Ferguson's whereabouts.

We had gone only a few miles when one of the scouts came galloping back up the trace, and headed for the clump of officers riding together. "Tories up ahead, sirs!" he called out. "A passel of 'em."

Shelby and I both looked at Campbell. It was hard to defer decisions to him when I was used to command myself, but so far I had no complaints about his judgment. He had not made any choices that I wouldn't have made myself.

"Is it Ferguson?" he said to the scout.

The fellow — one of Chronicle's men — shook his head. "Just locals as far as I can tell. But there's more'n a hundred, mounted and armed."

"Probably on their way to join up with Ferguson," said Shelby.

"How far from here?" said Campbell, still speaking to the scout.

The rider considered it. "Couple of miles, but down a different road. They look to be heading northeast, not south."

"Thank you, soldier," said Campbell. "You're dismissed. Ride on out again, and keep us apprised." When the scout was out of earshot, Campbell turned to us. "Well, gentlemen, is anybody spoiling for a fight?"

Shelby shook his head. "I reckon I am," he said, "but not at that price."

"It isn't Ferguson," I said. "We could attack them and win, but it would cost us powder and shot, and, above all, time. And if we stopped to fight them, word might get to Ferguson about our whereabouts, and we don't want to meet him until we have the South Carolina militias with us. At least, that's what I think. You asked for our opinion, Colonel Campbell. Well, there's mine."

William Campbell smiled. "Colonel Shelby, are you of the same mind?"

"I am, sir. Shall we ask the other commanders? I'd wager they'll tell you the same."

"Well, since you all put me in command, I needn't ask them," said Campbell. "As it happens, I agree with you. I think we would be wasting precious time if we allowed ourselves to be distracted by these local Tories. And every minute that passes increases the chances that Cornwallis will send Tarleton's dragoons to the aid of Major

Ferguson. We will fare better if we can catch him before that can happen. I say we ride on, and avoid the temptation of a lesser skirmish. Are we agreed, then?"

We nodded, and rode on for a while in silence. Making a decision is easier than living with it. Sometimes you don't find out until later whether or not you made the right choice, but I had to believe that we did act wisely, for second-guessing yourself only saps your courage and makes you slow to act. You decide, and you move on, and the devil take the hindmost.

The march went on without incident, although a few miles farther along, a scout again reported the presence of enemy troops in the area, but again we refused to be led into temptation, and we plodded on into South Carolina under gradually darkening skies and an insistent wind that turned over the leaves of the trees.

"It's going to rain," said Cleveland, who was riding beside me at the time. "My knee is aching, and that's always a sure sign that the weather is changing. Besides, the leaves are showing their undersides. Never fails."

I nodded. "We're on the move, though. Maybe the storm isn't going our way."

Cleveland looked up at the sky, an unbroken blanket of clouds stretching as far as we could see. "No matter which way we go, that storm will be there."

Chronicle's men knew the area well enough to guide us, and by late afternoon we heard the bawling of cattle, and we saw a wide green meadow ringed by trees and stock pens with cornfields stretching away to the river. We had reached the field of cow pens, belonging to Hiram Saunders, the wealthy Tory that Lacey had spoken of, but when we arrived neither the farm workers nor the owner himself was anywhere to be seen. Perhaps they had been warned that a large enemy force was approaching the land, and they had made themselves scarce. Better to lose a few of their cattle than to risk being harmed. We met with no resistance, and we set up camp in the great field without incident.

Once we had determined that the area was undefended and therefore safe for an encampment, we settled down on the grass to rest and to await the arrival of Lacey's militia. The men were hungry as well as tired, though. For most of a week we had lived on parched corn and whatever we could scavenge from the farms and forests along the way, so straightaway Campbell ordered some men to shoot a few of the cows so that we could have one good meal before we had to continue the journey. We also sent others to forage in the cornfield to get food for the horses.

Within the hour, the men had built campfires, and the wind carried the smell of roasting beef across the field. Just at twilight, Edward Lacey appeared with his militia and the troops of Colonel Hill, and trailing them at a remove of a couple of hundred yards were the men under the command of James Williams, the scoundrel who had tried to send us all the way to Ninety Six for his own benefit.

I had left my horse to graze near the river, and Isaac Shelby and I were stretching our legs by walking around the field, not so much inspecting the troops as encouraging them and assuring them that our quest would soon be over, for it was important to keep up their spirits. When we saw our reinforcements arrive, Shelby and I began to walk toward Campbell's campsite where all the commanders would soon confer, but we proceeded at a leisurely pace, because we had things to talk about between ourselves.

"We are now in the state of South Carolina," Shelby observed.

"I know it," I said. "Mighty warm here for October."

"Mighty warm," Shelby agreed. "And you also know that James Williams claims to have a commission from Governor Rutledge making him a general."

"Yes. He waves that paper around like a boy with a toy flag. What of it?"

Shelby waited a few moments before he answered. Finally he said, "Well, if Williams is a South Carolina general, and we are now in South Carolina, then according to military protocol, that means James Williams is entitled to be the commanding officer of this expedition, does it not?"

I turned the problem over in my mind, determined to find another solution. According to military protocol, that was indeed the correct answer, but to my mind it was by no means the *right* one. Choosing my words carefully, I said, "I think military protocol is beside the point, Shelby. We are not enlisted in the Continental Army. Our militias are made up of men who serve of their own free will, and because they trust the leader they have agreed to follow. If my men were ordered to follow that scoundrel Williams, I reckon they would all turn around and start for home, and I can't say that I would blame them!"

Shelby sighed. "And suppose he tries to

take over, which Lacey says he is known for doing?"

"We tell him that Colonel Campbell has been elected commander of our joint forces, and that Charles McDowell has been dispatched to Hillsborough to confer with General Gates. Until and unless McDowell returns with orders to the contrary from Gates, we will proceed as we have been — answering to Campbell."

"Fair enough," said Shelby. "That argument is sound and logical. I think we should pass the word to the other commanders so that they will all be prepared in case Williams tries to take over."

"Let's find them now," I said. "And with any luck we'll be out of South Carolina before the issue of Williams becomes a problem."

Just after nightfall, when all the commanders had come together for the customary strategy session, a misting rain began to soak the field, making the campfires sputter, and dampening the spirits of the weary soldiers.

"It will rain harder before it quits," said Ben Cleveland, peering up at the starless sky. "My knee tells me that."

Major McDowell laughed. "I wish your

knee would tell us where Ferguson is, Cleveland."

"I can tell you that, sir." A dark-haired man of about thirty had come up to the campfire. He walked with the rolling gait of one who is lame in one leg, and his clothes had the ragged look of beggars' garments. After twelve days of marching and sleeping rough, none of us was garbed like gentlemen, but even in our shabby midst he stood out.

When he announced that he knew the whereabouts of our quarry, we all turned to look at him, but before anyone else could speak, Major McDowell was on his feet, clasping the hand of the stranger, and bidding him welcome. Then he turned to the rest of us.

"Gentlemen, this is Joseph Kerr, a most able and valuable spy. Because of his bad leg, he was unable to serve in the militia, so he presented himself to my brother Charles, and offered his services as a gatherer of information. I am happy to vouch for him. We can trust anything he tells us about the enemy's movements."

Joseph Kerr nodded his thanks to McDowell. "Colonel Charles McDowell sent me to South Carolina to keep an eye on Lord Cornwallis a while back," he said.

"The general has crossed over into North Carolina, and set up headquarters in Charlotte Town, as I expect you know. So I have been watching Major Ferguson, who has spent the summer around Gilbert Town, for the most part. Now, though, he is making his way back to join Cornwallis. At noon today he was about fifteen miles northeast of here, having his midday meal at a plantation."

"Is he camping there?"

"No," said Kerr. "Ferguson was moving on closer to Charlotte Town later that afternoon. I talked to one of the servants at the big house and she claimed that, while she was serving dinner, she had heard the major say he wanted to find himself a big hill and dig into the top of it. If she was telling the truth, then he's going to stand and fight, reinforcements or no. If I were you, gentlemen, I'd try to catch him while he's still alone. I don't know how many men he has got with him now, but by all accounts, it's fewer than one and a half thousand."

Around the circle of faces, we looked at one another. "We must catch him," said Shelby. "We have almost as many soldiers as he does. If we can meet him on even terms, we can destroy him. But if we wait until Tarleton's dragoons join him, then we might be facing another rout like Camden. I would do anything to avoid that."

William Campbell looked up at the sky. The drizzle was steady now, and the night was growing colder. "It's dark," he said at last. "The men have come a dozen miles today, on little sleep, and their bellies are full for the first time in a week. Perhaps we should let them sleep tonight, and start off first thing in the morning."

"Daybreak won't come early," I said. "These low clouds will hold in the night for a long time."

Ben Cleveland wiped a trickle of rain off his cheek. "I can't see anybody getting much sleep tonight, boys. With no cover from this downpour, I think we'd be better off on the move instead of lying on the cold, hard ground getting soaked to the skin. I reckon the men would get up more tired than they were when they lay down."

Campbell looked at each one of us, waiting perhaps for someone to voice an objection, but no one did. A sleepless night in the rain seemed preferable to many more cold, wet nights in the wilderness as winter approached. Better to get it over with as quickly as possible and go home.

"All right," he said. "Though I hope the

men will be fit enough to fight after such a night as you propose to make them endure. Go and tell your men that we are breaking camp within the hour. The mounted troops can go first, and the foot soldiers can follow at their own pace."

"One more thing," said Joseph Kerr. "There's an encampment of Tories not more than four miles from here. Probably on their way to join Ferguson in the morning."

Campbell shook his head. "We passed several such groups on our way here this afternoon, and we decided then not to be distracted by these local Tories. We could fight until doomsday and never meet Ferguson if we went chasing every little nest of Tories in the area." He thought for a moment. "I suppose we'd better send someone to see about them, though." He turned to his orderly, the man that Ben Cleveland had playfully pretended to mistake for Campbell earlier in the week. "Please find Ensign Robert Campbell and ask him to come here." When the orderly had departed, Colonel Campbell turned back to us. "The ensign can form up a party of volunteers and see about these local Tories. When they have done that, they can rejoin us farther along. Anything else, gentlemen?"

We shook our heads.

"Then let us make ready. We will depart within the hour."

We made a sorry, sodden procession riding out of the cow pens' fields at nine that evening, with a cold autumn rain pelting down on us, and an overcast moonless night making our journey one long interval of stumbling through the dark. We rode mostly in silence, each man wrapped in his thoughts and his misery. We went slowly because we could not see far ahead, and if we followed the wrong trail, it would cost us time that we did not have to spare. We took off our hunting shirts and wrapped them around our rifles, for if we got a drenching in cold rain, at least we had done what we could to protect ourselves from the disaster of charging into battle with weapons that would not fire.

We would sacrifice everything for the chance to stop Ferguson — we had to. What did it matter if we were cold, hungry, footsore, and wet, compared to the prospect of losing the battle when it came? I had brought from home a company of men who trusted me to lead them well and see them safely back again. I had brought my brothers with me, and my two eldest sons, and their lives were in my hands as well. I knew what would happen if we fought Ferguson and lost. They would hang us for traitors, and then there would be no one left to protect our women and children from the Indian raids that would surely come, or from the invasion of Ferguson's regiment when he finally turned his attention to the land beyond the mountains.

If we lose the coming battle, everyone who depends on me will die. Dark thoughts indeed for a black night, but I needed to face that fact to strengthen my resolve. It had been my decision to force this fight — mine and Shelby's, though the others came along willingly enough — but now I was risking the lives of my sons and my brothers. There was no turning back, and they would scorn me if I tried to keep them out of the battle. We Seviers pride ourselves on never running away from trouble. *Huguenot.* The word rose unbidden in my mind. Yes, all right then, perhaps a century ago my ancestors the Xaviers did run to escape the persecution in France, but we are in a new world with a new name, and times are different now. There will be no running here.

As I rode along in the driving rain and the darkness, I had no recourse but prayer, trust in my comrades, and faith in our resolve.

We were heading toward the Broad River, some eighteen miles from where we had started, but there was no respite from the encompassing darkness, and on the narrow trace through deep woods, the militias became separated. Those who had become lost in the mists would have to push themselves even harder come daylight, in order to catch up with the rest.

Ten hours had passed while we picked our way along a broken trail awash with mud, and then the sky lightened to the color of pewter, and we could just make out the shapes of the trees around us, and then we could see the other riders on the road just ahead.

A messenger from Campbell's militia found me, and asked me to ride ahead so that all the commanders could confer without halting the procession. I threaded my way forward between the horsemen, until I reached the front, where Shelby, McDowell, and Cleveland were already gathered. It had been a hard night for all of us. Campbell's black horse was streaked with mud, and Cleveland's wet graying hair hung about his face like pond weeds.

"Before we left the cow pens, the spy Joseph Kerr told us that yesterday Major Ferguson was stopping at Tate's Plantation, and so we had intended to ford the river there," said Campbell. "But I have been thinking that there might be some danger in that plan. Ferguson may still be there, or he may have left some of his men behind to ambush us."

"There's another ford about a mile away," said Joseph McDowell. "We camped there with the Burke militia back in the summer. Cherokee Ford, it is called. I can take you there."

"How do we know that the Tories aren't waiting to ambush us there?" asked Shelby.

"We have a spy," said McDowell. "Let's make use of him. Enoch Gilmer can go ahead of us, and cross the river by himself, and let us know if it is safe to proceed."

Campbell turned to one of his young officers. "Find the man Gilmer. He is one of Major Chronicle's men. Ask him to come up."

"While we wait for the signal to proceed, we can have the men check their weapons and powder," said Cleveland. "I want to be sure we have working rifles before we need them."

"And we can send some of our best men

ahead to this side of the river," I said. "In case there are any enemy troops there, they can hold them back until the rest get there."

"Yes," said Campbell. "Time is short now. We must leave nothing to chance."

We kept riding, and presently Enoch Gilmer drew his horse up alongside mine. "Good morning, sirs. I believe you sent for me."

He was his ordinary self this morning, though wet and weary like the rest of us. I would not have known him from the rustic fellow he pretended to be when he offered me an apple at the Green River encampment.

"We have need of a scout," said Campbell. "We want you to ride on ahead of us, and cross the river. We're heading for Cherokee Ford, and you are to make sure that there are no Tories there waiting to ambush us. Give us a signal if the way is clear."

Gilmer nodded. "Reckon I can do that. Now for the signal. This is the time to use the Irish tune I told you about: 'Barnie O'Linn.' " To remind us, he sang a few lines of it. It was a jaunty, carefree air, and he sang it in a strong tenor that should carry a sufficient distance to serve well as a signal.

"Right, then," said Gilmer. "I'm off. Listen for my song before you approach the river and you'll be all right."

We watched him canter away, and then Shelby said, "Well, let's give him a few minutes to get there. This is the time for each of our militias to check their weapons."

We headed back to our respective troops, and oversaw the testing of the rifles. The rain had not stopped, but it would come and go as the clouds shifted above us. I saw not a patch of blue anywhere, though, and I feared that the storm would be with us throughout the day. The testing took only a few minutes, and then we headed off again, following McDowell to Cherokee Ford. By the time we were able to glimpse the river through a break in the trees, we could hear the lusty voice of Enoch Gilmer raised in song.

"Oo-oh, there once was a man name of Barnie O'Linn."

All clear.

The days of steady rain had swollen the river to a few feet higher than normal, but it stayed within its banks, and we made the crossing without any mishaps, losing no men or supplies in the endeavor. Once we were safely across the river, we found Gilmer waiting for the commanders in order to suggest his course of action for the morning, subject to our approval.

"If it suits you fellows," he said, slipping into his rustic persona, "I reckon I'll ride on ahead, and stay a ways apart from the rest of the bunch, until we find out exactly where Major Ferguson is keeping himself. Maybe I'll wander down a side road now and then to stop off at a farm, in case the folks there have any fresh news to impart about Ferguson. I reckon I'll tell them I'm an eager little Tory a-wanting to join up with his army, so they won't think they're making trouble by talking to me. And when I find out anything, I'll head on back and hunt you up."

"Good luck then," said Campbell.

We all wished him well, and Enoch Gilmer trotted off down the lane, singing another jaunty tune in a clear, carrying voice, as if he hadn't a care in the world.

We kept on going through the gray half-light of that dark morning, and the rain fell in sheets around us. They downpour hindered our progress, but we would have proceeded slowly anyhow, because we knew that Ferguson's army could be waiting for us around every bend.

Finally, we reached the farm of Peter Quinn, where, according to Joseph Kerr,

Major Ferguson's regiment had stopped yesterday at noon. As we expected, there was no sign of enemy soldiers now, so we kept on riding eastward, having now covered more than thirty miles since we set out from the Cowpens the night before. The men were hungry as well as tired, and as we rode past the fields of corn, nearly ready for harvest, some of them steered their mounts close to the rail fences, and pulled off ears of green corn, eating it as they rode.

I was riding close to Campbell in the front of the procession, trying to see the trail through the curtain of rain. I urged my horse nearer to his black gelding so that we could talk. "I don't see how we could fight in this weather," I said to him, as quietly as I could, so that the riders near us could not overhear.

His expression did not change. "I was thinking the same, Colonel Sevier," he murmured. "The men are tired, anyhow. Perhaps we could call a halt to the march, and see if the rain stops. If it doesn't, we could always wait one more day. Let's take it up with the others."

Colonels Cleveland and Shelby were within hailing distance behind us, for all the officers rode close to the head of the column, so we motioned them to come up, and

Campbell put the question to them.

"We have been more than ten hours in the saddle," said Campbell. "The men are exhausted, for they only rested an hour or two between the march to the Cowpens and the time we set out last night. The horses are nearly spent. And it is still raining steadily. Should we call a halt to see if the weather clears, and if not, postpone further pursuit? Or at the very least, give them rest for an hour or so?"

Before anyone else could offer an opinion, Isaac Shelby spoke up. "I speak for myself here, gentlemen. Whatever you decide I will not stop. By God, I will not stop until nightfall, not even if I end up following Ferguson all the way to Cornwallis's lines." He looked more like a hawk than ever with the rain dripping off his beak of a nose, and his black eyes snapping with anger and cold resolve. Shelby looked at us each in turn — Campbell, Cleveland, and myself — daring us to contest his decision, but no one said a word. A moment later, the silence still unbroken, we fell back into the usual formation, and the interminable march went on.

CHAPTER SIXTEEN
OCTOBER 7, 1780

Perhaps Shelby's declaration of steadfastness made our luck turn, for the rain began to fall more gently than before, and behind us to the west we could see a break in the clouds. The land here on the north side of the Broad River was gently rolling, but we were hemmed in by trees, making me long for the mountains back home where you could find a promontory and see the surrounding countryside for miles in the distance. Here, though, curtained off by pine woods, we scarcely knew what was around the bend. It gave me a prickly feeling, for I mislike surprises when I am soldiering.

We had not traveled more than another mile when we came to a little farm.

This territory was close to the home of Col. William Graham, commander of the local South Fork militia, and Campbell called him forward to see what he could tell us about the place's inhabitants.

"That is Solomon Beason's place," said Graham wearily. Either the wet night ride had taken its toll on him, or else he had eaten some of that green corn along the way.

"Can you tell us if this man Beason is a Whig or a Tory?" asked Campbell.

Graham managed a weak grin. "Well, sir, it depends on who's doing the asking. Some of my men have run across Old Beason before, and we reckon that he don't care who wins the war, so long as he personally doesn't lose anything by it. He tells us he's on our side, but when the Tories come through, I don't doubt that he sings the same tune to them."

"Cowards can be useful," said Cleveland. "They'll betray anyone to save themselves. Let's send a couple of men to put the fear of God in him. Ferguson must have passed this way, and this craven farmer is likely to tell us all he knows in order to get rid of us." He brightened as another thought struck him. "And if Beason doesn't inform on Ferguson, we could hang him to loosen the tongues of his neighbors."

Campbell shook his head. "We needn't harm the man, Colonel Cleveland. Time is short, and we have greater foes to contend with. Colonel Graham, instruct your men to question Beason, and not to come back without information about Ferguson."

A few moments later, half a dozen officers from Graham's militia peeled away from the column of riders, and cantered back toward the little farmhouse we had just passed. They could easily catch up with us when they had completed their task, for a few riders could move much faster along the narrow trace than our serpentine procession of hundreds. I glanced back and saw them pounding on the cabin door, and then they disappeared inside.

"It won't be long now," I murmured, and Shelby, who was riding closest to me, replied, "It has been long enough already."

We had not traveled more than half a mile or so, before two of Graham's officers returned, whooping, waving their hats, and urging their horses forward in order to reach the head of the column. They looked jubilant and unharmed, but immediately I looked back to see what had become of the other four riders who had gone with them to Beason's place. They, too, were heading up the road to join us, but their progress was slower because between them they were herding two prisoners, young men clad in farmers' garb, not military uniform, who shuffled and stumbled along, trying to avoid the hoofs of their captors' horses.

"Seven miles!" called out the first rider to reach us. "They talked, right enough. Beason and everybody we found there swears that the enemy is dug in on a little hill only seven miles east of here, and Beason says that Ferguson swore he wouldn't be moving from that spot."

The other rider had caught up with him now. "For good measure, sirs, we brung along two farmhands who know the lay of the land hereabouts. They're going to show us where Ferguson's holed up. Place called King's Mountain."

William Campbell nodded. "He must have taken the name as an omen. What better place for His Majesty's army to defend the royal holdings than on a mountain named in his honor."

The young officer laughed. "Yes, sir, except it isn't any such thing, begging your pardon, sir. I don't suppose Major Ferguson knows the rights of it, either, being a stranger in these parts, but one of our prisoners yonder told us that there little hill was named after a man by the name of Charles King who built himself a cabin at the base of it. So the place has nothing to do with King George at all."

Cleveland laughed. "There's his omen,

boys! Ferguson is in the wrong place, fighting on the wrong side, for the wrong reasons. Let's go show him the error of his ways."

"Bring the prisoners to the fore," said Campbell. "They can show us the way."

I went to join the Watauga boys farther back in the procession, so that I could tell them what we had just learned. We were barely out of sight of Beason's farm before we spotted another little cottage set back from the road in a little square of yard, bordered in autumn wildflowers, and fenced in to separate it from the adjoining cow pastures. A familiar sorrel mare was tied to the gatepost in front of the house.

One of my younger officers called out to his fellows, "Say, boys, don't that horse yonder belong to Enoch Gilmer, the spy feller?"

There was a chorus of agreement from the other riders. "Reckon he's trying to get some more news about Ferguson," said another. "He's a-claiming to be a Tory."

The first officer laughed. "What say we go and help him out with that?"

They all looked to me for permission to leave the column. For the first time in many days, their faces were alight with merriment, and so young — scarcely older than my Joseph. I was mindful, too, that within hours, we all would be going into battle, and chances were that not all of us would live to see the sun set. Knowing that I could not offer these brave boys any food, or even an hour's rest before the fighting, I could not bear to deny them this one last bit of fun.

"Go on then," I said, "but catch up with us as quick as you can."

They assured me that they would, and five of them wheeled and cantered off in the direction of the cottage in the flower garden. As we rounded a bend in the road, I glanced back and saw them pounding at the door, acting every inch the angry enemy soldiers.

We had gone perhaps another mile before, still laughing, the young officers caught up with the procession, and rejoined the ranks of our Watauga militia.

"You should have seen it, Colonel!" said the ringleader. "We pounded on the door, and purt near frightened the life out of them."

His comrade took up the tale. "When we got inside, there was Gilmer tucked up at the table, a-shoveling food in his mouth, fast as ever he could. And Will here hollered out, *'We have caught you, you damned scoundrel!'* Well, Gilmer knew who we were, of course, and he knew it was a jest right off. He played along with us without missing a beat."

I was not surprised. "Spies have to think on their feet," I told them. "Their lives depend upon it."

"Well, that Gilmer was a daisy, he was. He said scoundrel he may be, but he was the *king's* scoundrel, and proud of it. So after we swapped a few more insults with him, we took out a rope and threaded a noose in it. The sight of that sent the whole boiling of them into a frenzy."

"I draped that rope around Gilmer's neck," said the one called Will. "And quick as a flash, he commenced to hollering and crying, begging for his life. And the ladies who had been giving him dinner started bawling, too, pleading for us to spare him. It was all we could do not to laugh. I didn't dare look Gilmer in the eye, for fear that between us we would begin to giggle and give the game away."

"So, I told the ladies that on account of their delicate sensibilities, we would do them the kindness of killing the traitor elsewhere, so that his ghost should not disturb them by haunting their dwelling place. And with that, we half dragged and half carried him over the threshold and out the door. We set him up on his horse, with the rope still around his neck, and with the horse on a lead rein, we set off down the road, saying we were a-hunting a proper tree for the hanging. We could still hear them hollering for mercy from a quarter mile down the road."

"Of course, once we were out of sight, we shared a belly laugh and turned him loose. He's back a-riding with Major Chronicle's men now, unless he has set off again."

"Did Gilmer get anything out of his visit besides his dinner?" I asked.

"Yes, sir, Colonel. He sure did. Turns out that one of the younger women had taken a brace of chickens to Major Ferguson's cook this very morning. She told Gilmer that Ferguson had made camp on that King's Mountain we heard about already, but up on a ridge set between two creeks."

I nodded, and eased my horse out of line, heading again for the front. "Round up the other militia commanders and send them up to the head of the column," I told the nearest officer. "Did they say anything else about the place he's camped?"

The young man thought it over. "Just something about some hunters using that spot for a camp when they were deer hunting last fall."

"I know that place," said Maj. William Chronicle, when the leaders had come together to discuss this new information. "I was one of those deer hunters they talked about, and Captain Mattocks yonder was the other one. A year ago November it was when we pitched camp there. We hail from a place not too far from here — Armstrong's Ford, same as Colonel Graham. Let me go talk to Mattocks, and between us we will work out the best way to attack that position. We know it well."

When Chronicle veered off to consult with Captain Mattocks, the rest of us began to talk among ourselves about how to proceed against an enemy holed up on a hill above our position, but before we had got very far on the subject, someone pointed out a lone rider, galloping up the road toward us from the direction we had just come from. As he drew nearer, I saw that he was an old man, gap-toothed and balding, red-faced from the ride, and speckled brown from boot to chin with road dust. He looked too old and frail to have been part of a militia, so I reckoned he had been left behind to tend the farm for somebody.

He drew rein when he reached us, looked from one to the other of us, trying to decide who was in charge. When he finally managed to squeeze the message out of his throat between coughs, he had still not decided who outranked who, so he addressed us as a group. "Dispatch for Colonel William Graham, sirs."

Colonel Graham waved the man over, calling out to him, "Yes, Samuel, here I am. What is amiss?"

" 'Tis your wife, sir. She has commenced with the birthing of your child, and the women tending her think she is like to die. They've sent me to tell you to go home directly, Colonel."

The color drained from Colonel Graham's face. "My wife," he murmured. "It is our first child, and we knew there might be difficulties, but . . . dying! Are they sure? Oh, what should I do?" He had rightly addressed this last question to Colonel Campbell, who as chief commander of our makeshift army, had the temporary, but final say-so over each man's disposition.

Campbell seemed unmoved both by the news, and by Graham's distress at hearing it. "Why, I think you must stay, Colonel," he said calmly. "The women can get on with the business of birthing without a gentleman underfoot to hamper their efforts. Besides, babies take a long time to come, and this mission of ours will be over before sunset. Why, Graham, at the end of the battle, flush with victory, you may ride off home with a clear conscience and a light heart, and see about the state of your family. I'm sure you would be of no use at your wife's lying in, but once we are victorious, you can carry the good news to your lady wife. What a splendid gift that would be to reward her efforts in labor. You may each win a battle today."

Campbell's breezy suggestion did nothing to allay William Graham's fears for his wife's well-being. So distraught was he by the news that he scarcely seemed to heed Campbell's words at all. He simply kept saying, "But what if she dies in the birthing, and I am not there beside her? Surely, I must go to her. Oh, what am I to do?"

Campbell's face clouded over with impatience and annoyance, and it was evident that he did not like having his advice so blatantly ignored. He had no sympathy for Colonel Graham's domestic plight, and no time for any unforeseen distractions from the mission at hand. Campbell had given his opinion — that Graham should do his duty as a soldier, regardless of his personal concerns — but apparently he had not calculated that the poor man's agitation would render him all but useless for commanding his troops.

I wondered what I would have done in his place. My poor wife Sarah had passed away in the cold gray days of January, when the weapons of war are laid aside, in wait of better weather in which to fight. Thus, I was not called to be away from home, for Indian and Tory alike were likewise by their firesides, troubling no one in that bitter weather. I was with Sarah to the end, and followed her casket to the grave, comforting our weeping children for many days after their mother's passing. Nearly twenty years we had been man and wife, for I was a lad of sixteen in the great valley of Virginia when we married. What if I had been summoned to some not-too-distant battle, as my Sarah had lain fighting for her last breaths? Would I have gone with the militia, or stayed to comfort my dying wife? I was glad that Providence never tested me with such a sorrowful choice, but, after all, Graham's situation was not so dire. Women can and do die in childbirth, but mostly they don't. My Sarah survived it ten times, and from first to last I was never in such a frenzy with worry as Graham. I'm sure that Graham's working himself into a lather over the coming of a baby struck most of the older men present as a husband's foolishness borne of inexperience. If it were not for the fact that we had a battle to fight, I reckon we might have got him drunk to take his mind off his worries.

Ben Cleveland made a bearlike attempt at levity. "After all, Colonel Graham," he said, "your presence is not required at the end of the childbearing process — only at the beginning of it!" He slapped his thigh, and looked around for confirmation of his own wit.

Cleveland's remark drew grins from a few of us, but Graham would not be jollied or shamed out of his determination to go to his wife's bedside.

With a mighty scowl, Campbell called for Major Chronicle to come back into the group. When Chronicle had maneuvered his mount up near Colonel Campbell, the commander explained the situation with Graham's wife as succinctly and civilly as he could. Perhaps he meant for his account to be neutral, but there was no mistaking his impatience with this new difficulty. When Chronicle nodded that he understood the matter, Campbell stretched out his hand, inviting an answer, said, "Well, then, Major, what say you? Should your Colonel Graham be allowed to leave his post on account of women's business at home or should he not?" Campbell's expression and the mocking tone in his voice indicated that he expected only one answer to his question, but Major Chronicle was equal to the task of outstaring a Virginia gentleman, supreme commander or no. He took a long look at William Graham, and then turned a steady gaze back on Campbell. "Well, sir," said Chronicle. "Since you ask me, I say: let him go."

Campbell reddened, and for the duration of a thunderclap he kept silent. I thought he was biting back more harsh words on the subject, but finally he recovered his composure, and simply said, "Very well, Major Chronicle. Since you are acquainted with the terrain we are bound for, you may assume command of the militia in Colonel Graham's stead. And, Graham, you have leave to go attend to your ailing wife."

Having seen that there was some sort of commotion concerning Colonel Graham, several of the men of the South Fork militia, and one of Graham's officers, a German-born soldier named Frederick Hambright, had made their way up to the head of the column to investigate. They rode alongside, keeping a respectful distance, and listened in grave silence to the exchange between Campbell and Major Chronicle. They showed no emotion either on behalf of their leader or against him.

When the matter had been settled, Campbell motioned to Colonel Hambright and said, "I know that you outrank your fellow officer, Major Chronicle, but I am minded to put him in charge in Colonel Graham's place, because he is acquainted with this area. Indeed, he says he has camped at the very place where Ferguson is now entrenched to fight, and in that case his leadership may prove invaluable. Given these circumstances, Hambright, have you any objections to serving in battle today under young Major Chronicle?"

From the look of him, Frederick Hambright might well have had objections to being passed over for command in favor of William Chronicle, for in addition to Chronicle's inferior rank in the militia, he was no more than half the age of Hambright. A gray-haired man in his early fifties, Hambright seemed as fit as any of us, lean and wiry, with dark eyes and a countenance that spoke of wit and courage. If command had fallen to him instead of Chronicle, he would have acquitted himself well, I thought. But William Chronicle knew the mountain where Ferguson had chosen to take his stand, and that had decided the matter.

Many a man would jibe at being passed over in favor of a mere youth, even had their military ranks been equal. Many a man would have insisted on his well-earned rights, which were undeniable. But fortunately for all of us, Frederick Hambright was not the sort of thin-skinned man who would put his pride above his duty. Perhaps, too, he was mindful that the preferment of Chronicle over him would end at the close of day, for after the battle the separate militias would disperse, and Campbell's appointments of expediency would no longer matter to anyone.

Would the elder colonel object to serving under Major Chronicle?

"No, sir," said Hambright, his strong German accent barely discernible in that brief reply. "I do not object. Chronicle must lead."

"Good man," said Campbell. "Then you will assume the duties previously carried out by Major Chronicle, and Colonel Graham may go home to his wife."

William Graham looked no less agitated than he had before, and, indeed, in deciding on whether to stay or go, the poor man could only choose between two wrong answers, but now the choice had been made, and he must live with it. He turned to Major Chronicle, not to offer words of advice for the coming battle, but still preoccupied with his own troubles: "I must have an escort, Major."

"Granted," said Chronicle. "But you must choose one yourself, Colonel Graham. I won't order any man to go with you."

Graham looked back at the men from his militia who had come up to lend their support at the first sign of trouble. "I want David Dickey to accompany me, then."

At the sound of his name on the colonel's lips, the young soldier looked aghast, and then scornful. "Go with you, sir? Why, I'd as lief die in the coming battle as to desert my fellows and hightail it home with you and miss the fight."

"You must go, Dave," said his new commander, Major Chronicle.

Dickey spit on the ground. "Naw. Y'all can shoot me right here on the spot. I ain't going with him and miss this battle."

"You must go," Chronicle said again. He was more forceful this time, for this was his first order as the South Fork's commander.

Dickey was silent for a moment, returning

400

the major's stare, and then he looked away, shrugging. "Well, sir, if it is your order that I depart with Colonel Graham, then I reckon it is my duty to obey you."

"We must hurry!" said Graham, whose thoughts now concerned only his wife.

With one last regretful look at the column of soldiers, David Dickey raised a hand in valediction, turned his horse, and rode off into the woods after Graham. In a few moments they had disappeared from sight.

William Chronicle shook his head as if to clear all thoughts of the incident from his mind. He had more weighty matters to concern him now. He turned back to Campbell. "Captain Mattocks and I have been talking about that deer camp we had last fall up on King's Mountain. If that's where Ferguson is holed up, we could surround him. He's up on a narrow, flat place, a few hundred feet above the valley, so we would have to attack uphill, but that may be a stroke of good fortune. I reckon we'd be less likely to shoot each other that way. And if we do have enough troops to encircle that ridge, Ferguson would be caught up on that plateau with nowhere to go."

We were all silent for a moment, waiting, I suppose, to see if anyone could come up with any objection to this plan, and also in deference to Campbell, who had the final say. I looked around at the riders nearest me — Campbell, Shelby, Cleveland, McDowell, Winston — and to a man they were all smiling and nodding in agreement with Major Chronicle's suggestion.

"There are seven hundred of us in all, I judge," Campbell said. "Would you think that to be sufficient numbers to surround that ridge?"

"Yes, sir," said Major Chronicle. "To the best of my recollection of the place, I believe it would." He looked to his friend Captain Mattocks for confirmation, and received a slight nod from that young man in return.

"So you are agreed then?" said Campbell, looking from one to the other. "Good. We will plan accordingly. Let's divide the militias into three groups and surround the encampment."

It wouldn't be long now. We knew where we were going. And we knew how we would launch the attack once we arrived. Now there were only a few miles to cover, a little time for a silent prayer in the saddle, before we could accomplish what we set out to do, and then, God willing, we would go home.

When the newly appointed leader of Graham's militia had taken his officers and rejoined his men, no doubt to explain to them what had transpired, Joseph McDowell, who happened to be riding alongside me at that point, leaned over and said in confidential tones, "After seeing what just transpired, I expect you must think William Graham a coward, Colonel Sevier. He is devoted to his wife, and indeed I hope that heaven will spare her to be with him for many more years, but, for those of us who know him, Graham's courage is not in doubt. He was at Thicketty Fort with my brother's troops, and he acquitted himself well. I don't know, though, that we won't be better off in the end by having Major Chronicle take over his command, since he has camped at the very spot where Ferguson is now dug in. It may be that Graham's leaving is a blessing in disguise."

I thought that the leaving of Joseph McDowell's brother had been another such blessing in disguise for us, but I was not so uncivil as to say so. I smiled my thanks and rode on, content for the moment to commune with my thoughts.

"Look!" someone called out. "It has stopped raining."

We had been too preoccupied to notice, but now the sudden appearance of blue sky and autumn sunshine seemed like an omen, a celestial blessing upon our mission. At least, I hoped it was.

I kept thinking that in a few more bends in
the trail, the site of Ferguson's encampment
would be before us: King's Mountain,
whose name Major Ferguson had report-
edly taken for his own omen of good fortune. Major Chronicle and his South Fork
men had moved to the head of the column,
and we were proceeding under his direction. But though I looked upward to the left
and right of us, scanning what horizon I
could see, there was no peak rising above
the level of the surrounding terrain.

"Where is it?" I said to no one in particular. "I can't see a mountain."

"It's just a long ridge," said Joseph Mc-
Dowell. "I've been in these parts before.
After the mountains you're accustomed to,
this one won't look like much."

I nodded. Anyone from the Watauga settlement would scoff at hearing this little ridge
being called a mountain, for compared to
the mighty Roan, from which you can look
down upon the clouds, it was a sorry excuse
for one.

"Even if you could see it from here,"
McDowell was saying, "that little bump on
the landscape is more molehill than mountain. The long low ridge is perhaps three

miles long, and oriented northeast to south-west. But it is thickly forested, like the mountains you are accustomed to."

I considered the terrain in the light of my years of wilderness fighting. From McDow-ell's description, the thing sounded like a giant razorback hog asleep between two val-leys. So Ferguson was ensconced on a nar-row little summit, was he? And he thought he was safe? Well, it didn't look like it would turn out to be much of a climb for mountain soldiers. A couple of minutes would prob-ably see you to the top of it. And I would thank Providence for every single one of the trees growing along the entire length and height of the ridge. We would ascend that sorry little mountain, wherever it was, Indian style, darting from tree to tree, protected from enemy fire, while the Tories were on a flat open space above with no-where to run to. I hoped Major Ferguson liked his choice of battlefield as well as I did, and I could not resist remarking to Major McDowell: "Well, if the hill you describe is the king's *mountain,* then I reckon the king's *ocean* must be a mill-pond."

Joseph McDowell smiled, but before he could reply, we noticed a commotion going on ahead of us. No one made much noise, for Chronicle reckoned we were now about two miles from the site of his old hunting camp, close enough to the enemy's position to worry about being detected, but we saw that one lone rider, who had been heading down from the mountain, had been surrounded by men of the South Fork militia, and though the horseman had tried mightily to elude them, one of the men had grabbed the reins, and several others managed to pull the struggling rider out of the saddle.

"He looks about the age of my James," I said, trying to peer around the riders in front of me to see what was happening. I said to McDowell, "So it isn't Ferguson, nor even one of his officers. Still, if he has been up on the ridge he probably knows something worth hearing. I think we should find out what it is."

I wouldn't horn in on the capture, for Chronicle's men were all local to this area, and chances were good that they knew the prisoner and could get more out of him than a stranger. But if they did get him to part with any information, I wanted to be privy to it. I saw that Shelby and Winston had the same thought, for they, too, were approaching the head of the column. Frederick Hambright and several of the South

Fork men had taken the captured boy to the edge of the trail, and, judging by the sullen and tearful look on the face of the prisoner, they were not taking no for an answer.

After a few minutes, Chronicle's hunting companion, Captain Mattocks left the group around the prisoner and came to tell us what they had learned.

"That there's John Ponder, sirs," said Mattocks, nodding toward the prisoner. "Ponders are thick on the ground hereabouts, but Colonel Hambright recognized this particular one, and said that since this lad's older brother is an infamous Tory scoundrel, he figured this one was just as bad."

"Did he tell you anything?" said Shelby.

"Oh, he is a goose laying golden eggs, sirs. We searched his pockets, first thing. Why, he was headed for Charlotte Town, carrying a dispatch from Major Ferguson to Lord Cornwallis himself."

"I suppose Ferguson is asking for reinforcements and supplies," I said. "I would, in his place."

"Well, it's too late for him to get any," said Mattocks. "But yesterday our spy Joseph Kerr said he didn't think any were being sent. There's a rumor abroad that Bloody

Ban Tarleton is ailing, and cannot leave Charlotte Town."

"Probably choked on his own venom," said McDowell.

Major McDowell's bitterness toward Tarleton meant that he was thinking of the battle in the Waxhaws back in May, when Tarleton's dragoons caught up with the retreating forces under Abraham Buford of Virginia, and cut them to pieces. It was not so much the defeat that rankled — our side had lost its share of battles before and since — but Banastre Tarleton's refusal to give quarter to those who tried to surrender was an act of barbarism that shocked even those of us who were Indian fighters. Those who did survive said that while the wounded lay helpless on the ground, crying out for water, Tarleton's dragoons crisscrossed the field, running their bayonets through the bodies of the fallen. Their testimony had spread throughout the southern militias, and the shock and outrage at this tale of savagery had spurred us on to greater efforts against the enemy.

"I wish Banastre Tarleton was up on that hill," said McDowell, "but for the fact that his presence might tip the odds against us."

"Well, it's good to know that he isn't there," I said. "Our numbers should be about even without him."

I turned back to Captain Mattocks. "So Tarleton is still at headquarters. Did General Cornwallis send anyone else to reinforce Ferguson?"

"Ponder says not. He even reckons some of the men Ferguson had to begin with have begun to slip away."

McDowell and I exchanged glances. "Heard we were coming," he muttered.

"There was one other thing," said Captain Mattocks. "Major Chronicle wanted us to pass this information on to all the men. The Ponder boy told us what Ferguson is wearing so that we'll be able to pick him out in the battle."

"Isn't he in the regulation uniform?" asked McDowell. "I should think that a Redcoat would be easy enough to spot."

"So it would," said Mattocks, "only Major Ferguson has put on a long red-checkered hunting shirt over the top of his uniform. You need to look for a man on horseback wearing that red-and-white-checked hunting shirt. That's your target." Mattocks touched a finger to his hat by way of valediction. "By your leave, sirs, I'm going off now to tell the other commanders." Barely pausing long enough to hear our thanks, Captain Mattocks headed for the back of the column to deliver his message.

Joseph McDowell was looking up at the beginning of a forested ridge stretching out before us. "Less than a mile, by my reckoning," he said. "It won't be long now."

I glanced up at the sky. The storm had well and truly passed on, and the sky was still the deep blue of the best autumn days, with the warm afternoon sun beaming down on us as we rode. There was nothing now to keep us from completing our mission: we had information on the enemy's position and strength; a sound plan of attack from local men who knew the terrain; and clement weather in which to do battle.

The hour was at hand.

CHAPTER SEVENTEEN
OCTOBER 7, 1780

When we were still half a mile from the tree-less plateau where Ferguson had made his camp, our procession halted. Horses would do us no good in the ascent of a steep and rocky hillside, and they had earned a rest, anyhow. We ordered the men to tether them a little away from the trace. There was little else to leave behind, for we had made the last leg of the journey without provisions. We had only our weapons and the powder and shot to fire them. Ferguson, we had heard, traveled with a score of baggage wagons. A few miles back I had wondered aloud what he kept in them, and solemnly Isaac Shelby replied, "Why, enough provisions to last him the rest of his life." Owing to my utter exhaustion, we were another hundred yards farther along before the ominous meaning of his words struck me.

I would keep my horse, as would the other commanders, for we could more easily be seen by our men if we were on horseback. As the other Seviers tied up their mounts with the rest, I turned to my youngest boy. "James, you will stay here with the others who are minding the horses."

He gaped in astonishment. "But, Daddy, you said I could come!"

"And so you have, son, but this is as far as you go. When the fighting is over we'll come back for you."

James scowled at his brother, his eyes red-rimmed now with tears of vexation. "What about Joseph? Is he staying, too?"

I glanced at Joseph, suddenly tempted to keep him safe as well, but he was two years older than James, older than I had been when I married his mother. As a father I might wish to protect him, but as his commanding officer, I could not justify it. He could shoot as well as anyone, and he was old enough to do a man's job. "No," I said. "Joseph is eighteen. He will come with us."

James looked as if he wanted to contest the matter further, but I was giving him a stare that brooked no argument, and Robert ruffled his hair, and said gently, "You are a soldier now, James. It is your duty to obey an officer's order without question. And mind you look after my horses particularly, nephew, for I am too tired to walk home."

The sun had begun to tilt downward, the beginning of its slide toward an early autumn sunset. It was just before three o'clock then. We began our preparations for the battle. Our concerted intention was to surround that hill of Ferguson's, but, according to Chronicle and Mattocks, the thing was shaped like a washerwoman's battling stick — long and narrow — which meant that some of the militias had farther to go than others to take up their positions. We ordered the men to check their weapons yet again, for the early part of our morning journey had been through a steady rain. The old priming had to be cleared from the pan of each weapon, and new priming put in. The men examined their bullets, and many of them stuffed four or five of the bullets into their mouths, a trick learned in previous battles. Having the bullets so readily to hand made it easier to reload the weapon quickly, and some fellows even claimed that a mouthful of bullets kept them from getting thirsty, but in all the skirmishes I've ever been in, with Indian and Tory alike, I cannot say that I ever had a moment to spare to think of hunger, thirst, or relieving myself. Sometimes it is as if you are sleep-walking: you see things happening, and you are moving and firing and reloading, but it's as if you are watching it from somewhere outside yourself. Perhaps that feeling kept me from being afraid. I would only come back to feeling in my own skin when the danger was past; until then, I felt no bodily needs, not even the pain of a wound. There may have been men who did not experience battle that way, but perhaps they did not survive, while I lived through the dangers without feeling fear or pity, or even anger, and I was satisfied with my lot.

One last bit of preparation: a sign so that each man could show which side he was fighting for. There were likely to be some regular army troops in Ferguson's com-mand, but the majority of his men were lo-cal Tory volunteers, and they would be dressed same as we were — like hunters or Indian fighters, in buckskins or homespun shirts and leggings. It would be easy enough to mistake the enemy for one of our own, or the other way around. We had heard that the Tories generally put a sprig of pine bough in their hats to mark them as Loyal-ists to the Crown. There was nothing out growing — no wildflower or colored autumn leaf — that would supply the many hundred men in our command, so we settled on a bit of ordinary paper, stuck into each man's hat band, as our symbol.

As an extra precaution, because we were a citizen army lacking recognizable uniforms, we agreed upon a countersign that could be called out if a man needed to identify himself to someone from another militia and prove they were on the same side. The countersign we chose was "Buford," in memory of the Virginia commander whose men were slaughtered at the Waxhaws. Today we aimed to avenge them. Because of that, "Buford" was more than a code word: it was a battle cry. It reminded us not only of our reasons for fighting, but also of the consequences of losing.

Almost in silence, we formed ourselves into battle lines, mindful of our proximity to the enemy. This time there were no public prayers to consecrate the mission, as there had been for us at the outset at the Sycamore Shoals mustering, and none of the commanders made any rousing speeches, as Cleveland had done on the day after we left Quaker Meadows. Every man was now alone with his thoughts. I remember patting Joseph on the shoulder and shaking hands with my brother Robert as we walked away from the tethered horses. In hasty whispers we wished one another Godspeed, and then the preliminaries were done with, and we got on with the business at hand.

The commanders had discussed our plan of attack back when we received the information from the spy Enoch Gilmer about the whereabouts of Ferguson.

As agreed, we now divided our troops into four columns, each heading for a different portion of the ridge. My Watauga men were in the far right column, behind the Burke County militia, commanded by Major McDowell. We were heading for different points on the west-southwestern end of the ridge, and when we reached the summit, my troops would be positioned between the militias of Isaac Shelby and William Campbell.

According to Major Chronicle's recollection of his deer camp on that ridge, the western slope was the gentler incline, so we should have an easier time climbing up, but if Ferguson had a grain of sense, he'd be expecting the attack to come from that quarter, so it would be the most heavily defended area.

Benjamin Cleveland headed the column bound for the northern flank of the ridge, nearest to Ferguson's encampment, and the troops of Lacey and Hawthorn went with him. So did the ragtag band of men led by that scoundrel James Williams. They had trailed us from the Cowpens, keeping a little back from the rest of the column, but nonetheless with us. The rest of us didn't pay him much mind, after his antics earlier in the week of trying to send us on a wild goose chase to Ninety Six, and of attempting to take over Hill's command. Williams was not included in the discussions with the other commanders, but, although we made our disapproval obvious, we allowed him to accompany us to King's Mountain. We needed all the soldiers we could get, even from the likes of him, and, as far as I knew, no one had ever faulted his courage or his fighting spirit. So Williams led his men to the north flank of the ridge, to occupy a position between the forces of Shelby and those of Cleveland, Lacey, and Hawthorn.

Major Chronicle and the South Fork men and Major Winston's troops headed out before the rest of us, because they were headed for the northeastern end of the ridge, both the steepest and the farthest point away from our current position. Before they set out, some of our scouts had preceded them, creeping up toward the ridge, Indian style, to remove Ferguson's first line of defense: the pickets posted around the base of the King's Mountain plateau. If all went as planned, the scouts would sneak up on the unsuspecting sentries and dispatch them with a quick knife thrust to the vitals. We aimed to get as close as possible to Ferguson's camp before he knew we were coming.

It almost worked, but one of the last pickets must have managed to spot the scouts approaching him through the underbrush, and before they could reach him, he fired off a shot. Up on the ridge, Ferguson's men heard it and were forewarned.

The drums began to rumble.

We had lost the element of surprise.

VIRGINIA SAL

The attack had come. My heart was beating in time with the drums, and in the distance I could hear the whoops and yells of the rebel soldiers coming ever nearer.

The major had been mightily pleased the day he spotted this table of a hill. When they told him that it was called "the King's Mountain," he thought God himself was smiling down upon his mission and would deliver him and his regiment safely from the Backwater Men. In his certainty he was jubilant.

I hoped he was right. I'll allow that the major knows more about waging war than the likes of me, and, being the son of a lord, likely he is closer to Our Lord and Father as well. But I felt no joy in what he took as a sign from Providence. That feeling of summer's ending had never left me, and now I shivered even when the sun was blazing overhead.

Virginia Paul took no notice of anybody's sentiments, sharing neither the major's confidence nor my own misgivings. She glided about the new encampment, smiling her cat-in-the-cream-jug smile, and doing the officers' bidding, as if we were safely tucked in Charlotte Town, instead of camped on some godforsaken hill, with a ragtag army coming at us. Sometimes I heard her voice wafting up the hill from the little stream below, singing a queer tuneless air with words I could not make sense of.

"What do you reckon?" I'd asked her last evening, as we stared into the firelight. We knew that the rebels were coming. The major was alone in his tent, writing yet another dispatch to Lord Cornwallis, asking again for reinforcements, so we had the night and his campfire to ourselves.

Beside me, Virginia Paul kept humming her strange little tune for so long that I thought she had not heard me, but at last she said, "Well, girl, I told you what I thought a long time ago, did I not? I gave you the good and the bad, depending on how you take it."

I harked back to the talks we'd had over the summer, mostly while we were washing the major's linen in a forest stream. *You'll never pass a day of winter cold or hungry . . .*

You and the major will be together forever . . .
I looked up at her then, and she was no longer smiling.

"I won't see another winter, will I?" I whispered.

"You made your choice a good while back. You chose him. . . ."

I opened my mouth to say that I repented of it, but the words stuck in my throat. He would never have stayed with me, but I had chosen him, and what was there for me if I left him now? *A life of toil on a clay dirt farm, with a brute of a husband, and never quite enough to eat? Old at thirty, dead at forty, forgotten a week after my burying. Worth living for?* I fingered the green glass beads around my neck, and shook my head.

She answered me as if I had spoken my thoughts aloud. "So you know," she said. "Yes. I told you once: there are worse things than dying."

Now, in what had been a peaceful afternoon, the drums were rumbling and the rebels were upon us. I caught sight of the major, but he had no time for me. Elias Powell held the white horse while the major, clad in his checkered hunting shirt, hoisted himself in the saddle, always a painful thing to watch on account of his useless arm. He put the silver whistle to his lips, and rode off toward the red-coated regulars.

I looked around me, trying to block out the noises, so that I could think on what to do next. The piddling hill had become an ants' nest of activity, with the regulars and the local Tories scurrying first one way and then another, trying to hear the officers' commands over the din of the drums and the echoing yells from below.

Suddenly Virginia Paul was beside me, wrapped in her black shawl, but as serene and unruffled as ever. I wondered if she were deaf or mad to ignore the chaos about us, but her eerie calm made me turn to her for help. Grabbing her arm, I said, "What must I do? Tell me!"

She made to answer me, but then she shook her head.

"What will you do, then?"

Virginia Paul shrugged. "Oh, I'm away down the hill in a moment. There'll be no more work for us here, Sal. It is done, and you are free."

"But should I hide, or take up a musket, or run with you?"

She made no answer, but she embraced me quickly, humming in my ear her strange sad song. She hurried away toward the southeastern slope of the King's Mountain.

I watched her disappear over the brow of the hill, and then I heard the roar of the guns and the answering volleys from below, and the soldiers were enveloped in the smoke from the guns, and I stood alone.

My courage failed me then, and when I saw the first of the rebels scrambling up to gain the hill, I turned to run. I felt a sharp pain in my breast — no worse than the sting of a wasp, and then — nothing.

CHAPTER EIGHTEEN
3:00 P.M. OCTOBER 7, 1780

As we advanced toward the slopes of the mountain, we heard the roll of drums continuing to echo from the heights, and then the shrill sound of a whistle, blown in long blasts and then short ones, as if signals were being given. We had no time to consider any of this, though. With the enemy alerted to our presence, we had no time to spare.

Somewhere off to my left, I heard Shelby shout out, "Let every man be his own officer! Do not wait for orders, but . . ."

Then I raised my rifle and aimed it in the direction of the summit.

The attack began.

On the edge of the ridge above us, a line of troops with scarlet coats banded in green appeared. I was right about Ferguson's defense: knowing that this was the lowest and most vulnerable side of the encampment, he had positioned his best men

424

nearby in readiness. From the look of their uniforms, these men were regular army, and likely better trained than the local recruits. We could see them at the summit, standing out clear and bright from the surrounding greenery and silhouetted against the blue sky. Near them rode a boyish-looking Redcoat officer, waving a sword. It was not Ferguson, though, for this man wore no hunting shirt, only his green-trimmed scarlet uniform. The soldiers he commanded would be carrying regulation Brown Bess muskets, fitted with bayonets. Perhaps these soldiers had come south with Ferguson himself. Certainly, these were the troops that he would value most highly, for they were entrusted with the initial defense of his position.

We were not expected to get past them.

These defenders began to fire downward, mostly at Shelby's approaching men who were more directly in their line of sight, but their volley was not returned by Shelby's men. Because the men were not yet in their assigned place, Shelby would have ordered them to hold their fire a while longer. Many a leader would have lost his head at the first sign of enemy fire and cast the prearranged strategy to the winds, but Isaac Shelby was a brave man and a seasoned fighter, and he would not let the enemy dictate his moves or rush him into recklessness.

Our men kept climbing up the ridge, tree to rock to tree, and the firing from above went on, unanswered. From what I could see, though, the Tories' volleys were availing them nothing, for none of Shelby's men fell, and all seemed well around me. Ferguson's men were aiming too high. If those regular army soldiers were flatlanders, he had made an error in judgment by choosing to defend a hill. It takes skill and experience to fire downhill with any accuracy. If you are accustomed to shooting in a straight line on level ground, your aim will be off on hilly ground. I reckon my men and Shelby's could have managed it, if the situation were reversed, for we were used to high country fighting, but those redcoats firing down at us were not.

As I guided my horse up the slope, I looked upward, expecting to see a barrier of breastworks protecting the enemy's position. There were certainly trees enough hereabouts for them to have constructed breastworks for defense, and with a thousand men who had been encamped there at least a day, they had certainly had the time and troops to do so, but for whatever reason none had been built. On the opposite side

426

of the plateau, the part that Winston and Chronicle were headed for, Ferguson had set his baggage and supply wagons in a half circle, but that would afford him little protection from a massed attack coming at him from every direction. Did he not anticipate a battle taking place here, or was he simply counting on Tarleton's dragoons to come riding to his rescue? Now we knew that they would arrive too late, if they came at all.

The first of our troops to return fire were William Campbell's Virginians, for having less distance to travel to reach their assigned position, they were in place and ready to attack a little before the rest of us on the western slope. As they shot upward at the enemy, the Holston boys accompanied their volleys with piercing war whoops that echoed along the ridge and nearly drowned out the sound of the gunfire. The noise drowned out fear, too, for soon the men felt as fierce as they sounded. Moments later Shelby's men had taken up the cry, then my Watauga boys, and soon the whole of our force was yowling like wild men. Perhaps the aristocratic Scot up on the plateau found this behavior barbaric — we had heard that the flatland Tories sometimes called us "the yelling boys" — but so be it.

War is not a game for gentlemen.

Soon we heard, in counterpoint to our war cries, the shrill piping of a whistle coming from somewhere above us. In all the smoke and confusion of the battle, the one thing that stands out clear in my memory is that piercing sound. I might have mistaken it for a bird at first, trilling its warning of interlopers in the forest, but this sound was rhythmic, a series of sharp blasts in a patterned sequence, as if someone were using that noise to give orders. I had no time to think about what it was, though, because a battle is a storm, and it sweeps you along in its own noise and current until nothing else can get through. But the noise can also shut you inside yourself so that sometimes you may have odd disconnected thoughts as if you had all the time in the world.

As I took the pellets of shot out of my pouch, and rolled one between my fingers, I thought, *There's your proof that the world is round,* for if you know how round pellets of ammunition are made, the question is settled. On the bank of a river, you build a tower, maybe a hundred feet high, and from the top of that tower, you pour out molten lead. A white hot stream of liquid lead falls through the air and into a kettle of cold water to cool and harden the lead. The fall from a great height turns the molten lead into little round spheres of hardened metal. If at the beginning of creation, a molten earth had tumbled through the heavens, the fall would have made it round. But that thought flashed through my head in less time than it took to load the pellet and fire my weapon, and then the tide of the battle swept me away again.

On the plateau above us, something had changed.

The red line of defending soldiers had stopped firing their weapons. Now they were rushing down the slope to the right of us, straight toward Campbell's men, with their weapons straight out in front of them, for there was a bayonet affixed to the barrel of each musket. The British officers were partial to fighting with bayonets. They liked close combat and charging at the enemy rather than long-distance sharpshooting, maybe because those old Brown Besses weren't any great shakes at accuracy, but also I think because the sight of a sharp and deadly bayonet terrifies the opposing force. If you stand your ground, they'll spit you like a pig, and if you run, you lose the battle. It had worked at Camden and the Waxhaws.

My men weren't accustomed to it, though.

We fought with tomahawks, sometimes, same as the Indians did, but it wasn't the same. And we didn't have any similar apparatus tacked onto our Deckard rifles brought from home. We could outshoot them, but if we had to dodge a bayonet charge while trying to fire, I wouldn't give you a fig for our chances.

On our right, Campbell's men seemed frozen for a moment before they had the good sense to cut and run back down the hill. One of the Virginians waited too long to retreat, and before he could gain his footing, he was cut down by the sword of one of the mounted Redcoat officers.

They might have kept on running, rather than face those deadly blades in an uphill limb, but by the time the Virginians were back down on level ground, the shrill whistle blasted again from somewhere up on the plateau, and, hearing it, the Redcoats stopped their pursuit of Campbell's militia, and scrambled back up the hill. We managed to pick off a few of them as they climbed. They made good targets framed against the open sky above them.

As the Redcoats continued to make their way back to the plateau, the Holston boys stopped retreating and regrouped at the base of the hill. They, too, began to fire at the retreating enemy, sending a few more of them sprawling and tumbling down the slope. If he knew about it, this should have been Ferguson's first intimation that things were going wrong, for at the battle of Camden, when the bayonet charge scattered the Whig troops and sent them running, they did not stop. But here, while our men had the good sense to avoid impalement on those bayonets, they did not quit the field in panic. They simply withdrew to a safe distance, and waited for the chance to attack again, and that chance was not long in coming.

On the other side of us, Shelby's men had worked their way upward, over the wet leaves and fallen logs, and now they were nearing the summit.

This was the reason that the regular army Redcoats had been recalled from their pursuit of Campbell's militia: they were needed to defend the encampment from this new wave of attackers. As before, they fired down on Shelby's ascending soldiers, with little effect, and then, as they had done on Campbell's side, they assumed the same attack stance for a bayonet charge and set off down the hill again. Shelby's men had no choice but to pull back, slipping and scurrying back down the slope to safety, but, like Campbell's militia, they regrouped on level ground and fired up at their pursuers. More of the Redcoats fell.

Bullets from the summit buzzed over our heads like hornets, but few of them found a target. They were still aiming high. We weren't.

The air was filling with smoke from the discharge of the weapons, and the roar of so many guns all firing at once sounded like thunder, echoing over the hill.

While the Redcoats were driving Shelby's men down the slope again, Campbell's militia took advantage of the distraction, and started up the hill again, tree to tree, pausing to fire upward as they went.

The ridge was narrow, but it was a good quarter mile long, so we could not see what was happening at the other end of the plateau, where Ferguson's encampment stood. If all was going according to plan, the rest of our troops would be in position now, and beginning their own ascent. Ferguson's pet troop of trained Redcoats could not hold back all of us at once; sooner or later the homegrown Tories would have to join the battle, and they would be no match for us. If Tarleton's dragoons had been up on that hill, things might have gone differently, but Ferguson was on his own here, with an ill-trained local force, and an encircled hill that could not be defended against an army the size of ours.

I was not afraid. Whether I lived or died, we would carry the day, and that's what mattered.

I couldn't see much beyond my own patch of the hill, and it was only later, after the battle was over, that we were all able to piece together all our separate squares and fashion a quilt of the battle in our minds.

I caught a glimpse of Ben Cleveland early on, astride that great beast of a horse of his, with its broad back and hoofs like dinner plates, a fitting mount for its three-hundred-pound rider. The next time I saw Cleveland, when we had gained the plateau and a cloud of smoke parted for a moment, the big man was on foot, still at the head of his Wilkes militiamen, and mowing down enemy soldiers in his path.

When we reached the plateau, we saw that the other militias from all sides had also attained the ridge, and they were in the process of surrounding Ferguson's embattled soldiers, driving them back toward their encampment, until they had nowhere left to go.

The bayonet charge availed them nothing, for from all sides our rifle fire was cutting a swath through their ranks. As I stepped over the body of one of the fallen, a farmer dressed in hunting clothes, same as we were, I saw a sprig of pine bough in his hat — to show the other Tories which side he was on — and I noticed that the poor fellow had some kind of makeshift bayonet tied to the barrel of his weapon. Unlike the regular army soldiers, with their Brown Bess rifles, fitted with army-issue bayonets, these local recruits brought their hunting pieces from home, as we had, and apparently they had been ordered to whittle down their hunting knives to fashion homemade bayonets out of them. But I doubted that anyone had bothered to train them in the skill of fighting with bayonets, and judging by the piles of bodies dotting the clearing, those makeshift weapons had done them little good. Before they could get close enough to stab anybody, our backwater marksmen had brought them down with bullets. I doubt that they could even see what hit them. But I had only a moment to contemplate all that, for I was heading for the thick of the fighting.

There would be a thousand stories spun out of the confusion of this battle, for every man here would have his own narrow escape, his own sorrowful memory, or his little personal triumph to remember. To piece the battle together, like the women fashion the separate squares of a quilt, you would need to gather together all those stories. I had been in enough battles by now to know that someday I would know at least some of the stories that made up this one, but no one makes sense of a battle while it is happening. The best you can do is to try to live through it.

A Redcoat officer was heading up a troop of local Tories, dressed in homespun hunting shirts and hard to distinguish from our own men. They made a run at us and at Shelby's men with their homemade bayonets, but before they had accomplished anything, that piercing whistle sounded again, and the officer called out to them to stop, but they didn't seem to understand what they were being asked to do, or why. Perhaps they had never been told the code of the whistle sounds at all. They stopped, confused, glancing back up the hill as if for further orders, and when none came, they seemed to fall into a panic, ignoring the shouted orders of their Redcoat commander. Each man was trying to do what seemed best to him, which is exactly what we told our soldiers to do, but in the British army, they believe that an officer must always keep control over his men or all is lost. In order to restore order, the poor Redcoat officer was forced to cut down a couple of his own men with his sword in order to gain the attention of the rest. The ones in panic, those who would try to run away, must be stopped, before their frenzy infected the rest of the troops. The officer had to kill them to stop the stampede that would surely have followed if he had not.

I saw all this like flashes of lightning, while I loaded and fired my weapon, almost without conscious thought to my actions, and all the while in the back of my mind I was searching the field for a man in a checkered hunting shirt, astride a white horse.

Smoke . . . the roar of the weapons . . . the smell of blood and burnt powder . . .

Shelby's men, Campbell's, and mine all came together at the edge of the summit, all of us firing as we went, pushing forward to the northeast, toward Ferguson's tents and supply wagons. McDowell's Burke County boys and Cleveland's Wilkes militia were driving forward from their positions to the right and left of us, and Chronicle's men had emerged on the opposite end of the ridge, behind the wagons. We had made a noose and now we were slowly closing it around Ferguson's men.

Suddenly, from amidst a crowd of riflemen and mounted officers perhaps fifty yards away, I caught a glimpse of a white horse. The rider, a slight fellow in a red-checked hunting shirt, was urging the horse forward and down the slope, and four other horsemen trailed behind him, but no one had a thought to spare for them. Our quarry was the man on the white horse, and we had been searching for him for nearly an hour. Now he was on the run, and if he managed to break through our line, he would be down the hill and clattering up the trace toward Charlotte Town before we could stop him.

But we all knew who we were looking for, and as soon as he broke away from the cluster of his own troops, he headed for the steep slope on the opposite end of the ridge from where we had come up. A dozen men, mostly Burke County militiamen who were closest to his position, were aiming their weapons at the retreating form of Maj. Patrick Ferguson, as he urged his mount to take the slope at full speed.

One man might have missed his mark, but our men are hunters, sharpshooters, and Indian fighters, and their lives depend on their aim. The years of practice and experience served them well. The guns spat little bursts of flame, and the man shook with the force of the bullets as they struck him, tumbling from his horse. One booted foot caught in the stirrup, but Ferguson was past being able to free himself. The frightened animal plunged on down the hill dragging its rider, while several Redcoats chased the beast, grabbing for its reins in order to free their fallen commander. Within a few yards they had managed to stop its flight, and disentangle Ferguson's foot from the stirrup. They carried him the rest of the way down the hill, and set him down next to the little stream that ran along the bottom of the slope.

The major lay motionless where his comrades placed him, with puddles of blood staining the checkered hunting shirt. The fatal wound was the one to his head. He twitched for a few moments, as if he were trying to get to his feet, but after a few moments he fell back and lay still.

I saw none of this, for my militia was still fighting its way across that long swath of ridge, heading for the encampment at the other end. But I heard the story so many times in the aftermath that the image etched itself into my memory, so that it became indistinguishable from things I really had seen and heard.

At the time that Ferguson was shot by McDowell's men, a great cheer went up from those who were near enough to have witnessed it, and word quickly spread that the Tory commander was dead.

There was no time for any of us to dwell on this, though, for the battle was still raging around us. Patrick Ferguson was dead. That object of our mission had been accomplished. But we still had to end the fighting and get down off this mountain and home alive.

Battles are easier to start than they are to stop.

Another Redcoat officer, whom I took to be Ferguson's second in command, seemed to be trying to rally his men, but they, too, had heard the shouts announcing Ferguson's demise, and at this news, many of them were in disarray, not knowing what to do next. Some of them had thrown down their weapons — they had run out of ammunition.

Finally, the officer now in charge must have decided that it was useless to continue fighting — or perhaps he had wanted to surrender long before, but was unable to persuade the proud Major Ferguson to do so. He must have realized that he could keep going and sacrifice more of his men, but no strategy or rallying charge could change the outcome of the engagement. The officer produced a white flag and waved it in our direction, signaling the Tories' surrender. Others, seeing his action, took out white flags of their own, and waved them at the approaching troops.

But it takes time to stop seven hundred men who have spent the past hour fighting for their lives. They cannot hear shouted orders for the echoes of gunfire still ringing in their ears. Some cannot see the white flag, because they are looking at a soldier whose weapon is pointed at them, or the smoke obscures the scene, or they are out of the line of sight of the scene of surrender. And maybe some of them knew full well that the enemy had yielded, but, with the countersign of "Buford" fresh in their minds, they decided to give the Tories what we had come to call "Tarleton's Quarter," which is no quarter at all.

Cries of "Buford!" and "Tarleton's Quarter" rang out across the ridge, and the crack of gunfire went on.

The militia commanders attempted to stop the battle, shouting orders for a cease-fire, but for several long minutes, the shooting continued, and men who had laid down their arms died needlessly. Shelby even rode up between the Tory troops and our own troops in order to force them to stop fighting. He shouted for the Tories to lay down their arms, and he ordered our men to cease fire. The rest of us attempted to restore order to our own militias.

Finally the word spread, and little by little the firing faded to random shots from here and there across the ridge. I was heading down to inspect the body of Ferguson, when Major Tipton ran up and grabbed the reins of my horse. "You must come back, Colonel! He thinks you are dead, and he won't stop shooting."

"Who? Who won't stop shooting?"

"Your son. Joseph."

I dismounted, and followed Tipton back to the part of the ridge where the Watauga boys were situated. "Joseph?" I said. "But why should he think that I had been killed?"

"He misheard. Someone shouted that Sevier had been shot, and he thought it was you, sir."

Something in his voice made me shiver. "Tell me, Major."

His eyes met mine, and I could see that he wished he didn't have to be the one to say it. "It's Robert. He was hit in the back early on. He's still alive, though. We'll get the surgeon to see to him. But Joseph —"

"I'll see to him," I said. "Thank you, Major."

I was running now, toward the sound of the crack of rifle fire. At the edge of the ridge, Joseph was standing with his back against a tree, caked with dirt and sweat, but apparently uninjured. He was weeping, and trying to aim his weapon between heaving sobs, and I heard him crying out, "They killed my daddy! I'll get every one of 'em."

"Joseph! Stop this now."

At the sound of my voice, the boy turned toward me, and I saw streaks of tears across the dirt on his cheeks. Slowly he lowered his Deckard rifle, staring at me as if I were an apparition. "But they told me . . . I heard —"

"Yes. It's your uncle Robert. You need to find him and see that a doctor tends to him. I have to see about the surrender now, so I am trusting you to do this. When I can join you, I will."

I wanted nothing more than to turn my back on the aftermath of the battle and tend to my family, but when I accepted the job of militia commander, I had given up the right to put personal feelings ahead of duty. I told myself that if Robert was still alive, his wound could not be too serious. I would see to him as soon as I could.

Then I trotted back across the field to where the Tory army was penned in, some eight hundred of them, or what was left of that number, crowded on the last two hundred feet of the plateau, caught between the half circle of supply wagons and our own militias who surrounded their position.

Colonel Shelby and his brother Evan were standing beside the Redcoat officer who had first signaled for surrender. I dismounted and as I approached them, Isaac Shelby turned to look at me, and I blurted out, "By God, they have burnt off your hair!" The left side of his head was scorched and the hair singed away by the gunfire that had swirled around him.

Shelby simply nodded, and then, returning to the matter at hand, he said, "Colonel Sevier, may I present Captain DePeyster, who is the ranking officer for his troops now. Captain, I am glad to see you."

DePeyster muttered something about not being glad to see Shelby, but he drew his sword and held it out. It was Major Evan Shelby who took it from him, and he also seized the enemy's flag.

Sporadic shots still continued to ring out. Off to one side of me, I glimpsed a light-colored coat, and I knew it to be that of

Colonel Campbell. Sure enough, he was at my side a moment later. "We must get them to stop firing," he murmured to me. "I will see to it."

The defeated Tories had laid down their weapons, but they were huddled together, near a pile of bodies, and now and then one of them would be hit by a bullet and fall to the ground. Campbell approached them, waving his hands to get their attention. "All you who have surrendered, sit down!" he shouted. "Then we will know that you are no longer in the fight."

After a moment's hesitation, the prisoners began to obey this order, and when all of them were seated on the damp ground, Campbell turned to the soldiers nearest our position — McDowell's men and Cleveland's, I think — and he called out, "Send up a cheer of joy and thanks for this victory. The day is ours!"

Those within earshot of Campbell took up the cry first. "Hurrah for liberty!" Then the troops farther away heard it and joined in, until the cheer echoed around us, drowning out other, more terrible sounds, like the cries of the wounded.

When the cheering had faded away, a silence fell across that plateau. Now that the battle was won, all the other thoughts that had been tamped down into the darkest corners of our minds were allowed to seep back. *Who of our comrades had died in the fighting? Who was wounded?* And perhaps some of our number remembered to give prayerful thanks to the Almighty for our deliverance.

For the space of a minute, exhausted as we were from the night march and the rigors of battle, we stood there lost in the silence.

And then a shot rang out.

CHAPTER NINETEEN
OCTOBER 7, 1780

One single shot broke the stillness. But fired by whom? Our men had been ordered to cease firing, and they had shouted the victory cheer, signaling the end of the fighting. They knew it was over. We all looked toward the Tories who had surrendered, but they were still clumped together where Colonel Campbell had told them to sit, with their weapons stacked a few feet away. They looked as shocked as I felt.

Scarcely had these thoughts had time to form in my brain before a voice cried out, "I'm a gone man!"

I looked to the north side of the ridge, just beyond the encampment, in time to see James Williams sway in his saddle and pitch forward. One of his men ran to the horse's side, and caught Williams as he fell. Moments later, more of his followers were easing him down from the saddle, and shoulder high they carried him up to the camp and into one of the Tories' tents, calling out for a surgeon to attend their fallen leader.

I looked a question at Shelby, and he nodded, but neither of us spoke. *James Williams.* In the days before the battle he had been a nuisance, threatening the mission with his chicanery. First he had tried to take over Graham's command, and then he had come into our camp and tried to make us march nearly to Georgia by claiming that Ferguson had gone to Ninety Six — Williams's home territory — simply because he wanted us there to fight his personal battles against his Loyalist neighbors. Had we believed him and continued south, we would have missed Ferguson, and given him time to join forces with Tarleton. His trickery could have killed us all.

Yet even though we had shunned him and left him out of the commanders' meetings, he had stayed on. With his hundred followers, Williams had taken his place in the assault on the ridge, midway between the troops of Shelby and Cleveland, and I reckon he had fought as bravely as anyone. The victory was his, too.

He had lived through the battle, seen the surrender, shouted the cheer of victory — and then some unseen marksman had shot him out of the saddle.

I heard Campbell shout out orders for the men to fire into the crowd of Tory soldiers, and most of them were happy to oblige. They fired shot after shot at the helpless prisoners, and perhaps two score of their number fell wounded or dying into the wet leaves.

All this took only a minute or two, and by then Shelby came to the fore again, demanding that the shooting be stopped. The prisoners were still an arm's length away from their weapons, and he ordered them to stand up and move away from their guns. They did so, and in another minute or two, the crackle of gunfire ceased, thanks to Shelby's insistence, added to the fact that the Tories were obviously disarmed and defenseless. The battle was over. To shoot an unarmed enemy now would be not war, but murder.

Benjamin Cleveland stumped across the plateau and joined us. "They shot my horse, the blackguards!" he wheezed. "Roebuck. Finest horse in the county. Now how am I supposed to get home?"

I looked at him — red-faced, and wheezing, and three hundred pounds if he was an ounce — and indeed I could not imagine him getting much farther than the bottom of this hill on foot. But before we could pursue the subject of his dead mount, Shelby said, "At least you're unharmed yourself, Colonel Cleveland. My brother was shot — he's down there by the stream now, waiting for the surgeon."

I had just seen Major Evan Shelby, so I knew that it was the youngest brother, Moses, who had been wounded. I nodded. "My brother was shot as well. Not Valentine. Robert. When we get everything settled down here, I need to see to him. I lost two or three good men — John Browne, Michael Mahoney, and William Steele — and a few others are wounded."

"We must find a good surgeon to tend the wounded."

"Who else did we lose?"

"We have appointed some men to number the dead, so we shall know more when they have finished their accounting. From what I can tell, perhaps fifty of our men killed in all," said Shelby. "A goodly number wounded. Poor Major Chronicle, whose hunting camp this was, died leading his men to the summit. His old hunting companion Captain Mattocks was killed as well."

"Brave fellows," I said. "Theirs was the hardest climb."

Shelby nodded. "And nearest to the en-campment. Lieutenant Colonel Hambright, who assumed command after Chronicle fell, is wounded in the thigh, but he is a tough old rooster, and he bids fair to recover."

"I hear that we also lost the spy Enoch Gilmer," said Cleveland.

We were silent for a moment, remembering the larking about of just a few hours ago, when my officers had hauled him out of a Tory farmhouse, pretending that they were going to hang him. How strange are the ways of Providence that in those carefree moments, Gilmer had only hours left to live.

A cry went up from the tent where the South Carolina boys had carried James Williams. A young man, who looked about the age of my James, pushed his way through the tent flap, his face streaked with tears. "It's bad," he said. "He's hurt real bad."

The men who had followed Williams into battle in spite of everything began to weep openly. He had the loyalty of his followers, and that was a testimonial to his life as much as anything. In this battle, at least, he had been trustworthy and brave.

I looked at Shelby and Cleveland. "Williams was shot after the enemy had surrendered their weapons. They were all sitting there together in front of us."

"A stray bullet from one of the soldiers

who was still shooting?" Shelby said this in a toneless voice, his face carefully blank.

We were thinking the same thing: someone — perhaps one of Hill's men — had not forgiven or forgotten the attempt of Colonel Williams to assume command. Perhaps someone had hoped that Williams would be killed in the battle, and when that did not happen, he had taken advantage of the confusion and the continuing gunfire to deliver his own form of retribution. James Williams was shot by one of our own men — there was not a doubt in my mind about that.

After an awkward moment of silence, Ben Cleveland spoke up, his face alight with eagerness. "It was them foragers, boys!" he declared. "Didn't you see them? Down at the bottom of the ridge, a party of Tory foragers rode up just as the battle was ending. I expect Ferguson had sent them out earlier in the day for supplies. They returned too late to aid their side in the fighting, but one of them got off a shot at a likely target on horseback, and it happened to be Williams who was hit. Then they faded away again into the woods. Didn't you see them?"

Shelby and I shook our heads. *And neither did you,* I thought. But Cleveland's hopeful theory was both plausible and unverifiable, and I found myself trying to conjure up an image of those Tory foragers in my mind's eye.

"It must have happened that way," Shelby said solemnly.

Yes, I thought, *when we tell the story of the shooting of James Williams, we must say it happened that way, because the truth would tarnish our victory.* A troublesome officer shot by some resentful compatriot would make a sorry footnote to this glorious day.

"Foragers," I said. "If he dies, it will be a tragic end to a fine soldier." In that event, we would speak well of him, and praise his valor, and mourn his loss — in public and in print, that is — but I confess I would like him better dead.

"Where is Ferguson?" I asked one of the Burke County men, for they had been on the side of the ridge where the major had begun his last desperate ride. This fellow, who was guarding the prisoners, pointed to the eastern end of the ridge, only a few yards beyond the camp. "Still down there near that little spring, where his men laid him out."

There was a score of other things to be done in the aftermath, but having come so far on account of the taunting of this arrogant man, I meant to see him *in extremis,* if only for a moment. I might have saved myself the trouble of asking for Ferguson's whereabouts, for there was a steady stream of men making their way down the steep slope to stare at the corpse of the Redcoats' commander. Even wounded men were limping down the hill to view the body; others, too badly injured to walk, were being carried to the scene by their loyal comrades. Perhaps they felt that, even if they died of their wounds, they had been rewarded by the sight of their enemy brought low through the efforts of a makeshift army.

I edged through the crowd, the more easily done because many of the men recognized me and parted their ranks to let me through.

Now that Major Ferguson was diminished by death, he looked as insignificant as a child, sprawled out in the weeds, his hat and his checkered hunting shirt in tatters from the weapons fire, and awash in blood. Half of Ferguson's face sheared away by the force of the bullet that killed him, and his arms lay at twisted angles to his body — broken, both of them, either by the shots or by his fall from the horse. He had been shot eight or nine times, though, judging by the blood and the holes in his clothing.

The men who crowded around Ferguson's body were still angry. It did not matter to them that he had been a brave soldier, doing his duty as he saw it. I'm not sure it mattered to me, either. He had called us *banditi,* and threatened to burn our homes and kill our families. An honorable death in battle did not even the score in the minds of our citizen soldiers. They were busy parceling out Ferguson's possessions — his checkered shirt, his boots. The pistol, sash, and his sword would be reserved as trophies for the commanders.

Shelby had come down the hill to see the remains as well. He stopped a little above me on the slope, and said in the manner of one pronouncing a eulogy, "Well, Ferguson, we have *burgoyned* you."

Someone in the crowd touched my arm. "I think I'm the one that took him down, Colonel. I had a clear shot, and I aimed for his head."

I turned and recognized the speaker as one of my own Watauga men — Robert Young, a good soldier and a marksman to be reckoned with.

"Very likely you did," I murmured.

"It was John Gilleland — I reckon you know him, Colonel, 'cause he's from Washington County as me — well, sir, it was Gilleland that spotted Ferguson first. He yelled out, 'There he is in the big shirt,' and he tried to take a shot at him, but all he got from his musket was a flash in the pan, so he called for me to shoot, and I did, and I believe I brought him down, though there were half a dozen of us all taking aim at him at once. Gilleland is sorely wounded, though, I'm sorry to say."

"We'll see that he's looked after," I said. "But you did well."

Robert Young flushed with pleasure. "Well, Ferguson had it coming, especially after that letter that was read to us on the trail a few days back. The one where he tells the rich planters, If you don't stop those Backwater Men, you will be pissed upon forever.

Half the crowd grouped around the corpse overheard Robert Young's remark, though I'm sure someone would have remembered that phrase sooner or later.

"Pissed upon forever!" The words became a chant and then a taunt, and as I turned and made my way back up the slope, I heard raucous laughter, and an acrid odor reached my nostrils. The men were suiting the action to the word. I did not turn back. I did not particularly want to see it happen, but I did not stop it, either. Ferguson had made me feel like a bear tied to a stake, and I

thought a quick and easy death was more than he had deserved.

Chapter Twenty
OCTOBER 7, 1780

The spell of the battle was wearing off now, and I became aware of the smell of blood, and for the first time I really saw the piles of bodies I had passed before as if I had been sleepwalking. One of the dead was a young woman, shabbily dressed and sprawled out on the wet grass with an arm outstretched reaching out for something that could no longer matter now. I stopped to look down at her. She had fallen close to the baggage wagons; perhaps she had been trying to reach one for safety. She looked young — perhaps twenty — with a face unmarred, for she had been shot through the heart, and the red curls that tumbled about her face were tipped with blood. Perhaps that blaze of hair had made her a tempting target for some coldhearted marksman. The pall of death had not yet settled over her features, so that at a glance one might think that she was merely sleeping. *A servant,* I thought, from her ragged clothing. I wondered why the Tories had not sent her away before the fighting began, but then I realized that there had not been time. They had only minutes from the time their sentry fired the warning shot until the first of our militias began to climb the ridge. No one had spared a thought for the wretched young woman caught in their midst. She must have spent her last moments in blind terror, and because of that, I thought of my bride, bonny Kate, who had also been caught in a battle when Old Abram's men attacked Fort Watauga four years back. I had saved her that day, but this young lass was not so fortunate, and the memories of my Kate's peril moved me to pity.

"We must see about burying this woman," I called out to a passing officer.

"That's Ferguson's doxy, that is," the fellow replied, nudging the body with the toe of his boot. "I heard one of the prisoners say so. Reckon she got hit early on. Probably got caught up in all the smoke, so they couldn't properly see her."

"Yes." I hoped it was quick, and that she did not suffer.

One of the prisoners stood up. "I'll do it, with your permission, sir."

A short mousey-looking man stood looking at me, with an expression that mingled fear with sorrow. "It's Major Ferguson I'm thinking of, but I could put her in the grave with him. He wouldn't mind that, I reckon."

He wasn't in uniform, and he didn't look like he'd done any fighting. "Who are you?" I said.

"Elias Powell, sir. I am — was — Ferguson's manservant. I'd like to do this one last thing for him and bury him proper. He was a good officer."

I considered it. We had settled the score with Ferguson in the battle, and answered his "pissing letter" in kind, and that was an end to it. Now he could have his honor back. "All right," I said to Powell. "See what you can do to help your wounded comrades first, but when time permits, bury the both of them. You may take some of the prisoners to help you dig the grave, and we will send a guard with you. Find something to make a shroud. We have to see to our own wounded, and then bury our dead."

Elias Powell nodded his thanks. He looked down at the red-haired woman crumpled at my feet. "She wasn't a bad woman, sir," he said. "She was just trying to live through this war, same as the rest of us."

"Yes. It is a great pity that the innocents must suffer as well."

As I started to walk away, another thought struck Elias Powell, and he called after me, "Did you happen to see the other one, sir?" I looked back and he went on, "There was another washerwoman. Virginia Paul. We called that one laying there Virginia Sal. I only wondered what became of the other one."

"Yes, I remember her. She came running down the ridge just as the shooting started. We asked her how we could recognize Major Ferguson, and when she told us, we let her go. If she got hold of a horse, she may be halfway to Charlotte Town by now. Or perhaps she ran into our soldiers down the road and they detained her. I wonder why the other one didn't go with her."

Elias Powell shivered. "I don't reckon any of us could follow where that one was going. But I thank you for the news, Colonel, and I'll see to the burying when I can." He knelt down and scooped up the body of the young woman, and, staggering a little under its weight, he shuffled off to lay her body in the pile with the others.

Perhaps the young woman had not suffered but others did, and were suffering still. I could hear the feeble cries of the wounded, Whig and Tory alike, all over the plateau.

They begged for water, or called out to their comrades to help them.

A few yards away I saw a dark-haired young fellow in muddy blood-smeared clothes, kneeling beside one of the blood-soaked Tories, probing for wounds. I judged that he must be the Redcoats' surgeon. We would have need of him. I needed him now.

I started toward the Tory physician, but big Ben Cleveland came stumping across the field, and reached him first. Scarlet with rage, Cleveland hauled the doctor to his feet and slapped him across the face with the back of his hand. "You're a prisoner now! You'll treat our wounded, not yours!"

The fellow rubbed at the mark on his cheek, but he faced Cleveland with calm resolve. "I'll treat any man who needs me, sir."

I stepped in before they could quarrel further. "Pardon me, Cleveland, but I have need of this prisoner. My brother is gravely wounded. Come with me, please, Doctor."

Cleveland sighed. "Is it Valentine?"

"No. My younger brother, Robert."

"It's a curse, I tell you," Cleveland declared. "I mean, think on it, Colonel Sevier. My brother Larkin was wounded on the way here. Isaac Shelby's youngest brother was wounded this afternoon, and now you tell me that your brother is a casualty as well. Mighty like a curse, ain't it?"

"Mighty bad luck, anyhow. I hope they all recover quickly. May I borrow the doctor here?"

"Take him and welcome," said Cleveland.

"Thank you. Doctor, come with me."

The Tory surgeon stood still for a moment, glaring at Cleveland, but I touched his elbow, and murmured, "Please. My brother needs help."

The doctor glanced at me, and nodded. "Lead the way, sir."

He stooped to pick up his leather bag, and then he followed me back across the plateau, hesitating every now and then when we passed a wounded man, but I gave him a look that said I would brook no diversion from the task at hand, and he made no trouble about it.

As the doctor and I made our way toward the southwestern slope, I heard voices whooping and cheering behind me. I turned and saw that some of the men had managed to catch Ferguson's white horse, and they were leading it over to Ben Cleveland. I suppose they meant to present it to him to make up for the one that had been shot out from under him during the battle. I was glad of this. Now we could be sure that the big man would make it home safely to Wilkes County.

At last we threaded our way past the fallen soldiers, and reached the edge of the hill. As we began to make our way down, the doctor's foot slipped on a pile of wet leaves, and he nearly fell, but I braced myself against a tree and caught his arm, steadying him until he regained his balance.

He muttered thanks, and I said, "I am Colonel Sevier, commander of the Watauga militia. What's your name, Doctor?"

"Johnson," he said, scraping the mud off his boot on a fallen log. "Uzal Johnson. From New Jersey. I was commissioned by the New Jersey Volunteers before I came south." The bitterness in his tone suggested that he regretted this decision.

"And you have studied medicine?"

"Yes, I qualified at King's College in New York." He gave me a mirthless smile. "I think I am equal to the task of treating the wounded, sir. Heaven knows I've had enough practice at it by now. Bullet wounds and smallpox — I've seen enough of them for two lifetimes of doctoring."

We were where my militia had fought only a few hours ago, though now it seemed to me as if a week had passed, for much had happened, and weariness was fogging my mind. A moment later I heard Valentine calling out for me, and I could see him waving from the edge of the stream among the trees at the base of the ridge. Near him, I saw our younger brother Joseph kneeling beside Robert, who sat propped against a tree, pale but conscious. Joseph had taken a dipper of water from the creek, and was dabbing at Robert's face with a bit of cloth.

When he saw me coming, Robert raised a hand to hail me, but then his face contorted with pain, and he let it fall again. I took the last few yards of the slope at a run, and the little Tory surgeon followed me as best he could.

"Hello, Bob," I said, willing myself to sound cheerful. "You never could stay out of trouble, could you?"

He managed a faint smile. "I got hit when my back was turned. I reckon they were aiming at you, Jack, for that's the part of me that most resembles you."

I laughed. "Well, now they can tell us apart both coming and going. I have brought you a surgeon, Bob. We'll soon set you to rights."

While Dr. Johnson knelt beside Robert and began to study his patient, I drew Valentine and Joseph aside for a whispered

464

discussion a few yards away. "When did he get hit?"

"Early on, Jack," said Joseph. "He was right close to me as we went up the slope. It was sheer bad luck. He was stooping to pick up his ramrod, and just then someone let fly with a load of buckshot, and got him in the lower back."

"Can you tell how bad it is?"

Valentine shook his head. "Hard to tell. He never passed out. There's blood, but the shot went in deep. He's hurting, of course, but we both know that's no sign. Sometimes flesh wounds can pain you more than mortal ones. Now that you've come, I reckon I'll go look for some whiskey. We can cleanse the wound with whatever he doesn't drink."

"Round up my boys when you get a chance," I told Joseph. "It'll soon be dark, and I want all of us together by then. We'll be staying here tonight."

Joseph glanced up the hill, and I knew that he was thinking that sleep would be hard to come by on that battlefield amongst the dead and dying, but he made no comment, and merely nodded and hurried away.

When Valentine and Joseph had gone, I got some water from the stream at the doctor's request, and then I knelt down beside him as he probed the wound with a small, sharp instrument. Robert was paler now, but he seemed determined not to cry out. When Uzal Johnson had washed the wound, I noticed that there didn't seem to be overmuch blood, which led me to hope that the wound wasn't mortal.

"How do you feel?" I said, patting my brother's shoulder.

"There's a good many hurt worse," he said, trying to turn a grimace into a smile. "At least I'm not yelling my head off."

The doctor looked up, as if he intended to say something, but then he thought better of it, and went back to probing the wound. The sun was low in the sky now, and there was more shadow than light in the woods. It was colder now, too, as night was setting in — not cold enough, though: the stench of spilled blood and the odor of dead bodies would soon fill the plateau with a new horror, when darkness finally hid the sight of the carnage.

We sat there in silence for a few minutes, while the doctor concentrated on his grisly task, and in my weariness I nearly sank into sleep, despite my worries for Robert.

At last, Uzal Johnson sat back on his heels and flung the probing tool down on his coat, which he had laid next to Robert when he began. "Well, I can't find it!" he snapped.

"I doubt I could find a cannonball in this darkness."

"Shall I build you a campfire?"

He shook his head. "The pellet is in too deep. Even if I could see well enough, I think I might do more harm than good by digging around trying to get it out. We don't want him to lose any more blood."

He stood up and headed for the stream to clean his hands, and I followed him, so that I could ask about Robert without his overhearing us. "How is he?"

The doctor sighed, and, fishing a scrap of linen out of his bag, he swirled his hands in the creek water and began to wipe them. "The pellet went into his kidney, best I can tell." I waited for him to tell me the implications of that, and after a moment he went on, "It's a grave wound, but it could be worse. He has two kidneys; he can live without one of them if he has to."

"Yes, better to be shot there than in the head or the heart. But what of the injury itself?"

"Time will tell. I have cleaned the wound as best I could. I can sew it up, and bandage it to keep it uninfected. After that . . ." He shrugged. "He has not gone into shock, which is a good sign, considering the hard few days he has had. He is young and strong. He might recover if he will stay somewhere close by and rest for a week. Two weeks would be better. Put him with a farmer hereabouts, and let them keep him in bed until the wound heals, and he should be all right."

From his resting place by the stream, Robert called out, "Where have Joe and Valentine gone?" he said. "I could use that whiskey they promised."

"They should be back soon. They've probably gone back to get James and the horses. Then we can see about getting you lodgings with some local Whigs. How far can he travel safely, Doctor?"

Uzal Johnson shook his head. "Impossible to tell, Colonel. Any time spent on horseback might jog that pellet loose and do more damage. I wouldn't go three miles if it was me."

Robert tried to laugh. "In my place, Doctor, I'll wager that you would. We are half a day's ride from Charlotte Town, and if Tarleton isn't here now, he could be at any moment. And if the Redcoats were to find me laid up in a cabin in these parts, I reckon I wouldn't have to worry anymore about this gunshot wound, 'cause they'd hang me before you could say Jack Robinson."

Johnson nodded. "You must weigh the

risks, sir."

Robert looked up at me, and braced his arms as if to push himself to stand up, but a spasm of pain must have hit him, for he thought better of it and settled back down against the tree. "I want to go home, Jack."

"This man advises against it," I said, nodding toward Uzal Johnson. "He's a good doctor, Bob. He has been to college up in New York."

My brother shook his head. "I'm sure he's a daisy, Jack, but I can't take his advice. All the rest of you will be heading out tomorrow. I don't want to be alone and helpless down here at the enemy's back door. I want to get home. I want to see my boys. Keziah can take care of me."

I looked over at the doctor. He met my gaze with a shrug and an expressionless stare. He was a Redcoat: it was no business of his what the rebels did. Or perhaps he had enough experience with headstrong patients to know that you cannot talk them out of a course of action if they are dead set upon it. After a moment's silence, he said, "Well, I have done all I can for your brother, Colonel. I hope he makes it. Now, by your leave, I'd like to go and tend to the rest of the wounded."

"You'll have a long night of it," I said.

He nodded. "I hope so. I hope they live long enough for me to get to them."

I thanked him, and he made his way back up the hill, where most of the dead and injured lay. He would have a long night, I knew, for there were perhaps a hundred men in need of his care. Our work was done, but his was just beginning.

By sunset, fatigue had caught up with us, although we still had much to do in the aftermath of the battle: bodies to bury, spoils of war to parcel out, prisoners to be dealt with, and wounded men to be seen to. We had done very little of any of it before darkness came. Some of the men took it at turns to stand guard in case Cornwallis had sent reinforcements to Ferguson. After the long march, a day and a half without sleep, and then the battle, we were too weary even to quit the field to make camp. As gruesome as it sounds, we simply lay down on that same ground we had fought on, and slept there amongst the dead and the dying. It felt like reliving the battle over again. Our exhaustion was our salvation, though, for even had we wanted to heed the cries of the suffering, fatigue pulled us into oblivion, for a few hours at least.

The last thing I remember is seeing a little

lantern bobbing across the field, as Uzal Johnson made his way from patient to patient amongst the dead and dying.

Come sunup, it was quieter.

CHAPTER TWENTY-ONE
OCTOBER 8, 1780

The morning after the battle, I awoke on the cold ground of the battlefield, roused more by hunger and sunshine than because I was rested. As I sat up, blinking through the mists at the pale morning sunshine, I heard shrill cries that sounded like women weeping. I scrambled to my feet and looked across the field, where the wounded still lay, mingled with the dead. In the distance through the swirling morning mist, I could see a crowd of people wandering along the ridge, stooping to turn over bodies for a look at their faces, and crying piteously as they went. In my half-waking state, I thought of spirits of the dead, still roaming the place where they had died, but an instant later, I was fully awake, and I knew who they were: the inhabitants of the nearby farms, who had come in search of sons and husbands who had fought in the battle. Many of those who fought here — for both armies — came from settlements within a few miles of King's Mountain. Some had come unwillingly, for we had heard tales of the Tories forcing men into service. These people must have waited by their firesides through a long night, not knowing the fate of husband, son, or brother, and now at first light they had ventured here to learn the worst.

As the women wandered over the battle-field, searching for a familiar face amongst the dead and dying, their screams and lamentations drowned out the cries of the wounded, and bid fair to be louder than the battle itself — or perhaps it only seemed so to me because I had less to distract me now. Some of these people set about to do what they could for the wounded, fetching water and dressing wounds. I suspect that others were there to rob the dead, out for what profit they could make from the misfortunes of others, but we had no time to spare for such concerns.

There would be no time to recover from the march and the fighting, not with Char-lotte Town and the army of Cornwallis a day's ride away. Word was sure to reach them soon, and they might come after us to avenge Ferguson. We had to make ready to move out.

We killed some of the Tory cattle, though there were precious few of them for so many mouths to feed, and we took whatever food we could find for our morning rations. On our journey across the mountains and down to King's Mountain, while we were eating parched corn, half-cooked meat, and whatever else we could scavenge, the men had kept themselves going by imagining the splendid feast we would have once we took possession of the Tories' food supply, but once we had it, we were disappointed to find that Ferguson's army had little more to eat than we did. The Carolina border country had been picked clean by the predations of the various armies until there was almost nothing left to take. We would go hungry a while longer.

After that hasty and meager breakfast, we began the business of tying up the loose ends, to make ready for our departure.

We assigned some of the men to burial detail, first to inter the fifty of our own men who had perished in the fighting. The enemy dead numbered more than two hundred, and there would not be time to properly bury them all before we needed to move out. Colonel Campbell announced that he and some of his men would stay behind to finish the task, and they would rejoin us as soon as they could finish their grisly labors.

Some other soldiers spent the early morning hours fashioning litter poles out of stout tree limbs and blankets so that we could transport the most gravely wounded. My brother Robert had refused this means of conveyance, though, and insisted on being given his horse.

Early in the day we had a family conclave to try once more to reason with him, for though he had insisted yesterday upon going home, I had hoped that a night to consider it might change his mind. It had not.

"The rest of us can't go straight home, Bob," I told him. "If we could we'd give you an escort, but we have eight hundred prisoners to contend with. Still, it's dangerous for you to try to make a long ride with a bullet in your back."

Valentine nodded. "Jack is right. Wouldn't it be better if you stayed hereabouts for a while? That Hambright fellow lives somewhere near here. He could keep an eye on you until we could come back this way."

Robert looked worse than he had yesterday for despite the whiskey Joseph found for him, he had slept little the night before, and the effects of the wound were beginning to take hold. There were dark shadows under his eyes, and though he was the youngest of us, he looked a decade older.

My sons Joseph and James had joined us on the hillside, but they knew better than to say anything in this discussion. They gnawed at their food, big-eyed and solemn, while their elders debated the fate of their uncle.

I wished I could simply order Robert to bed rest in a nearby farmhouse, for after all he was but a captain and I was the colonel in command of our militia, but though I outranked him both in war and in the family, Robert paid little heed to me on this matter. In the face of my arguments, coupled with Joseph's and Valentine's, he set his jaw in a mulish scowl and said, "I'm going home, boys. Just fetch me my horse, and some of the rations and gunpowder, and I'll be off."

I looked at Valentine and Joseph, hoping for more brotherly support, but they simply shrugged. Glancing nervously at me, Joseph said, "Well, Bob may be right about the Redcoats swooping in from Charlotte Town. Maybe he could get a little farther away from here, and then rest up where it's safer."

Robert shook his head. "I'm going home."

There was no reasoning with him, and no way that the rest of us could abandon the militia to escort him home. I could tell, though, that his mind was made up, and we could argue all day without making a dent in his resolve. I thought the matter over for a few moments. "All right," I said at last. "For the last time, I tell you that I wish you would not do this. But if you are hell-bent to get back over the mountain, then I will let James accompany you."

The boy brightened at the mention of his name, because he had always set a store by his Uncle Bob, who was a scant fifteen years older than he. Joseph, two years the elder of James, opened his mouth to protest my decision, but then he closed it again. He had probably intended to argue that as the more mature of my sons, he ought to be given the responsibility of looking after Bob, but then he must have remembered his behavior in the aftermath of the battle, when he had shot at the defenseless prisoners in a fit of anger over the rumor of my death. My choice of James was not a punishment for Joseph's rashness, but it was a consequence of it.

I turned again to my injured brother. "Mind you, Bob, this pup of mine is only sixteen, and he'll be little help protecting you from Redcoat soldiers if you happen to run into any, but I think you should be safe on that account. I wish I could send the surgeon along with you, but there's only the one, and there are too many other wounded among the ranks to spare him."

Bob nodded. "He said himself that there's nothing more he can do. If he tried to take the pellet out, I might die from that. I'll take my chances on the trail. But I'd be glad of James's company. He can round up food for us, and make a campfire, and that's as much as I reckon I'll need. Once we get past Quaker Meadows, it'll be three or four days at most to make it home. We'll make better time without an army and a herd of cattle to slow us down." He looked over at the boys, sitting together on the slope under a stunted tree. "Do you think you can manage that, James?"

The boy nodded, trying to temper his excitement with concern. He was being given a man's share of responsibility, and he relished it, even though it came under circumstances he would never have wished for.

Valentine spoke up. "One of Hambright's men told me that there's a Whig farm not too far from here. A fellow by the name of Finley. He told me where it was. Make for there, Bob, and don't try to go any farther today."

"That's fine, then," said Bob. "We'll find the Finley place. So, we'll be off directly, boys. And we will meet up again over the mountain when you finally make it back."

I swallowed my doubts. "Sure we will," I told my brother, clasping his hand. "Have a safe journey and take it slowly. We'll get home just as soon as we can. Once we leave here, we'll be moving slow enough, with eight hundred prisoners to slow us down, so you should be well ahead of us before long. There should be no need for you to hurry. Any pursuers Cornwallis sends will be coming after us."

Valentine touched my shoulder. "They'll be needing you up the hill, Jack, so you go ahead and see to the preparations for the general decamping, and Joseph and I will get James and Robert ready to go."

I said my farewells and hurried up the ridge to where Major Tipton was waiting. I did not look back because I didn't want to make too much of this parting. *If I look back,* I thought, *I may never see Robert again.*

The one diversion we permitted ourselves that morning as a reward for the victory was to cast lots among the commanders for the spoils of war. We did this as we ate our portion of the breakfast rations. Ben Cleveland had already received Ferguson's fine white horse, to replace his own mount, which was killed in the battle. William Lenoir got the major's sword with its silver handle, a beautiful weapon. Joseph McDowell got Ferguson's china plates and an eggshell-thin coffee cup and saucer; we reckoned such fine goods were more suited to the splendor of Quaker Meadows than to our frontier cabins in the backcountry. Ferguson's little silver whistle went to Isaac Shelby, and the major's papers and his correspondence were given to William Campbell, who was more of a scholar than the rest of us. Ferguson's silken sash and the sword of Captain De-Peyster went to me.

Other possessions of the defeated enemy — Tory horses, powder and shot, clothing and the like — were distributed among the rest of the men, who drew lots for them. Sharing the spoils is a custom of war as old as time; I had a fleeting thought of the Roman soldiers on Calvary, casting lots for the possessions of Jesus. I'm sure the comparison would have amused Ferguson, but it was not apt. Patrick Ferguson's besetting sin, Pride, is of the devil, and, true to the adage, it went before a fall.

"As much as we could use the supplies, we have to burn those baggage wagons,"

Campbell was saying. "We cannot let them slow us down, and we can't leave them for the Tories to recover, either. All agreed?"

We nodded, but with heavy hearts, for in the backcountry we made or grew everything we had, except for salt and nails, and those we generally traded for. Passing up the enemy's treasures was indeed a sacrifice, but it had to be done.

"We'll pull them across the burning camp-fires when we go," said Shelby.

"What about the prisoners?" said Cleveland. "There's a veritable multitude of them. It'll take us a week to hang them all."

There was a little silence, in which we carefully avoided looking at one another. We could settle that matter later. The sun was climbing higher in the sky, and we needed to be off.

At last Campbell said, "We'll herd them away like cattle, I suppose. Post guards to keep them from getting away. They'll have to carry their own weapons, for we can't do it for them, and we certainly cannot leave them here where other Tories might retrieve them."

Shelby said, "I'll assign some men to collecting all the flints from their guns. Then they can carry them without endangering anybody. I have been looking over the captives this morning, and I find that I know some of these fellows. They fought with me at Musgrove Mill. When I saw them sitting there among the prisoners, I asked them how they came to be in Ferguson's army, and they swore they had no choice. They had been rounded up and forced into service. I'll vouch for them. We needn't treat them like the others. They'll be useful to help with the burying and perhaps do some of the guarding."

"All right," said Campbell. "And the wounded prisoners? What of them?"

"We can't take them," I said. "There's only one surgeon still alive, and he'll have his hands full looking after our own injured men."

Campbell nodded. "They'd be better off not having to go with us anyhow. Let's take them with us off the ridge, and then leave them at some nearby farm. Some local Tory ought to think it is his duty to take them in. I suppose Cornwallis's men can go and collect them when they get here. Perhaps that will slow them down in their pursuit of us."

McDowell turned to Campbell. "And I believe you said that you are remaining to oversee the burial detail?"

Campbell nodded. "I am. We'll do as much as we can, but we daren't stay long enough to make a proper job of it. You see that hillock yonder, about eighty yards down from Ferguson's headquarters? My men will dig a trench there, and we'll put the bodies in together with blankets over them. Some of the prisoners can dig the trench for their own dead. It won't be churchyard proper, but Cornwallis may already be heading this way, and the living must take precedence over the dead."

"And what of Major Ferguson?" I asked.

"He is buried already," said Campbell. "His orderly, a local man named Powell, said he spoke to you yesterday about burying his commander, and this morning I gave him leave and a few prisoners to help him. They wrapped him in the hide of one of the beeves we killed, and laid him to rest along with that unfortunate young woman who was caught in the crossfire." He paused for a moment, and looked out across the field, which was still strewn with the bodies of the dead and the mortally wounded. He sighed and wiped his forehead.

Cleveland understood the gesture, and smiled. "Winning a battle is a deal easier than cleaning up after one, isn't it, Colonel?"

When we reached Gilbert Town on Wednesday, the eleventh, in order to give ourselves a rest from guarding the prisoners, we put some of them in a pen there in the town. Ferguson, when he had occupied Gilbert Town earlier in the summer, had used this same pen to imprison some Whigs, and we felt that this small act of retribution was well deserved.

The news of our victory at King's Mountain had preceded us, and many of the inhabitants of Gilbert Town came out to meet us with cheers and words of praise. A hunk of bread would have gone down a good deal better than empty words, but we thanked them for their good wishes. Others, who had been sure of a Tory victory, were frightened and sullen to see us coming in triumph from the battlefield. Some of them had friends and kinsmen among our prisoners.

The townspeople came bearing news as well. A recently paroled soldier, newly arrived from imprisonment in South Carolina, approached Shelby, whom he remembered from a previous sojourn, with more grim tidings: "I was lucky to be let go, sir," the fellow said, leaning against Shelby's horse as if to prop himself up, and indeed he looked gaunt enough to warrant it. "I'm glad to hear that you'uns whupped Ferguson there at the King's Mountain. I wish you could do away with the whole boiling of them while you're about it. A few days back, the scoundrels done hanged eleven of our men down at Ninety Six, sir."

Shelby received this news tight-lipped, and with the briefest of thanks. The paroled soldier's story was overheard by a number of those nearby, and they in turn spread the tale like fleas among their fellows. The rest of us heard it and the rumblings occasioned by it before we had progressed another half mile along the road, and we steered our mounts up alongside Campbell to consider what must be done.

Nearing Bickerstaff's Old Fields, Cleveland nodded with grim satisfaction. "I told you so, gentlemen. We must do something to even the score, before they take it out on the prisoners themselves."

Colonel Campbell sighed. It was evident that he wished there were some other way to bring peace to the militias, but he could see that nothing would answer but a show of retribution. "We are in North Carolina, whose laws I am not fully conversant with," he said. "Can someone get a copy of the state statutes. I wish to determine how we may legally conduct a trial."

Chapter Twenty-Two

"*Two magistrates may summon a jury, and forthwith try and, if found guilty, execute persons . . .*" Campbell looked up from the statute in question in his compendium of North Carolina laws. "Well, that settles it, I think."

Joseph McDowell smiled. "Oh, yes, indeed. Two magistrates with jurisdiction in North Carolina? I should say we're spoiled for choice there. I am a magistrate myself, and Cleveland. Shelby? Sevier?"

We nodded. Lawyers may be sparse in the backcountry yet, but we do have laws and we ordinary citizens enforce them.

After we passed through Gilbert Town, we had made camp Wednesday evening on the land of Colonel John Walker, some five miles northeast of town, less than a mile from Cane Creek. We stayed there through Thursday as well, for the wounded needed a respite and the rest of us were by no means in fighting trim, either. Hard travel and meager rations were taking their toll.

"We have magistrates aplenty among us," said Joseph McDowell. "More of the militia officers than you can shake a stick at, in fact. Since you are asking about this, is it in your mind to have a trial, Campbell?"

William Campbell's craggy face looked haggard, and, though he was my age exactly — five years shy of forty — there were dark circles under his eyes and faint lines about his mouth. The cares of command and the privations of the journey were outweighing the joy of victory in his countenance. He had been reading the book of North Carolina law by the flickering light of the campfire. At McDowell's question about a trial, Campbell sighed. "Yes, a trial. I think we must, gentlemen. Despite my general orders, the tormenting of the prisoners goes on, and this grim news of the hangings at Ninety Six will only enrage them more. Colonel Cleveland was right. We must mete out justice to the guilty ones. Not to the ordinary soldiers, mind you, for some of them were forced to fight. But among us we know who the scoundrels are — the men who use the war as an excuse to pillage, the murderers, the house burners who make war on helpless women and children. Yes, I think we can hold them to account for their crimes."

We fell silent for a moment. No one objected, some of us because we knew this step to be inevitable and the rest because they wanted their enemies to be punished.

McDowell spoke up again. "There's a place about ten miles up from Gilbert Town, on Robertson's Creek. We fought the battle of Cane Creek not far from there, and it's on our way. We could make it there by nightfall, and make camp. Bickerstaff's Old Fields. There used to be a plantation house there, but it's long gone. I think it would serve. It's secluded. Some of the Bickerstaffs still live nearby, though. They're Tories."

"I believe someone of that name was among the wounded Tories," said Shelby.

"Yes," said McDowell. "He died, though, before we left the field. I don't suppose his kinfolk will be glad to see us camping on their land, but that's their hard luck."

Again, no one had any alternatives to suggest. McDowell knew the area better than any of us, for it was perhaps a day's ride from Quaker Meadows. A day's ride, that is, if you didn't have to herd eight hundred prisoners on foot as you went. This pace was especially hard on the wounded men, for each day of green corn and jolting travel weakened them further.

The night before, as we camped in Gilbert Town, we had talked about billeting our wounded men in homes around Gilbert Town, but there was so little food and so much unrest in the area, that we decided against it. They would be better off taking their chances on the trail with us.

We reached Bickerstaff's Old Fields at dusk, and camped within sight of two stark redbrick chimneys, all that remained of the plantation house that had once stood there. I wondered if it had fallen victim to the running battles that had crisscrossed the area in recent years, and, if so, whether one of our militias had torched the place.

As the men sat around their campfires, settling down for the night's rest, we sent officers around to each group, to tell them that tomorrow we would hold trials for the prisoners who were known to have committed crimes or outrageous acts of cruelty in the course of the war. If any of them wanted to denounce any of the prisoners before the tribunal, they should inform their commanding officer without delay. We heard the murmurings as the word spread.

In anticipation of the response from the men, the militia commanders sat together, waiting to see who would accuse the prisoners. McDowell had acquired a jug of whiskey, probably from some well-wisher back in Gilbert Town, and he shared it out amongst us, carefully pouring a dram or two into the battered tin cups from our knapsacks. As I sipped mine, I thought about the coming trial and what would inevitably follow.

"I wouldn't like to be in the prisoner's position, if the situation were reversed," I said. "Many of these men are well-acquainted with one another. They have been neighbors and even kinsmen since well before the war began. They may have disputes and resentments that have nothing to do with the present hostilities. How are we to know the difference?"

"Well, I for one don't care," Ben Cleveland declared. "The fact that they fought against us is all I need to know. The ones we kill — we won't have to fight 'em again."

"No, Sevier is right," said Shelby. "We mean to punish thieves and killers, not honest soldiers. I think we will have to consider the accusations very carefully before we agree even to try a man, much less condemn him."

"I want veto power," I said. "Over the men from the Watauga settlements, I mean. I have known some of them as friends and neighbors — fought alongside them, helped with their barn-raising, danced at their weddings. I think among them I'll know a thoroughgoing scoundrel from a misguided Tory."

"Fair enough," said Campbell, and the others saw the sense of my argument, and nodded as well. "We all have the power to stop a man from being hanged if it is warranted."

We were talking of the weather and the journey ahead, when a contingent of officers from both sides of the Carolina border approached us, hats in hand. "We heard that you were asking for charges against some of the prisoners, sirs," said the spokesman. "And we came to make our report if you gentlemen are ready to hear it."

They addressed their remarks to Joseph McDowell, for he was the commander they knew best, being from this area of the state, but William Campbell took charge of the meeting. "Go on," he said. "No . . . wait a moment." Then he called out to one of his own junior officers. "Major, have you the wherewithal to make a written record of this? We shall need one."

The Carolina officers waited while the Virginia soldier secured paper and ink.

When he had got them, he sat down near the fire with a leather-bound book propped on his knees, nodding that he was ready to make note of the names and charges against the prisoners.

The leader of the Carolina officers, a dark-haired, cadaverous-looking fellow who put me in mind of a goose, spoke up. "I'm from South Carolina, sirs. Well, about half of us are," he gestured toward the rest of the group, who stood a little behind him, shuffling their feet and looking ill at ease.

"You may recall that battle at Camden, some six weeks back or so. Well, sirs, that was dark days for South Carolina. Cornwallis had just about wiped out all the Whigs in the state, and there was no one left to stop his army from doing anything they wanted to the helpless citizens. They went after the known Whigs in the area like hounds after a fox. Some of them tried to hide, of course — it's only sense to do that — but if the Tories came to a man's house and found him gone, why, they'd burn it right down to the ground. And if a father or a son refused to say where the absent man was hiding, the Tories would hang him without a second thought."

Another officer spoke up, "I heard that when one fellow's wife wouldn't say where he'd gone, they ripped open her stomach with a bayonet."

"That's right," said the leader. "And that is what we've been living through, from Camden to Gilbert Town, everywhere in the path of Cornwallis's army. Maybe we killed some of them at King's Mountain, but we know for a fact that there's some of the ringleaders penned up here with the prisoners, and we want them to pay for what they did."

"You have to deal with them," said the second officer. "If you let them go in an exchange of prisoners, I reckon they'll go back home and do worse than before, on account of being furious over losing the battle. I say we put them down like the mad dogs they are."

"They did the same to our men after Camden, and just lately down at Ninety Six," the leader reminded us. "Maybe if we hang a few of them here, it will make the rest think twice before they go to tormenting their neighbors again."

William Campbell had listened to this recitation in tight-lipped silence. When the officers finished speaking, Campbell turned to look at the rest of us, and in our faces he saw the same angry resolve. "Very well, gentlemen. I am persuaded. We will convene

493

a court-martial in the morning to try those accused of such crimes. Field officers and captains can serve as jurors. Tell the men to bring us the names of any they wish to see tried for these offenses."

"We'll be at it all day," said Shelby.

Shelby was right about that. The trials did last all day. So many accusations were brought against Tory prisoners that, even though the proceedings were as swift and efficient as we could make them, the hours dragged on, as our soldiers took the oath and then told their harrowing tales of torture and murders perpetrated upon the helpless citizens caught between two armies. One Tory after another was brought in and made to hear the charges against him, then the jurors would deliberate and pronounce the accused innocent or guilty. There was no need for them to deliberate about the punishment to be given, for that was the same in every case: hanging, immediately following the trials.

I think if we had intended strict justice, untempered by mercy, we might have hanged a hundred of the prisoners, and I think Ben Cleveland would have been glad to see it done, but the rest of us had decided to settle for a token retribution: hang the worst of the offenders as a warning to the rest.

There was one man, though, that we all agreed must be punished. Col. Ambrose Mills was the highest ranking Tory officer to be tried, and, even before testimony against him had been presented, his reputation preceded him. One of the South Carolina soldiers, who had served with Colonel Williams, stepped up to testify that Mills had incited the Cherokee into attacking frontier settlements. The jury duly — but briefly — deliberated on the truth of this accusation, and announced that they found the prisoner Mills to be guilty as charged. Of that particular crime, I am by no means sure that Ambrose Mills was guilty, but that was of no consequence. What we did know beyond a doubt was that Mills had been the commanding officer of the Tories who raided Colonel Charles McDowell's camp on the Pacolet River, back in August. Young Noah Hampton was killed in that raid, and his father was here, an officer in the Burke County militia. Was it a crime to lead a raid on an enemy camp, even one composed of sleeping men? Strictly speaking, it was not. But Andrew Hampton, grieving still for his murdered boy, expected that incident to be avenged, and so it would be. Ambrose Mills was sentenced to die, and he would be the first man to mount the gallows tree.

In all, thirty-six men were condemned to death. Many of those accused were unknown to me, because over the mountains we had no raids from Loyalists to the king. The British sent the Indians to do their dirty work in the backcountry. But in Burke County and in Gilbert Town, and especially over the border in South Carolina, the hostility had been great, and the bitterness was an open wound. Much of the testimony came from the men from those areas.

When two Burke County brothers, Arthur and John McFall, were put before the tribunal, the first witness described the McFalls' raid on the home of a Whig named Martin Davenport. They had gone to his farm to kill him, but, finding him gone, they had abused his wife and ordered her to cook breakfast for them. Davenport's ten-year-old son was ordered to feed the McFalls' horses. When he told them to feed their own horses, John McFall whipped the boy.

At the end of this recitation, William Campbell turned to Joseph McDowell. "Major, you must be acquainted with this fellow, as he comes from Burke County. What do you have to say about him?"

Major McDowell reddened, looking from

the jury to the accused brothers, and then back at Campbell. "Well, sir . . . I do know the McFalls, yes, but . . ." He seemed reluctant to say that the offense did not warrant the death penalty. At least, that's what I was thinking, but before anyone could voice that opinion, Ben Cleveland roused himself, red-faced and wrathful. Looking up from his notes, he bellowed, "Well, I know John McFall! Martin Davenport, whose home he invaded, is one of my soldiers, one of the best. McFall insulted Davenport's wife and whipped his child. Such a man ought not to be allowed to live!"

"And what of the other McFall?" asked Campbell.

Now Major McDowell did speak up. "I don't think we need hang the both of them," he said. "After all, Arthur McFall was wounded in the battle. Between that and the execution of his brother, I think he will mend his ways. I say we let him off."

No one voiced an objection, so after a few moments of silence, Campbell said, "Very well, Major. John McFall is sentenced to be hanged, but Arthur McFall will be spared. Who is next?"

"James Crawford," said the officer acting as bailiff.

I looked up, and saw one of the few men

on trial that I did know. The last time I had seen James Crawford was in the shadow of Roan Mountain on the second day of the march. He had been the man who deserted my militia and persuaded young Sam Chambers to abscond with him. He had given us many uneasy hours, worrying what he might have told Ferguson about our plans and whereabouts, but in the end it did not matter. Forewarned that we were coming, Major Ferguson elected to take a stand and fight, and that was the end of him, so perhaps, with some help from Providence, Crawford did us a good turn after all. But he had not meant to. What he did was treason, pure and simple: he deserted one side and went tattling to the other. He could have got us all killed with his treasonous folly.

But, although he most certainly was a traitor, Jim Crawford was no coward. I had fought beside him in skirmishes with the Indians on the frontier, and it might be that I even owed him my life a time or two. Back then he had fought bravely and well.

Now here is where I differ from my comrades, the rest of the men who settled the backwater country. Most of them are Scotch or Irish, and they are brave to a fault and loyal to the grave, I'll give them that, but here's the thing: they will hold a grudge tighter than a gold sovereign. If you ever do them a kindness, they will consider themselves in your debt forever, and that is an admirable sentiment, but the converse of it is that if you incur their anger by injuring either their pride or their person, they will neither forgive nor forget your transgression. Never. If they lived long enough to see the mountain crumble to dust and the river run dry, they would still be holding on to that grudge, and it would be as fresh and green as the day it was conceived.

Perhaps it is that strain of French Huguenot blood that makes me differ from my Scotch-Irish neighbors, but, though I am as quick to anger as any one of them, I get over it. Let a few days or weeks pass, and my resentment withers away. I can forgive. You never know when someone who has trespassed against you will turn up in some later hour of need and become your angel of deliverance.

So there it was . . . If we could have run James Crawford to earth in the day or two after he had deserted the militia, or even any time before the battle took place, I could have killed him myself and then eaten a hearty dinner immediately thereafter, such was my wrath at him. But now, more than two weeks had passed, and tempered by the joy of our victory over Ferguson, my anger toward Crawford had cooled. My sense of justice told me that the man was certainly guilty, and in strict accordance with the law, he deserved the same fates as the other guilty men, but I kept remembering what a good soldier he had been in former days.

Our eyes met.

In his, I saw no hint of fear or supplication. He expected nothing from me, and I knew that his defection to the Loyalists was not an act of betrayal toward us, but an act of allegiance toward a king whose divine right he must sincerely believe in. If he had begged for mercy or cursed and blamed me for his fate, it would have hardened my heart. But he did not.

The jury foreman was saying, ". . . find the prisoner James Crawford guilty of treason, and sentence him to hang . . ."

I held up a restraining hand. "Just a moment. James Crawford is one of my men, and I wish to exercise my right of veto. Let him go."

Shelby, seated to my right, gave me a look of mild surprise. "There can be no one here with more witnesses to his treachery than James Crawford," he murmured.

"I know it. But I have been in other battles

with him, and he acquitted himself well in them. As long as the frontier is in danger of attack, Crawford's is a life worth saving." I could see Ben Cleveland's scowl of disapproval, and I knew that by his lights, the man should hang with the rest of them, but Cleveland lives far from Indian country, and so in this case he and I were using different measures to pass judgment.

William Campbell made a note of my veto, and nodded for the guards to escort Crawford back to the prisoners' camp. "Well, Colonel Sevier, you have spared Crawford. Now what of his partner in treason, Samuel Chambers? He is next to be tried."

"He's little more than a boy. He does what he's told, and his misfortune was listening to Crawford's bad counsel. I don't think we can spare the dog and kill the pup."

"He has learned his lesson, I'll warrant," said Shelby.

"Yes, sirs, I have!" Sam Chambers called out, tears running down his cheeks. "I was sorry before we had gone ten miles that day, but I was afraid to turn back."

"Take care whose advice you take from now on," growled Cleveland, but he made no objection to our decision.

"Reprieved," said Campbell. "Next case."

The trials went on and on, until they began to run together in my mind. Most of the crimes were the same — violence against the wives and children of Whigs, robbery, and destruction of property. One case is etched in my memory, though I did not know the accused. Capt. Walter Gilkey, a Tory officer who lived somewhere near Gilbert Town, had gone to the home of one of his Whig neighbors, and when he asked if the man was at home, the man's son, aiming a pistol at the intruder, replied that his father was gone. Captain Gilkey drew his own weapon and shot the boy, wounding him in the shoulder and confiscating his pistol. The chief witness against Gilkey was the wounded boy himself. The lad had recovered from his injury, and, perhaps inspired by it, he had joined the militia and fought with us at King's Mountain. When he was called upon to testify, he bared his shoulder, revealing the scars from the gunshot would. "He done that to me, that Gilkey. He made life a misery for all the Whigs he knew of in the settlement."

The testimony was compelling, and the prisoner unrepentant, so after a short deliberation the jury sentenced Gilkey to hang.

"Oh, please, no!" cried a voice from the

spectators.

A white-haired man made his way up to the front of the crowd, his shoulders heaving with sobs. Before anyone could stop him, he threw his arms around Walter Gilkey, still crying, "No. No. No!"

When two of the guards pulled him away, he turned to those of us sitting in judgment. "He's my only son," the elder Gilkey said. "All I have in the world."

"Are you a prisoner, too, sir?" asked Cleveland.

"I am not. I'm too old and infirm to take any part in this war, and glad of it, for it has brought nothing to us but sorrow. I came along here, because you have my son in custody." He nodded toward Captain Gilkey, whose arms were now pinioned by guards. When the captain's sentence was pronounced, he had shown no emotion, but now his features contorted with anguish for his father. I do not think he was sorry for what he had done, nor afraid of the punishment to come, but he grieved to see the pain he had caused his father.

"Please, sirs, you mustn't kill him. If you will spare him, I can pay you a ransom. I'll give you all I have." The old man was speaking to Colonel Campbell, whom he perceived to be in charge of the proceedings. "I rode here on a fine saddle horse. You can take him. Saddle and bridle, too. All of it. And . . . and . . . I have a bit of money, too. That is, I think I can raise a hundred, if you'll give me just a little time. I'm sure I can. Just a little time."

I could not look at the poor man, pleading for his son's life. I felt embarrassed for him, and, as I listened to his entreaties, I wondered what I would have done in his place. And suddenly I realized that I *could* have been in his place. A week ago, in the aftermath of the battle, my oldest son had fired upon defenseless, unarmed prisoners. I don't doubt that he killed one or more of them — he's a fine shot. Surely Joseph's transgression was the equal of the crimes committed by many of those on trial today. If this were a Tory tribunal, it might well be my son who was facing the gallows. But I did not know Captain Gilkey. It was up to others to decide his fate. I did know, though, that not a one of us here would be tempted to neglect our duty for the offer of a ransom.

Campbell, too, looked discomfited by the old man's display of grief. Apparently deciding to overlook the grieving father's offer of a bribe, he spoke gently. "I am sorry for your misfortune, Mr. Gilkey, but your son was convicted on the testimony of the boy

504

he shot, and the sentence has been passed. I cannot in good conscience go against the decision of the officers on this jury. But if you will accompany the guards, they will allow you to spend a little time with your son, before his appointed time. I can do no more for you."

The poor man turned away to hide his tears, and when the guards led the condemned man away, he shuffled after them. I hoped that he would mount that fine saddle horse he spoke of and ride straight back to Gilbert Town. I hoped he would not watch the hanging. After that, we all paid particular attention to the next prisoner, in order to banish the image of the Gilkeys from our minds. I never forgot them, though.

By the time we had finished trying all the accused prisoners, the afternoon light was fading and a chill night wind stirred the fallen leaves. Perhaps it would have been better to wait until morning to carry out the death sentences on the prisoners, but tomorrow was the Lord's day, and it seemed a sacrilege to hold executions on the Sabbath. We could not wait here another day, either, for again rumors had arisen that Tarleton and his men were in pursuit.

An officer from the local militia directed us to an ancient, spreading oak at the edge of our encampment. The tree had a low heavy branch, about the size of a tree itself, and it stood beside the road to Gilbert Town with space enough around it for the hundreds of men who would comprise the solemn assembly: witnesses, guards, executioners, and the thirty condemned prisoners. Some of the other prisoners, too, would be brought out to watch the executions, so that they could bear witness to the proceedings. The ranking officer among the prisoners was DePeyster, the man who had surrendered to us at King's Mountain, ending the battle. He and Ferguson's aide Lieutenant Allaire were among those chosen to bear witness for the Tories. Both of them protested that the executions were illegal and barbaric, and they demanded that the men be offered in a prisoner exchange between our side and theirs, but Campbell told them that no such consideration had been shown to the Whig prisoners, lately executed at Ninety Six, and that we were taking a leaf from their own book on warfare.

It was full dark when we escorted those about to die to this gallows tree, but the way was lit by scores of burning brands fashioned by our militiamen. These pine knot torches sputtered and blazed, casting strange and terrible shadows upon the scene, and turning the nearby woods into a twisted host of demons.

"A dark deed, done in darkness," Shelby murmured to me as we walked out to the gallows oak.

"We must set an example," I said. "Over the mountain, we have been spared all this in-fighting between neighbors, but McDowell's people and the South Carolinians have suffered greatly. The Tories have hanged a good many of their men as well."

"I wish somebody was keeping score," said Shelby, "so we'd know when to quit."

Col. Ambrose Mills was the first prisoner slated to die. The officers in charge of the execution had secured a farm cart from the Bickerstaffs', and they had rolled it into place directly beneath the massive low branch of the oak. Because so many prisoners were to be dispatched, the executioners decided to hang the condemned men in groups of threes, launching them into eternity in quick succession, and then putting up three more, on and on, until all of them had been hanged.

The men assigned as guards stood in lines four deep surrounding the gallows tree. The officer in charge called out the names of the first three prisoners. "Colonel Ambrose Mills, Captain James Chitwood, Captain

Wilson . . ."

The guards helped the three condemned officers up onto the farm cart and secured the ropes around their necks. They seemed determined to set an example for the men who would follow them to the grave, for they did not cringe or cry out as the preparations were made. Mills stared straight ahead into the torchlights, his face expressionless, and his body as rigid as if he were standing at attention before a general. Heartened, perhaps, by his example, Chitwood and Wilson showed similar courage.

They, too, stood erect and still, staring over the heads of the crowd until at a signal from the executioners, the cart was pulled away, and the three men dropped, swaying perhaps six feet from the ground. Mills did not struggle — an admirable force of will when one is being slowly strangled at the end of a rope. The other two twitched and writhed for a long time before they finally stopped moving.

From somewhere in the crowd — among the South Carolina militias, I think — I heard a raucous voice let out a war whoop, and then call out, "Would to God every tree in the wilderness bore such fruit as that!"

Out of the tail of my eye, I saw Shelby shudder. "One might wonder who is setting an example for whom," he muttered.

Walter Gilkey was among the next three to take his place on the cart, alongside Captain Grimes, who was one of our backwater settlers, and Lieutenant Raffery, who lived near Gilbert Town. I did not look for Gilkey's aged father in the crowd, for I did not want to see him in his anguish.

These three did not die as bravely as the others. The first three bodies still hung from the limb, and I think the sight of them in the flickering torchlight, one still twitching in its death throes, sapped whatever courage they had mustered for the ordeal.

They struggled when the ropes were put around their necks, and they cursed the guards and tried to kick at them. The executioners finished their preparations as quickly as they could, and jerked away the cart with undue haste. After the drop, they tried to kick with their bound legs, and one succeed in tangling the rope, so that he twirled slowly round and round as he strangled.

If I had not felt it my duty to stay and watch the proceedings that we as commanders had sanctioned, I would have spared myself the sickening spectacle of watching men die slowly and painfully for acts of war that may have been no worse than some of those committed by our own men. Shelby, too, bore a look of disgust, but we stood there in the front of the crowd, trying to witness the horrors without betraying any emotion.

Three common soldiers were next to mount the cart: John Bibby, Augustine Hobbs, and the scoundrel from Burke County, John McFall. One of them wept and begged for his life, calling out to those in the crowd that he knew from home. The others howled and fought.

"I cannot stomach much more of this," said Shelby. "I'm not disputing the justice of it, but if it incites our own men to further acts of cruelty, the game is not worth the candle. How many more are left to hang?"

More than twenty. "Oh . . . quite a few," I told him, but my heart was as heavy as his.

With nine bodies spiraling slowly in the shadows beneath the oak branch, three more men were brought forward for their turn on the cart. The hemp ropes were tightened around their necks and their hands tied behind their backs, but before they could be hauled up onto the cart, a young boy broke through the ranks of prisoner witnesses and flung himself at one of the condemned men, sobbing bitterly, and wailing that his brother must not leave him.

I recognized the prisoner from the afternoon trials: Isaac Baldwin, one of the Burke County Tories, accused of being the leader of a gang of raiders, who would attack the homes of local Whigs, steal their goods and clothing, and often tie them to trees and whip them soundly, leaving them in this piteous condition to be rescued . . . or not.

The man was indeed a villain, but his young brother lamenting over him was an affecting sight, and I think many of us looked away, embarrassed to witness such a wrenching scene. An instant later, the weeping lad's intention became clear. As young Baldwin embraced his brother, he managed to cut the cords that bound him, and before anyone could react, Isaac Baldwin shook free of his bonds and dashed into the dark woods.

But in order for Baldwin to run even those few yards into the woods, he had to get past hundreds of soldiers, many of them holding their rifles, loaded and ready in case the prisoners had tried to revolt. But not one of them raised a hand to stop Isaac Baldwin's escape. Not one shot was fired. The boldness of this bid for freedom outweighed all the anger at his past deeds.

Prisoner and soldiers alike simply stood there, frozen with shock, perhaps, at what had just happened, but even when that wore off, no one set off to pursue the fleeing prisoner, and no officer gave an order that it should be done.

The executioners, as stunned as the rest of us, shuffled uncertainly for a few moments, waiting to see if someone would issue orders. After a few more moments of silence, the guard standing in the cart shrugged and began to hoist the next man up into position.

Isaac Shelby stepped forward, at the same time that I did. "That's enough," he said.

His features looked more hawklike than ever in the flickering light of those pine knot torches. He motioned for the executioner to remove the prisoner from the cart. That soldier was one of my Backwater Men, and at once the fellow looked to me for confirmation of this order.

I nodded. "Yes, soldier. Stand down. These proceedings are ended," I said. To the others I added, "Take the rest back to the prisoners' camp. They will not be hanged."

In the silence that followed my words, I fully expected to hear Cleveland object to our order, or Campbell to protest that he was the final authority here, but no one spoke up. The silence persisted for a few moments longer, and then the men began to turn away from the gallows tree, and in small groups they began to make their way back to their own camps. I stood there for a long time and watched the trail of pine knot torches moving across the field like fireflies, and gradually fading into the wooded darkness.

Chapter Twenty-Three
OCTOBER 15, 1780

I went back to my campfire, where Valentine, Joseph, and Jonathan Tipton awaited me, but I had no heart for conversation. I settled under my blanket, hoping that sleep would come and banish the horrors I had witnessed that night, but before I could drift off to sleep, one of the guards came up and, with apologies for disturbing my rest, said that he had brought one of the prisoners who wanted to speak to me.

I sat up, and shook myself back to full wakefulness. In the glow of the firelight I recognized the prisoner as one of those men who had been sentenced to hang tonight, but whose life had been spared when we stopped the executions. He looked haggard and swollen-eyed, and I heartily wished I was downwind of him, for he stank like a cesspit, but I greeted him in a civil manner and asked what he had come about.

"I want to thank you for my life, Colonel,"

he said. "And I feel like I owe you something in return."

I wanted to tell him that he was not in my debt, but I understood the sentiment. The men in the backwater country cannot stand to be "beholden" to anyone. They will repay a debt of honor as quickly as they will repay the loan of goods or money. The kindest thing that I could do for him would be to allow him to discharge his obligation. It was obvious that he had come up with some way to square things with me, so I waited to hear him out.

After a moment's pause, the man went on, "I have some information, Colonel Sevier, and maybe by telling it to you, I can save your life."

"I'd be much obliged to you then."

He glanced up to make sure that no one was close enough to overhear our conversation. And then leaning in on a wave of sour breath, he said, "Word is going around among the prisoners that Tarleton and his dragoons have ridden out from Charlotte Town, and that they will overtake us soon."

Well, they could overtake us if they'd a mind to. With eight hundred prisoners, give or take, to herd along, we couldn't make much more progress than a pregnant sow. Now, this fellow meant well, but the rumor he had heard might not be true. "Where did you hear this?"

"A woman come to camp this evening, and told some of the officers that Cornwallis's men would attack at dawn. Word got around."

There was no way to prove or disprove his tale, but I didn't want to bet a thousand lives on the possibility that it was a lie. I thanked the fellow, and he slipped back into the darkness. Moments later, I was on my way to rouse Campbell and Shelby to tell them the news.

They listened gravely while I reported the rumor from the grateful prisoner. "I think we have to assume it is true," I told them. "We can't let them catch us. We are too tired and weak for a second battle."

"I doubt we have the powder and shot to effect it, even if we tried," said Shelby. "We have to break camp, but it's so almighty dark I doubt we could see the trail to follow it."

"The clouds moved in sometime after sunset," said Campbell. "It is too dark to travel tonight. We will have to wait for first light to move out, but we can use the hours until then to break camp and be ready. Pass the word among your officers."

"I'm taking my men back over the mountains," I said.

"And mine," said Shelby. "If we can make it to the Catawba River, I think we can get to safe territory before they overtake us."

We never got a proper sunrise, but the sky did lighten up enough so that we could see the unbroken skein of low hanging clouds stretching as far as we could see. We had not gone far down the trail before the rain began, showering us with cold pellets, and adding to the general misery, but we could not wait it out in the sheltering woods or in some farmer's outbuildings. We had to reach the river before another day passed. The path became a stream, and the horses fought the mud with every step they took.

For a while I rode along next to Shelby, glad of his company to take my mind off the misery of the journey. We rode in silence for a bit, and then we heard a sloshing behind us, and turned to see the ranking officer among the prisoners overtaking us. Some of the Redcoat officers had been allowed to keep their mounts, though they were not noticeably grateful for the favor. DePeyster drew rein alongside Shelby, his weasel face slick with rain. "The men are too tired and ill-fed to be out in such punishing weather. Where are you heading in such undue haste?"

Shelby pointed northwest. "Back to our natural element," he said. "The mountains."

DePeyster thought about it. He stared at Shelby's impassive expression, waiting, but neither of us said anything more, and at last he ventured another remark, "So, Colonel Shelby, you smell a rat?"

Shelby permitted himself a tight-lipped smile. "We know all about it, yes."

"Well, it will serve you right," said the Tory, and turning his horse, he trotted back to rejoin his own men.

We had hanged only nine prisoners at Bickerstaff's Old Fields before Shelby and I called a halt to the proceedings. I hoped we had dispatched those most deserving of execution, but I suspect that it was a matter of chance. Considering how many of our supporters had been executed by the Tories in similar circumstances, I thought we showed a measure of restraint that bordered on celestial mercy, but DePeyster did not see it in that light. He had complained bitterly that we had no right to execute soldiers who were doing their duty, that we had no authority, that the trials were not properly conducted.

We had ignored his objections before the

executions and since. Shelby was philosophical about it. "DePeyster is from one of
the northern colonies," he pointed out. "As
are Allaire and the little Tory doctor, Uzal
Johnson. They think the British are going to
win the war, and that all their army's actions are justified on account of that."

I shook my head. "I don't think they're
going to win."

He smiled. "Why not, Sevier? Has Providence vouchsafed you with a vision of the
future?"

"No. I worked it out for myself, thinking
about my farm."

Shelby raised his eyebrows. "Your farm,
Sevier? Pray tell."

"It's this way: my farm is only a hundred
miles or so away. Just a day's ride past the
mountains yonder. I've been gone three
weeks now, and even though it's harvest
time, I think things will be all right when I
finally do get home. But three weeks is
about the limit that I can trust things to get
along without me there to run them. And
I'm only a couple of mountains away. Now,
these American colonies are an ocean away
from England. And they're being troublesome. The British may be able to keep their
hold on us for a few years, if they really put
their minds to it, and if they're willing to

spend the fortune it will take to maintain an army so far away, but they can't run this country from the other side of the ocean, any more than I can run my farm from the other side of the mountains. Sooner or later, I have to go home — and so do they."

Shelby smiled. "But, as you said, the British are winning up north against the Continental Army."

"Well, they didn't win here. We proved that we can beat them. And sooner or later, they'll have other things to worry about. They have a whole continent full of enemies over the water. All we need is for one of them to start a war with the British, and that will distract them from our little revolution. I think that when they have to pick their battles, they'll leave us be and fight enemies closer to home."

"So will you and I, Colonel Sevier," said Shelby, no longer jesting. "It cannot be long before the Indians notice that we are gone, and lay plans to attack the backwater settlements."

The rain continued steadily all day and into the night, and still we plodded northwest, heading for the river. Judging by the swollen creeks we passed along the way, the river would have risen many feet higher than its normal depth. We would need all the help that Providence would give us if we were to cross it safely. I pitied those who were making the journey on foot.

It was only two hours until midnight by the time we reached the Catawba, and as I feared it was rising steadily.

"Well, this is a heaven-sent blessing," said Joseph McDowell, coming up beside me as we surveyed the rushing brown water.

"I'd hate to see one of its curses then," I said, shivering in my sodden coat.

McDowell laughed. "No, Colonel, think about it. We have come in the nick of time. The river at this stage of the flood is just fordable. But if Cornwallis has troops riding in pursuit of us, they will be unable to follow us. By the time they get here, the river will be impossible to cross. We are safe. And Quaker Meadows lies just beyond the river. You can stop, and rest, and eat in safety, before you continue your journey home."

"Thank God," I said.

EPILOGUE

The Battle of King's Mountain ended, but the fighting did not. I got back over the mountain only to learn that Nancy Ward, the Cherokee Beloved Woman, had sent word that the Indians planned to attack. So instead of getting to rest on my laurels at Plum Grove, I had to haul myself right back into the saddle and ride out again to fight.

The dying hadn't ended, either. Before I had even set foot in the house, my boy James met me at the door with tears in his eyes. He had made it back safely, but my brother Robert had not. Nine days into their journey home from King's Mountain, just past the Gillespie Gap, on the road to Roan Mountain, Robert had suddenly taken ill and within minutes, he had died there in a little field beside the river. They buried him there.

The little Tory doctor had been right when he counseled him to rest and recover before he had tried to head for home. Robert had been afraid of getting caught by Cornwallis's men if he stayed, but the irony was that instead of coming after us, Cornwallis had left Charlotte Town, going the other way. He wrote off North Carolina as a lost cause, and was heading up to Virginia, hoping to join the fighting up north where things were going well for the British, I suppose. But I had been right about how hard it was to run a war from across an ocean. The British got tired of the trouble and the expense, just as I thought they would. The war sputtered on for almost exactly a year after King's Mountain, and then Cornwallis surrendered to Washington at Yorktown, and the United States was officially a new country.

William Campbell did not live to see it, though. He was on his way to Yorktown for the last gasp of the Revolution, when he was suddenly taken ill — I heard it was apoplexy — and he died at a farmhouse not far from his destination.

We stopped fighting the British then, but it seems there's always somebody who needs sorting out. The Indian wars went on.

Seven months after King's Mountain, old Ben Cleveland got kidnapped from one of his tenant properties by some Tory rascals, who wanted him to sign safe conduct passes for them, so that they could come and go through enemy territory. They stashed Ben in a cave some thirty miles up the mountain from Wilkesboro, and set him to copying out the passes. He wrote as slowly as he could, knowing that his brother and some of their militia would be on his trail. Sure enough, as he was writing the last one, his deliverers discovered the cave up on Howard's Knob, and they succeeded is rescuing Ben and taking his captors prisoner.

Ben Cleveland hanged them all, of course, back in Wilkesboro, on what they call "the Tory Oak." I wonder if he misses the war.

Isaac Shelby is doing well. He has moved west into the Kentucky wilderness, and talks of gaining the territory's independence from Virginia. Once you learn that you can prevail against the powers-that-be, it's hard to stop challenging the authorities to get what you want. If he gets his territory to statehood, he'll be the first to govern it, I'll warrant.

The Seviers continue to prosper. In addition to the brood I had with Sarah, now well on their way to being adults, my bonny Kate and I have five children, beginning with George Washington Sevier, born a few months after the war's end. Robert's widow

Keziah, left with two young boys to raise, married Maj. Jonathan Tipton a year after King's Mountain, and they have gone back to the Carolina side of the mountain. I wonder if the major moved out of this area in order to avoid being swept up in the conflict between his older brother and myself. I wish them well. I like Jonathan as much as I dislike his older brother, and that is a great deal indeed.

It was on account of John Tipton that, eight years after the battle of King's Mountain, I ended up back in Morganton — in jail.

The Overmountain Men had their own little war of independence, but it did not go as well as the first one. Four years after York-town, those of us in the three counties west of the mountains decided to declare our independence from North Carolina. The state had ceded its territory west of the mountains to the Continental Congress to pay off North Carolina's war debts.

It was not all my doing, this drive for separation from North Carolina, but those in favor of secession put me in charge of it, and after that my fate was bound up in the fledgling state, whether I wanted it to be or not. We had heard about the establishment of Kentucky, independent of Virginia, and it seemed to us that what we were doing was just the same as that, and ought to be no more difficult to accomplish. But politics is even more troublesome than war, because most of it is done while your back is turned, and the enemy isn't always easy to spot.

The upshot of it was that some of the people in the backwater counties wanted to get away from North Carolina's governance and some of them didn't. So that political distinction — of whether or not to stay with North Carolina — did what the British and the Indians before them could not effect: it made us turn against one another.

Suddenly instead of battling a faceless enemy, I was in contention with some of my neighbors, most notably with the brother of one of my most trusted officers. Major Jonathan Tipton had been my second in command at King's Mountain, placed even above my brothers in the ranks of the militia, and now his older brother John was my sworn enemy. His excuse was that he did not want the western counties to separate from North Carolina, but I suspect that he did not want to be a citizen in a state of which I was governor.

It came to battles between his supporters and mine. Finally he came up with a reason to call for my arrest. When North Carolina changed governors, the new one opposed the creation of Franklin, and my political enemies — Tipton chief among them — accused me of all sorts of crimes and finally arrested me for treason.

I went off to jail over the mountain in Morganton, knowing that the penalty from treason was hanging. But if I had enemies back in the western counties, I had friends in Burke County, those who had fought at my side at King's Mountain, and when my deliverers came to fetch me, my old comrades from the war let me go.

I spent the days of my Morganton captivity visiting with Charles and Joseph McDowell of Quaker Meadows. I take care not to make enemies needlessly, and this habit probably saved my life this time. Charles McDowell bore us no ill will for sending him off to Hillsborough and choosing another commander in his stead. We are all still friends and allies. Charles has married that brave young widow he so admired, Grace Bowman, and they are raising a new family of McDowells. They tell me that Frederick Hambright, that staunch German-born soldier who took command of Chronicle's militia, has enlarged his landholdings so that he now owns the acres of King's Mountain where the battle took place. I'll bet he got it cheap. McDowell says that the hastily buried bodies were soon dug up by the wolves and stray dogs in the area, and that the field is now strewn with human bones and still haunted by the wolves, so that the local people dare not go near it.

That arrogant little Scotsman Patrick Ferguson is still lying beneath a cairn of stones there on the battlefield, and if his ghost walks abroad, I reckon it must do it in his native Highlands, for he is as gone from here as the Union Jack, and good riddance to both. We have a nation to build, and we'll do it ourselves.

ACKNOWLEDGMENTS

When I studied American history at a North Carolina high school, the chapters on the American Revolution covered the war from Concord Bridge to Valley Forge, and, with the exception of the British surrender at Yorktown, the history book did not mention any events that took place farther south. Yet King's Mountain, a battle fought on the North Carolina/South Carolina border, was hailed by Thomas Jefferson, and by other scholars since then, as the turning point of the American Revolution.

In October 1780, in response to a belligerent letter from a British officer, a volunteer force composed of the militias of several states marched to King's Mountain, and accomplished in an hour what George Washington's Continental Army couldn't seem to do up north: they won.

These thousand men, who came from the mountains of North Carolina, South Caro-

529

lina, north Georgia, southwest Virginia, and the territories that would later become Tennessee and Kentucky, were not soldiers in the Continental Army. They had no uniforms, no food, no horses, and no weapons supplied to them. No one ever paid them for their military service, nor did they expect to be paid. After the battle, the makeshift army dissolved, and its soldiers went home to their farms.

The 1780 victory of the Overmountain Men has long been a source of pride to the people of Appalachia, and I decided to tell the story for a wider audience. In addition to its importance in the course of the Revolutionary War, King's Mountain is a veritable "Who's Who" of the frontier South. The roster of the Overmountain Men included: the first governor of Tennessee; the first governor of Kentucky; the brother-in-law of Virginia governor Patrick Henry; Davy Crockett's father; Robert E. Lee's father; and the grandfather of North Carolina's Civil War governor, Zebulon Vance.

In researching this book I received help and encouragement from a number of people, many of whom are descendants of a soldier in that battle, as I am. My seven-time great-grandmother Keziah Robertson was married to Robert Sevier, who died from a wound incurred in the battle. A year later, Keziah married Maj. Jonathan Tipton, who had been second-in-command to John Sevier at King's Mountain, and I am descended from them.

I decided to write this book two years ago, when I spoke at the convention of the Daughters of the American Revolution in Washington. The enthusiasm and encouragement of the Virginia DAR convinced me that King's Mountain was a story that needed to be more widely known.

I began by consulting all the written records I could find about King's Mountain, as well as the many nonfiction books that have been written on the subject. If you are ever tempted to think that "nonfiction" means "gospel truth," read three accounts of the same historic event and note all the discrepancies between one book and another. (For example, most books stated that William Campbell was the brother-in-law of Patrick Henry, but one book claimed that Campbell was Henry's son-in-law.) I sorted out the conflicting accounts with more research and more reading, but when I could not absolutely verify a disputed fact, I tended to believe the original source from which many of the subsequent books are derived: *King's Mountain and Its Heroes* by

Lyman C. Draper (Cincinnati: Peter G. Thomason, 1881).

The Battle of King's Mountain Eyewitness Accounts by Robert M. Dunkerly (Charleston, SC: The History Press, 2007) provided valuable insight into the minds of the soldiers themselves. For the general reader, who wants a clear and engaging account of the battle, I recommend *King's Mountain* by Hank Messick (New York: Little, Brown and Co., 1976).

My thanks to the many people who enriched the book with their advice and expertise. The parks at Sycamore Shoals in Tennessee and the King's Mountain National Battlefield Park have excellent exhibits, helpful to anyone trying to understand the particulars of the battle. My husband, David, and I walked the battlefield, figuring out which militia attacked from which position, so that I could visualize the terrain in the context of the battle.

Blair Keller, a Revolutionary War reenactor in Virginia showed me how to load and fire a flintlock. Leigh Anne Hunter, director of Abingdon Muster Grounds, gave me a tour of the site and provided information on William Campbell's southwest Virginia militiamen, who began their journey there. Librarian Mary Gavlik took me on an expedition near Jonesborough, Tennessee, in search of John Sevier's house, Plum Grove, now only a lone chimney in the weeds. She also took me to the grave of Mary Patton, the woman who made the black powder for the troops of Sevier and Shelby. My distant cousin Alan Howell took me to Elizabethton, Tennessee, to show me the place on the creek where the Pattons' powder mill once stood. Research librarian Robin Caldwell searched historical and genealogical records for the story of Grace Bowman. Bill Carson, at the Orchard in Altapass — where the Overmountain Men camped — is a descendant of Robert Young, the man credited with shooting Major Ferguson, and I am grateful for his advice and encouragement. North Carolina historian Michael C. Hardy helped me to trace the first days of the 1780 journey — from the first night's encampment at the shelving rock to the trek over Roan Mountain on Bright's Trace, and along the road that is now U.S. 19 to Spruce Pine, where the militias of Shelby, Sevier, and Campbell left the mountains for the river valleys of the Carolina piedmont. Musician Richard Cunningham traced the eighteenth-century song "Barnie O'Linn," the all-clear signal from the scouts to the militias.

Dr. Randy Joyner of Wilkes County, North Carolina, showed me the spot by the Yadkin River where Benjamin Cleveland's house, Roundabout, was once located. The house itself disappeared long ago. We also traced the route taken by the Wilkes County militia, who joined up with the Overmountain Men in Morganton: they traveled down the same river road, where some eighty years later, Thomas Dula — Tom Dooley — lived.

Finally, I thank all those descendants of the Overmountain Men who shared their family stories, their genealogical records, and their enthusiasm with me. This is a story that needed to be told.